UNSWEET CHARITY

KEITH WATERHOUSE

UNSWEET CHARITY

Hodder & Stoughton
LONDON SYDNEY AUCKLAND

BRITISH LIBRARY CATALOGUING-IN-PUBLICATION DATA

Waterhouse, Keith
  Unsweet charity.
  I. Title
  823[F]

  ISBN 0-340-53299-8

First published in Great Britain 1992

Published by Hodder and Stoughton,
a division of Hodder and Stoughton Ltd,
Mill Road, Dunton Green, Sevenoaks, Kent TN13 2YA.
Editorial Office: 47 Bedford Square, London WC1B 3DP.

Photoset by E.P.L. BookSet, Norwood, London.

Printed and bound in Great Britain by
Mackays of Chatham PLC, Chatham, Kent

UNSWEET CHARITY

1

This could be the longest suicide note in history. Maybe I should get it sponsored at so much a page, all proceeds to the Samaritans. And instead of o-d'ing on gin and sleeping pills as I've been contemplating ever since Bananaskin Week went wrong (not that it was ever going right), why don't I drown myself in a bath of custard in aid of a new hospital scanner? Or is Dallas so rich you don't need a new hospital scanner?

I don't know how many of the inquest jury will ever have been to England. The chances of any of you having passed through Badgers Heath I would say are remote. It's a pleasant enough community of some 67,000 souls but with nothing for the visitor except our annual bonfire when unlike the rest of the country which burns Guy Fawkes and the nearby town of Lewes where they burn the Pope, we put a different effigy to the flames each year. The tradition goes back to the end of the war when the Badgers Heath Bonfire Society re-formed itself and we burned Adolf Hitler. Since then we've incinerated Tojo, Colonel Nasser, Burgess and Maclean, President Nixon, General Galtieri, Yasser Arafat and Saddam Hussein to name but a few, plus a sprinkling of home-grown left-wing politicians no one on your side of the Atlantic will have heard of. The victim is always decided by popular vote and next Bonfire Night the honour will most likely fall to yours sincerely, Oliver Kettle.

Badgers Heath is an expanded market town quite near the South Coast, fifty minutes by SupaShuttle from Victoria and too close to Gatwick airport for comfort. But convenient when you want to get away. That's how I come to be ending my days in Dallas – it was the first long-haul flight out. Had the M23 not been reduced to single-lane traffic because of road works I should probably be writing this to the coroner of Dubai. I didn't care where I went so long as it was far enough away.

There's not much you need to know about Badgers Heath. A typical English High Street – council offices, gas showrooms, estate agents, banks, building societies, shoe shops, McDonalds, Savewise Supermart and the newish Cherrytree Shopping Mall – surrounded by a *cordon sanitaire* of car parks beyond which radiate pleasant crescents and avenues of mainly postwar homes, starting at not much change out of £80,000 on the inner perimeter and working up to no change at all out of a quarter of a million where the town peters out into farmland. The High Street leads up to the Heath itself, or what's left of it – a biggish stretch of parkland once surrounded by Victorian villas which have been gradually extracted like blackened teeth to be replaced by low-rise, high-tech office blocks. That's how we make our living. Owl Insurance is in Badgers Heath and so are Credit International and EuroFund and a whole raft of others. We have a thriving trading estate which we're supposed to call a business park, turning out everything from software to garden furniture. Unemployment is minus nil. So we're prosperous – the last issue of the *Badgers Heath Herald*, which I've edited, past tense, since the year the Bonfire Society got into trouble with the Commission for Racial Equality by burning the Ayatollah Khomeini, carried eighty-four pages of advertising. And our prosperity – or maybe our guilt, as that old soak Eric Barlow would have it – has made us a caring community. Maybe that's been the trouble.

The town pretty well runs itself, with a little help from the local council and a little hindrance from the county council which is always trying to make our roads lead somewhere other than where we want to go. We've a Chamber of Commerce but it doesn't do much beyond complaining about business rents. The Parish Church of St Michael and All Angels, at what has become the unfashionable dog-end of the High Street, is little used except for weddings and funerals, although the Vicar, the Rev Basil Thrush, or Basil Brush as we call him behind his back, is on the committee of the Bonfire Society which is the driving force of Badgers Heath's social life, a kind of unisex Rotary if you like.

These Bonfire Societies, some of them going back a hundred years or more, are very much a feature of our part of the world, but the Badgers Heath Bonfire Society is a bit more enterprising than most. I suppose there was a time when it concerned itself solely with arranging the Guy Fawkes Night bonfire and the traditional Roast Potato Supper that follows it – or rather parallels it, since after the fireworks display its five hundred members are to be found with their feet tucked firmly under the trestle tables in the supper marquees while the rabble continue to surge around the bonfire, the rowdier elements pushing one another into it. But besides this obvious *raison d'être*, the Bonfire Society these days operates just about every major community activity going – the Fun Run, the Easter Egg Hunt, the Motocross Marathon, the Summer Fayre, you name it. We have a corner in leisure a theme park operator would envy. And all, but of course, in the sweet name of charity.

The story of my decline and fall starts at the funeral of Ted Greenleaf – the first sponsored funeral I've ever attended, incidentally – when I decided to have a fling with his widow; or to be more precise, Rosie Greenleaf decided to have a fling with me and I did nothing to discourage the idea and everything to encourage it.

There was not much wrong with my marriage, which had pottered along happily enough for ten years or so; but availability probably rates next to lust among the most common motivations for adultery – and I was available. My wife's name, Lydia Sheridan – Sherry to her friends – doesn't yet mean anything over here but she was a biggish name at home, the star interviewer of one of the national dailies and a minor television star. It wasn't a nine-to-five job and so she couldn't reasonably be expected to trudge back to Badgers Heath every evening, especially if there were extra-marital calls upon her time in London, as it was my not-much-considered belief there were. But she was always home for the weekend and whatever she might be getting up to at her *pied-à-terre* in the Barbican didn't seem to inhibit the zest she brought to the marital bedroom, and so I was content enough, the more so in that Sherry's inflated salary paid for most of life's little luxuries such as the mortgage on a property poised almost exactly between the £80,000 and the £250,000 brackets. Time does not hang too heavily on the hands of a small-town editor, who is expected to do his regular crawl in the social swim – particularly if his newspaper is one of the chain owned by Sam Dice, who happens to live in the district. But Badgers Heath has usually put up the shutters by ten, and I do not need all that much sleep. Rosie Greenleaf would make a welcome change from watching videos.

Ted couldn't have picked a better day for his sponsored funeral. The high summer sun bouncing off the white forecourt of the Texaco service station opposite the parish church was so dazzling that it blinded the driver of the leading limousine which in consequence rammed the hearse. Fortunately Rosie wasn't on board, having gone on ahead to set up her begging bowl. Her over-ripe farmer's wife figure sheathed in black, she had stationed herself in the church porch with an old-fashioned milk churn into which, having been forewarned by a story Rosie had got me to run in the *Herald*, you were expected to drop a minimum of a tenner. Coming face to face with the grieving widow, under whose sad, unrelenting gaze they were obliged to dip into their wallets or purses while mumbling condolences, most of the startled mourners gave at least double that. Anyone less smart than Rosie would have delegated the job to the sidesmen and halved the takings.

"You gave the appeal a very good write-up, Oliver," said Rosie as I dropped a twenty pound note into her milk churn, hastily topping it up with another one as she telepathically conveyed the impression that it didn't seem very much to her for a man of my standing. "Thanks to the paper we're off to a flying start, we must have a good thousand in the kitty and the church isn't even half full yet. I'm more than grateful, Oliver, because without people knowing in advance style of thing it would have been very awkward asking them for money. Thank you, Mr Helliwell!" This, with a flash of teeth, was to the manager of the D-I-Y Mart practically next to the church, a notorious skinflint, who was trying to sneak in without paying. Looking as if he would have liked to say "Our cheque is in the post", he clattered a fistful of pound coins – nearer five than ten, by my reckoning – into the milk churn and slunk into the church.

Having been a prominent member of the National Farmers' Union as well as Appeals Secretary of the Bonfire Society, Ted Greenleaf was a popular figure in Badgers Heath and the church was soon full. We raised nearly £3,000 so it was a successful funeral all round, except perhaps for the Rev Basil Brush who was frustrated in his hopes of rich pickings from his usual collection during the choir's tambourine obligato of "I am the Lord of the dance said he". Ted had expired of a heart attack – while enjoying Rosie's favours, she later confided to me – so the proceeds were going to Heartsearch – not a dating agency but a benevolent fund for heart attack victims. It was what he would have wanted, Rosie said. Personally I think he would have liked the money to go to the Bonfire Fund. Ted's love for bonfires stopped only just short of arson and he had been in trouble more than once for hanging a pall of black smoke over the South Downs in the course of burning his stubble.

Rosie wanted a funeral and memorial service rolled into one and so Ted got the full send-off. We gave him "Fight the good fight" and a couple of prayers, and then the Chair of the Bonfire Society, Len Quartermouth MBE FIAV as he always styled himself, the first crop of initials being his gong for thirty years of unremitting good works and the second his qualification, as a Fellow of the Institute of Auctioneers and Valuers, to run the town's biggest auction rooms out by the old cattle market. The reading was from Paul's letter to the Corinthians. Slumped next to me, Eric Barlow, the whisky already on his breath even though it was still half an hour off opening time, muttered, "Why can't we have the Corinthians' reply to St Paul for a change?" Like me, he was irritated that we couldn't have the authorised epistle as remembered from school assembly and more orthodox funeral services: Though I speak with the tongues of men and of angels and all that. Basil Brush prefers the paperback version: Whatever my language, if I don't have love I'm only a resounding gong or a clanging bell . . .

Barlow, having extracted a smirk out of me for his quip, looked set to milk the entire service for one-liners. To discourage him I turned my head, and found myself exchanging smiles with the chief mourner across the aisle.

Now although I am no more footloose than the next over-forty editor of a country weekly whose boss is a born-again Christian, I do know when I am being given the eye, and I was being given the eye. I was surprised to say the least. Not only was it the most spectacular advance I had ever come across on the old social cliché, "I know this is neither the time nor the place . . . ", but Rosie Greenleaf had an almost blemishless reputation for not having a reputation. With her pneumatic figure, straw-blonde hair and general air of having just straightened her raiment after a lusty afternoon in the apple loft, she was probably such an easy target for gossip that, Caesar's wife style, she had to be doubly careful to avoid scandal. Although the odd mud pie was flung – she had a fancy-man over in Lewes, she and Ted's pigman had been seen climbing the wall of Far Meadow with grass on their backs – none of it had ever stuck. The fact was that Rosie, in her mid-thirties, was twenty-five years Ted's junior but he was game to the last and she had had little need – let alone opportunity – to stray. That, I was to find, was what all this was about.

Her strawberry lips formed fleetingly into a sensual moué which said, as explicitly as if she had addressed me from Basil Brush's pulpit, "I want you to sleep with me. Soon. It's quite urgent." Then she demurely lowered her eyes in meditation.

I was as stunned as if she had openly winked at me. But accompanying the sense of shock was a tingling in the soles of my feet, a sensation at once of excitement and danger, a kind of sexual vertigo. Being mentally chatted up at a funeral is an erotically exhilarating experience, if a depraved one. With Ted not only not yet in his grave but lying in his box but twelve feet away, I felt that Rosie and I were on a par with a notorious pair of visiting exhibitionists still talked about in Badgers Heath, who had openly honeymooned in an upstairs bay window of the Euro-inn Dolphin Arms Hotel. So, I was soon to learn, did Rosie, who was experiencing in her heaving bosom stirrings even more bizarre than those expressed by her brazen pout.

At the lectern, Len Quartermouth MBE FIAV, with that famous leisurely delivery which Barlow had described as half the speed of sound, had finally got to the last verses of Paul to the Corinthians – Now we see through a glass darkly, as it used to be. "Just now we see ah but a poor likeness in the ah mirror; but soon we shall ah see one to one . . . " Listening to Len's interminable summings-up at our Bonfire Society committee meetings I did sometimes wonder whether he had found his true vocation as an auctioneer; I meant one day to drop into the auction rooms to see if he took as long to sell a second-hand tractor as to declare a motion carried. "And now of ah these three remain: ah faith, ah hope, and ah love. But the greatest of these is ah love . . . "

"Charity!" I prompted in an involuntary growl.

"Dear Paul, we gaveth at the office," rumbled Barlow.

There were no other signals from Rosie. During her request number, Ted's favourite song "I did it my way" – not a particularly adventurous choice considering some of the pop rubbish Basil Brush habitually got away with under the umbrella of Songs of Praise – she put all she had into the role of mourning helpmeet of the dear departed. Then came a eulogy from the pulpit with Basil Brush laying it on with a trowel, followed by his standard disclaimer before Prayers for the Dead: "Now whether we believe in an afterlife or not . . . " After a barbershop rendering of a negro spiritual by a nubile-looking quartet of the Farmers' Ladies Guild, the service went conventional again with "Now the day is over", and then we followed the coffin out into the graveyard where Badgers Heath still buries its selected dead, lesser ex-mortals being consigned to Bellevue cemetery out by the council housing estate.

As Basil Brush led the pallbearers and family mourners to the plot Ted was about to share with his long-departed parents – I am sure he would have preferred a cremation with a send-off of rockets and catherine wheels – the congregation divided itself into those who considered it all right to shuffle off back to work or across to the Goat and Compasses, and those sticklers for good form, perhaps a third of our number, who felt that one should hang around at a respectful distance until the bereaved had been chauffeured away. I didn't mind much one way or the other but editors of country weeklies are supposed to be upholders of the traditional values, which in this instance meant

firmly distancing myself from the company of Barlow as he made
tracks through the lych gate and across to the pub as fast as his
legs could decently carry him.

As the burial service got under way and we stood with heads
reverentially bowed in the brilliant morning sunlight, I found
myself wondering what, on the assumption that I had read Rosie
Greenleaf's come-hither look correctly, could be reasonably
judged a respectable interval before I responded to it. The
Badgers Heath Herald runs a syndicated etiquette column but I
couldn't remember it ever tackling so delicate a problem.

I tried to put unworthy thoughts out of my mind as Basil
Brush's nasal, off-cockney Good News Bible tones wafted across
the churchyard. "In the middle of life we are never far from
death . . . " But then his voice was lost in a tremendous clatter
from behind the cluster of secondary mourners straggling the
church pathway. Looking round, I saw one of Ted's farm
labourers, sweating in his thick Sunday-best dark suit, trundling
Rosie's offertory milk churn out of the church porch. Unrespon-
sive to scandalised shushes from our ranks, he dragged the
clanking receptacle down the path towards the lych gate.

Ted having been deposited among his forebears, Rosie, the
Vicar and assorted Greenleafs from far and wide made their way
back through the thicket of gravestones with that slow, plodding
gait that mourners have as if walking through mud, the phalanx
of remaining supporters parting respectfully to let them through,
and Rosie shaking hands at random like royalty on a walkabout.
Giving the family a head start to get into their funeral cars,
everyone began to drift out of the churchyard. Perhaps not as
badly as Barlow a few minutes earlier, but badly enough, I
needed a drink. Suspecting the Rev Basil Thrush of over-doing
the handshakes, I was irritated to find myself logjammed in a
slow-moving queue to get through the lych gate, until I identified
the true cause of the hold-up. Rosie had wedged herself and her
milk churn right inside the gate, where she was crying out to the
departing congregation like a barker at a fair, "Now come on, all
you lovely generous people, we've given Ted a smashing send-off
but I'm sure like me he'd want to see this milk churn full."

*   *   *

14

So that was the start of it. As I forked out my supplementary fiver exit fee, Rosie babbled in her unstoppable way, "Ooh, it's been a fantastic morning, Oliver, Ted would have loved it, now I want you to come over to Mill Farm on Thursday for the cheque presentation, I know you'll be sending a reporter and photographer but I'd very much like you to be there personally and stay on for lunch, because there's something I really need to discuss with you." But for the net-sheathed nail she was digging into my palm on the pretext of shaking hands, I would have made my excuses there and then. Widows who really need to discuss something are usually looking to circumvent their expensive professional advisers by getting a free and time-consuming opinion on their affairs. Maybe Rosie, with her peculiar requirements, should have gone to the appropriate professional. It would have saved me a lot of trouble.

The *Herald* office used to be where any country newspaper office ought to be – bang in the middle of the High Street, in a mellow mock-Georgian building next to the council offices. But when the bricks and mortar became more valuable than what they were accommodating, the council's activities expanded to fill the space available and the *Herald* moved into a custom-built brick box off the motorway slip-road. Streamlines distribution, according to Sam Dice – come press day, we can get copies out to every village within our circulation area in half the time. On the other hand, it takes twice as long to get them into Badgers Heath where sixty per cent of the sales are. But that's just the swings and roundabouts. There is also a big dipper and dodgems effect which left Sam a reputed million or so richer on property wheeler-dealering and gave some undisclosed councillors the opportunity to expand the borough's flourishing trade in patios, granny flat extensions and time-sharing schemes in Portugal.

It is not an office to hurry back to, especially after a funeral. Avoiding the Goat and Compasses where Barlow would be looking for an argument by now, I set off for the Dolphin Arms, which despite all the Euro-inn chain's ingenuity in trying to gut and refurbish a listed building including conniving with the council fire officer to have it declared a death trap, still manages to look like a not entirely Disneyfied version of its original coaching inn self. They do you a reasonable sole-goujons-in-a-basket in the Buttery, and if my luck was in my raffle ticket would be called – the Dolphin Arms Buttery is run on democratic lines where the serving wenches periodically interrupt their conversation to call out a number, and you go up to the bar and get it – before my ear had been too much bent by supplicants for the *Herald*'s editorial space. But first I had to shake off Crabbe.

Nick Crabbe was a mistake. He was not my mistake, he was the parental Crabbes' mistake. But he had been bequeathed to me by my wife Sherry – she likes to be known by that diminutive of her surname: it goes with her power-dressing – upon being fired as the high-flying gossip columnist of her esteemed journal for paying large sums of money to non-existent contacts. Massaging one's expenses is an accepted Fleet Street Spanish practice but Nick had been doing it on such a breathtakingly grand scale that no other national newspaper would touch him, at least not until the heat was off. Sherry said he had only done it to cover gambling debts incurred at Royal Ascot and such places in the course of duty, and she felt sorry for him. If you asked me, the truth was that he knew where too many bodies were buried, with particular reference to those buried under the duvet in a certain flat in the Barbican, not necessarily excluding his own. At all events I gave him a job, which meant that for a third of his former salary and a fraction of his former expenses he could use the *Herald*'s fax and telephone facilities to bootleg diary stories to his former Fleet Street rivals, against the day when his transgressions were forgotten and he returned as the overpaid prodigal son.

I had put Crabbe on covering Ted Greenleaf's funeral. It meant establishing himself opposite Rosie in the church porch and taking down names and "organisations represented" in a spiral notebook. While I confess I enjoyed humiliating a bumptious young man in this way – there is a good deal of satisfaction to be got out of cutting an upstart down to size, especially when your own dreams of glory have not been entirely fulfilled – I knew he would turn in a livelier story than anyone else on the paper was capable of, myself included.

"A good yarn, boss, the sponsored funeral angle," Crabbe enthused as he caught up with me in the High Street.

"Yes," I agreed. "And I don't want to see it in the national dailies before the *Herald* comes out on Friday." Strictly speaking the story was the *Herald* group's copyright, but when you are paid as badly as Sam Dice pays his hired hands, you are entitled to your perks.

I was about to remark acidly on the striped blazer and gaudy cricket club tie selected by Crabbe from his extensive wardrobe as fit wear for a funeral, but thought better of it. The Rev Basil Thrush, after all, had worn his customary bomber jacket, which he maintained helped him to meet his dwindling congregation "where they are at".

We paused under the illuminated hanging plastic sign of the Euro-inn Dolphin Arms Hotel where I had no intention of inviting Crabbe in for a drink. He took the hint.

"By the way, boss, not now because I've got to interview this pantomime cow, but some time when you have a free moment, could I have a quiet word?"

A quiet word with Nick Crabbe usually meant that he was after me giving him his own column or a pay rise or both, or that he wanted me to allow him to accept a freebie to some exotic place from Heath Holidays, our friendly neighbourhood travel agents, in exchange for a lavish plug.

"Have as many words as you like," I responded pleasantly, "so long as you don't mind a one-word answer."

"I can't see you turning this one down, boss. It's a great idea. Here comes the pantomime cow now – it was that kind of stunt that put it into my head. Then Mrs Greenleaf and her milk churn reminded me. *Bananaskin Week!*"

The pantomime cow, housing two students from the agricultural college, was lumbering up the High Street towards us with a pail around its neck, collecting money for a kidney dialysis machine for the hospital.

"Which week?" I half-echoed, bemused.

"Bananaskin Week. I won't say more for the moment, I just thought I'd whet your appetite. By the way, boss, talking of appetite and talking of Mrs Greenleaf, I have a shrewd idea she fancies you. Whoops, sorry, hardly the day for that sort of talk, is it, boss?"

Crabbe's familiarity, bordering on impertinence, grated on my nerves, as did his irritating use of the term "boss" which contained no hint of deference but had a smack of the second-hand car dealer calling his potential catch "squire".

I said sourly, "No, it isn't, and incidentally, cock, that jazzy outfit may be all very well for interviewing pantomime cows but it's hardly the correct attire for a representative of the *Badgers Heath Herald* covering a funeral."

I could almost hear Crabbe uttering "Balls!" to himself as the pantomime cow plodded up and whimsically cocked its head.

"Moo. Well well well, if it isn't Mr Kettle, the editor of our wonderful local rag. Now there's a generous man if ever we saw one." The voice inside the papier-mâché head boomed with megaphone effect, drawing amused smiles from passers-by. I flung some loose change into the bucket and went into the Dolphin Arms. It had been an expensive morning.

It continued as expensively as it had begun. No sooner had I ordered a gin and tonic, avoiding eye contact with the clutch of local businessmen at the other end of the bar and adding "Make it a large one" in a loud tone to discourage anyone who might feel inclined to come over and stand me a drink in exchange for a bit of intensive lobbying against the gypsy encampment or in favour of a new zebra crossing, than in walked the Rev Basil Thrush and Len Quartermouth MBE FIAV, both of them on double scotches. The Vicar said funerals were always an ordeal and Len said he needed a stiff one after making a public spectacle of himself at the lectern.

After Basil Brush and I had assured him half-heartedly that he had read the Lesson very well we clinked glasses and murmured, "Well, to absent friends"; then Len said, clearing his throat, "We were ah talking about ah Mrs Greenleaf on the way up."

I thought for a moment they had some observations to offer on her eye-fluttering performance in church, but that had seemingly gone unnoticed, except by the audience it was aimed at – plus, at a guess, Nick Crabbe.

"While we don't want to be accused of acting with undue haste," said Basil, "we have been having a word with our worthy

Treasurer and the consensus does seem to be that we must think very quickly about electing a new Appeals Secretary." Our worthy Treasurer was then Dennis Reason, a local bank manager and so by definition totally incompetent – but on this occasion he happened to be right. Fireworks don't grow on trees and the Roast Potato Supper couldn't rely on miracles equivalent to the loaves and fishes and turning water into real ale. The town had to be chivvied and coaxed into funding the enterprise, which it did more or less cheerfully on the pledge that for every pound spent on this annual display of self-indulgence, at least a hundred would go to good causes such as sheltered accommodation for Badgers Heath's frailest old folk or the endowment of new hospital beds (some of which would certainly be filled by future casualties of Bonfire Night). But what with a popular health scare which occupied him in slaughtering and disposing of his pigs, plus the attendant paperwork followed not altogether surprisingly by his heart attack, poor old Ted Greenleaf, while adept at getting blood out of stones, had left it a mite late this year.

"With the ah committee's approval, I couldn't think of ah a better choice than ah Ted's ah widow," said Len, coming what in his terms was straight out with it.

Had I not already got him a drink I should gladly have stood him a treble. If I had chosen to write my own scenario I couldn't have come up with a better one. Rosie didn't drive. Mill Farm was but five minutes from the *Herald* plant out by the motorway. What more natural, on committee nights which were weekly at present but twice and even three times a week as bonfire fever took hold, than that I should pick her up for our meetings and chauffeur her home again? Within the last hour, of course, I had already fantasised myself into a full-blown affair with Rosie. And a fairly tame fantasy it was to prove to be.

"Well," I said judiciously, "she certainly knows how to raise money."

"She certainly does," said Basil Brush with feeling. Not only had she deprived him of his collection but she had stung him for a tenner into the bargain.

Not to sound over-keen, I asked, "Have you sounded out Eric Barlow?" Barlow, for reasons lost in the mists of time, was a member of our unofficial committee within a committee which effectively ran the affairs of the Bonfire Society.

"We were ah hoping he would be ah joining us but he must be ah." Pissed.

"I'm sure he'd go along with the idea," I said.

"Then ah if one of you will formally ah propose and the other ah second, I don't ah anticipate any ah difficulty with the ah committee," said the Chair of the Bonfire Society.

"Moo."

Its interview with Nick Crabbe concluded, the pantomime cow was shuffling around the Buttery with its clanking pail. The three Bonfire Society stalwarts hastily drank up and left.

2

I fetched up in Dallas with a briefcase stashed with papers, mainly the minutes of the Bonfire Society committee dating from the election of Rosie Greenleaf up to and including the committee's sensational mass resignation, plus all manner of bumph about Bananaskin Week. They are of no sentimental or any other kind of value, except perhaps as an *aide mémoire* for this my letter to whom it may concern. But the real reason for my briefcase accompanying me on this last journey is that airport check-in desks and hotel reception clerks look askance at the traveller lacking even hand baggage, and there was no time to pack a suitcase. So a small chunk, no, a large chunk, of Badgers Heath life came with me.

Here, for example, is the file of clippings from the *Herald* compiled by Nick Crabbe with the aim of proving, for his own devious purposes, that Badgers Heath is a bottomless well of human kindness. I never doubted it.

Regulars of the Pop Inn Fun Pub, I see, are to stage an all-night karaoke marathon in aid of the Mental Health Foundation, an appropriate enough fund I would have thought from what I have seen of karaoke fanatics.

Verity Snell (13) raised cash for Age Concern by running on the spot all through her lunch hour wearing snorkel and flippers.

Students from the agricultural college raised £250 for Walk For Life, a sponsored walk to help the Aids Crisis Trust, by pushing a double bed to Brighton.

Badgers Heath Casuals cricket team will dress as rabbits for a charity match with the EuroFund Eleven, who will dress as chickens.

Terry Pawcett (31) was the winner of a blindfold darts knock-out match which raised £80 for the visually challenged.

And farmer's widow Mrs Rosemary Greenleaf (36) raised £2,985 for Heartsearch from the sponsored funeral of her husband Edward (61).

"Do you think I'm wicked?" asked Rosie invitingly.

This was immediately after the cheque presentation ceremony at Mill Farm. My over-creative, denim-enshrouded photographer Gavin Pyle, once I had persuaded him that the occasion did not warrant his perching perilously on top of the Welsh dresser in order to capture a fish-eye lens study of all present, had got his picture of Rosie supposedly handing over a six foot by three replica of the cheque to the Heartsearch chap up from Brighton, and the sundry local worthies rounded up for the occasion had sipped up their sherry and departed. As the last car door slammed, we were already using the giant Three Counties Bank cheque for £2,985.48 as a mattress on the stone-flagged kitchen floor, being quite unable to make it to the bedroom.

While the question was rhetorical it did seem to merit an answer. I said, "No, not wicked. Impulsive."

"If it hadn't been you it would have been the pigman or somebody," said Rosie.

"Thank you very much."

"Ooh, dear, I shouldn't have put it that way but you know what I mean, Oliver, it was definitely desperation time."

"Yes, I can understand that." Or at least I could appreciate it. All through her little sherry party Rosie had been semaphoring her requirements so wildly that the man from Heartsearch, catching a stray purple passage of body language and thinking it was meant for him, could not believe his luck. I murmured in his ear that Mrs Greenleaf was still in a state of controlled hysteria following her bereavement.

Rosie guided my hand back to her plump thighs. "It's ever since Ted passed away, I've been like a cat on hot bricks, I wake up some mornings feeling ever so ashamed of myself after the dreams I've been having, ooh, just there Oliver, a bit harder, in fact I've got to the state where I've been wondering if there's anything I can take for it."

22

I could have felt ashamed of myself too had lust not figured higher in my sense of priorities. Having Rosie on a sheet of cardboard on the hard stone floor had been but a brief and uncomfortable curtain-raiser and I was anxious for the perform-ance to continue, but at my age, on the wrong side of forty, preferably on a less unyielding surface.

"I know just the cure," I said, quite unnecessarily trying, and failing, to put a seductive note in my voice. I settled for the matter-of-fact: "Let's go upstairs."

"Unless you'd prefer the barn?" She sounded like a hostess offering a choice of tea or coffee.

"I get hay fever," I said.

"It's such a lovely day," persisted Rosie. "Why not in the orchard?"

"Someone might see us."

"That's the idea," she purred coaxingly. "It's the chance of being watched that makes it all the more exciting, ooh, put your hand back where it was, it's one of my symptoms I'm afraid."

"You mean wanting to be watched?"

"Not exactly wanting it, Oliver, ooh, I can't go on calling you Oliver, it sounds so stuffed shirt, can I call you Ollie? No, I mean just taking the risk style of thing. I was never like that with Ted, it was all very much behind closed doors. Mind you," added Rosie, rolling her eyes, "what went on behind those doors was nobody's business."

Before I answered Sam Dice's advertisement for a dynamic editor to charge the batteries of a talented team of self-starters – a bit of an oxymoron that would have been, had either job descrip-tion been accurate – I did a spot of features work for one of the tackier Sunday papers, and among my assignments was ghosting a series by a tame psychiatrist. It was, of course, all about sex, with drooling emphasis on nymphomania in its myriad forms. As I recall, while straight exhibitionism, if you can call it straight, is more of a male kink than a female one, there are women who enjoy the possibility of being watched or disturbed, especially, for some reason connected with the womb I seem to remember, on beaches. Badgers Heath's nearest beach is twenty miles away and uncommonly pebbly, so I supposed Mill Farm's apple orchard,

23

with the sporting possibility of being overlooked by scrumpers, was Rosie's idea of the next best thing.

In the end we compromised by repairing to the bedroom but with the curtains drawn back and the windows wide open, so that anyone who chanced to be on the roof of the adjoining farm's cattleshed with a telescope would get a grandstand view.

"Ooh, that's wonderful, that's marvellous," Rosie was crooning as we slithered about on her duvet. "Are we going to be doing this again, Ollie?"

"We haven't finished doing it this time yet," I pointed out.

"No, but I like talking about it, pet. You know I had a very healthy sex life with Ted and I can't speak for other widowed ladies but my physical needs didn't die with my husband so I'd very much like a very healthy sex life with you, ooh, don't stop. Just so long as it's understood that's all it is, that it's just appetite style of thing."

"There's nothing wrong with appetite, provided nobody gets hurt," I said sententiously, between grunts.

"Which nobody will," promised Rosie – as inaccurate a forecast, I was to find, as it was possible to make. "But we will do it in the open air sometimes, pet, won't we? To please Rosie? And you do know how to please me, Ollie, ooh, like you're doing now, ooh, slower, I want to make it last."

"It depends what you mean by the open air," I said cautiously. "There's secluded spots on the Downs, I suppose."

"The golf course is nearer," breathed Rosie, a suggestion which so stimulated her that it was not until I was lying on my back next to her, panting and bathed in sweat, that I had the chance to give her my reply, which I made an ironic one: "Why not in the middle of the Heath?"

"Ooh, don't say that, you'll get me going again before I've time to get my breath back, but after all why not the Heath, Ollie? I'm not saying in broad daylight, I'm not that stupid, but one of these warm dark nights after a committee meeting, that's if I get elected, or even if I don't I could always meet you in some nice quiet pub."

"Of course you'll be elected. It's a rubberstamp job." I certainly hoped so, anyway. Had not Rosie agreed with alacrity to

24

be co-opted as Appeals Secretary of the Bonfire Society I should have had to invent a society for us both to become officials of, the Extra-marital Union perhaps, to give me a cover whenever I chanced to be seen nipping into Mill Farm, if not whenever I chanced to be seen writhing about with Rosie in the clubhouse bunker of Badgers Heath golf course.

The Bonfire Society committee met every Monday evening, so it was evident that any other business was firmly set as a regular item on my agenda. We fell to mentally consulting our diaries for the rest of the week. "Tuesdays are bad because I've got my Farmers' Ladies Circle, but I can always do Wednesdays," said Rosie as if planning a bridge afternoon. Wednesday was fine by me too. The paper was usually in as good a shape as it was ever going to be by then, and I could always sneak off for a few hours on the pretext of going home to write the next issue's Badger's Babble, the so-called hardhitting opinion column which Sam Dice insisted I inflict on the *Herald*'s readers.

"And being as how I'm a Fifth Day Adventist," said Rosie with a saucy wink, "Thursday is my day of rest."

"From me?"

"No, you chump, *with* you, that's unless you're too exhausted and have to send in a deputy. Preferably somewhere in the long grass."

"You forget about my hay fever."

"Then we'll wait till winter and roll about in the snow."

Thursday suited, even if the long grass didn't. It was my press day, so I could always put the paper to bed and then come round and put Rosie to bed, trusting that not too many inquisitive friends of the proprietor noticed that I had begun to vary my routine of having a few jars at the Dolphin on Thursday evenings.

Mondays, Wednesdays and Thursdays seemed a pretty full itinerary to me, considering that Sherry was usually home for the weekend quite early on Friday. I thought, to avoid misunderstandings, that I had better mention this fact to Rosie. "Ooh, dearie me, then I'll just have to make other arrangements," she said with what I was supposed to take as a mock sigh. But I believed her.

"You're all sweaty," Rosie went on, managing to make a

25

clinical statement of fact sound like a provocative *double entendre*. "Come into the bathroom and let me soap you down under the shower, ooh, you'll like that, so will I."

I followed her willingly, feeling unbearably smug. If ever anyone had it made, I reckoned, I did. If I didn't yield to any fanciful demands Rosie might make to put on a performance in the window of the D-I-Y Mart or on the hard shoulder of the M23, I could be reasonably sure that a discreet little fling would run its course without anyone being the wiser, or anyway without anyone being able to prove anything, which in a gossip mill like Badgers Heath is the best one can hope for. What Sherry didn't know wouldn't hurt her, and furthermore, I concluded virtuously, I should be doing Rosie a service by keeping her out of the arms of her pigman, at least on Mondays, Wednesdays and Thursdays. There were no snags that I could think of. It was my firm editorial policy to keep clichés out of the paper, and so maybe that is why I failed to register the one about not seeing the wood for the trees.

"Yes, Bananaskin Week, boss."

I would not normally have encouraged Nick Crabbe to join me for a ploughman's at the Harvesters, the jumped-up farm labourers' pub which is the only oasis within staggering distance of the *Herald* plant. Sam Dice likes his executives to mingle with the staff but you can take democracy too far, and I knew that Nick would make the most, in office politics terms, of having been seen lunching with the editor. But I had put him down to cover that evening's meeting of the Bonfire Society committee meeting, and he had been proposing a drink afterwards for what he persisted in calling a quiet word. I had other plans. Even as Nick Crabbe ferried his half pint, my large g-and-t and two ploughman's lunches across to my usual table well away from the dartboard – if he wanted quiet words he could pay for them – I was wondering if Rosie Greenleaf would insist on keeping her bedroom light on and the blinds up. I could always take to wearing a mask, I supposed. She would probably enjoy that.

"If this is another charity stunt, forget it," I said sourly. Had he but known it, he had picked a bad time. My wife had arrived home on Friday evening in a filthy mood and returned to London that morning in a sulk, and it was all down to Badgers Heath's preoccupation with charity.

"Did you know they're flagging down cars near the Garden Centre?" she had asked as she threw down her briefcase and flopped on to the sofa.

I mixed her a generous gin and tonic to match my own. "The police?"

"The bloody students. There's a tailback going half way back to the roundabout. There's a whole gang of them, all dressed up in smocks like village idiots, and they insist on washing your windscreen or rather squeezing a filthy sponge over it so it's more mud-streaked than it was before, and then they wave a plastic bucket in your face."

"Oh yes, the kidney dialysis machine. I would have thought they'd bought the thing five times over by now."

"I wish I'd run the silly sods over. Can't you do something about them, Kettle?" Sherry and I had been on second name terms all the ten years we'd known one another. "Write a leader, run a campaign. They're an absolute public menace."

"Bit curmudgeonly, wouldn't it be?" I demurred. "All in a good cause and all that."

"Good cause my eye. It's coercion."

That was on the Friday. On Saturday Sherry came back from her weekly shopping expedition livid, having had her Savewise Supermarket trolley forcibly seized and wheeled to the car park by urchins who then demanded a forfeit for War on Want – or so they said, but Sherry didn't believe them. "If you ask me they'll take a Stanley knife to their collecting boxes and spend the money on glue or whatever turns them on these days. They're just taking us for a town full of mugs." And on Sunday, when we went across for pre-lunch drinks with our neighbours Percy and Betty Spruce, an estate agent and his wife who were both what they liked to be called leading lights of the Bonfire Society committee, no sooner had we crossed the threshold than we were accosted by their plump and owlish twelve-year-old daughter Kimberley and invited to become subscribers to a sponsored swim for the Save the Children Fund. As I signed her dog-eared exercise book, committing myself to fifty pence per Olympic length, Sherry said quite loudly, "Why don't we sponsor the drinks table instead, Kimberley, then you'd really clean up now the Kettles have arrived." She had had a couple of large ones before we left the house and the interview she had been writing up was not going well.

The Spruces, who must have heard her from opposite sides of the room, made a pincer movement towards us, Percy bearing glasses of Tio Pepe. "Is she being a nuisance? Now what did I say to you about not pestering our guests, Kimberley?" chided Betty, a refrigerated smile signalling to Sherry whom the reprimand was really aimed at.

"Make yourself useful, young lady, and take some of these crisps and olives round," ordered Kimberley's father.

"And don't forget to say it's in aid of Oxfam — you could make a bob or two!" called Sherry after the confused, moon-faced child. She was a good deal more pissed than I'd imagined. She must have had a kick-start after breakfast to get her interview piece going — it was not unknown. Returning Betty's glassy smile with a winning one that nevertheless had all the sincerity of an official handshake, she said, "She wasn't being a nuisance, poor lamb, no more nor less than all the other little do-gooders in this town."

The Spruces, both upright members of Basil Brush's select and dwindling flock, flinched as if my wife had said "in this fucking town", which in essence, of course, she had. I could see the self-defensive yet conciliatory phrases forming ready-congealed in Percy's not very original mind — culled, most probably, in his social panic, from Basil Brush's last Parish Pulpit slot in the *Herald*:

"Yes, I do take Lydia's point, there's a lot of it about as the old saying goes and your wife is quite right, Oliver, one can have too much of a good thing," he waffled, wisely refraining from addressing Sherry directly. "But after all, if they weren't doing good, what else would they be doing? One shudders to think, in this day and age. The devil finds work, as my grandmother used to say."

"Sententious crap," Sherry mouthed to me as she turned away.

Betty Spruce stiffened, not at her boorish behaviour, or rather not at her boorish behaviour directly, but at the sight of Kimberley stumbling about the room with a bowl of olives like one of the visually challenged for whom she had no doubt collected in her time. The wretched child's spectacles were misted with tears.

As Betty Spruce hurried over to steer her daughter into the garden out of my wife's orbit, Percy said, "She's an over-sensitive girl, unfortunately. She takes these things personally." I brandished my empty glass but there was no offer of a top-up.

Sherry and I had words about the episode afterwards.

"It's all very well you coming the big noise from London," I said, "but I have to live with these buggers, besides which old Percy is one of our biggest advertisers."

"Oh, piss off, Kettle, he has to sell his poky little semis for Christ's sake – he needs the *Herald* as much as the *Herald* needs him. More so."

"Perhaps, but there's such a thing as live and let live."

"That's the point I've been trying to make all bloody weekend. Why can't people leave people alone? And if they want to wear their hearts on their sleeves or on their lapels rather, whatever happened to flag days?"

She then tottered off to bed to sleep it off, leaving me to my own devices. I thought viciously that it would serve her right if I took myself down to Rosie Greenleaf's for the afternoon, but it was a bright day and Rosie would probably fancy a walk in the fields. Foraging for a scratch lunch I decided that Rosie could wait until tomorrow, and in the meantime I would pray for rain.

At the Harvesters, now only a few hours away from my second bout with Rosie Greenleaf, I presented Nick Crabbe with a carefully-edited resumé of Sherry's experiences over the weekend and her observations thereon. "So you see, cock," I concluded, "while not concurring with my wife's view that we should slag off the agricultural students and all the other assorted collecting-box janglers in our pages, I'm not just at this moment inclined to give them more houseroom than I can help."

"But that's just it, boss – I'm *agreeing* with Sherry!"

Here was another example of Crabbe's over-familiarity. Non-intimates of my wife were expected to call her Lydia. But I was forgetting: I had never established quite how non-intimate she and Nick Crabbe were.

"Get to the point," I said.

"The point is this, boss. Do you know how many charity events there are in this town in the course of a year?"

"Too many."

"The Bonfire Society alone organises six, starting with the Easter Egg Hunt and climaxing with the Bonfire itself, all raising money for spastics, starving kids, the old, the lame and Christ knows who else."

"Yes, well, all that's got a bit out of hand," I had to admit. "Fixtures like the Easter Egg Hunt and the Crazy Gymkhana were never meant to be in aid of anything except having a bit of a lark. But then the craze for sponsorship set in and now as the scintillating Lydia Sheridan puts it in her inimitable way, you can't even have a fuck in this town without making a donation to Ethiopia." I reflected, at the same time wondering if the smirk that flitted across Nick Crabbe's face at this sally had any hidden significance, that had this particular weekend been a typical one in my marriage, Ethiopia would remain in a bad way.

"Then there's a good dozen orthodox tin-waving collections a year," Crabbe went on, "plus the agricultural college Rag Week which your wife's just had to endure the tail-end of, plus as you say all these sponsored swims and sponsored bike rides and sponsored stilt walks and sponsored this, that and the other, plus – "

"Yes, all right, all right." The Harvesters' ploughman's lunch gives me indigestion at the best of times without Nick Crabbe's ear-bending as a contributory factor. "So what's the solution?"

"Bananaskin Week."

"You keep saying Bananaskin Week, but what the hell are you talking about, cock? One more charity junket on top of all the others, it sounds like."

"Not on top of, boss, instead of."

Catching just a whiff of a patronising sigh I made a mental note to appoint Crabbe holiday relief amateur dramatics correspondent, with strict instructions to cover every village production of every Agatha Christie play ever written, plus the

Badgers Heath Operatic Society's gala performance of *South Pacific*. That would teach the cocky young bastard.

"All right, I hear you," I said. "Roll all the local charity events into one week-long orgy and get them over with, is that the idea?"

"Sponsored by the *Badgers Heath Herald*," said Crabbe, all but prodding my chest in his eagerness. "It'd get massive coverage on the local telly and radio – it would have to, because we'd make them take part. Great publicity for the *Herald* Group and nobody would dare run another charity event for the rest of the year."

"And why Bananaskin Week?"

"We'd make it a really whacky festival, boss. Clowns, street theatre, jugglers, slapstick, jelly-wrestling, all that sort of thing."

"I think Miss Sheridan would divorce me."

"Plus there's no reason why we shouldn't get some really big names. Steve Selby, the alternative wheelchair comedian – ever heard of him, boss?"

"No."

"He's a big mate of mine, he'd come down." I munched my foam-rubber French bread and had another go at removing the cling film from my second cube of plastic Cheddar, nodding from time to time as Crabbe rattled off a list of famous comics, rock stars and TV personalities, all known to him but hardly any of whom I had ever heard of. I always let the showbiz pages run on automatic pilot.

"Think about it, boss." Crabbe at last rose to recharge the empty glass I had been twirling pointedly for the last five minutes. "It'd be a week to remember."

"Sounds like a good week to go on holiday," I said. It was either a brilliant idea or a terrible one – I would need to know more about it. I should have scotched it there and then.

The bar telephone rang. It was for me – it was always for me. I hoped it would be a fire brigade tip-off on a hay-rick fire in some distant parish to which I could despatch young Crabbe and thus curtail his lunch hour. Instead, it was Rosie.

"Would you like to come over if you haven't got anything on at the moment, which I certainly haven't?" I feared, with no great prescience, that this was to be the shape of things to come, and that confining Rosie to Mondays, Wednesdays and Thursdays would be like trying to confine a quart to a pint pot.

"I'm afraid I have an editorial conference at two," I said guardedly. "We'd better stick to the original arrangement."

"So what do you think, boss?" persisted Nick Crabbe as I knocked back my fresh gin and tonic in one to show what I thought of hacks who tried to get away with buying their editors singles the second time round.

"Send me a memo," I said.

The co-option of Rosie Greenleaf as Appeals Secretary of the Badgers Heath Bonfire Society in succession to her late lamented husband went through on the nod, with congratulations and condolences offered to the absent incumbent in equal measure. Despite the usual efforts by our Chair Len Quartermouth MBE FIAV to spin out the agenda until past closing time, we were down in the lounge bar of the Dolphin Arms – we meet in the Tudor Room upstairs – by half past nine, leaving me only with the problem of how to get out of the place with all possible speed.

As Eric Barlow privily ordered himself a treble at the waiters' serving hatch, and Basil Brush and Co hovered by the bar rubbing their hands and making joshing remarks about talking being thirsty work, while at the same time failing to catch the barman's eye, I hissed to Nick Crabbe, who had been covering the meeting for the *Herald*, "Get a round in and put it on your expenses," then marched off in the direction of the Gents. Out in the lobby I wheeled smartly left and hurried off down the High Street.

I had arranged to meet Rosie, or she had arranged to meet me, in a mean little tavern in what we are pleased to call the Old Town, a tangle of shabby cobbled streets behind the Texaco service station, dedicated to the sale of bric-à-brac and antiques. On the pretext of wanting to catch a new film at the Cherrytree Cannon 1-2-3 she had insisted on joining me after the meeting rather than waiting for me back at Mill Farm in something black and lacy.

"What if someone sees us?" I had protested, but that of course was the idea.

"You can always crack on you've just bumped into me and say in a loud voice, Well well well, what are you doing here Mrs Greenleaf, fancy meeting you!" teased Rosie. In fairness the likelihood of running into anyone I knew in such a dump was remote. By night the area was abandoned to drunks and derelicts and the only real danger was of finding my car vandalised on the piece of waste ground where I had discreetly parked before the Bonfire Society meeting.

I found Rosie sitting in a corner of what I supposed was the snug, sipping what proved to be harmless Coca-Cola but which her aura somehow conspired to suggest was a large port and lemon. While her low-cut, blue silky dress could not otherwise be called exactly blowsy, it did have an air of being well used to being hurriedly taken off at odd times of day. That and the slash of orange lipstick gave her the air of a lady of the town. Any other pub would have refused to serve her and I was glad now that she had not taken up my alternative suggestion of meeting openly in the lounge bar of the Euro-inn Dolphin Arms where the conclusion of our acquaintances, so ran my dubious reasoning, would be that if we had anything to hide we should have gone somewhere else.

My idea was to gulp down a swift drink and then bundle her into the car, preferably with my jacket over her head, and drive at high speed down to Mill Farm. The plan did not match Rosie's.

"It's a lovely evening, Ollie. I've been sitting here thinking why don't we go over to the graveyard?"

No one would ever call Rosie a mistress of euphemism. Had she said "go for a walk through the churchyard" I might have been a degree or so less shocked. As it was, I was so aghast that I could barely keep my voice down. "Good God, Rosie, it's not a week since you buried your husband there!" I muttered fiercely, already desperately fighting off an unshaped black magic fantasy of making love in a desecrated tomb.

"It's a big place, that graveyard," said Rosie, unconcerned. "We could go round the far side, by the back of the vestry. It'll be quiet there."

"I should bloody hope so. No, I'm sorry, Rosie, it's not on. Anyway, it'll be locked up for the night."

"I know, but there's a spot where the railings are down, I noticed on my way over from the pictures."

"What was the film – *The Return of the Bodysnatchers?*"

Rosie put a podgy hand in mine, applying pressure to my palm with her painted Jezebel nails. "I'm quite serious, Ollie, because if we don't go over there where can we go? We can't go back to the farm unfortunately on this one occasion, because as luck would have it I'm having to give a bed to Harry the pigman for the night, with his cottage being fumigated. And I don't suppose there's any question of going back to your place?"

No, there certainly was not. I knocked that one firmly on the head at once, then went on weakly, "But surely that doesn't leave the churchyard of all places as the only alternative?"

"It's nearest, pet," said Rosie simply. And bringing her bright orange lips close to my ear so that I had a bird's eye view down the Grand Canyon of her cleavage, she whispered, "I don't want to go too far because I've got very little on under my dress and I shouldn't like to catch my death of cold."

"If you do," I said, "at least you'll be in the right place."

Plainly the alternative in Rosie's fevered mind was not the geographical one between the church graveyard and somewhere else, but the physical one between me and Harry the pigman back at the farm. I succumbed. We drank up and threaded our way through the mean streets, with Rosie's silk-swathed thigh rubbing so insinuatingly against mine that it was I, rather than she, who called a pit-stop in the doorway of Bygones Bazaar for a panting foretaste of what was in store across the High Street and through the railings of the Parish Church of St Michael and All Angels. Rosie's sexual tastes may have been a little too advanced for me but they never failed to elicit a response.

An almost full moon was coming out from behind the clouds as we found the gap in the railings, uncomfortably close to where Ted Greenleaf rested in his all too recently-earned everlasting peace, and picked our way through the gravestones round to the other side of the church. We trod in Indian file, Rosie leading the way and it seemed to me that moonlight or no moonlight her step was pretty confident.

From taking short cuts through the churchyard – it backed on

to one of Badgers Heath's over-profusion of car parks – I knew
that on the approach to the far gate there was a jumble of older,
neglected graves whose blackened slabs, carved with names like
Ebenezer and Obadiah and Martha, contrasted with the rows of
white headstones and occasional stone angels shining like alabas-
ter in the moonlight. Obscurely, it seemed to me that if you were
going to have sex in a graveyard at all, it was more decent to have
it in that sector whose inhabitants had been dead the longest.
Rosie evidently felt the same, for it was to this patch of untended
graves, set in an undergrowth of brambles and nettles, that, with
firm tread, she was leading me.

We sank down on the unyielding marble slab of some accommodating Ebenezer or Obadiah. Too late, as the moon shed
another drifting bank of cloud, I realised that we were laid out
like a pair of kippers in a fishmonger's in the most exposed part
of this side of the graveyard, a good six yards from the protection
of the undergrowth. At least we were not lying in a six-foot plot
of marble chippings.

If the undergrowth did not protect us, however, it was well
capable of protecting others. In the shadows, behind a clump of
shrubbery, a twig crackled.

I stiffened, a reaction registered by Rosie who was already
guiding my hand beneath the hem of her dress. Given that it had
ridden up to her hips as she sank back on Ebenezer's marble slab,
the manoeuvre was guaranteed to get me off to a head start.

"Just another courting couple, ooh, a bit further up," she
whispered reassuringly.

"Or a peeping Tom."

"Well then, we'd better give him something to peep at, hadn't
we, ooh, you'll have to give me a hand with this zip I'm afraid,
Ollie, I'm all thumbs tonight."

There is a point of no return on these occasions and even if I
hadn't reached it Rosie certainly had, and with the recklessness of
lust we began to make love in earnest. Even as the climax was
marked with her all too shrill cry of "Ooh, ooh, ooooooh, there's
nothing like a hard surface, what is it, granite?" a new fear
sprang fully-formed into my head, that of the policeman's torch
and the subsequent appearance in Badgers Heath magistrates'

court of Oliver Kettle, 44, described as a journalist, charged with public indecency and desecration of the grave of Ebenezer Obadiah (1782–1859).

But there was no sudden beam of torchlight as I began to adjust my clothing while Rosie ostentatiously refrained from adjusting hers – just a quick flash of light from somewhere behind the shrubbery.

"What was that?" I tried vainly to tug Rosie's dress down to somewhere approaching the Plimsoll line of decency.

"That light, do you mean? I don't know, pet, it went off before."

"Why didn't you say so? It was a camera flashlight, I'm sure of it."

"Is that what it was?" murmured Rosie happily, her hand seizing mine and using it to bulldoze her dress back up to her hips. "I thought I was seeing stars."

3

Among my briefcase souvenirs is a copy of my memo to Sam Dice outlining my plan for Bananaskin Week. Yes – my memo, my plan, my noose round my own neck. There is an explanation, and part of it lies in the personality of Sam Dice.

Sam is a self-made man who by rights ought to be a professional Yorkshireman, a wool millionaire turned publisher presiding over the fortunes of the *Pontefract Chronicle and Osset Bugle* from a crag-top granite mansion, and delivering fire and brimstone lay sermons from the lectern of the Foursquare Baptist Tabernacle. In fact he comes from Essex where he made his fortune in packaging materials, and now lives in a custom-built ranch-style bungalow, complete with swimming pool, overlooking the golf course. But the lay preacher bit would be true enough if only he could find a church narrow enough to contain his primitive, punitive Christianity, a philosophy formed at the hands of a visiting evangelist when he was in hospital with a bad case of pancreatitis a few years ago. Lacking a congregation, Sam directs his sermonising at his dinner guests. He no longer drinks or smokes, and no pin-up pictures have appeared in any *Herald* Group newspaper since he saw the light.

Sam owns six weeklies spread across the county and it is his custom to dine their editors and deputy editors in rotation each Tuesday evening, an alcohol-free endurance test that every sixth week left me longing for Sam to expand his little empire with the acquisition of a seventh, an eighth, a ninth, a tenth title, even an entire ready-made newspaper group with enough editors and their deputies to set him up in weekly dinners for six months without duplication. At least Tuesday was not one of my nights out with Rosie.

Although one heard idle speculation about the possible subsidiary role of his not unhandsome cook-housekeeper Mrs Bishop, there was no lady in Sam's life, Mrs Dice having left him shortly after – according to the *Daily Telegraph* report of the divorce proceedings of which each of Sam's editors kept a private photocopy under lock and key – he began to require her to kneel with him in fifteen minutes of prayer before breakfast and after supper. Consequently his dinners were always bachelor occasions, with no wives present. His purpose in inviting deputy editors, however, was not to make up a nice little dinner party but to keep his editors on their toes. It was Sam's practice, when discussing the fortunes of his newspapers, to encourage his deputy editors to chip in with sales promotion ideas which, if they appealed to him, would leave his editors wondering uneasily whether they might not shortly be eased out for a younger, brighter man.

My deputy Douglas Boxer was neither younger nor brighter than I, in fact he was a good five years older, but there was no love lost between us. He had already been deputy editor for a decade or so when I took the paper over, and like all incumbent number twos felt that he should have been given the post. It was easy to see why he hadn't. He had a plodding, flatbed-press mind; his idea of a good story was the Women's Institute jam-making competition results and the best promotion stunt he had ever put before Sam Dice was to suggest that the paper present runner-up medals at the annual Cattle Show. He was to surprise me.

Sam likes to eat early so as to get in an hour's Bible-reading before bedtime, so as always I arranged for Boxer to pick me up at the Euro-inn Dolphin Arms at 6.45. Since our proprietor never gave us anything to drink there was no reason to leave the car at home, save that if Boxer and I arrived independently, he would be sure to arrive first. There was nothing I feared from my deputy but I did not want him bending Sam's ear without my being present to make prudent adjustments to whatever gloomy profile he might be putting over of life on the *Badgers Heath Herald*.

I found Boxer in the lounge bar in conversation, as was pretty well usual, with Nick Crabbe, who displayed himself almost nightly at the Dolphin under the delusion that he was holding court there as he used to do in the West End champagne bars in ritzier days. At least, on these sixth Tuesdays, I was guaranteed a free gin and tonic before giving Boxer the nod to be making tracks.

"Our young friend here's been mentioning his charity week concept," said Boxer as I joined them. I still hadn't made my mind up whether Bananaskin Week was a possibility or a prattish idea – I had yet, in the absence of the memo I had demanded from Crabbe, to give it a second's thought as a matter of fact – but you could trust Douglas Boxer to put it in the dreariest light possible by calling it a charity week concept.

"And what was your reaction?"

"He thinks it's a non-starter," said Nick Crabbe with a twitch of the right cheekbone which would have developed into a full-blown wink had I not discouraged him with a cold stare.

Boxer just would, I thought. He would think the idea of the London to Brighton veteran car run, the Grand National and the Marathon non-starters. Aloud I said, "You could very well be right, but what have you got against it, Douglas?"

He sealed my fate, and in a roundabout way his own as things shaped out, with his reply: "Sounds too much like hard work." If any one thing persuaded me to look seriously at Nick Crabbe's crackpot brainwave, it was that lackadaisical reply of my deputy.

Driving at a moderate 25 mph to counterbalance the effects of the half of lager he'd just enjoyed, Boxer got us to Sam's place promptly at seven. Mrs Bishop showed us in and, clutching a glass of Malvern water apiece, we had our feet under the dining table by three minutes past. In socialising as in business, Sam was a man for coming to the point. I was all for it: it meant I could be back in the lounge bar of the Dolphin sinking a much needed brandy by nine at the latest.

Sam, a squat, podgy figure in a grey plaid suit, looked and dressed like a bookie, and it was always an incongruous moment when he pressed his pink, sausage-like fingers together in prayer. As Boxer and I deferentially lowered our heads, Sam favoured us with what I called his lightweight grace – "For good food and good company we thank the good Lord." An encouraging sign: it meant that the evening was not about to be as heavy going as it might have been. When he was in moralising mood and about to do some heavy denouncing of the sins of the flesh, he would pronounce a grace so long, unctuous and pious that it might as well have been in Latin.

"The figures are disappointing, gentlemen," said Sam, getting down to brass tacks even as Mrs Bishop served the grapefruit with glacé cherry. He meant the circulation figures. They were not down but they were not up. That, to Sam, was a disappointment.

"It's August, Sam," I pointed out. "A lot of people go on holiday in August."

Sam set down his spoon with great deliberation and turned his round, pink face towards me in an expression of almost comic exasperation, fixing me with his baby blue eyes. "Yes, I know it's August, Oliver, but these are the July figures we're talking about."

I could see Boxer trying not to smirk. His turn would come: I would see to it.

"Of course they are, silly of me." Silly of me to think I could get away with it. Nothing gets past Sam Dice – except the implication of one of his editors in the embezzlement of a quarter of a million pounds: but we are coming to that.

"So what are you saying to me, Oliver? That the August figures will be even worse than the July figures?"

"I hope not, Sam, but I'm afraid they won't be very much better."

The *Herald* on the road to ruin and the need for stringent economies took up the rest of the first course and I nearly forgot that I was editing the most prosperous weekly in the south-east. With the main course, which reflecting Sam's simple taste was invariably a casserole indistinguishable from the Harvesters pub's cottage pie, Sam took as his theme the need to improve our circulation in the villages. At least he was not embarking on his pet theme of Aids being a visitation from God, a connection I had at one of these dinners once had the greatest difficulty in persuading him was not a suitable subject for a leading article. Improving our circulation in the villages was Douglas Boxer's hobbyhorse, so even as he licked his lips in anticipation of launching on his master plan for extending our news coverage by establishing a better relationship with our village correspondents, in other words paying them, I chipped in hastily with: "As it happens, Sam, a ten-point plan for improving circulation in the villages will be on your fax machine by the end of this week. I don't really want to anticipate my recommendations because they've yet to be fully worked out." Point one would be Boxer's proposal to pay our village correspondents by results, and I would cast around the office for the other nine points.

"I'm delighted to hear it," beamed Sam as Boxer sulked into his glorified cottage pie. "It means we can get down to what I was hoping would be the main business of the evening." Sam put down his knife and fork. Important pronouncements were always preceded by a laying down of cutlery. "Gentlemen, two nights ago I had a vision."

While the announcement was portentous in tone, it was as matter of fact as if our proprietor had said, "Gentlemen, I am switching the ink contract." In the unquivering bosom of Mrs Bishop, entering at that moment to replenish the Malvern water, it plainly generated an emotive effect equivalent to a declaration that we might smoke.

Boxer and I exchanged uneasy glances across the table. The lightweight grace had lulled us into believing that we should be spared any heavy dollops of evangelism; but Sam's visions were even harder going than his religious homilies. They were the stuff of dreams – the kind of dreams that the kind of people who talk about their dreams insist on inflicting upon their friends and acquaintances at parties. All Sam's executives had heard about his original vision, wherein his late mother had come and sat by his bedside and urged him to diversify from padded envelopes and cardboard cartons into the newspaper business. His mother still visited him from time to time to give him advice but most of his visions were now of the religious variety. When he had first seen the light it had happened literally, if what goes on in the fevered brain while one is tossing and turning in one's sleep may be termed literal: a door had opened in Sam's mind and beyond it there shone a blinding light, as seen in the Book of Revelations. Since then he had encountered angels and the odd saint. Sam's visions had to be taken seriously. Legend had it that when one of my predecessors had been asked by Sam whether he had ever had the pleasure of meeting a saint he had replied with a straight face, "Yes, St Crispin – the patron saint of cobblers" – and that was why he was one of my predecessors.

"St Urban – ever heard of him?" asked Sam. I shook my head. When Sam is recounting his visions you learn to say as little as possible. It did occur to me to wonder, though, how St Urban had identified himself. Perhaps he had presented his card.

"One of the two patron saints of drinkers, the other being St Martin," Sam went on, drawing, at a guess, on one of the popular books of lists which adorned his shelves rather than on the Lives of the Saints. Apart from the Good News Bible and the newspapers he controlled, our proprietor was not a big reader.

"But you don't drink, Mr Dice," pointed out Boxer sycophantically.

"I don't drink now, Douglas, but I did once upon a time. Not that I ever drank to excess, I was too busy building up a business," said Sam with his self-made smugness. "If I did still take a drink, you'd both be entitled to ask just how many I'd consumed before I had this experience."

There was no answer to that but it did not prevent Boxer from attempting one. "I'm sure no one would ever accuse you of all people of falling by the wayside," he all but chortled. I was glad to see Sam's blue eyes fix my deputy with a glance of loathing before, otherwise ignoring the remark, he launched upon an account of his latest vision while the unperturbed Mrs Bishop cleared away the dishes.

"Yes, I was in a garden, not your gardening correspondent's idea of a garden, Oliver – and why, when we have a quarter page advertisement for a thornless climbing rose, does he choose to write about compost bins, and when compost bins are advertised he writes about tomatoes? Remind me to come back to that. No, it was a garden of what I'd describe as mossy rocks and peculiar twisted trees and olive bushes I should think they were, though I couldn't see any olives; but you'd be right if you said it was a

42

biblical garden, probably on the plain of Jordan which we know from the Book was well-watered like the garden of the Lord.

"And I was sitting on this stone bench by this gravel path when who should come walking along in his long flowing robes but St Urban as I somehow knew him to be, although he didn't introduce himself. He said he was glad to find me because he'd been wanting to have a word, and he sat down and we had quite a chat." Sam sounded proud yet blasé, as if describing a visit to some foreign country where our embassy had fixed him up with a twenty-minute audience with the president.

As we paid studious attention to Mrs Bishop's bread and butter pudding, Boxer and I were briefed on the St Urban–Sam summit meeting. St Urban, it emerged, was greatly concerned about the hordes of lager louts who swarmed through Badgers Heath and outlying villages on Saturday evenings. Whether the co-patron saint of drinkers had been making visitations to other newspaper proprietors with the same problem on their doorsteps, or perhaps dividing the task with his colleague St Martin, Sam did not say. At any rate, St Urban had expressed the view that the youth in our locality had lost direction, and in the light of his vision it now seemed to Sam that in choosing to settle in Badgers Heath and make a second fortune from the *Herald* and its associated titles, he had been unwittingly responding to divine guidance to move among us and do something about it.

"Or if you regard that as too fanciful," Sam concluded as Boxer and I continued to avoid eye contact, either with our proprietor or each other, "I'll give you a more down to earth point of view, gentlemen. I've been feeling for some time now that I ought to be putting back some of what I've been fortunate to get out of Badgers Heath, and this hint I've been given to do something about the youth may be just the nudge I've been needing. So I'm looking for inspiration, Oliver and Douglas, and if it's something that puts on sales, so much the better."

"Douglas is our youth expert," I said promptly, unloading responsibility upon my deputy with all possible speed. Although we were always looking for young readers, anything to do with youth had for me the galvanising effect of a recycled bottles drive and I wanted nothing to do with it.

43

"We could always extend our youth club coverage," said Boxer cautiously. "Perhaps we could even run to a Youth Page."

I gave him an over-my-dead-body look. Fortunately Sam didn't think much of the idea either.

"We're not talking about the kind of youngsters who go to clubs and play ping-pong, they're no problem, Douglas. It's the ones Titus was told off by Paul to exhort to be sober minded, the ones you see roaming around in packs, drinking lager and shouting obscenities – that's who we should be concerned about."

This was more up my street. "A clean up Badgers Heath campaign. Last call for the lager louts. The police must get tough now."

But Sam was still impatiently and dismissively waving his podgy hand. "Too negative, Oliver, too negative by half. What we have to do is take them under our wing in some way, give them a sense of direction."

"With the greatest respect, Sam," I felt I had better feel emboldened to say, "I don't know what you have in mind but I doubt whether adopting a couple of hundred lager louts would do much for the *Herald*'s image."

"I don't know what I have in mind either, Oliver, that's the trouble, but there must be some way of putting meaning back into these young lives, a way of showing them what they're missing. What is it the Book says? This is the way, walk you in it."

If Sam was going to start quoting his Good News Bible it was time for me to glance surreptitiously at my watch. Having done so, noting that we had about ten minutes to go before curfew, I glanced up at Boxer and noted that a mad, faraway look had come into his eyes. Had I not known he was on Malvern water I should have sworn he was pissed.

"A youth rally!" cried Boxer, as a man inspired – very possibly, under Sam's influence, in communion with St Urban.

Sam did not condone swearing, or I should have retorted "Don't talk such balls!" Unable to reach far enough to kick him under the table I had to content myself with a withering look and a world-weary, "Oh, really, Douglas – you'll be inventing the boy scouts next."

"Now don't put him down, Oliver," said Sam impatiently. "This is the one semblance of an idea we've had all evening, and here you are pouring cold water on it." He turned his chair towards Boxer, laying down his pudding spoon. "Tell me more, Douglas. What kind of a youth rally?"

Boxer, having already bitten off more than he could chew, wildly bit off a whole length more. "Why not a youth prayer rally?"

Sam's transfixed expression as he digested this clownish proposal warned me not to react in the most constructive way I could think of, namely by throwing the remains of my bread and butter pudding in Boxer's face. Instead, pretending to consider the idea and deal with it on its merits, I asked, "And who would conduct this youth prayer rally? Billy Graham?"

"If I may presume to make a suggestion," said Boxer with a cringing smirk, "who better than Mr Sam Dice?"

I was so furious that I could not bring myself to speak to Boxer as we headed back to the Dolphin Arms where I had left my car. I ignored his contented burblings of "Well, that wasn't too bad as these evenings go" and "I was afraid for a moment he was going to make more of a meal of the circulation figures".

The deed was done. Sam had swallowed Boxer's crackpot scheme whole. The Youth Prayer Rally – it had already acquired capital letters – would take place on Badgers Heath on an unspecified evening under the auspices of the *Badgers Heath Herald*. There would be hymns, probably from some guitar-twanging young evangelists from East Croydon who sometimes made a nuisance of themselves in the Cherrytree Shopping Mall. Sam Dice would speak, but the thing would be professionally organised with the crowd whipped up by a religious rabble-rouser yet to be named. The Rev Basil Thrush and ministers of other denominations would be invited to chip in their two-penn'orth.

Any objections I had tried to raise, such as that whoever else turned up the youth of the district certainly would not, except to throw beer cans and disrupt the proceedings, fell not so much on deaf ears as on ears growing ever more prickly at what their owner termed my negative approach. After making the point that religion did not sell newspapers, to which Sam's sharp retort was that it had not done too badly for the *Christian Science Monitor*, I lapsed into a sulky silence, knowing that I was unwisely leaving the running to my deputy but, even as he elaborated on his plan, plotting my revenge.

I would make the bastard's life a misery. I would put him in sole charge of organising this bloody rally, without assistance and on top of his editorial duties. He was not the most energetic of deputy editors, in fact lazy sod was the phrase I would have used in any career assessment, so that would get him well below the belt. Every letter written about the rally would be written by Boxer, every phone call received answered by him, every contact contacted by him. He would be responsible for safety, lighting, sound amplification, police liaison, seating, platform construction, catering, dressing room accommodation, artistes' contracts, transport, and any other arrangement that might go towards making the event marginally less of a fiasco than it might otherwise have been, not forgetting the lavatories. I would chivvy him from morning till night. And when the whole nightmare experience was over and Sam Dice came crawling out of the wreckage, I would remind our proprietor whose brilliant idea it had been.

The persecution, I resolved as Boxer pulled up outside the Dolphin Arms, might as well start right now. "All right, Douglas," I said. "I won't ask you to join me for a celebratory drink but I'd just like to know what the fuck you mean by springing this harebrained stunt on Sam without discussing it with me first."

"You would have killed it," Boxer said, correctly enough.

"I would have killed it and I would have killed you, but that's not the point. I don't want to sound pompous but how dare you commit the paper to such a step without consultation with the editor?"

"Sorry if I trod on your toes, Oliver," said Boxer, with the same fawning smile he always used on Sam Dice. "But it was very much a spur of the moment thing and a heaven-sent chance to leave my mark on the paper."

"What do you mean, leave your mark on the paper? You're

not going anywhere."

"But you see I am. I was going to mention it anyway before we parted company this evening, as a courtesy before you got my letter tomorrow."

"Letter, what letter?"

"My letter of resignation, Oliver. I've been appointed editor of the *East Sussex Advertiser*."

"Congratulations, cock," I snarled, climbing out of the car. "And take your fucking Youth Prayer Rally with you." I slammed the door and swung into the Dolphin Arms, where Nick Crabbe was still propping up the bar with some council cronies.

"A large brandy," I said through clenched teeth. "And if you so much as mention your pestilential Bananaskin Week, you're fired."

"There was a phone message for you, boss," reported Nick Crabbe, having prudently ordered my drink. "Mrs Greenleaf of Mill Farm. She said if you dropped in would you call her?"

A feeling of being pressurised fought with the prospect of being pleasured. The pleasure principle won. At least she hadn't rung me at Sam Dice's.

Mumbling something about Bonfire Society business in response to the knowing look on Crabbe's face that was half way to a leer, I went out to the reception area and called Rosie.

"I thought you had your Farmers' Ladies Circle on Tuesdays?"

"I do, but I'd rather have you, sweetheart, ooh, that's really good."

Meeting me at her front door, fully dressed rather to my surprise and disappointment, Rosie had conducted me straight up to her bedroom, where she turned out not to be so fully dressed after all.

"So what have you done with the Farmers' Ladies?"

"Oh, they're still downstairs, watching one of Ted's old dirty videos," said Rosie carelessly. "I told them I'd someone coming in to look at the bedroom ceiling, well it's true in a way, isn't it, ooh, don't let me raise my voice in all the excitement, will you, pet?"

4

From the minutes of the Badgers Heath Bonfire Society Standing
Committee, August 14. Item 1: Treasurer's report.

Mr L. Quartermouth MBE FIAV (Chair) said that before asking the Treasurer to report, he knew that Standing Committee
would wish him to extend a welcome to Mrs R. Greenleaf as
Appeals Secretary. He only wished that her co-option, which had
been unanimous, could have been undertaken under happier
circumstances.

Thanking the Chair Mrs R. Greenleaf (Appeals Secy) said that
she was more than happy to serve Standing Committee. It would
give her something to do and it was what her late husband would
have wanted.

Chair called upon the Treasurer to report.

Mr D. Reason (Treasurer) said he was afraid the picture was
an even more gloomy one than usual. Since his last report the
Society's overdraft had increased by some £200, no incoming
monies whatsoever from the Bonfire Society Appeal having been
paid into the account.

Mrs Greenleaf said that if a new girl might interrupt the
Treasurer, that was because her husband had been very ill, in fact
at death's door, during the period covered by the Treasurer's last
report.

Mr Reason said no one appreciated that more than he did, but
that did not alter the fact that the Society remained seriously in
the red. Speaking with his bank manager's hat on, he would be
quite frank and inform Standing Committee that had the Bonfire
Society been an individual, its account would have been closed
months ago.

Mr E. Barlow said that if the Bonfire Society had been a South American banana republic, its overdraft facilities would have been extended by five billion pounds.

Through the Chair, Mrs P. Spruce asked the Treasurer who was in charge of emptying the many Bonfire Society Appeal collecting boxes to be seen on every shop counter and, it was to be presumed although Mrs Spruce did not herself go into public houses, every bar counter far and wide.

Mr P. Spruce said that while he was by no means a frequenter of public houses himself, he could confirm that collecting boxes were very much in evidence on licensed premises.

Mr Reason said that the responsibility for emptying the boxes was his own as Treasurer, with the help of young members of the staff of the Three Counties Bank who very kindly gave up one Saturday morning a month to do the rounds. To be brutally frank, however, the collecting boxes attracted so few contributions nowadays that they were barely worth emptying. To give an example at random, the box at Dorothy's Pantry in the High Street, an establishment one would imagine was patronised by decent, charitable citizens ever willing to donate their small change to a good cause, had when last emptied yielded the princely sum of four pence and an Italian telephone token.

The Rev B. Thrush (Secretary) said he could well believe it. Whenever he paid his bill for morning coffee at Dorothy's Pantry it was to be confronted by a battery of collecting boxes, five in number, for such worthy causes as the Blind, the NSPCC, the Red Cross and the Salvation Army, as well as the Bonfire Society Appeal. In addition, the entrance to the café was flanked by plastic effigies of a child with her legs in calipers and a spaniel on its hind legs, both clutching collecting boxes for their respective charities. The plain fact was that there were too many collecting boxes chasing too little cash.

Mr Barlow said he believed the Church of St Michael and All Angels had a similar problem.

Calling the meeting to order, Chair said that the Treasurer had drawn Standing Committee's attention to a serious state of affairs. The Press was present and he would not wish to overstate the situation, but the day was fast approaching when the Society might be forced to consider cancelling its traditional annual Bonfire for the first time in its 90-year existence, bar of course the war years.

On a point of information, the Society Archivist Miss N. D. Bellows said this was not strictly the case. The Bonfire had been cancelled on police advice in 1957 when so-called Mods and Rockers had threatened to descend upon the town in force. However, irresponsible elements had taken matters into their own hands and not only lit the Bonfire but started several other unauthorised bonfires about the Heath, setting the gorse ablaze and hampering fire appliances which arrived to extinguish the conflagration before it reached the Maternity Home.

Mr O. Kettle (ex-officio Member as Editor of the *Badgers Heath Herald*) said that this time, if similarly thwarted, they would probably set fire to the Maternity Home and overturn the fire engines.

Mrs Greenleaf asked, through the Chair, exactly how much cash had to be raised to ensure the survival of the Bonfire.

The Treasurer said that each Member of the Standing Committee should have a copy of the Treasurer's Report in front of him or her. He did not wish to burden Mrs Greenleaf with figures but the Society was looking to her as Appeals Secretary to clear the Society's overdraft and provide sufficient cashflow to cover the organisation and running costs of this year's Bonfire and the various activities connected with it. In round figures the Society was talking about finding the sum of around £10,000 within the next ten weeks at the outside.

Mrs Greenleaf asked what proportion of such a sum would go to charity.

Chair said that for the benefit of the new Appeals Secretary he would explain the position, if other members of Standing Committee would bear with him. The position was that under its constitution the first duty of the Bonfire Society, principally through its Appeals Secretary, was to raise monies sufficient to build, Miss Bellows would correct him if he had got the wording wrong, "a great Bonfire that shall be visible from the parish of East Hustling to the south, the parish of South Hustling to the north, the parish of West Merdley to the east, and the parish of

North Merdley to the west; with a pyrotechnical display visible far beyond these same points; and a Roast Potato Supper for the honourable Members of the Bonfire Society".

Chair continued that any surplus monies went to charities from time to time nominated by Standing Committee, as did the proceeds of the sale of tickets for the Roast Potato Supper, together with the proceeds from side events such as raffles, Guess the Weight of a Pig and Guess the Number of Currants in a Cake competitions and so on and so forth; from advertisements in souvenir programmes very kindly printed by the *Badgers Heath Herald*, and sale of same; from monies paid by concessionaires for permission to set up hot potato and soft drinks stalls; from the sale of Badgers Heath Bonfire Night T-shirts, ashtrays, eye patches, commemorative plates and the remainder; and last but not least from collections taken from the many hundreds of people attending the Bonfire. On a good year the Society expected to donate a handsome five-figure sum to charity.

Again under its constitution, the Society was not permitted to touch any of these monies for its own maintenance or for any future provision. Therefore, and first and foremost as the Treasurer had explained, the Society urgently required a lump sum to keep its head above water and to create the wherewithal for all these fund-raising enterprises to be set in motion, said lump sum having been estimated by the Treasurer, and there was no reason to question his assessment of the situation, at some £10,000. The marquee people, to take but one example, would not erect so much as a tent peg without being paid in advance, charity or no charity. Chair trusted that Mrs Greenleaf now grasped the position. If there was anything she did not understand, Chair would be only too happy to explain.

The Secretary reminded the Chair that the room was booked only until 10.30 pm.

Mrs Greenleaf, thanking the Chair for this detailed explanation, said that if £10,000 was what the Society needed to "get its act on the road", then £10,000 was what the Society would get. The Treasurer had only to give her a deadline by which the money had to be in the bank.

The Treasurer said no one doubted Mrs Greenleaf's

enthusiasm but he wondered if she realised the enormity of the task she was setting herself. She was undertaking to achieve in two and a half months what her late husband, for all his dedication, conscientiousness and unflagging application to the job had been unable to achieve in ten.

Mrs Greenleaf reminded Standing Committee that her late husband had not been a well man. Speaking for herself, Mrs Greenleaf had never felt fitter. She was full of beans. She was raring to go.

Chair asked nevertheless, was the new Appeals Secretary biting off more than she could chew?

Mr Barlow asked whether the Chair and the Treasurer were not underestimating their worthy Appeals Secretary's capabilities. Judging by her "form", if he might make so bold as to use a horse-racing expression in this context, it only needed three or four funerals in the town with Mrs Greenleaf in a strategic position with her milk churn, and the money was as good as in the bank.

Mr Kettle said that while he could not go along with the idea of the Society's Appeals Secretary presenting herself at funerals like a busker working cinema queues, if Mr Barlow was being serious for once he would go along with him in begging Standing Committee not to underestimate Mrs Greenleaf. She was a lady of considerable resources and remarkable energy.

Mrs Greenleaf asked if she could have that testimonial in writing so she could frame it.

The Secretary reminded the Chair that time was getting on and that Standing Committee had as yet reached only Item One on the agenda.

Chair said that while sharing the Treasurer's cautious evaluation of the difficulties involved in raising so large a sum in so short a time, he would agree with Messrs Barlow and Kettle that the new Appeals Secretary would make up for in enthusiasm what she lacked in experience, and he was sure that Standing Committee wished her well in her endeavours. Certainly the Society had no option but to accept her undertaking to raise the required £10,000 in the required time at its face value, since the money was not otherwise likely to fall out of the sky. There was

no point in chasing moonbeams further and he would ask someone to propose that the Treasurer's report be adopted.

"Thanks ever so much for standing up for me, Ollie," said Rosie.

"You mean at the committee meeting or just now?" I quipped
crudely. We were back at the farmhouse, on the living room sofa.
The curtains were drawn, but with a two-inch gap affording an
excellent front stalls view to any peeping Tom or peeping pigman
out in the blackness of a cloudy night.

"Both, cheeky thing, ooh, that was good, I'm still throbbing
away like one of those vibrators, incidentally have you ever tried
one? Molly got one for me out of her sex aids catalogue but it
needs new batteries."

Abandoning, from lack of essential research data, a passing
attempt to estimate how long a vibrator had to vibrate before its
batteries ran down, I asked who Molly was.

"You know Molly, pet, yes you do, Len Quartermouth's
daughter, married her Dad's valuations manager or whatever he
calls himself, you ought to know if anybody did, you had their
wedding photo in the paper. Strictly speaking she's not entitled to
belong to the Farmers' Ladies Circle but as her married name
happens to be Farmer we made her an honorary member."

Wondering what manner of stuttering song and dance Len
Quartermouth MBE FIAV would make if he only knew, I said,
"And she brings all of you these sex aids, does she? So that's what
you get up to at your Farmers' Ladies Circle!"

"Well, we don't sit around discussing the price of feeding
stuffs, if that's what you mean." Rosie went on with matter of
fact coquettishness, "Anyway, what's wrong with sex aids? I
mean to say, out of the ten of us, three are widows, two have
husbands who are past it and the other five count themselves very
fortunate indeed if they get it once a month, you see that's
farming for you, pet – there's that much paperwork you don't get
to bed till all hours."

"Going by what you tell me, Rosie, that wasn't among Ted's
chief worries," I suggested.

"Thank God for the lap-top computer," said Rosie. "Have you
ever tried it across the back of an easy chair, by the way? Not that

I ever have, because Ted only liked it in the bedroom, don't get me wrong, he was passionate enough for three but orthodox with it style of thing, but Janey, she's another of our ladies, recommends the position most highly."

The idea of having Rosie across the back of one of her easy chairs had immediate appeal but I needed a breathing space. To make conversation I said, "Janey, Janey. Let me guess. She can't be one of the two whose husbands are past it so she must be one of the five who get it only once a month. I wonder she needs the variation."

"Ah, well that's just where you're wrong, sugar," said Rosie. "She's one of the widows and guess what killed her husband, no I mustn't say things like that even in jest, I'll be struck down dead one of these days. But you mustn't mock the afflicted either, because the Farmers' Ladies are going to be a great help to me in raising that £10,000, a very great help indeed, Ollie. If there's one thing they've all got going for them it's what you quite rightly told that committee I've got – surplus energy."

"That was my little private joke for your benefit, Rosie." Not so much out of idle curiosity but because, sensing Rosie's surplus energy stirring again, I needed a few more minutes' grace, I went on hurriedly to ask, "But how are your Farmers' Ladies going to help you find all that money?"

"That's *my* little private joke," said Rosie seductively. My own surplus energies coming unexpectedly into play at that moment in response to hers, I gave little thought to what she meant by that enigmatic remark. It makes no odds. Even had I pursued the question I doubt if events would have panned out any differently. They might, had I been able to deflect Rosie from her course, have taken a different route, that's all.

For the present, my mind was concentrated on conquering the previously unclimbed back of the easy chair by the window. So was Rosie's. Unfortunately the operation required something more than dedicated complicity, it needed a dress rehearsal. We were both taking her friend Janey's word for it that the exercise would work smoothly, but doubtless Janey was of a slighter build than Rosie, and we had made no calculations allowing for Rosie's generous weight, combined with mine, against the distributed weight of an uncut moquette easy chair. As the chair tilted backwards, depositing us on the carpet in a tangle of naked limbs, there was a flash of white light through the gap in the curtains.

This time Rosie was aware of it too. "Summer lightning," she gasped in response to a shudder of alarm from me as we both lay recovering our composure. "Ooh, dearie me, Rosie girl, I think you'll have to go on a diet before we try that one again, and so will you, Ollie."

"That was no lightning," I said. I was of a mind to leap up and peer out into the darkness, but in the tumble, or very possibly before it, my legs had become inextricably intertwined with Rosie's.

"What was it, then, clever Dick? You'll see, there'll be thunder in a second or two."

On cue, there was a distant rumble that might have been thunder or, much more likely in retrospect, the sound of a goods train rattling over the viaduct far across the Downs. While I was trying to remember whether lightning really did come before thunder or was it the other way round, it occurred to Rosie to make a virtue out of misfortune, if what she had in mind could be described as virtuous. Observing, "Well, since we're down here we might as well stay here, ooh, come on, Ollie, get me going again," she initiated an exploration of the possibilities of an easy chair tipped on its back. Doubtless she would report her findings, favourable or otherwise, to her friend Janey later. For myself, I found the position a little cramped but it did have the advantage that, saving possibly a glimpse of Rosie's thick ankles, it was unlikely that we could be visible through the gap in the curtains.

The editorial floor of the *Badgers Heath Herald* was designed on what one of my more waggish reporters called the open-plant principle. That is, it was conventional open plan but with lines of potted plants acting as space dividers. The more exotic and impenetrable the plants, the more important the person or persons they screened. The reporters worked from within a perimeter of geraniums, the sub-editors behind a low wall of Busy Lizzies. My sports editor and show business editor faced one another across a bank of weeping fig while Douglas Boxer, my future ex-deputy and prospective fellow-editor, lurked inside a spinney of Swiss cheese. As editor, I surveyed my little domain through a barrier of rubber plants.

This morning, the morning after the toppled easy chair esca- pade with Rosie, there was little to survey. The magistrates' court sits on a Tuesday, as does the council, and there was an inquest on a farmer who had accidentally set himself on fire while burn- ing stubble – another merry widow for Rosie's Farmers' Ladies Circle? I wondered in passing – plus all the sundry meetings and comings and goings of a small town with too much time on its hands, every one of which had to be covered. Except for Nick Crabbe, who was writing up last night's meeting of the Bonfire Society committee ("Badgers Heath Bonfire Society's buxom new Appeals Secretary, farmer's widow Mrs Rosie Greenleaf (36), this week made an amazing pledge – to raise £10,000 single- handed at the rate of £1,000 a week . . . " I would have to have another word with Crabbe about his snappy style), the news- room was left to the geraniums. Behind their Busy Lizzies, my three sub-editors, plugged into their VDU terminals like cows into a milking machine, silently converted the week's hard copy into pap.

My style of editing was to delegate – a constructive way of saying that as far as possible I let my subordinates do the work. My leading article, moderately criticising the council planning department for its well-intentioned but to the *Herald*'s mind ill- considered decision not to allow the Owl Insurance Co to pull down yet another listed Victorian villa for an office extension (Owl Insurance are big advertisers in the *Herald*'s sits vac pages), was already written. I had little to do that could not be done by Boxer, and I might as well get my money's worth out of him before he went. I fell to brooding about Rosie and those flashing lights.

It was rather worrying if I cared to apply my mind to it – which was why, until now, I had been reluctant to allow my mind anywhere near the riddle. The light in the graveyard, caught only by the corner of one eye while the brain was actively engaged on other business, could be explained away: fellow-lovers, having made a bed of an adjoining tombstone, striking a match for a post-coital cigarette perhaps, or even a stray peeping Tom with a torch. But what about the flash through Rosie's window last night? Given a week or so I could probably persuade myself that it was lightning as she had suggested, or the lights of a passing car (it would have to be driving across a five-acre field, since Rosie's living room faces away from the road). But with the incident fresh in my memory I knew it could only have been a camera flash.

It didn't make any sense at all, or rather it didn't make the kind of sense that I had any wish to contemplate. If the light outside Rosie's window had been a camera flash, then so had the light in the churchyard. Same flash, same person. I could easily imagine some mackintoshed observer lurking around Mill Farm with a view to compiling a portfolio of happy snaps of Rosie and escort (or escorts?) at play – Harry the pigman, perhaps: Rosie's pro-nounced streak of exhibitionism, even if newly acquired as a side effect of widowhood as she dubiously claimed, could not have escaped the notice of any farmhand with eyes in his head and access to a ladder. But what was the mysterious candid camera-man doing in the churchyard? I knew that serendipity attends many photographers, with the exception of the *Badgers Heath Herald*'s trendy snapper Gavin Pyle who was so busy thinking up arty camera angles that he was never in the right place at the right time, but this was something more sinister than the luck of the devil. He must have been following us – to what purpose, it was not difficult to hazard a guess. Unless, that was – and here I began to hatch a theory which while fanciful was preferable to the alternative scenario of my having to leave a huge sum in used notes in a hollow tree – he had turned up by appointment. I would not have put it past Rosie. From what I knew of her sexual tastes, and I was in turn appetisingly and apprehensively aware that so far I had only seen the tip of what in any other context I would have called the iceberg, she was quite capable of persuad-ing a friend with a camera, or even engaging a professional photographer, to compile a souvenir album of our little fling over which she could browse on long winter evenings, once she had acquired new batteries for Molly's vibrator.

These ruminations were interrupted by the appearance of Nick Crabbe as he leered through a gap in my rubber plants on his way to the coffee machine. "Any reaction, boss?"

He was referring to the memo I had requested on his Banana-skin Week brainstorm, which had lain unheeded on my desk for several days. However, open-plant etiquette decrees that you do not part the leaves of a colleague's rubber plants should you want a word with him, especially if that colleague happens to be your superior: the correct form is to hover at the proper place of entry until invited in. I ignored the interruption.

I was sitting at my desk doing nothing at all, not even pretending to read a newspaper. Crabbe was emboldened to persist: "I could always take the idea to Radio South if you didn't like it, boss."

Using the word that I had been trying to push to the back of my mind before Crabbe had broken my uneasy train of thought, I said, "That sounds like blackmail, cock."

"If you'd just read my memo, boss. You did ask me to give you a memo and I've spent a lot of my own time putting it together."

"All right, I'll read it. Now piss off and write what you're paid to write."

Having nothing better to do and worse things to contemplate, and reflecting that an idea dismissed out of hand by my deputy Douglas Boxer must have something going for it, I plucked Crabbe's memo, as I thought, out of my tray. "Can't you cut this down, cock?" I groaned aloud as I leafed through a good dozen closely-typed pages. But it was not Nick Crabbe's memo on Bananaskin Week, it was Boxer's memo on the Youth Prayer Rally. I had not read that either, for all that it had been submitted on the instructions of Sam Dice himself. Nor did I intend to, until Sam broached the matter again. By then, with any luck, Boxer might have departed to screw up the sales of the *East Sussex Advertiser*, when I could feed his memo to the shredder, claiming to Sam that when it came down to it the Youth Prayer Rally wheeze had proved so full of holes that he had found it impossible to produce a proper blueprint.

As I tossed the document back into my tray it suddenly occurred to me that what I should have had from Boxer and hadn't got was his letter of resignation. Glaring out through my rubber plants I saw him sitting contentedly behind his allocation of Swiss cheese plants like a member of a protected species. Brandishing a pair of scissors, he was placidly and methodically going through the other weekly papers that impinged on our circulation area, carefully snipping out items that might be plundered.

It always annoyed me to watch Boxer performing this chore with the happy concentration of a stamp collector busy with his hobby. I got up and went across to him, choosing to plough through his curtain of greenery rather than use his entrance space. This was calculated to annoy Boxer in turn.

"I'm not trying to hurry you, Douglas, but wasn't I expecting a billet doux?"

A shifty look was superimposed on his naturally anxious features.

"My memo? It should be on your desk."

"Yes, I've got that, though I haven't had time to read it yet. I didn't say memo, cock, I said letter. Dear Oliver, with regret I must ask you to stick my position as deputy editor up your jacksey."

Upon my entry Boxer's left knee had begun to jerk violently as if keeping time to Ravel's Bolero played at three times its normal speed. This sign of acute agitation was now supplemented by other body language distress signals such as backside-wriggling and tie-fiddling.

"Yes, I was going to have a word with you about that, Oliver. What's the drill, would you say – if one hasn't in fact submitted a formal letter of resignation, how does one go about withdrawing it?"

"You're saying you're not going after all?"

"There's been a hitch."

A hitch. The expression, "Well, well, fucking well!" formed on my lips but I contented myself with a self-satisfied smile and the words, "Oh dear me!"

"Yes, I'm afraid when it came down to the nitty gritty the offer was far less attractive than it at first appeared, at least the fringe benefits were."

"No tape deck in your office car?" I couldn't resist scoffing.

Boxer was notoriously a stickler for all the allowances he could screw out of his puny appointment. He talked about golden handshakes with the wistfulness that older men talked about loose women.

"You may laugh, Oliver, but these things are important when you get to a certain stage in life. No, the fact is the advertisement clearly promised a generous relocation allowance, but what it turns out is that they were simply talking about removal expenses. All the expense of selling up No 4 The Ridgeway and buying a new house in East Sussex somewhere, all the solicitors' fees and stamp duty, conveyancing and estate agents' commission and so on would all fall on me. Plus, what guarantee is there that I'd get more for my house here than I'd have to pay out for my house there? East Sussex property's very pricey these days, Oliver, very pricey indeed. I could have ended up seriously out of pocket. Besides which," concluded Boxer lamely, "what if my face didn't fit? They were only offering a one-year contract — where should I be then?"

To prevent Douglas Boxer from taking up his new appointment and rub his nose in the Youth Prayer Rally mess he had proposed to leave on my doorstep, I had daydreamed of writing a series of anonymous letters to the management of the *East Sussex Advertiser*, drawing attention to their editor-designate's supposed drinking habits, sexual deviations, driving convictions, bungling incompetence, bad breath and wonky heart condition. I might have known that in the end Boxer's own natural caution and career vertigo would draw him back, at the eleventh hour, from this terrifying step into the unknown and the traumatic migration from a semi with carport and d-i-y patio on one side of the Downs to a semi with carport and d-i-y patio on the other side of the Downs.

"So at the death, cock, you got cold feet," I said, coming on like the hardboiled Fleet Street veteran.

"I had second thoughts, if that's what you mean. I faxed them a letter this morning, saying I'd thought it through very carefully and decided to stay with the devil I know."

"But you're not staying with the devil you know, cock," I pointed out with malice. "You're staying with his opposite number." I jabbed a finger heavenwards.

Boxer understood the allusion. "The Youth Prayer Rally. Yes. That's something else I wanted to have a word about."

"Hoist with your own petard, chum. Whatever a petard may be."

This time it was the turn of Boxer's right knee to twitch convulsively. To stop himself from another compulsive bout of tie-straightening he thrust his hand into his pocket and began to jangle change.

"I know you think I was trying to land you with a giant headache, Oliver, but I honestly and truly did think it was a good idea, good for the paper and good for Badgers Heath."

"Bollocks."

"You say that, and I know you won't believe this, Oliver, but I genuinely did want to leave Badgers Heath with something to remember me by."

I was going to savour this. "You'll be remembered all right, cock," I said grimly. "For as long as this paper exists, cub reporters will speak your name with awe, and do you know what they'll say? They'll say, 'There went a man who couldn't even trust himself to move house from one part of the county to another without incurring a loss, yet the prat tried to organise the biggest outdoor event the south-east has ever seen since the Rolling Stones concert on the Downs.' If that prayer rally ever comes about, Douglas, I'm putting you in sole charge. And may the star of the show have mercy on your soul."

On that triumphantly vindictive note I was about to make a forceful exit through Boxer's Swiss cheese plants, but he had propelled himself to his feet and nervously grabbed his paper scissors, with which he began to make violent stabbing motions in the air. Doubtless he would like to have lunged them at my private parts. "If I can just beg one more moment, Oliver. You say you haven't read my memo?"

"No, but I hope for your sake it's watertight."

"That's the trouble – it is."

I knew exactly what the devious bugger meant. Thinking he was shaking the dust of Badgers Heath off his heels he had put the case for the Youth Prayer Rally in the rosiest possible light,

61

glossing over the possible snags and pitfalls and playing down the organisational problems and cost – not to mention the possibility, the certainty I should say, of our born-again proprietor, whose public speaking experience was limited to the annual dinner of the Regional Publishers' Association, making a raging fool of himself.

There was more than enjoyment to be got out of my deputy's discomfiture, however. I could see a way out.

"Let's not piss about with one another over this, cock. I meant it when I said I'm putting you in charge. Sam wouldn't want it any other way – it's your baby. Now I'm going to ask you a straight question. Are you up to it?"

"You know I'm not, Oliver – I don't have the organisational skills. But then I didn't intend to be here, did I?"

"So who did you propose should mastermind this bloody shambles?"

"As I say, Oliver, you should read the memo."

I interpreted this correctly. "You mean you swung it on to me?"

Boxer treated me to one of his fawning grimaces. "Well, you are after all the editor, and considering all your experience with the Bonfire Society . . . "

He tailed off, leaving me wondering what, if anything, he had decided to leave unsaid. " . . . I thought I'd land you in it" seemed to fill the gap.

It was a time to be decisive. I knew I had him by whatever passed for balls in the Boxer anatomy. "Douglas," I said. "I'll tell you what we're going to do, by which I mean what you're going to do if your life's to be worth living. You're coming across with me to my desk and you're going to repossess that memo. Not only have I not read it, I have not seen it. It does not exist. Burn it, shred it, eat it, flush it down the loo, but get rid of it. Then I want you to write me another memo, explaining in detail why your Youth Prayer Rally is a non-starter. We all thought it a good idea at the time but you've now had a closer look at what we'd be letting ourselves in for, you've costed it, you've taken advice from the experts, you've had a word with God himself even, and he's given it the thumbs down. And you keep my name right out of it, cock – you put all the blame on yourself, right?"

"I'm sure that would be the best solution," Boxer practically whimpered in his gratitude. "I shan't forget this, Oliver."

"Too bloody true you won't, cock."

I trampled through the Swiss cheese undergrowth with the subdued Boxer trotting after me like a baby elephant following its leader through the jungle. Passing Nick Crabbe busy at his VDU and wondering whether I ought to make Boxer shred his memo too while he was about it, I cut a swathe through the rubber plants and reached my office space.

Reception had not rung to warn me that Sam Dice was on his way up. Maybe he had told them not to: he liked to catch us on the hop sometimes.

He was sprawled on my sofa, reading a closely-typed document intently. He reached the last paragraph of Douglas Boxer's memo just as its author, taking the conventional route rather than trample the editorial foliage, joined me at my desk.

"You're to be congratulated, Douglas," said Sam, tossing the memo back into my tray. "You'll be letting me have a copy of this, Oliver?"

"Of course, Sam, as soon as Douglas has added some qualifications."

"What is there to qualify? It's all there, laddie. I must say," said Sam, "that thinking over Douglas's Youth Prayer Rally, first-rate idea that it is, I did begin to wonder whether it was the kind of area our newspaper ought to be getting into, whether we might stand accused of ramming religion down our readers' throats. But this reassures me. I was a doubting Thomas and I was wrong. It's what I was sent here to do and it's a circulation builder."

"That's if it comes off, sir," warned Boxer, catching my eye and following my unspoken instruction.

Sam permitted himself a fat chuckle. "It'll come off, laddie. And do you know why I know it'll come off? I had a message. The seal of approval. D'you know what I mean?"

Boxer and I nodded glumly. With God on the other side we were outnumbered.

5

A typical Saturday morning in Badgers Heath. An eight-foot Yogi Bear lumbers along the High Street, waving at children and scattering leaflets advertising a Whale Sale at Bancroft's, our local department store, where every pound spent on selected items will yield ten pence to Greenpeace. A banner stretched across the street from Dorothy's Pantry – now proudly proclaiming itself holder of the National Heartbeat Award for healthy food choice – and the Cumbria, Badgers Heath and Acorn Building Society, and somewhat obscuring the southbound view of the Brook Lane traffic lights, counsels careful driving during National Safety Week. Outside the Scent Shop two young women in boiler suits solicit signatures for a petition against animal experiments for the cosmetics industry, while outside the Wine Mart a girl dressed as a can of low alcohol beer offers handbills advocating sensible drinking. Pedestrians negotiating their way around the three pavement bottle banks encounter a further obstruction in the shape of four scouts of the third Badgers Heath troop posing as statues for the Scout Association Promise Appeal. At their various time-hallowed strategic corners, middle-aged ladies hawk trays of smiling paper sunflower faces in aid of the Sunshine Shelters for Disadvantaged Children. On a chalked grid in the Cherrytree Shopping Mall, marked off by traffic cones, half a dozen schoolgirls including the myopic Miss Kimberley Spruce are engaged in a sponsored hopscotch marathon, their latest initiative for the Wildlife Fund. A four months premature female Santa Claus wearing net stockings and ringing a bell, patrols the Mall collecting for the homeless. Over the throb of disco music from the clothes boutiques may be heard, intermittently, the merry clink of coins falling into collecting boxes. Our Town.

My Saturday morning routine is – was – to drive my wife into town, or more accurately to be driven by my wife into town since she has a superior class of car, and then, after pottering about for a bit, to repair to the lounge bar of the Euro-inn Dolphin Arms Hotel where in due course she would join me and my cronies for a stiff drink after the ordeal of shopping. I did hope I was not in for yet another rant from Sherry about having to run the gauntlet of flag day collectors and today's selection of exhibitionists moved by charitable impulse.

The Rev Basil Brush, selfconsciously nursing the pint pewter tankard he affected as the plain man's parson, was already at the bar with Len Quartermouth MBE FIAV and Dennis Reason the bank manager, all of them sporting the county businessman's off duty uniform of tweed jacket, cavalry twills and cravat or dog collar according to vocation. For myself, I favoured the smartly-casual sweater and slacks affected by ministers of state for weekend photo opportunities. Soon, after he had fortified himself at the Goat and Compasses down the street, we should be joined by, and sartorially let down by, Eric Barlow in booze-stained blazer and flannels. This would complete the quintet, or clique as some called it, that was the Bonfire Society's unofficial steering committee.

I had expected Rosie's progress as Appeals Secretary to be high on the lounge bar agenda, and so it was, although it was to prove that we had even more important business to deliberate before the morning's drinking session was over.

"If I had Mrs Greenleaf in charge of my Steeple Fund, chaps, my troubles would be over," said Basil waggishly, as with two extended fingers a wafer's distance apart he indicated to the barman the nominated size of the gin he had hastily ordered me so as to conclude his round before the arrival of Barlow demanding doubles. Still in jocular mode he added, "I wonder if she'd take to the suggestion of co-option once again!"

"Suggestion of copulation again?" This could be nobody else but Barlow making his fairly well-oiled entrance. A spasm of irritation flicked across Basil's face, probably more at the prospect of having to buy Barlow a drink after all than at the fellow's bad taste. The Rev Basil Thrush counted himself a broadminded man.

Dennis Reason, on the other hand, did not. "Rather an offensive observation to make about a fellow committee member, one would have thought," he said shortly, addressing a framed photograph of Morris dancers infesting the Dolphin Arms courtyard.

"We were talking about Rosie Greenleaf," I explained in response to Barlow's blank look.

I had misinterpreted it: it was simply the physical manifestation of an alcoholic haze. "Yes, I thought you might be," Barlow chortled.

"Really!" protested Reason.

Basil hastened to pour oil on troubled waters. He did not hasten, I noticed, to pour scotch into Barlow. Barlow, however, was already waggling a hand at the barman, a pantomime gesture indicating not only that he required a scotch at the double, but that he required a double scotch at the double. "It's early days yet," said Basil, "but our Appeals Secretary shows every sign of bringing home the bacon."

"She's been in office what, ah, twelve days?" said Len Quartermouth MBE FIAV. "And ah how much would either of you guess she's ah?"

"In round figures," said Reason.

"*Very* round figures," murmured Basil.

"Now then, naughty naughty," said Barlow, misunderstanding, or choosing to, and Basil buried his face in his beer tankard in his determination not to blush.

"I won't guess," said I with a certain amount of smugness, "because I already know the answer." Considering it could only have come from one source, I wondered fleetingly if this admission, boast rather, was wise.

"Two hundred," hazarded Barlow.

"Higher," said Reason.

"Three."

"Keep going."

"Is Mr Barlow's order down to you, Vicar?" the barman asked

pointedly, noting that Barlow had already downed most of his large scotch.

With either feigned or mock innocence, it was hard to say which, Barlow said, "Oh, were you getting them in, Basil? I would have asked for a small one if I'd known you were pushing the boat out." He went on, as Basil reluctantly fumbled in his pocket, "Go on, then, how much?"

"Three pounds exactly, if you please," the barman said.

"A thousand," I said.

"One thousand pounds precisely," said Reason.

Eric Barlow expelled whisky fumes in an attempt at an astonished whistle. "Stone me! A thousand quid in less than a fortnight! How does she do it?"

"I can tell you how she raised the last thirty pounds of it," I said with a good show of ruefulness. "She was on her way to Dennis's bank with nine hundred and seventy smackers stuffed into her handbag when she had the great good fortune to run into Muggins here. She twisted my arm to make it up to an even grand."

"Well done! Splendid!" congratulated Basil, giving me the kind of beam I would have got for bringing an unusually large marrow to the harvest festival. I wondered if he would have grinned as broadly had he known in what sense, and in what circumstances, Rosie and I had bumped into one another. "Ooh, that makes me feel really horny," she had crooned as I tucked the cheque into her stocking top. "Did I ever tell you I get a kick out of pretending I'm on the game sometimes, ooh, do you think it's warm enough to go outside and do it against the wall?"

"Be that as it ah, that leaves nine hundred and ah unaccounted for," said Len Quartermouth MBE FIAV.

"When you said you saw her going into Dennis's bank, Oliver," said Barlow with a wink, "she wasn't by any chance wearing a stocking mask at the time?"

"I think I should have been informed," said Reason bleakly.

"Well God blimey, there's got to be some explanation. Just go out and look at that High Street – there's so many collecting tins out there that one of these Saturdays there's going to be a very nasty accident with the crush of shoppers crossing the road to avoid them. Yet our Rosie's only been on the job twelve days, if Dennis will excuse the expression, and already she's managed to screw a thousand quid out of the tightfisted sods. How?"

"We're getting perilously close to looking our gift horse in the mouth," pronounced Basil Brush. "Perhaps we'd better move on."

"Where to, the Goat and Compasses?" quipped Barlow.

"Strictly between ourselves and these four walls, Dennis has an announcement to make."

"Hardly an announcement," said Reason. "The place for that is in committee."

"Call it a preview," Barlow suggested. He signalled for a fresh round of drinks. Basil Brush unsuccessfully tried to evolve a signal instructing the barman to take his time and if possible miss Barlow out of his own round.

"You won't say anything about this in the *Herald* for the moment, Oliver," requested, or rather commanded, Reason, in too conspiratorial a tone for my liking. I gave him the standard guarded response of small-town editors to saloon bar confidantes: "Not if it's between ourselves, Dennis, but that's not to say the paper might not have heard whatever you're about to divulge from another source."

"That's just it," said Reason. "That young fellow Crabbe seems to have got wind of it. At any rate he buttonholed me as I was going into the bank after lunch yesterday and wanted to know if I'd anything for the *Herald*. I referred him to Head Office if it was bank business and to the next agenda of the Standing Committee if it concerned the Bonfire Society, and sent him packing."

I frowned. Doorstepping, as it is known in the trade, was not encouraged on the *Herald*. Sam disapproved of it and so did I. Besides, I wasn't paying Nick Crabbe to stroll around the town digging up dirt on his own initiative. Yesterday lunchtime, as I recalled, should have seen him at the Badgers Heath Museum and Heritage Centre buffet lunch to welcome a travelling exhibition of folk art. I would study his report keenly for indications of his having left before the speeches.

"And which was it?" I asked.

"Both," said Reason. "As Basil and Len here already know, I'm afraid I have no option but to tender my resignation as Treasurer of the Bonfire Society."

My first thought was what I had no doubt must have been Nick Crabbe's first thought upon hearing the news, if heard the news he had: that Reason had been on the fiddle. I at once dismissed the notion as the figment of a journo's fevered mind. Two signatures, Reason's as Treasurer and mine as his deputy, were required on every Bonfire Society cheque. Besides, apart from the thousand pounds lately deposited by Rosie, the Bonfire Society didn't have any money, if our worthy Treasurer were to be believed. Unless he was into forgery and had been falsifying the Society's bank statements, which I conceded was not entirely out of the bounds of possibility, his enforced resignation was of a more pedestrian order.

So it proved – or so I was led by Reason to believe it proved. "It's a fearful nuisance, but the decree has come down from on high that branch managers are no longer allowed to undertake treasurerships or handle funds on a personal rather than professional level for any local organisation."

"Oh dear me, afraid you might mix their money up with ours, are they?" sniggered Barlow with another of his winks.

"Evidently the Three Counties Bank's head office regard it as undesirable to serve two ah," bleated Len Quartermouth MBE FIAV.

"Not quite to serve two masters," said Reason sharply. "But there could be a conflict of interests – where, for example, an individual wearing his hon treasurer's hat might be tempted to speculate short-term with a society's funds using knowledge obtained while wearing his bank manager's hat. Such cases have been known, though not in Badgers Heath I hasten to add."

While Barlow made some facetious remarks about hat tricks I speculated that maybe Nick Crabbe was on to something after all. Reason wouldn't swindle the Bonfire Society but it wasn't beyond the bounds of possibility that he had tried to improve its finances with a spot of insider trading. I was wide of the mark as usual. I should have realised that a treasurer stroke bank manager as inept as Dennis Reason who tried to juggle the funds would have lost the lot within hours.

"As Dennis says, it's a great nuisance, but it seems we shall have no option but to accept his resignation at the next committee meeting," said Basil, interrupting Barlow's seemingly endless flow of hat jokes.

"With an appropriate vote of ah, it goes without saying."

"I should be grateful if any vote of thanks that was thought appropriate didn't sound like a valedictory," said Reason. "I shall of course hope to be invited to continue to serve as an ordinary committee member."

"No invitation necessary," I pointed out. I didn't count myself a constitutional authority on the Bonfire Society but I had read the rules. "You're an elected member."

"Which leads us to the thorny question of Dennis's successor," said Basil, who really was a constitutional authority, having nothing better to do. "All offices as we know must be filled from the existing committee, except in the event of death or resignation when we may co-opt from outside, as in the case of Mrs Greenleaf."

"Pity you're not prone to heart attacks, Dennis – we could co-opt your grieving widow and solve all our problems," offered Barlow.

I cannot say Reason physically flushed but he certainly gave the impression of flushing. "If that's going to be the standard of your wit for the remainder of the year, Eric, perhaps I should offer my resignation here and now and as you say solve all your problems."

"It would not be accepted," said Basil Brush firmly, an exasperated sideways glance intimating that if on the other hand Barlow cared to proffer his resignation it would be accepted with alacrity. "Now let's I beg of you stay within the realm of practicalities. Of the nine committee members, only four do not already hold office, if we exclude Dennis but include Oliver who is nominally Deputy Treasurer by virtue of countersigning the cheques."

"But who is also only an ex-officio member by virtue of being editor of the *Herald* with access to a very big printing set," I chipped in hastily, already seeing what was coming.

"Nothing in our constitution disqualifies you from office," said Basil with misplaced reassurance. "Now of the other three contenders, I'm afraid that with the best will in the world and saving your presence, Eric – "

"Thank you very much for your support, I shall always wear it," said Barlow in something of a huff.

"If the cap fits," murmured Reason with quiet malevolence.

"Although lending sterling support in other ah," put in our tactful Chairperson.

"So if we eliminate the other two candidates as not quite Treasurer material, that leaves us with you, Oliver," said Basil.

I was lumbered and I knew I was lumbered. The other two candidates so rightly dismissed by Basil were our neighbours the Spruces, and I would sooner have had Barlow than either of them. Indeed I would sooner have had Barlow in the first place than Dennis Reason, or either or both of the Spruces for that matter, but there was little point in going back on that. I was lumbered. The fact that at this stage in the game I did not know by whom I had been lumbered, or why, is neither here nor there. I trotted out my lame protestations but to no avail. I came, apparently, with Reason's warmest endorsement of my work as his deputy, a recommendation based entirely, it seemed, on my having once in an idle moment added up the right hand column of the draft accounts and found a discrepancy of £7.30, an item for petty cash carelessly overlooked, in the best tradition of the Three Counties Bank, by my prospective predecessor. To seal his testimonial, Reason went to the unusual lengths of standing me a drink, unasked. As Barlow and Basil Brush, with meaningful glances at the barman, included themselves in the round, Len Quartermouth MBE FIAV said, as always when we had finished carving up the Bonfire Society's business between us, "Of course, all this has to be formalised by the full ah."

That seemed to conclude the meeting. Basil Brush and Len fell to talking about parish matters while Barlow accosted a crony across the room. On the strength of having bought me a gin and tonic, Reason drew me aside.

"Referring back to that young fellow-me-lad Crabbe, I'm sure he's one of your brightest sparks but I should keep an eye on him, if you'll take a word of advice."

I was already keeping an eye on Nick Crabbe unprompted by Reason, but I asked, fishing for anything he might have to tell me, "Keep an eye on him in what sense?"

"He strikes me as a young troublemaker. I'll say no more," said Reason with cryptic significance, all but tapping his nose. Nor did he say more, for at that moment Sherry entered with a sustained denunciation of the Cherrytree Shopping Mall multi-storey car park system that took her all the way through a large Bloody Mary and towards the hour when I had rashly agreed to take her out for lunch.

Badgers Heath's only entry in the *Good Food Guide* is the Old Forge, an establishment noted more for what the *Herald*'s restaurant critic Trencherman (aka Douglas Boxer) calls "ample portions" than for the subtlety of its cuisine. Its position on the edge of town overlooking what was formerly a village green but is now a traffic roundabout would be ideal for discreet liaisons were it not that the few Badgers Heath residents gourmet enough to make the expedition are all known to one another. Saturday lunchtime, however, despite the recommendations of Mr & Mrs P. Spruce, Rev B. Thrush, Mr LQ MBE FIAV and others, usually finds the place experiencing one of its frequent lulls, which is why Sherry preferred it to the Dolphin Arms Buttery for what she termed "one of our little talks". An idling waiter cocked an ear as my wife asked over the boeuf Wellington, "By the way, are you having an affair?"

Although I had been expecting the enquiry sooner or later, I had not anticipated that it would be so soon, and indeed had not even included it on my shortlist of possible subjects for debate. After all, my fling with Rosie was only into its third glorious week — barely time for rumours to start circulating, let alone reach the ears of a practising non-member of the tea-and-gossip circuit who in any case spent most of her time in London. However, I had prepared my answer.

"No," I said. "Are you?"

"If I were," said Sherry evenly, "it wouldn't threaten my career. You know what Sam Dice is like, Kettle. If he so much as suspected you were putting yourself about you'd be back doing casual shifts on the tabloids."

"Where at least I'd be able to keep an eye on my wife." I had no pressing curiosity about what she got up to in her Barbican hideaway, but I had decided, musing on my possible response should she ever get wind of Rosie, that if not attack then a spot of sabre-rattling would be the best form of defence.

Sherry saw through my show of belligerence to my reluctance to awaken sleeping dogs. "You don't really want to pursue that line of thought, do you?"

"Not particularly. But sauce for the goose and all that."

My companion, as Trencherman would have dubbed her, prodded a forkful of pastry into the brown goo on her plate. "Talking of sauce, would you say this was Bovril or Oxo stiffened with cornflour?" I took this as an indication that a truce had been arrived at, and with relief turned to some piece of Fleet Street gossip gleaned from *Private Eye* to encourage my wife to start talking shop. This she obligingly and entertainingly did until we had waved our food away with the usual explanation to the maitre d' that the meal was excellent but our appetites small and the portions too ample. Ordering decaff and sending the pudding trolley on its way, Sherry then resumed hostilities without warning.

"If you *were* having an affair, and the party of the second part was your friend Mrs Greenleaf, it really would be incredibly stupid."

I did my best not to look startled, for with Sherry safely prattling away about which editor was due for the chop and which reporter had involved his paper in a possible £1,000,000 libel suit, it was towards my friend Mrs Greenleaf that I had allowed my thoughts to drift. Having by this time assimilated my unexpected elevation to the treasurership of the Bonfire Society, it was now dawning on me that the appointment was no bad thing. With a pocket calculator to hand and without the disadvantage of a branch bank manager's training, the Bonfire Society's books could not occupy me for more than half an hour a month at most; as for the non-book-keeping side of the job, the Treasurer's duties tended to throw him into the company of other officers, notably the Appeals Secretary. I would be free to move to and from Mill Farm without arousing suspicion.

Except, of course, that I appeared to have aroused it already. "We've already agreed that it would be incredibly stupid whoever else was involved," I said carefully. "But why single out Rosie Greenleaf?"

"I ask myself the same question, duckie. For anyone granted the experience, it must be like screwing the Goodyear Blimp."

No point in trying to dodge the issue any further. "Come on, Sherry, let's stop fencing. What's the point you're making?"

"You mean apart from accusing my husband of sleeping with another woman? Only that she's barking mad. I hope you realise that."

The thought had crossed my mind; but then I had reflected that it was only in her sexual tastes that Rosie was notably eccentric. Out of bed, or off the kitchen table, she was a plump, uncomplicated if somewhat exuberant but essentially nice personality who was coping well with widowhood.

It would be Nick Crabbe, I guessed, who was feeding my wife her information. He always went up to London on his days off and while I had never bothered to make enquiries I had no reason for supposing he would avoid the company of an attractive former colleague who remained a good Fleet Street contact, possibly in more than one sense. But unless he had taken to following me about with a flash camera – a theory I could not entirely rule out, if I cared to dwell on it – he had only conjecture to go on.

"Who's your source?" I asked.

"You should know better than to ask a fellow-hack a question like that. Just watch your back, Kettle. Subject closed." Good advice. I should have taken it.

But before we did leave the subject I could not resist asking, "Talking of affairs, did you ever have it off with Nick Crabbe?"

"Credit me with some taste, Kettle. I'm not the toy boy type and anyway he would certainly have exploited the situation for all it was worth – just like your Rosie Greenleaf, if you let her. They'd make a good pair."

Perfectly on cue, into the empty restaurant walked Rosie

Greenleaf, looking as usual as if she had just risen from a bed of pleasure, escorted by Nick Crabbe, looking on this occasion like the cat that has swallowed the cream. As he spotted us across an uncrowded room, the expression switched to that of a cat that has stolen the cream.

"Talk of the devil," I said with lame heartiness as the maitre d', with that unerring instinct waiters are born with for seating all but the most favoured customers at the worst table in the house, placed the newcomers in the middle of the floor well within conversational reach of our table.

"Snap," smiled Crabbe. I noted with reluctant approval that he did not make the mistake of explaining, even in the most round-about way, what he was doing out with Rosie in the most expensive restaurant within a forty-mile radius, though doubtless he would in time. Rosie, for her own part, was being every inch the discreet mistress, betraying neither with confused glance nor stammered word that she had stumbled unexpectedly across her lover and his wife. It could only be an aplomb born of practice.

"You mean you were talking about us too?" responded Sherry with just a hint of cattiness in her smile as she gathered up her things. "A pity you couldn't both have got here sooner – we could have made up a foursome."

It was only then that Rosie permitted herself a swift, covertly lascivious glance into my eyes and I knew exactly what was flashing through her mind.

6

"I had ever such a naughty thought in that restaurant yesterday."

"Yes, I thought you might have done," I said guardedly, not caring to add, in the peculiar circumstances, that Rosie's naughty thought was what had sustained me through an otherwise lackadaisical patch of lovemaking with Sherry the previous evening.

The peculiar circumstances were that it was now Sunday afternoon, Rosie was ringing me at home, and my wife was upstairs resting. Either that or she was listening in on the bedroom extension, a possibility so horrendous that it had to be checked out at once.

"Hold on, the papers are in my briefcase," I loudly added in the shakily officious tones of a fraudulent stockbroker maintaining that he can prove his innocence. There was a mischievous giggle at the other end of the phone, but otherwise Rosie tactfully held her peace.

I dashed out and grabbed my briefcase from the hall table, then, clutching it against my chest as a talisman against awkward questions, tiptoed up the stairs and peered round the open bedroom door. Sherry was lying on the bed either asleep or feigning sleep, it mattered not which: the point to establish was that she was not in reach of the telephone extension. I tiptoed back downstairs and resumed my cryptic conversation with Rosie. Cryptic on my side, that was.

"I'll keep this short if you don't mind, because I don't want to wake my wife."

"Why not?" snickered Rosie. "She might like it, ooh, I wish you were waking me up, Ollie sugar, and not with a cup of tea either."

"I have the report in front of me but there are rather too many points to discuss over the telephone."

"Would you like to ring me back from outside, pet?"

"No, I don't think I could do that." The nearest payphone, in an area blessed with an over-abundance of telephone subscribers, was nearly a mile away and I had no reputation for taking Sunday afternoon walks, especially when it was pissing with rain.

"I'd better get straight to the point then, hadn't I, lover boy? How would you like to come round for tea?"

A slight creak from behind me made me look sharply across at the mirror over the bookshelves. It reflected a view of the doorway where Sherry stood yawning elaborately. In a panic I dived into the briefcase which I had set down on the chair beside me, and drew out the first batch of papers to hand, which happened to be Nick Crabbe's Bananaskin Week memo. It had made several fruitless trips between office and home without my yet getting round to reading it. Now I tossed it down on my desk and, telephone cradled on my shoulder, leafed through it in an aimless frenzy. Praying that I was conveying a sense of danger to Rosie while simultaneously not conveying an impression of agitated babbling to Sherry, I said into the receiver, "There's a good deal of ground to cover, Sam. You wouldn't rather we tackled it at the office tomorrow?"

Mentally kicking myself for having handed Rosie such overt *double entendre* material as "a good deal of ground to cover" and "tackle it at the office" to play with, and giving myself an extra kick for dragging Sam's name into it when there were a dozen *Herald* staff I could be pretending to be speaking to, I turned with instantly-induced nonchalance to take in Sherry as she crossed to the sofa, and made an eyebrow-raising, yawn-stifling pantomime of irritated boredom. Sherry picked up one of the Sunday pop papers lying on the coffee table.

"I'm all for tackling it tomorrow, honeybunch, but how about tackling it today first?" purred Rosie. Pitched low in a seductive key, it was unlikely that her voice was reaching Sherry. The disadvantage was that it was reaching me soft and clear. Despite, or because of, the knife-edge I was on, I was beginning to feel distinct stirrings.

"So you're suggesting teatime?" I said recklessly.

"With jam on it," whispered Rosie.

Sherry, I saw, was browsing through a double-spread feature on what purported to be a newly-discovered medical condition known as sexoholism, a kind of sexual equivalent of alcoholism to which Errol Flynn, President Kennedy and Marilyn Monroe, among other celebrities too dead to be able to sue for libel, were said to have been addicted. If such a condition existed, Rosie certainly suffered from it. Now I wondered if I did too.

"I'll be there, Sam," I said.

Suppressing a stupid urge to volunteer, "That was Sam" as I hung up, I said to Sherry with a show of mock-petulance, "If you'd had the consideration to wake up five minutes ago you could have got me out of that."

"Pull the other one, Kettle – when did you last refuse to speak to Sam Dice?"

"I would still have talked to him, sure, but when he asked me round for tea I could have called over to you, 'Darling, can't we put off your bridge afternoon?' or something."

"So why didn't you? I was sitting here, reading the paper."

"It was too late, I was committed by then."

"So why didn't you call up to the bedroom? I shouldn't have minded – except that putting it about that I hold afternoon bridge parties is what I'd call cast-iron grounds for divorce."

"Sorry. I should have said sex orgy," I quipped with daring flippancy.

"That'll be the day. What's he want, anyway?"

"Oh, a stunt of Nick Crabbe's that's caught his fancy," I extemporised, Nick's memo still in my hand. "Bananaskin Week. Hasn't Nick ever bent your ear on the subject – he's bent everyone else's?"

"Bananaskin Week?" echoed Sherry, either evading or ignoring the question. "Sounds suspiciously like street theatre to me."

"It is. With collecting boxes."

"Tell Sam to steer clear of it."

Curling her legs up on the sofa and resuming, this time more closely, her study of the sexoholism phenomenon, Sherry indicated that she had had enough of the discussion. The all-clear had sounded, and provided I remembered my briefcase in my hurry to get to Mill Farm, I could leave the house without arousing suspicions, or at least without arousing any more suspicions than were already implanted.

Or was I being over-sanguine? One reason why alarm bells hadn't sounded for Sherry, not the most gullible of wives, was that it was by no means unusual for Sam to call me on a Sunday; nor, if he were feeling bored, to invite me over to the house for an hour. Sam's beliefs didn't preclude him from working on the Sabbath: if challenged he would explain that since all the work he did was the Lord's work, he was no more breaking the fourth Commandment than was the Rev Basil Thrush in conducting his morning service.

So just supposing he rang when I was ostensibly visiting him? The remote possibility became a distinct probability even as I contemplated its grisly outcome. There was only one thing to do, and that was to drop in on Sam on my way round to Mill Farm. That again would not be so unusual: indeed, I had made a grovelling point of voluntarily calling on Sam every six months or so to seek his advice on this or that project, and thus demonstrate what a keen and conscientious editor he had appointed. Normally, of course, I would ring him first. I could still do that from the distant paybox.

I would need an excuse for calling. I flicked through the unread Bananaskin Week notes. Sam would prefer his Youth Prayer Rally as a topic but I didn't have Douglas Boxer's memo with me. Besides, Boxer had been so typically lukewarm about Nick's project that it would give me perverse pleasure to push Nick's interests at the expense of his.

I stuffed the Bananaskin Week file back into my briefcase. By now I was so caught up in waterproofing my alibi that I had almost forgotten the purpose of it. I felt a tingling in the loins as there bounced back into my mind an image of Rosie waiting for me at the farm, flaunting God knows what rig from one of the saucy mail order catalogues that were passed around the Farmers' Ladies Circle. While I fervently hoped that Rosie did not propose to make a practice of ringing me at home, I was fervently glad she had done so on this occasion. I gave no thought to the consequences – not the consequences of being found out, which with the cover I had worked out for myself seemed a pretty unlikely possibility, but the consequences of selling Sam on an idea I had no faith in, which were to be profound and far-reaching. The article on sexoholism that Sherry was now lapping up mentioned as one of the symptoms a reckless disregard for its effect on work and career prospects. I would have made a good case history.

So it came about that twenty minutes later I was sitting in Sam's drawing room sipping tea and nibbling one of his favourite oatmeal biscuits while he ploughed through Nick Crabbe's memo. Sam is a slow reader but a meticulous one and I found myself drifting back to Mill Farm and wondering, none too idly, what new gyrations Rosie had in store. I choked on my oatmeal biscuit as I summoned up a variation from the norm that was probably anatomically impossible.

"He seems to have put a lot of work in this," said Sam approvingly, at length.

"He has," I said, taking Sam's word for it since I had not myself got past the first paragraph.

"But won't we have enough on our plate with Douglas's Youth Prayer Rally?"

At this point I should have said, "You're absolutely right, Sam, as always," got to my feet, apologised for wasting his time, and driven at speed to Mill Farm. But Sam had been uncharacteristically grumpy on the telephone and had said that whatever I had to say to him he hoped for my sake it was important since he had been just about to take his afternoon nap. I had to put on a show.

"That's what I'm coming to, Sam," I ad-libbed wildly. "I've been giving a lot of thought to the Youth Prayer Rally and the conclusion I've come to is that terrific though the concept is, we do need to sugar the pill in some way."

"The Lord God is not a pill," Sam reproved with a wag of a chubby finger.

"What I'm driving at is that we could combine the two events – make the Youth Prayer Rally the high spot, the culmination, of Bananaskin Week."

"Chalk and cheese, laddie."

Again I should have left it at that. I could have got away with wasting Sam's time by buttering him up and saying I bowed to his experience, sagacity and shrewd commercial sense. But having started, I felt an obligation to plough on.

"With respect, Sam, I don't think so. What is it that St Paul has to say about charity?"

In reply, Sam quoted from Paul's first Epistle to the Corinthians at such length that, imagining Rosie adjusting her stocking seams in her cheval mirror and then adjusting her cheval mirror to reflect the bed, I began to regret my choice of illustration. Furthermore, Sam's recitation came from the same tarted-up Good News version of which Len Quartermouth MBE FIAV had made such heavy weather at Ted Greenleaf's funeral service, and which makes no mention of charity whatsoever. It did not help my case.

" . . . Love is patient, love is kind, it does not envy, it does not boast, it is not proud, it is not rude, it is not self-seeking, it is not easily angered, it keeps no record of wrongs . . . " droned Sam. I waited for him to draw breath and plunged in anew.

"No record of wrongs, right, right. But isn't St Paul saying, Sam, that love and charity are one and the same thing?"

"He's not saying that, laddie, no. He's saying that if he speaks in the tongues of men and angels but has not love, he might as well save his breath to blow his porridge with – I'm paraphrasing there. Now you, Oliver, will have been brought up to say, how does it go, 'Though I speak with the tongues of men and of angels and have not charity' and so on and so forth – but do you see he's not talking about charity in the flag day or sponsored jogging sense, he's using the word as it's meant to be used . . . "

As the theological lecturette continued I began to wonder why I didn't stop arguing with Sam and just clear off. The answer seemed to be that I didn't want him to think I'd interrupted his day of rest with a harebrained idea. Besides, I was by no means any longer certain that it was a harebrained idea. Other things being equal, I should probably have opted for the quiet life, let Nick sell Bananaskin Week to Radio South or the local TV station and then milked it for all it was worth in the *Badgers Heath Herald* without having to take any of the responsibility.

But other things were not equal. As I had unwisely blurted out to Sam, Bananaskin Week could sugar the pill of the Youth Prayer Rally with which I now seemed well and truly lumbered – with any luck, could even wash it down virtually unnoticed by my readership. All right, so it would be a major headache, but weighed against prudence, sound judgement and common sense were the ample proportions of Rosie. In some unformulated way I felt that if Bananaskin Week ever did get off the ground, the organisation involved would provide the perfect smokescreen for my liaison with Rosie, whom I had already mentally appointed to the steering committee, exact nature of appointment to follow.

"All right, Sam, I'd be a fool to try and score points off you on the Good Book. But if St Paul didn't say it, I'm saying it now. Charity and love are the same thing. You only have to see those kids out in the town centre working their little butts off for Romanian orphans, earthquake victims, starving peasants, and they're not doing it for kicks or because they're bored, it's because they're genuinely involved with humankind, they truly do love their fellow creatures." The bit about humankind rather stuck in my gullet but I roughly meant what I was saying. I had used the same sentiments in the *Herald*'s leader on more than one occasion.

"So you've said often enough in your leaders, Oliver," said Sam, who didn't miss a thing. "And I agree with you one hundred per cent. But what's all this to do with the Youth Prayer Rally?"

"They're your congregation. You must have noticed that apart from your common or garden flag days, nearly all the charity work in this town is done by the under-25s. If we can get them mobilised, get them to be in certain places at certain times, you've got your Youth Prayer Rally ready made."

"You think so?" I could see that Sam was beginning to bite.

"I'm positive," I enthused, sounding more like Nick Crabbe by the minute. "One of my reservations about the Rally has been persuading the right kind of youngster to turn up. Get them involved in Bananaskin Week and you've got a captive audience."

Sam folded his leg of mutton arms and raised his eyes to the ceiling, very possibly seeking guidance. If he was, it was favourable. "Yes, I can see that, Oliver, but I wouldn't want to be preaching only to the converted."

"You wouldn't be, Sam. These kids may channel all their energies into good causes but they don't go to church." I was about to add, "That's if by church we don't mean some of these far-out weirdo sects that have been springing up lately," but bearing in mind Sam's own extremist form of religion I decided against it. Instead I went on, "If it's a crusade you're starting, they're just the material you're looking for. They're idealistic, they're enthusiastic, they have a strong sense of right and wrong, they believe in changing the world. Potential born-again Christians, Sam, every bright-eyed one of them."

Carried away, I was becoming a more powerful advocate for their respective causes than Douglas Boxer and Nick Crabbe combined. What I had said, now that I had said it, was so patently true that it rather frightened me. Only the thought of what lay ahead with Rosie saved me from wondering seriously whether, in my eagerness to experience it, I had not deliberately opened an evangelical Pandora's Box.

"All right, I've heard you out, Oliver. I'll think it over," said Sam. He was impressed.

I rose to leave, but my employer waved me back into my chair. When Sam had said he would think it over, he meant here and now. Lying back on the sofa he closed his eyes. His hands clasped on his waistcoat, his Pickwickian stomach rose and fell rhythmically. My eyes strayed to the mantelpiece clock. It was coming up to half past four, considerably past the hour which Rosie euphemistically chose to call tea-time. A snort brought me back to Sam. Mouth lolling open, he began to snore loudly as he belatedly enjoyed the Sunday afternoon nap of which I had earlier deprived him.

I contemplated giving him a sharp kick on the ankle but ruled it out as imprudent. Tiptoeing out of the house without saying goodbye would have been a breach of etiquette and, more to the point, an affront to Sam's sense of self-importance. Even when they arrived unbidden, Sam liked to dismiss visitors formally from his presence rather than allow them to leave at their own discretion.

The clock ticked slowly towards a quarter to five. Presently Sam's cook-housekeeper Mrs Bishop entered to clear away the tea things. Evidently the situation of Sam enjoying a catnap was a familiar one, for she moved with practised soundlessness, setting down her tray so quietly that it might have been fitted with a silencer.

"Let me help you, Mrs Bishop," I said loudly, rattling my cup and saucer as I passed it to her. Sam did not stir. Mrs Bishop, putting a reproving finger to her lips, gestured to me to leave the job to her. Crockery and teapot silently loaded, she picked up her tray. Sam snored on. There was nothing else for it – as Mrs Bishop passed my chair, I shot out a foot and sent her flying, tray, cups and saucers, plates, cakestand, teapot and all.

Even then Sam did not awaken immediately. It was not until I was on my hands and knees, babbling apologies as I scooped up bits of broken china, that he gave a sharp, terminal-sounding snort and I heard him grunt, "It's a good job that's not the Clarice Cliff." Had it been the Dresden, even, it would have been in a hundred pieces by now, I was so desperate.

Mrs Bishop having been despatched to her kitchen, not without a look of combined exasperation and acute suspicion in my direction, Sam rubbed his podgy hands together to signify that what he was about to say was of a jovial nature. "Now you're going to say I was asleep, aren't you?"

"I certainly had an impression of closed eyes, Sam," I ventured diplomatically.

"What would you say if I were to tell you I've been receiving a very important visitor?" asked Sam roguishly.

Not having the remotest notion how to answer, I decided to treat the question as rhetorical and nodded sagely and sympathetically, as one does to the ramblings of the senile. With a prefatory chuckle, Sam went on, "You're going to laugh at me now, Oliver, but you know who sent you here this afternoon, don't you?"

Yes – Rosie Greenleaf.

I gave him a weak, indulgent smile. Sam chuckled again, indulgent in return. "You're a heathen, laddie, what are you? But even so, you've been guided here as a messenger, and the message you've brought has been received loud and clear and you can go home to your wife now and tell her it's been taken on board. Off you go."

"This is Molly and this is Janey and this is Suzie and this is Wendy and this is Paula and this is Barbara and this is Kathy and this is Beverley."

Rosie was always a one for surprises but finding her Farmers' Ladies Circle taking tea in her living room was more of a jolt than I had bargained for. At least she had not, as on a previous assignation, sneaked me upstairs while they tucked into their hostess's home-made banana and walnut loaf below, leaving me wondering how I was to be sneaked out again, let alone how Rosie proposed to explain away the sound of bouncing bed-springs. In the event, her guests were so engrossed in the video film bequeathed by Ted Greenleaf, "Satisfied Desires", that they appeared to notice neither my arrival nor my departure.

On this present occasion my imagination had been so stoked up in the enforced interval since Rosie had rung up inviting me for tea that, expecting her to answer the door in a state of provocative undress and finding her fully if not demurely clad in a plunging green silk blouse and hip-hugging skirt, I assumed the ensemble to be but a detachable outer covering intended to be removed there and then on the doorstep. Rosie, allowing herself a moan as I struggled with a button, would have needed little persuading; but a peal of girlish laughter from within reminded her of her responsibilities.

"I'm afraid we'll have to bottle it up for a little while, precious, I've got visitors, ooh, do that once more and I won't be answerable for the consequences." Assuming a coy expression negated by two unfastened top buttons, she led me by the hand into the living room.

The Farmers' Ladies Circle, taking their title literally, were disposed in a wide ring around the living room, some sitting on sofas and easy chairs, others draped on the carpet or sprawled on cushions. Their average age was about thirty-five, their average degree of attractiveness fair to striking. A good deal of knee and not a little thigh were visible. As I entered, teacups froze between saucer and carefully made-up lips, and genteelly-held finger sandwiches were poised in mid-air. The tableau could have been an indoor picnic scene by some latterday Manet.

"Now, ladies, you all know Mr Kettle, the Editor of the *Herald*." In fact none of them did to my knowledge, with the exception of a large-boned lady, Mrs Molly Farmer as she now was, whom I had met occasionally in her capacity as daughter of Len Quartermouth MBE FIAV without ever suspecting that she might lead another life as supplier of vibrators to the Farmers' Ladies Circle from her sex aids catalogue. I wondered if she got commission.

As Rosie performed the introductions, I turned slowly around the circle of Farmers' Ladies like a clockwork man, treating them to a variety of grimaces, bows and suchlike gallant gestures. My 360-degrees course completed, I searched my swimming head for some polite scrap of conversation less pointed than "So what's all this about, then?" but more substantial than "Well, the rain seems to have passed over". Out of an emergency well of archness, often dipped into on those social occasions when I had to mingle with readers and advertisers, and remembering that the Farmers' Ladies were supposed to be ten in number, I dredged an observation as likely to break the ice as any: "But this is like Agatha Christie's Ten Little Indians, Rosie. There are only nine of you."

"That's what you think!" exclaimed a bejeaned, Barbie-doll figure earlier identified as Janey, who I recalled was the young widow — surprisingly young — on whose recommendation Rosie and I had tried the not very successful easy chair position. One could now see that a degree of youthful suppleness would be a help. Janey had sprung up from the fireside rug where she had been not so much reclining as posing, and now threw open the hall door leading to the stairs. Through it, to a ragged, raucous "Da da da, di da da da" rendering of "The Stripper" led by Rosie and taken up by the other Farmers' Ladies, shimmied an ample, black satin-clad vision which seemed, at first astonished blink, to be a wiggling, souped-up version of one of those advertisements for wired corsets for the fuller figure with which our department store Bancroft's used to titillate its potential customers, if not its potential customers' husbands, in the days when it was locally owned with partners known as Mr Cyril, Mr Ronald and so on. Mr Cyril and Mr Ronald both, however set in their ways, would have recognised a change in the times when they saw one. My neighbour Mrs Betty Spruce, for it was she, surprisingly sported, considering her full figure, a black basque clearly selected from one of the risqué mail order catalogues left lying around Rosie's premises like copies of the *Farmers Weekly*. The confection was augmented by suspenders, black stockings and little else.

"Da da da, di da da da!" chanted the Farmers' Ladies. "Da da da, di da da da!" responded Mrs Spruce, gyrating. Then she saw me, and with a cry of "Oh, my godfathers!" was out through the door like a bat.

Over the chorus of ribald, earthy laughter, Rosie called, "Don't be shy, Betty, he's a married man, he's seen it all before!" And to Janey, with a leer, she added, "Or maybe he hasn't. Shall we give him one of your catalogues to take home?"

"Now don't go giving Mr Kettle wrong ideas," urged Molly Farmer, née Quartermouth, the only one of the party who, with Mrs Spruce's rapid departure from the room, seemed a shade embarrassed. To me she offered, "It's only a bit of fun – Betty was doing a spot of modelling for us."

"Before she goes home and does a spot of modelling for Mr Spruce!" chortled Rosie. "They're neighbours of yours, aren't they, Oliver? Now don't you go round calling unexpectedly tonight or you'll spoil their bit of fun!"

The boisterous chaff continued, getting even nearer the knuckle until, not only by way of changing the subject but because I felt entitled to an explanation, I said to Rosie with a failed attempt at lightness, "You didn't tell me you'd be entertaining your Farmers' Ladies."

"Ooh, did you want me all to yourself, then?" pouted Rosie, eliciting a fresh gust of titters. I flashed her a danger signal, for she was by now not so much skating on thin ice as performing figure eights on it. I strove for a neutral, not to say neutered, form of words that would discourage further pirouettes.

"It's very agreeable to see you all, and I feel highly privileged to be let in on the secret of what really goes on at these meetings," I said with what I hoped was just the right touch of roguishness, "but I understood we had some Bonfire Society business to discuss."

"You're not in a big hurry, are you?" asked Rosie, giving me a meaning look the significance of which I was none too clear about. Presumably she was signalling me to wait until her Farmers' Ladies had gone, but with Rosie's track record she could equally well have been hinting that in the fullness of time she might invite me upstairs while the ladies continued their tea, for which after all there was something of a precedent – or even that, for the Farmers' Ladies Circle's further amusement, the pair of us might continue the cabaret started by Mrs Spruce. "Only seeing that the girls here are helping me with the Bonfire Society Appeal, I thought it only fair they should get to meet our new Treasurer."

Interesting. Besides our little consortium in the lounge bar of the Dolphin Arms yesterday, each member of which was tacitly sworn to secrecy until the appointment was endorsed by the committee, only Sherry knew I had allowed myself to be railroaded into the post of Treasurer (and a pretty weak decision she had called it, but that was by the way: the point was that she was hardly likely to have transmitted the news to Rosie Greenleaf).

"News travels fast," I said.

"Nick Crabbe told me at lunch yesterday."

Yes, but who told Nick Crabbe?

Fruitless rumination on this score was interrupted by the re-entry of Mrs Spruce, now fully, and conservatively, dressed, and once more looking every inch my God-fearing suburban neighbour complete with hubby and kiddy.

"Oh dear, I was praying you'd be gone, Mr Kettle," said Mrs Spruce with downcast eyes. "I hope the girls have explained I was just doing a little modelling. Just my luck, it would have to be what you saw, wouldn't it, when it could just as easily have been a quilted dressing gown?"

I did not see much of a market for quilted dressing gowns among those present but I kept the thought to myself and tried to put both Mrs Spruce and myself at ease by chatting about the educational progress and prospects of the dumpy Kimberley, always a reliable topic of conversation with the Spruces. With the conclusion of the fashion show, the circle of Farmers' Ladies had by now broken up into three of four chattering little groups, like a cocktail party without the cocktails. For this I was grateful, and not only because it relieved me from having to deal with arch questions such as "Now we've got a bone to pick with you, Mr Kettle, why does the *Badgers Heath Herald* never report our activities?" (to which Rosie's response, to general mirth, had been, "Because it's a family newspaper, you silly cat!"). There was something that had to be said to Mrs Spruce.

"By the way, it's of no importance but in case you should bump into my wife before she goes back to Town in the morning," I said as casually as I was able, considering that this was by way of transition from Kimberley's difficulties with maths, "I ought to explain that I shouldn't be here. I've already squandered most of Sunday afternoon on a meeting with my boss and I see little enough of her as it is."

"I shan't say anything," said Mrs Spruce, with rather too much alacrity for my liking. I did not want her running away with the wrong idea — or more accurately, I did not want her running away with the right idea.

"She likes me to keep work, even voluntary work, down to the minimum at weekends," I thought it politic to add.

"Percy feels the same, even though he does a lot of charity work himself, as you know," volunteered Mrs Spruce. I now sensed from her twitching expression that I had read her air of complicity wrongly, and that her eagerness to fall in with my request stemmed from an urgent wish to make a similar request of me.

To ease her path I said, "I must say you're the last person I expected to find at a meeting of the Farmers' Ladies Circle."

"You mean considering Percy's only an estate agent, well not *only* an estate agent but you know what I mean?" flustered Mrs Spruce. "That's just it. I was more or less press-ganged into joining by Rosie — she would insist that as Percy has one or two farmhouses on his books it qualifies me to be a member."

"Rosie is very accommodating," I said, thinking more of the honorary membership accorded to Molly Farmer as she now was than of her generosity towards myself.

"It's good fun and it makes a nice change, and the Circle does do a lot of fund-raising so it's all in a good cause, but I don't think Percy would quite understand, so of course he thinks I'm down at the church doing the flower-arranging."

"We'll each keep one another's secret," I said with a not-so-mock conspiratorial wink; upon which Rosie descended upon us like a party hostess about to inflict some enforced mingling among her guests. The glint in her eye, however, told me that mingling was not what Rosie had in mind.

"I'm going to steal Oliver away from you, Betty," said Rosie with a firmness born of what I feared was desperation. To me she said boldly, "We've got to get down to those figures you wanted to see, Oliver, or I'll be in a hell of a mess. Let's pop into the dining room where we won't be disturbed."

Grabbing my briefcase which had remained at my heels, and brandishing it like the Chancellor of the Exchequer clutching his red box on Budget Day, as an indication to all and sundry that anything about to take place between Rosie and me would be of a business nature, I followed her into the adjoining dining room. Even as I set my briefcase down on the sideboard and turned to face her, she was feverishly unbuttoning her green silk blouse.

"For Christ's sake, woman!" I hissed. "The whole bloody troop of them could burst in at any second!"

"It's all right," whispered Rosie, shedding her blouse to reveal a creation that Mrs Spruce must have been glad she was not modelling when we came face to face. "I've locked the door."

"That's almost as bad. What if one of them tries it and can't get in – what are they going to think?"

Unzipping her skirt, Rosie nuzzled my ear. "That would be exciting, wouldn't it?" The skirt slid to her ankles. "Make your mind up, precious, you can't have it both ways. Leastways, you can as far as I'm concerned but I think we've only just got time to do it this way, ooh, down here on the carpet."

Half past seven is no time to get home from afternoon tea and I was apprehensive, though not altogether astonished, to find the house in darkness. Maybe Sherry had taken herself off to the pub.

Maybe she was across the street comparing notes with Percy Spruce. If she had repaired to the bedroom, I trusted it was with no other plan in mind than sleep.

There was a note on the hall table. "Sorry, I've had to go back to London. Tomorrow's interview has just literally died on us and I have to turn it into an obituary, but I stupidly don't have the copy with me." Did I believe this? Not really: Sherry was umbilically attached to her laptop computer and never travelled without it. I believed the next sentence, though. "I tried to reach you at Sam's place but he said you'd left nearly two hours ago."

7

Although the *Herald* boasts three pages of local entertainments in its Saturday Weekender section, it is always as well to check the display type of the attraction advertised against the small print of the venue named. Apart from the Hot Potato disco and the Cherrytree Cannon 1-2-3 cinema, little of the night life listed in What's On In & Around Badgers Heath runs to a custom-built hall, particularly if it is in aid of something, as most events in the neighbourhood usually turn out to be. Thus when Nick Crabbe invited me to see the alternative wheelchair comedian Steve Selby In Concert, all proceeds to the Children of the Brazilian Rain Forest Appeal, I should either have resigned myself to enduring an evening in a draughty disused hangar out at the Badgers Heath Flying Club or, better, pleaded flu.

This was subsequent to, and the consequence of, an hour with Nick Crabbe at the Harvesters where I had reluctantly agreed to meet him to discuss Bananaskin Week. The moment had come. On Sunday evening, slumping in front of the TV detective series I normally watched with Sherry and finishing off the weekend bottle of gin that would otherwise have been shared with her, I had drunkenly resigned myself to having committed the paper, and more to the point Sam Dice, to Bananaskin Week – and in exchange for what? An anxiety-induced premature ejaculation in Rosie Greenleaf's locked dining room – or which she claimed to be locked: had I realised that the key didn't work, the brief physical peak necessary to precipitate such an embarrassing mishap would never even have been reached.

Accordingly, when Nick Crabbe's head appeared above the shrubbery of my office space, as it did at regular intervals, and he asked for the fourth or fifth time that week whether I had yet read his memo, I nodded glumly; and accordingly, when work was done, we met as agreed for what Nick was pleased to call "a jar".

I was glad to observe that the only inhabitant of the jumped-up little taproom was Rosie's pigman Harry. While I did not care for his knowing look, I had to accept that my comings and goings at Mill Farm must be the subject of nods, winks and nose-tappings around the out-buildings, and I preferred Harry's smirk to the superior smile that would have played on Nick Crabbe's lips had he had the luck to be observed by any of his colleagues having a confidential drink with his boss.

Before congratulating Crabbe on his Bananaskin Week coup, or more accurately allowing him to congratulate himself, I had bones to pick – the first of them so delicately as not to give him any clue why it was being picked.

"That looked a very classy wine you were treating Rosie Greenleaf to at the Old Forge on Saturday, cock."

"Just a nice drop of Fleurie, boss."

"I must be over-paying you."

"I felt like splashing out. Don't worry, boss, it won't be figuring in my expenses."

"Why should it do that?"

"I'm saying it won't."

"I know that, cock, but I'm bloody sure that if you were given the slightest encouragement it would. I'm asking why."

"Oh, I see, boss, you want to know what I was doing out with Rosie?"

Yes, you smart little bugger, but I didn't want you to know that I wanted to know. Too late now. Press on.

I said, recalling that he and Rosie had arrived not separately but together, and very late for lunch at that: "It's none of my business, cock, just so long as you didn't duck out of covering the Chief Librarian's daughter's wedding in your hurry to get your leg across." I was tolerably certain that he had been nowhere near the Chief Librarian's daughter's wedding but that he would have gleaned sufficient on the telephone to compose a diligent enough caption to accompany the picture of a startled bride and groom staring down at the ground where Gavin Pyle was wont to spreadeagle himself in the hope of capturing an unusual angle, that would adorn this week's issue. I was less certain that he did not have designs on Rosie.

"All right, boss, I'll come clean. But don't let the other hacks know I've been seen working in my lunch hour or they'll probably send me to Coventry for being too keen." Crabbe's face, as he raised his glass with a silent "Cheers", was a study in dumb insolence. I made a note to put the cocky young bastard on some good long evening assignments.

"Go on – I'll buy it."

"I've been hearing about Rosie Greenleaf's valiant efforts on the appeals front. I thought she'd make a good profile."

"Mention it to Douglas Boxer, did you?"

"Not yet, no."

"Mention it – he is in charge of features, after all. But it's a good idea. Do it." That would teach him to work in his own time, I thought with satisfaction. Or to pretend to have been working in his own time, which was nearer the mark. I decided to drop this line of enquiry and pursue it with Rosie at the first opportunity. Since this was a Wednesday evening, that would be as soon as I had got rid of Crabbe.

"So Bananaskin Week," he said, briskly rubbing his hands.

I too wished to change the subject but only by a notch. "We haven't left Rosie Greenleaf yet," I said. "She tells me I'm to be Treasurer of the Bonfire Society."

"So I hear. Congratulations," said Nick with no uneasiness that I could discern.

"She says she got it from you."

"That's right, boss, and I got it from Molly Farmer – you know, Len Quartermouth's daughter." Either easily or glibly – I would have put my bets on the side of glibness – Nick echoed what I had said to Rosie in the same context on Sunday: "News travels fast in this town." And if Molly Farmer had really passed it on to Nick Crabbe, why hadn't she passed it on to Rosie who was her friend?

"Not fast enough to fill the *Herald*, cock," I said sourly. "And while we're on this subject, what's all this about your pestering Dennis Reason?"

"Does he say I've been pestering him? I heard he was resigning as Treasurer so I saw no harm in asking him for confirmation. It turns out I was right."

"Who told you he was resigning as Treasurer?"

"Molly Farmer."

Ask a silly question. It was all so plausible, it all fitted together, and what did it matter anyway? But this interrogation of Nick Crabbe, superficial though it was, had left me feeling uneasy. Had it not also left me with the slight headache habitually induced by Crabbe's ducking and weaving, I should probably have dug deeper and got no further, but felt even more uneasy.

I nodded to the barman to refill our glasses. Rosie's pigman Harry, I noticed, was ostentatiously draining his own pint pot. I gave the barman another nod. No harm in keeping in with the hired help, just so long as he made no reciprocal offer, seeing it was a Wednesday evening, to give me a lift to Mill Farm on the back of his swede cart.

"So Bananaskin Week," I echoed belatedly, raising my warm gin and tonic, the Harvesters having exhausted its stock of ice on the first round. "Here's to it."

"That sounds encouraging, boss."

"I was over at Sam Dice's place on Sunday," I said, not managing to keep the self-importance out of my voice. "I may have sold him on the idea." Pausing only to allow my junior to pay for the drinks – if he could afford to take my mistress to the Old Forge, he could run to two rounds in succession – I gave him a prudently edited version of my conversation with Sam, allowing our proprietor the credit for tying his Youth Prayer Rally in with Bananaskin Week.

"That's great, boss. That's marvellous. Thank you very much."

"You don't mind the Prayer Rally angle?"

"I think it's fantastic. The kids will really go for it."

"Exactly what I told Sam."

"I thought he said it to you."

Nettled though I was at not being given credit for my own idea, I was not going to bandy words with one of my reporters, however smart-arsed. "I shall want a memo," I said shortly.

"I've already put in a memo, boss."

So he had, as Sam Dice would be the first to confirm. Not having read it, it cut no ice with me. "A proper memo," I insisted. "I want chapter and verse for the whole thing." What I meant by chapter and verse I had no idea. Perhaps Nick Crabbe would know. He had better, since it was his pigeon. "For example," I said, remembering our earliest conversation on the subject, "these big names you said you could get down here. Give me a list."

Perhaps it was all in his memo. But apparently not: Nick looked shifty and I caught the agreeable odour of chickens coming home to roost. "To tell you the truth, boss, I've been ringing round a few agents and I've no idea what our budget would be but these guys don't come cheap. I mean no way are we going to get Paul McCartney."

"Who are we going to get?"

"I believe I mentioned Steve Selby, the alternative wheelchair comedian."

"I told you, I've never heard of him."

"With respect, boss, ask anyone on the staff under the age of thirty," said Nick, his words carrying a whiff of the contempt such suggestions always convey to those well beyond the age of thirty, "and they'll say he's the best news since Freddie Camp."

"Who's Freddie Camp?"

With a "you're joking, of course" grimace, Nick sighed, "Only the biggest thing since Dave Gloss."

This could have gone on indefinitely. I let him continue. "Plus, Steve is a big mate of mine as I say, plus, being physically other-abled as they call it in wheelchair circles, he does a lot for charity. In fact, it so happens he's penned in to do a Sunday gig down here, so maybe you'd like to catch his act. It's in aid of the Children of the Brazilian Rain Forest Appeal."

"The what?"

"You're winding me up, boss. Don't say you've never heard of the Children of the Brazilian Rain Forest Appeal?"

Reflecting that for this young upstart's editor I had displayed enough ignorance for one evening I murmured vaguely, "Oh, that," and ordered what I hoped would be the last round of drinks. Rosie Greenleaf beckoned.

"All right," I said, having been cornered into agreeing to see the alternative wheelchair comedian at work if my diary permitted it, "you'd better liaise with Douglas Boxer and cobble some kind of draft programme together. Oh, and I don't want this beano to clash with any of the Bonfire Society activities."

Nick Crabbe looked blank, as if he were about to emulate me by asking, "What Bonfire Society?"

Instead he said, "But haven't *you* talked to the Bonfire Society, boss?"

"About what?"

Blankness turned to exasperation. "I thought you'd read my memo?"

A difficult one, this. "I said I'd read it, not that I'd memorised it," I bluffed. "I get scores of memos, cock. I'm hounded by memos. What, in two sentences, does yours say about the Bonfire Society?"

Nick allowed me to save face. "I can give it to you in one sentence, boss, and in fact did so in my memo, which is why you probably skipped it. Bananaskin Week should be sponsored by the *Herald* but organised by the Bonfire Society."

Obviously. No wonder Sam had swallowed the idea. They would do the work and we would get the credit. They would leap at it. Our Standing Committee was only the top dog of a whole kennel of sub-committees that spent the whole year organising charity bunfights of one kind and another and generally falling over themselves to do good works. Bananaskin Week would be the juiciest bone of all.

"Oh, I see," I said. "Yes, I'd taken that on board, cock. I thought you were talking about how the Bonfire Society will get involved in the general merriment. That's your pigeon."

Had Nick Crabbe wished to be hard on me, or rather had he not thought it politic not to be hard on me, he could have reminded me, as I was to discover when I did at last get round to skimming through it, that his memo covered that point too, and at length. He settled for knocking back his beer and declaring briskly, "Then the sooner I get cracking the better. Thanks again for the back-up, boss. I won't let you down."

I was in two minds whether to warn him that he had better not or to hope, as I had hoped for Douglas Boxer and his Youth Prayer Rally, that he would make an almighty hash of the enterprise. On balance, though, I wished him as well as I could be expected to wish Nick Crabbe. If it all mapped out it would reflect well on the paper and that meant it would reflect well on me. Or so, neglecting to read one lot of rats' entrails with another, I allowed myself to believe.

It was still light as I climbed into the car, ignoring Rosie's pigman Harry who, having finished his free pint, had come out ahead of us without so much as a goodnight but was now hanging around in the hope of saving his bus fare with a lift down to Mill Farm. Nick, with an over-familiar wave, got into his blue Ford Escort XR3i, a vehicle he could only have paid for out of his expenses in his Fleet Street days.

I turned right at the end of the narrow B-road where the Harvesters nestled – skulked would be a better word – into the marginally A-road that would take me to Mill Farm. Nick should have turned left to take him into the town centre where he had a flat in a converted tea warehouse just off the High Street, another luxury I wondered he could afford. But he didn't; or if he had, another blue Escort was tailing me or, not to be too paranoiac about it, was going in the same direction as myself, while making no attempt to overtake me.

The road is a winding one and at each bend I would lose the Escort only to have it back in my rear mirror on the straight, but never long enough to establish whether it was Nick at the wheel or not. We were coming up to the lane, no more than a track, leading down to Mill Farm and the hamlet beyond it. There was no particular reason why Nick Crabbe shouldn't know that I was paying Rosie a visit, except that she had figured large in the earlier part of our conversation and I had said nothing about seeing her – and besides, the less he knew about anything I was involved in the easier I was in my mind. At least instinct was looking after me in that regard if in no other.

I drove straight past Voles Lane, as it is called, and drew into a layby some two hundred yards round a sweeping bend in the road, where I pretended to be consulting a map. If Nick pulled up alongside I would pretend to be looking for a mythical farm selling free range eggs. But the only vehicle to appear was the Badgers Heath Shoppahoppa which could not conceivably have overtaken any car behind me. I did a three-point turn and drove back to edge down Voles Lane. There was no need to slow down as I passed the gate of Mill Farm, since it was unwise to exceed more than five miles an hour along the potholed track. A blue Escort XR3i was parked on the gravel forecourt of the farmhouse, and the studded front door was just closing on a glimpse of black stocking. Rosie's pigman, plodding homeward from the bus stop up the lane to his hovel in the hamlet down the lane, cackled evilly as he caught my eye.

Extracts from the minutes of the Badgers Heath Bonfire Society Standing Committee, September 4.

Item 1. Resignation of Treasurer and election of new Treasurer. Mr L. Quartermouth MBE FIAV (Chair) announced with regret the resignation of Mr D. Reason as Treasurer, for professional reasons. Mr Reason had given sterling service to the Society and it was with pleasure that the Chair was able to say that Standing Committee would continue to be the beneficiary of his wise counsel as an ordinary, though a more appropriate word might be extraordinary, member of that Committee.

The Rev B. Thrush (Secretary) proposed a vote of thanks to Mr Reason for a difficult row well hoed. Seconded by Mr P. Spruce, this was carried unanimously.

The Rev B. Thrush then proposed that Mr O. Kettle be elected Treasurer in succession to Mr D. Reason. He was sure there was no need to remind Standing Committee of Mr Kettle's many qualities and he was sure that one excellent Treasurer would be followed by another.

Chair said that if there were no other nominations he would ask for a seconder.

There being no other nominations, the motion was seconded by Mr Spruce and carried unanimously.

Miss N. D. Bellows (Society Archivist) enquired through the Chair whether there would not now be a vacancy for the office of Deputy Treasurer.

Mr Reason said that saving Mr Kettle's presence, the Deputy Treasurership had always been something of a sinecure, its only real function being to provide a second signatory for the cheques. As manager of the Three Counties Bank he (Mr Reason) was in a position to monitor the Society's funds in an ex-officio as well as in a professional capacity. It had always been something of a nuisance to go chasing after a second signatory, and he was sure Standing Committee would be happy to leave the day to day handling of the Society's funds to Mr Kettle. He was not going to run away.

Miss Bellows said that nevertheless she would rest easier in her mind if there continued to be a Deputy Treasurer, and she would propose Mr E. Barlow.

Mr Barlow said that Miss Bellows must be joking.

Chair said that if it was the feeling of Standing Committee that there should be a Deputy Treasurer, he would not waste time putting it to the vote but would ask for a seconder for Miss Bellows' motion.

There being no seconder, the motion was withdrawn . . .

Item 4. Report by the Appeals Secretary (Mrs R. Greenleaf).

Mrs Greenleaf (Appeals Secy) reported that the Appeal Fund had now topped £4,000 and was well on target. (Applause). If Standing Committee wanted the exact figure, the exact figure was £4,127.60. Mrs Greenleaf said that as she saw the Press was present, she would like it very kindly mentioned that she wished to thank the generous people of Badgers Heath most warmly, they had been marvellous, but having said that the donations had to keep rolling in if the target was to be reached. Mrs Greenleaf said that she would also like to thank the Badgers Heath Farmers' Ladies Circle, of which she had the honour to be honorary secy, for their tireless efforts and for giving up so much of their time in a good cause . . .

Item 9. Any other business.

Mr O. Kettle (Treasurer) having asked permission of the Chair to table a discussion paper, "Bananaskin Week", Chair reminded Standing Committee that the paper had already been circulated to Committee Members and its contents were self-explanatory.

He was not at this stage calling for a motion as to whether the Society should say yea or nay to the proposals contained therein, but was so to speak testing the water. He would take comments round the table on the subject of the so-called Bananaskin Week in general and the wisdom or otherwise of the Society's proposed involvement.

Mr Kettle (Treasurer) said that as the Chair had intimated, the discussion paper spoke for itself. All he would add was that if in consequence of Bananaskin Week it became possible to walk ten yards in Badgers Heath on a Saturday morning without a collecting tin being rattled under one's nose, it would have served its purpose. On a more serious note the Treasurer added that charities would benefit far more from one concerted effort over the space of a week than from sporadic flag days and sponsored walks et cetera over the course of a year. The enterprise would be excellent publicity for the town, displaying as it would the warm heart of Badgers Heath to the world, and in the Treasurer's view the Bonfire Society could be associated with no more worthwhile scheme than Bananaskin Week.

The Rev Basil Thrush (Secretary) said he thoroughly endorsed the Treasurer's sentiments. It was thanks to that very warm heart of Badgers Heath to which the Treasurer had rightly paid tribute that charity collections in the town had got out of hand. The Secretary was reminded of the Sorcerer's Apprentice. Bananaskin Week would at one and the same time contain and encourage the desire of the good people of Badgers Heath to give until it hurt. The Secretary was reminded of the parable of the talents.

Intervening, Chair said he was sorry to interrupt but as the Secretary himself had often had cause to point out, the room was only booked until half past ten, when a penalty payment would come into play. He would suggest that Members speak for no more than two minutes, confining themselves strictly to the matter at hand.

Mr E. Barlow said that the Chair himself had already spoken for three minutes.

Chair asked Mr Barlow whether he had anything to add before Mr D. Reason was asked for his views.

Mr Barlow having no further comments, Mr Reason gave it as

101

his view that as the Vicar had already pointed out, Bananaskin Week would contain or if Standing Committee liked corral what quite frankly had become a considerable nuisance in the community's life. If Members endorsed Bananaskin Week, as he himself did, then he would earnestly recommend that the Bonfire Society be involved in the scheme to the hilt, otherwise it (the Society) would miss the bus and be left out in the cold.

Chair appealed to Committee Members not to express views that had already been expressed, adding that he would now call upon Mrs Greenleaf.

Mrs R. Greenleaf (Appeals Secy) thought it (Bananaskin Week) a lovely idea. The town needed a shake-up and this was the kind of shake-up it could do with. Mrs Greenleaf thought the Bonfire Society should definitely be involved. She herself would be definitely involved and she knew a lot of people who themselves would be definitely involved. As Mr Reason had said, the Bonfire Society must take care that it did not miss the bandwagon.

Mr P. Spruce said that he did not want to throw cold water on the Treasurer's pet project, but he would ask what guarantee there was that it would be successful? Supposing Bananaskin Week's operating costs left it with a deficit, would the Bonfire Society be liable? The Society ought to know what it was getting into. There was no absolute certainty that the scheme was viable as regards making a guaranteed profit.

Mr E. Barlow said that the only certain thing in this life was that if anyone was going to pick holes in anything, it was Mr Spruce. If Mr Spruce were shown a gift horse, he would not look it in the mouth, he would poke it in the eye.

Urging Standing Committee not to descend to personalities, the Chair reminded Members that this was a discussion, not a debate. He would call upon Mrs Spruce for her views, and after Mrs Spruce, Miss Bellows.

Mrs Spruce said that her husband had only said what needed to be said and for her own part she agreed with him. These things had to be looked into. Having said that, she agreed with Mrs Greenleaf. It was indeed a lovely idea and she (Mrs Spruce) would support it to the full, always supposing that it turned out to be viable as her husband had put it.

Miss Bellows expressed the opinion that there was little point in her expressing an opinion one way or the other. It was the same old story. The clique, the inner circle, call it what you would, had made its mind up long before Standing Committee had been given a chance to consider the matter, and the whole thing was "in the bag", as the saying went.

Chair, pointing out that Miss Bellows was straying far from the point, said that he would give her the opportunity either to withdraw her remarks or to explain them.

Miss Bellows said that if the Chair did not know what she meant by clique or inner circle, then nobody did. She was referring, as all present knew, to those insiders as she would call them who met in the bar downstairs to decide what decisions were to be taken – for example that a certain person was to be the next Treasurer, or, in this latest example, that a so-called Bananaskin Week was to be foisted on to the Bonfire Society – and then expected Standing Committee to rubber-stamp their deliberations. Miss Bellows for one had had enough of this plotting and scheming and was not having it.

Ruling Miss Bellows out of order, the Chair assured Standing Committee that there was no clique or inner circle attempting to manipulate the Committee. As for Bananaskin Week being foisted on to the Bonfire Society, this was if he may say so rubbish. The motion had yet to be put. He would call upon Mr Kettle (Treasurer) to frame a resolution for the next meeting when everyone, including Miss Bellows, would have ample opportunity to air their views.

There being no other business, the meeting was adjourned.

Owl Insurance clerk Terry Brett (24) will sit in a dustbin for twelve hours in aid of the St John Ambulance Brigade.

A Knobbly Knees competition among senior citizens of South Hustling raised £48 for the Keep Our Village School campaign.

Seven Badgers Heath postmen are to stage a wobbly-wheel unicycle race to raise money for the aurally impaired.

Members of the Church of St Michael and All Angels Women's Guild held an austerity lunch of lentil soup, dry bread and Malvern water in aid of Famine Relief.

Steve Selby, the alternative wheelchair comedian, will appear in concert at the Badgers Heath Flying Club – all proceeds to the Children of the Brazilian Rain Forest.

"If he's the hottest thing since sliced toast," I muttered sourly, "why is there nobody here?"

In fairness an audience of five hundred and odd on a rainy night isn't a bad turn-out by Badgers Heath standards, but they were lost in a makeshift auditorium that could have held five times that number. Besides, I was in a bad temper. Cold seeped up through the cracked concrete floor of the disused aircraft hangar, and heavy drops of rain exploded, as if by some computerised sequence of leaks, on whichever spot one may have shifted to for refuge. It was the only indoor concert I had ever seen with puddles.

"The gig was fixed at short notice," explained Nick Crabbe. "Plus his manager's dying of Aids so the advance publicity's been zero. With a few more fly-posters and an interview in the *Herald* he could have packed this place."

"So why didn't we have an interview in the *Herald*, cock?"

"I thought we'd keep him up our sleeves, boss, for the big week."

Not for the first time I reflected with irritation that Crabbe had an answer for everything, even when no answer was particularly called for. It was all the same to me whether Steve Selby played to an audience of five or five thousand. It was a Sunday evening, I was going to miss my TV detective series, and I had had no supper, Sherry having once again decided to take herself back to London, probably in the belief that the concert was a front for a rendezvous with Rosie Greenleaf. Furthermore the supporting or warm-up act was a group of folk singers from the town of Crawley known as the Crawlies, and I do not like folk singers.

As the Crawlies, feet tapping and violin bows going like piston rods, ploughed nasally through an endless dirge about how good it was to be alive on the M25, it began to infiltrate my mind that a rendezvous with Rosie would be no bad way of rounding off the evening. With any luck she would have cold beef and pickles on offer as well as the usual tariff. Mumbling to Nick Crabbe that the leaking roof was sending subliminal messages to my

104

bladder, I slipped out to the cavernous bar or "refreshment area" as it called itself, an arrangement of trestle tables dispensing canned beer and soft drinks, and called Rosie from the sticky wall phone.

She was in and available: "Ooh, what a lovely surprise, pet, and here's me been thinking there's nothing for it but have an early night, I've only just this minute got into my winceyette nightie but don't worry, I'll slip into something a bit more glam."

My damp spirits lifted and I hoped the alternative wheelchair comedian would not be doing encores. I bought a warm beer and helped myself to a plastic glass from the stacks still piled up in their cardboard carton. The catering arrangements for Sam's Youth Prayer Rally, I guessed, were going to be somewhat on these lines. Maybe I was previewing the very venue. I hoped he got a bigger audience.

The Crawlies, courtesy of the amplifiers rigged up in the "refreshment area" in forlorn anticipation of an overflow, were now repetitively expressing their wish to be back home in the Blue Ridge Mountains. Dearly wishing them home in Crawley, I allowed myself to muse, as I had been musing on and off ever since I had registered his blue Escort XR3i parked outside Mill Farm, about Nick Crabbe's involvement with Rosie. She had explained his visit, or explained his visit away, with the claim that he had come to do his interview with her for the *Herald* profile I had told him to go ahead with. She knew I usually came round on Mondays but after my bonus visit on the Sunday, "I thought you must have reckoned you'd had your ration, silly me, how wrong can you get?" Nick himself, departing from his usual technique of always apologise, always explain, had said nothing about the episode but had simply handed in his Rosie Greenleaf profile a day or two later. It was adequate, with a short inventory of the fixtures and fittings of the farmhouse kitchen plus a tribute to Rosie's potato cakes serving to demonstrate that he was making no secret of his visit. That in his devious way he was either up to something with Rosie or paving the way to getting up to something with Rosie I had no doubt. I was hazier on whether he was as familiar with her bedroom as he was with her kitchen, or was hoping to be so familiar. If he was, and I could not claim it to be very much of my business, then obviously Rosie would be a pushover for a presentable young fellow ten years her junior, particularly since he had already figured in one of Rosie's erotic fantasies concerning herself, himself, Sherry and me. Whether Nick had the nerve to rise to the occasion when he must have a pretty good idea that he was trespassing on his boss's territory was another matter.

These idle ruminations were terminated by a half-hearted ripple of applause for the Crawlies, and, after a request from a dismembered and, as it sounded, disembowelled voice to give a big welcome to one of the success stories of the Caring Nineties, an even more lukewarm response for Steve Selby, the alternative wheelchair comedian.

"I've heard a better reception for the blind accordionist outside Badgers Heath Parkway station, cock," I murmured as I rejoined Nick Crabbe.

"Bad acoustics, boss."

The Crawlies had regrouped themselves at the side of the stage and were now playing what was presumably Steve Selby's signature tune, a souped-up version of "We shall not be moved". Taking his time about it, the alternative wheelchair comedian propelled himself from the wings to the centre stage microphone. It had been adjusted to accommodate his sitting position, but not by very much for he was very tall, a six-footer I would have said had he been able to stand upright. He sported, not to my surprise, a black beard of the style affected by D. H. Lawrence, to whom, with his gaunt cheeks and staring eyes, he bore a strong resemblance. He wore faded denim over a T-shirt bearing a steam-transfer of a child almost as hollow-eyed as himself, and the legend CHILDREN OF THE BRAZILIAN RAIN FOREST. The tattered jeans encasing his thin and what I had to suppose were wasted legs were embellished with the emblem of CND and the panda logo of the World Wildlife Fund. He looked in his late twenties or early thirties.

As he fiddled further with the microphone I idly put the question to Nick Crabbe that had never crossed my mind until now. "What's he doing in a wheelchair anyway, cock? Multiple sclerosis or what?"

106

"M25, boss. He was driving home from a gig and this juggernaut rammed him up the bum. Spinal cord gone. He mentions it in his act."

"That should bring the house down," I said.

The comedian was ready, a fact he proclaimed by announcing "All right!" in a DJ sort of way. This was followed by an unexpected, fanatical bellow of "Who cares?", to which the Crawlies and one or two members of the audience responded raggedly, "We care!"

It now became clear why the Crawlies were still hanging about instead of going back to their dressing rooms or better still back to Crawley. Steve Selby's act required a response that was not, as yet, forthcoming from his audience, and the function of the folk group, at this stage, was to act as his cheerleaders or claque.

"Who cares?"

"We care!"

"Who cares?"

"We care!"

This primitive litany, now accompanied by hand-clapping, went on until a fair number of the audience had twigged what was required of them and were joining in with something approximating gusto. Steve Selby then changed tack.

"Do we care about the whale?"

"Right!" chorused the Crawlies, one of them shaking a tambourine. "Right!" echoed the audience or, by now, a good section of it, getting the idea.

"Do we care about the trees?"

"Right!"

"Do we care about the ozone layer?"

"Right!"

I turned up my collar against the cold and the dripping wet. "Is this supposed to be funny?" I asked Nick as the alternative wheelchair comedian solicited pledges that his audience cared about acid rain, the greenhouse effect, dwindling world resources, Planet Earth and finally the children of the Brazilian rain forest.

"It's his warm-up," explained Nick.

"He isn't warming me up, cock." I had to admit to myself,

107

however, that Steve Selby had by now whipped up a degree of enthusiasm in the draughty hangar to the point where the hand-clapping was augmented by a certain amount of foot-stamping. It was possible, of course, that the stamping element were stamping only to keep out the cold, in which case he could claim to be warming them up merely in the literal sense. "I'll give him five minutes," I warned Nick.

"Don't expect Jack Benny, boss," counselled Nick with something of a sneer at my implied simplistic and out-of-date taste in humour. "This boy is different, you've got to give him a chance to get through to you."

"It's the last chance he'll get, cock."

Having got enough caring underwritten to his apparent satisfaction, the alternative wheelchair comedian now led himself into what appeared to be the burden of his act, which he did by assuring his audience, "All right, you've got it!" and then calling for another big hand for the Crawlies who, their warm-up duties concluded, trooped off.

"Listen!" It was the standard opening of the stand-up comedian, yet it was clear, even had he been in a position to stand up, that we were not in for a string of mother-in-law jokes. "Whoa! Listen, how many of you caught my segment of the Channel Four Green Show last week? Segment, it was more like a sliver. They give you a minute to get the audience on your side, then they give you another minute's start. OK, so how many faithful viewers? Now's the time to stand up and be counted, gang. Put your hands up if you watch the Channel Four Green Show. All right, so we know some pervs were watching the late-night movie, snooker even! But how many greenies have we got here? Come on, gang, how many of you watched Channel Four Green?"

Eight hands at maximum had gone up, two of them to waver and be lowered again, leaving Steve Selby with a net grand total of six. He was in no way fazed. "So the rest of the gang were conserving electricity, right? Whoa! Don't be embarrassed, you were conserving electricity, at least that's your story and you're sticking to it! All right! So far so good! But let me ask you this, gang. While you were conserving electricity, while you were very considerately not watching Channel Four Green and learning how not to waste Planet Earth's resources, what else were you doing? You were bonking, right? Be honest, gang, how many of you were bonking?"

A rather better show of hands this time, from a sheepishly macho element in the back rows, yielded ironic cheers. As the comic continued – to what, I was wondering, was his alternative comedy supposed to be the alternative? – with a semi-serious warning to the self-confessed bonkers that they risked adding to the world's already over-swollen population, I turned to Nick Crabbe who was sniggering and snorting in dutiful appreciation.

"And you think Sam Dice is going to wear this kind of stuff, do you?"

"He'll clean it up, boss. He's very careful to tailor his material to the occasion."

" . . . Unless you were very sensible and used a condom," Steve Selby was continuing. "OK, I'm not about to take a head count on this one, gang, not even a prick count. Let's just look on the bright side and say you were all using condoms. All right? And do you know what you're doing to the dwindling rubber supplies of Malaysia? Right! You can't fucking win, gang!"

"This material doesn't need a tailor, cock," I grunted, getting to my feet. "It needs his shears. I'm off."

It was an effective way of wiping the grin off Nick Crabbe's face. He grabbed my sleeve. "He's only just getting into his stride, boss! Besides, I've arranged for you to meet him after the show."

"Arranged it with who?"

"Steve and his manager."

"Next time arrange it with me, cock."

My quick footsteps clacking on the concrete as I headed through the cavernous bar towards the car park were an echoing underscore to the alternative wheelchair comedian's echoing voice: "Listen, I was really knocked out to hear the Crawlies singing my theme song tonight. My theme song, Good to be alive on the M25. We came round the M25 only this evening, gang. All the way round the M25. Now for me that's an improvement. The first time I was on the M25 I came round in hospital. I was driving this snazzy little motor. Unleaded petrol of course. I said to my girl friend, 'This car is catalytically converted.' She said, 'Cataclysmically converted.' I said, 'Listen, I've read the leaflet, I watch Channel Four Green, it's catalytic.' She said, 'Cataclysmic. Your clutch has just gone and that bastard behind us is coming straight up your arse . . . '"

8

When Sherry eventually asked just what the hell was going on, she meant, of course, in the narrow sense of what was going on between me and Rosie.

Had she posed the question in a more general way I should have had to reply, "I have no idea." That something was indeed going on was by now clear. That Nick Crabbe was the pivot or vortex of at least some of the goings-on was equally obvious. Whether all the goings-on were connected I could not have begun to say.

This was not for the want of trying. I had even sat down one evening and made a list of the mysterious events, trivial and otherwise, that had begun to trouble me, an attempted mind-clearing exercise prompted first by the return of the lights and secondly by an unexpected visit from Miss Bellows, our Bonfire Society archivist and token spinster.

The return of the lights reminded me of an intermittent tooth-ache I had once experienced. It followed a very similar course. Just as I had resigned myself to a visit to the dentist the nagging pain vanished. I put it down to an injudiciously-chomped after-dinner mint and forgot about it. Then, weeks later, I was awakened in the small hours by a persistent throbbing at the back of my mouth. By morning it had gone and I put it out of my mind again. That evening it returned, but I persuaded myself that I was subject to ultra-sensitive teeth as identified by an oral hygienist in a toothpaste commercial on the box. By the following morning I knew that what I had there was an impacted wisdom tooth.

So it was with the lights. I had forgotten how many explanations I had offered myself for the mysterious flashes occurring from time to time concurrent with my sexual congress with Rosie. I knew that I had never examined any of them seriously – had indeed refused to examine possibly innocent explanations in any depth for fear of finding no depth there. And I had forgotten, or chosen not to remember, the reporter's cautionary axiom that the more explanations there are on offer, the unlikelier is the possibility that any of them holds water.

And soon, helped along by a series of other vaguely troubling events which claimed priority, I had forgotten the lights too. Until, on the night of my bonus visit to Rosie following the alternative wheelchair comedian's Sunday concert in the aircraft hangar, there they were again.

As my headlights swept the gravel drive of Mill Farm, they picked out Rosie as unerringly and revealingly as the spotlights of the Badgers Heath Purple Pussycat Club locate Suzy Fluzy the resident stripper. In full exhibitionist flow, she was posed plumply in the open doorway, one hand on rounded hip, the other resting on the door-frame, naked except for the latest number from her friend Janey's mail order catalogue – a kind of harlot's set, probably sold displayed on stiff card like the nurse's set I had once bought a niece for Christmas. It was an all-pink outfit comprising elbow-length net gloves, net stockings and a satin confection encasing her waist but spectacularly excluding her bosom. Above and beneath its pink trappings, her body gleamed whitely in the beam of my headlights.

As I hurriedly switched off and climbed out of the car, Rosie stepped out to greet me – or rather to meet me, since it was apparent with every seductive crunch of knee-length boot on gravel that she had more than a routine greeting in mind. She threw her net-sheathed arms around my neck, producing the not-unerotic sensation of being in the embrace of a roll of wire netting.

"Ooh, I thought you'd never get here, I've been waiting and waiting, ooh, it won't take long to get me going tonight I can tell you, pet, ooh, let's do it out here."

"For God's sake, Rosie, you're going to get yourself arrested one of these days!" I protested, trying ineffectually to disentangle her. "Come on, let's get indoors."

"You're always wanting to be indoors, Ollie, what's wrong with out of doors for a change, or weren't you ever a boy scout?"

"For one thing it's freezing cold."

"Get away with you, it's a lovely warm night. Look at the stars."

"Stars don't shed warmth, Rosie." I said pedagogically.

"Oh, well maybe it's being on hot bricks that keeps me nice and warm. Come on, love, where's your sense of adventure – and if you think I'll catch cold what's wrong with your car bonnet? Ooh, you just feel, it's so hot you could make toast on it, do you think you ought to have your engine checked, ooh, I'm glad you haven't though, ooh, it sends tingles all through me, come on, precious, I can't wait."

Rosie, if she put her mind to it, or even if she didn't, could have seduced a eunuch, provided his resistance level was on the low side. Mine, I had to admit, was pretty well at its ebb tide. Had Rosie been less blatant, less ripe, less obviously the answer to the tired businessman's prayer, I might have let prudence or conscience have a look in. Despite a far from blemishless life I was not so sexually sated that I really needed the kick-start of Rosie's erotic exuberance; but when she was on offer like fruit in a dessert bowl I could not resist it. Draped across the car bonnet in a shaft of light falling from one of the farmhouse windows, she was not so much an invitation as a command.

I had been peripherally aware, before being distracted by the pink and white vision in the doorway, of two yellow dots like fairy lights glowing in the long black shadow of an outbuilding. Out of the corner of my eye, as I hastily switched off my headlights, I had subliminally identified one of the farm cats slinking across the driveway. Now, as I fell across Rosie on the car bonnet and my trousers slid down around my ankles, I felt a velvety, purring presence rubbing against my calves.

While Rosie had awakened in me a latent mildly exhibitionist streak, the fascination, such as it was, lay more in the slight risk of being seen than in actual self-exposure; and in any case I drew the line at performing in the presence of a farmyard cat. Pleading cramp, therefore, I was in the act of relinquishing my awkward, sprawled embrace when I became acutely aware of a sudden

113

silence. With hindsight I realised that I had been hearing, in the background of my mind, the sound of a car approaching down the lane, and that it had now stopped and the engine been switched off. As I straightened up, disregarding Rosie's moans of "Ooh, don't stop now just as we're getting to the best part," and reached down to tug up my concertina'd trousers, there was a stealthy scratching of gravel down by the farmhouse gates, followed by a brilliant flash illuminating what must, assuming a reasonably efficient long lens, have been a very intimate close-up of my horrified face in proximity to Rosie's fat white buttocks, an additional touch of farce being provided by the trousers round the ankles. The cat scuttered off, there was another slithering of gravel, and Rosie moaned my name for all the world as if volunteering caption material to the visiting photographer.

Hauling up my trousers as best I could, I lumbered down the driveway after the flitting shadow heading for the lane. Whether I had any chance of gaining on him I would never know, for, as I spurred myself on, my hand involuntarily released its grip on my waistband, the trousers corkscrewed around my shins and I went sprawling face down in the gravel. The slam of a car door, an engine's purr not much louder than the farmhouse cat, and the intruder was off into the night.

As I lay spreadeagled on the drive, I heard Rosie's boots hurrying along the gravel, a sound not unlike a platoon of soldiers moving at the double. In a moment she was kneeling by my side. "Ooh, have you hurt yourself, pet? Never mind, love, we'll soon have it kissed better, and whoever it was you can see he's gone so come on, Ollie precious, we can relax now. Ooh, does the feel of this gravel send a thrill through you the same as it does me? Ooh, just stay where you are, pet, it's giving me ideas is this."

Later — not very much later, for I was in no mood to accommodate Rosie's feverish new living fantasy — as I suffered my kneecaps, grazed and pock-marked like a schoolboy's, to be dabbed with iodine, I said: "So, Rosie. Not lightning. Not a passing car. Not a courting couple lighting a cigarette. Not even an honest peeping Tom with a torch. It was a bloody flash camera."

To know it for certain was almost a relief – a relief to be briefly savoured while it lasted, for the implications were by now so alarming that they could no longer be left unregarded in the hope they would go away.

"No, you're right, pet, I've got to admit there was somebody here, and it definitely was a camera flash that time, there's no denying it. Now I hope you've got a touch of the masochist running through you, Ollie, because I've just got to hurt you a little bit while I dig these specks of gravel out of your knee."

Wincing, I pursued what I knew would be a fruitless line of enquiry: "So who was it, Rosie?"

"How the thump should I know? It could be anybody or nobody."

"No, it couldn't be nobody, Rosie, because we've established once and for all that we're being watched by a flesh-and-blood somebody who's hellbent on making a photographic record of what we get up to. The question is who and why?"

"Search me, pet, but whoever it is they must be some sort of weirdo."

This struck me as a bit rich, coming from Rosie. I had a further thought in the same area: Rosie seemed remarkably unconcerned about the incident. It was as if it were a passing embarrassment like being spotted frolicking in the woods by a distant stranger – a moment to raise a blush, perhaps, but not a matter of lasting concern.

I said, flinching again as she dabbed on more iodine, "Rosie, I've got to ask you this. I know you like doing it out of doors and in odd sorts of places. Is there by chance any connection between your exotic tastes and the phantom snapper of Badgers Heath?"

"Well, there does seem to be a connection, pet, I've got to admit. I mean to say he does seem to pop up when the mood takes us to go beyond the confines of the bedroom, doesn't he?"

"That's not what I meant, Rosie." In fact it was exactly what I meant, but for Rosie I had to spell it out. "What I'm getting at is this. Did you put him up to it?"

Rosie, not at all offended, chuckled earthily. "Now would I do a thing like that? Well yes, I suppose I would come to think of it, but not without telling you first."

115

I pressed on regardless – regardless, that is, of the certain knowledge that I was getting nowhere.

"So just what the hell is it all about, Rosie? Are we being set up, or have we just happened to fall prey to some slimy character's kinky hobby?"

"I'm sure I don't know, ducks, except that I should watch who you're calling slimy," said Rosie charitably. "It could be a case of the pot calling the kettle black."

Resisting the temptation to ask which particular utensil represented Rosie herself in this magnanimous imagery, I plodded on: "So you don't reckon it's blackmail?"

"I don't know I'm sure, pet."

"I don't either. If it is, you would have thought he'd have shown his hand by now."

"Perhaps he's not used up his roll of film yet," giggled Rosie.

"It's not funny, Rosie. Supposing it does turn out to be blackmail – what do we do then?"

"I've got four lads work on this farm," said Rosie thoughtfully. "That's one for each arm and leg. And there's a nice scummy duck pond two fields away."

I could see that she meant it. A weight lifted. Rosie's bold approach to life could be very reassuring on certain occasions.

"And if it turns out he's only doing it for kicks," added Rosie, "good luck to him is all I can say."

"Meanwhile we'd better find an indoor alternative to our alfresco adventures, don't you think so, Rosie?"

"Depends what you had in mind, treasure, ooh, does the smell of this iodine do things to you because it definitely does things to me, ooh, it really turns me on, let's play at doctors and nurses, shall we?"

Steve Selby was apparently staying overnight in Badgers Heath to fulfil an engagement in Lewes the following evening. Nick Crabbe had promised, or threatened, to see if the alternative wheelchair comedian could call in at the office to meet me before he left town. So when the reception desk, as we rather grandly called the classified advertisements department whenever we had visitors, rang up to say there was someone waiting to see me, I braced myself for the ordeal and went in search of Nick Crabbe.

"I think he's in the darkroom," said Douglas Boxer carelessly.

"What the bloody hell's he doing in the darkroom – he's not a photographer?" It couldn't be. Although Nick was my number one suspect, in so far as I had one, even he would not have the audacity to develop his incriminating snaps in my own editorial darkroom.

"Apparently he knocked off a few pictures at that concert you were both at last night."

Not in my presence he hadn't, but I supposed he could always have taken them in Steve Selby's dressing room before or after the show. And then used up the rest of the roll at Mill Farm.

"All right. When he comes out tell him his hero's arrived and we'll be down in the waiting area. And tell him to fetch some coffee." There was a communal secretary to do that sort of thing but I enjoyed the prospect of Nick Crabbe performing a menial task. "Oh, and don't forget I've got my weekly conference with Sam at eleven, so if I don't surface, come and rescue me."

The waiting area on the ground floor was a small annexe separated from classified ads-cum-reception by the usual bank of greenery, in this case expensive indoor palms to remind editorial types passing by their advertising colleagues where the money came from.

"Surprised you're not lining up for autographs," I quipped to the two pouting young things who staffed the department. They looked even blanker than usual, as well they might have done, for when I stepped through the grove of palms it was to be confronted not by the alternative wheelchair comedian but by Miss Bellows, the Bonfire Society archivist and scourge of the Standing Committee, who sat twisting her handkerchief in her bony, seemingly translucent hands and looking as if she had either been quietly snivelling or was on the verge of doing so.

Except when she raised one of the footling objections which were her only contribution to our committee proceedings, I don't suppose I had ever given a second's thought to Miss Bellows. Outside the upstairs room of the Dolphin Arms I knew her only as a permanent, unremarked-upon fixture of Dorothy's Pantry, where the only difference between her and the hatstands was that you nodded to Miss Bellows on the way out. She was what used to be described as a lady of a certain age, a professional spinster whose natural role in life was that of a walk-on part in a body-in-the-library detective novel. Her address in the Bonfire Society handbook was given as some cottage or other in Voles Bottoms, the hamlet just down the lane from Mill Farm, and I had no doubt that it had roses around the door.

"Miss Bellows, what a surprise. I'm sorry if I look taken aback – I was expecting someone entirely different."

"Oh dear, I knew I should have made an appointment," whimpered Miss Bellows, or anyway gave the impression of whimpering. "But since I was just passing, I decided to call in on the off-chance of your having a moment to spare." This seemed highly improbable. Anyone chancing to be passing the *Badgers Heath Herald*'s brick box could only be heading for the motorway, and Miss Bellows, as I knew, ran only to a bicycle.

"Now you *are* here," I said with feigned warmth, slightly stressing the verb in case she proposed making it a habit, "what can I do for you?"

She was the kind of woman to use the phrase, "I scarcely know how to begin," and looked set to do so. I cut in quickly: "But I'm afraid we'll have to make it brief, as I have an editorial meeting in a few minutes."

Miss Bellows took the hint and got to the point, or adjacent to it. "Mr Kettle, you'll be aware that I am the honorary secretary of the Badgers Heath Cat Sanctuary."

I wasn't, but I could well imagine it to be the case. Indeed, now that I came to think of it, given that a Badgers Heath Cat Sanctuary did exist it would have come as a considerable surprise had Miss Bellows not proved to be its honorary secretary.

Nick Crabbe would be down in a minute or so. Whatever she was after – a plug for funds, I imagined, like just about every other caller – I would put him on to the story, and serve him right.

"Yes, I hear it does very good work," I bluffed. "I have a man who's very hot on cats. He'll be down in a moment." I could see the headline already, the one we always used on cat stories: JUST PURRFECT.

118

"Mr Kettle, I'm in great trouble," pronounced Miss Bellows.

It was an unexpected yet familiar enough gambit which could mean only one thing. She had been caught watching television without a licence or riding her bicycle on the pavement, and she wanted the case kept out of the paper.

"Go on," I said, assuming an expression of magisterial gravity. It did not do to let the *Herald*'s supplicants think I was a push-over for suppressing the news, although I did tend to turn a blind eye upon drunks and disorderlies and public indecency involving consenting adults. There, I would think, but for the grace of God . . .

"I'm afraid I've been very foolish, Mr Kettle."

"We all are at times, Miss Bellows."

"In fact anyone not knowing the circumstances might even say wicked."

"Come along, I'm sure it's not as bad as that."

Miss Bellows gave a little snort of indignation. If she considered that she might be judged wicked, it seemed to imply, then who was I to argue the toss? "It depends what you call bad, Mr Kettle. To some, I dare say, a hundred and twenty-seven pounds is a trifle. To me, it is a fortune."

Where the hell was Crabbe? "We have very generous readers, Miss Bellows. With a little help from the *Herald*, I'm sure you'll raise your hundred and twenty-seven pounds in no time at all." As so often when having my editorial arm twisted by fund-raisers, I wondered where all the money came from that poured in from our readers. Generous was an understatement. They were profligate. If we had started a fund for sick cockroaches, they would have over-subscribed it.

"We're not talking about raising it, Mr Kettle," said Miss Bellows, a shade too petulantly considering what she was about to reveal. "We're talking about embezzling it."

The light, as I thought, dawned. "Oh, I see. Your cat sanctuary. All right, Miss Bellows, who's your treasurer and how many people know about this?"

"I am myself the treasurer and soon the whole world will know about it, Mr Kettle. One of my subscribers has threatened me with the police."

Here Miss Bellows broke into sniffs and sobs, displaying alarming expectations of my patting her hand. Trusting that the girls on the other side of classified advertising's Coconut Grove were not listening in, I mumbled, "All right, Miss Bellows, take it easy," and eventually the whole story came spilling out, exactly as she had quite obviously rehearsed it before chancing to be passing on her bicycle.

The money represented the entire funds of the Badgers Heath Cat Sanctuary. She had not, it goes without saying, abstracted the money for herself: the Miss Bellowses of this world rarely do. It seemed that she had a sister, a spinster like herself, living in Brighton. The idea of there being more than one Miss Bellows in existence so stunned and depressed me that I nearly lost the thread of her narrative; but I gathered that her sister was of a somewhat flightier disposition. That was presumably why she had taken herself off to Brighton instead of sharing a cottage in Voles Bottoms where she could have looked after the cats and kept out of trouble. The sister had always liked a flutter, and in short, working her way up from bingo and the betting shop, she had blown her modest savings at the roulette table. The rent on her flat – it would be a depressing basement masquerading as "the garden flat", I surmised – had fallen due and she had appealed to the Badgers Heath branch of the family to help. Miss Bellows kept to a tight budget and the cat fund was her only source of ready cash. End of story, or nearly.

"I know my sister is very anxious to repay the money, and she is earnestly looking for work, no matter how lowly – cleaning lady, deck chair attendant, anything, Mr Kettle – so as to be able to pay me back at so much a week. But meanwhile, I'm afraid, the discrepancy has been discovered."

"Oh? How?" I was mildly intrigued. Miss Bellows' cat sanctuary was so obviously a one-woman band that I doubted whether even her best friend, if she had one, was privy to its affairs. Maybe she had been shopped by a hungry tabby.

"The money was banked with the Three Counties. The account became overdrawn."

Dennis Reason. A bit brutal to threaten the poor old bat with the police, it seemed to me. A bank manager had his responsibilities, I supposed, and no one came more officious than the former Treasurer of the Badgers Heath Bonfire Society; but presumably Miss Bellows had a pension fund or securities tucked away somewhere, and he could very easily have called her into his office, given her a good talking-to, then siphoned a hundred and twenty-seven pounds from her own nest egg into the cats' nest egg.

Perhaps he just wanted to give her a good scare. "And you're seriously under the impression that Mr Reason is threatening you with exposure?"

"He was very angry, Mr Kettle. As I said, he's a subscriber to the cat sanctuary fund, or rather his wife is, she pays us five pounds a year by standing order in memory of a ginger tom she once had, and as Mr Reason says, as custodian of the account he has a duty to my other subscribers."

So now we came to the point, as I thought, of Miss Bellows' visit. "And you want to know, if it comes to it, whether I can keep the case out of the paper? Well, I can't make any promises, I'm afraid, Miss Bellows. The most constructive approach is to try and see that it never gets into court. I'm sure Mr Reason would be open to suggestions." It would make a bloody good story if it ever did come out. Cat Woman Stole to Pay Sister's Gambling Debts.

Miss Bellows stared. "Mr Reason has already made a suggestion of his own, Mr Kettle. That is why I am here. He says he can see his way to keeping the matter dark on two conditions. Firstly, that I pay the money back, which I fully intend to do, and secondly, which is far more difficult, that I resign."

"From your cat sanctuary?"

Miss Bellows' lower lip quivered. "From the Bonfire Society, Mr Kettle."

If Miss Bellows thought I was a close buddy of Reason's and could intervene on her behalf, there was only one thing I could tell her. Reason was a stickler for correctitude and the Bonfire Society committee he regarded as the Badgers Heath equivalent of the Privy Council. She would have to go.

"He – he said quite rightly that there were others better fitted for the office," gulped Miss Bellows. I felt sorry for her. I could imagine Reason banging on about responsibility, accountability and all the rest of it, the kind of lecture he read to anyone caught running the smallest of unauthorised overdrafts, never mind with their hands in the till.

"Did he have anyone in mind?" I casually wondered aloud. There must have been any number of upright pillars of Badgers Heath society with a healthy deposit account at the Three Counties to whom Reason owed patronage.

"Why, yes," replied Miss Bellows as Nick Crabbe stepped through the shrubbery bearing a canteen tray containing three polystyrene beakers of coffee and a heap of packeted sugar, sachets of powdered cream and plastic stirrers. "Strangely enough he mentioned this gentleman here."

So far I had caned a good two thirds of a bottle of gin and it was beginning to show in my deliberations.

It was the middle of the night after a gruelling evening with Rosie when she had insisted on making love in the bath. My knees, already tender from their contact with the gravel drive earlier in the week, felt as if I had been accompanying Sam Dice on one of his prayer marathons. The notes I had set out to make were increasingly rambling and progressively illegible as they reached the end of the page.

Nick Crabbe, Nick Crabbe, Nick Crabbe. It all came back to Nick Crabbe, but it was like a whodunnit where one knows the criminal without knowing the crime. If there was a crime, that was to say. For there was an innocuous explanation for practically everything. That was the trouble. The explanations were far too innocuous.

Take Reason's unexpected nomination of Nick for the Bonfire Society committee. What did it amount to? Nick, coming down to the office waiting area to find himself unexpectedly confronting Miss Bellows instead of his pal Steve Selby the alternative wheelchair comedian, had looked decidedly unflustered, not that he ever did look flustered. A civil word or two with Miss Bellows and he had smartly withdrawn, leaving me to reassure her on what at that moment I felt far from reassured about myself, namely that there was no conspiracy afoot; furthermore, and here I was on easier ground, that the Bonfire Society was not in the hands of an élitist clique, and above all that no whiff of the cat sanctuary scandal would reach the columns of the *Badgers Heath Herald.*

As for Reason, no one could have been more straightforward and above board when, dropping in for a liquid lunch at the Dolphin Arms Buttery as was my custom after my regular Monday morning conference with Sam Dice, I found him tucking into the salmon fishcakes with Len Quartermouth MBE FIAV. He made no attempt to pretend that Nick Crabbe had not been on the phone to him the moment I was out of the office.

"I gather you're already in the know about Miss Bellows having to resign for health reasons," he said almost before my first gin and tonic had reached my lips, a combination of grimaces and jerks of the head appraising me of our Chair's ignorance of the real reason for her departure. "She's probably told you that I brought up the name of that young protégé of yours, Nicholas Crabbe, purely on an informal and unofficial basis of course, as a possible successor. He is more than willing to serve – I had words with him this morning."

If we were not beating about bushes this morning, I saw no harm in not coming straight to the point myself. "I thought you didn't like Nick. In fact you went so far as to warn me against him."

Reason was in no way put off his stride. As bland as they came he said, "He's an ambitious young man, anxious to be a big fish in a small pond. To that extent I'm on my guard against him, just as I'm wary of all these yuppies who come down here overstretching themselves on big mortgages they can't keep up with. But he's a chap with bright ideas, one of them being this Banana-skin Week venture you've been canvassing, Oliver. Now if that goes through as he seems to think it will and we the Bonfire Society give it our blessing, who better to serve on Standing Committee than its only begetter?"

"We could go farther and fare ah," said Len Quartermouth MBE FIAV.

So Nick Crabbe would be nodded through – Miss Bellows was absolutely right in her conviction that the Bonfire Society was run by a clique – and then what? He would secure the chilli-bean-filled baked potato concession for himself under a false name? He would accept monetary considerations from a fireworks manufacturer? Under the influence of the gin bottle I laughed crazily aloud as I considered the minuscule scale of the possibilities. Dennis Reason, when he had talked of Nick Crabbe wanting to be a big fish in a small pond, had unwittingly put the whole situation into perspective for me. These were parish pump matters, trivialities. I tried to imagine selling the story to the news editor of one of the national dailies: "There's some kind of hanky-panky, I'm not sure what, at the Badgers Heath Bonfire Society . . . " and again I laughed aloud.

What else did I have to go on? Nick had known about Reason's resignation from the treasurership either before or very shortly after Reason's inner wheel colleagues, myself included. But so what? Then Reason had proposed me to succeed him as Treasurer – or had he? Come to think of it, hadn't the suggestion come from Basil Brush? I was getting fuddled. At any rate, I was now Treasurer and there was nothing sinister about that, so why should there be anything sinister about Nick Crabbe succeeding Miss Bellows?

Then there was Nick's involvement with Rosie, which had yet to be satisfactorily, or even unsatisfactorily, accounted for by either of them. Once again, so what? She could well be a purely, if that was the word I was looking for, recreational pursuit on his part. Even a blackmailer, in the remote event that such was his moonlighting job, is entitled to a social life.

I had an uneasy hunch that even as I fitted the jigsaw together there were pieces, important pieces, that I had not even taken out of the box. But I was tired. There was, at a pinch, a perfectly reasonable explanation for everything, and at this time of night and at this stage of inebriation that was good enough for me. Except for the lights. There was no explaining away the lights. If the prowler with the flash camera had anything to do with all this then my non-conspiracy theory went out of the window.

But my gut feeling, which was to turn out not entirely as misleading as it might have been, was that the puzzle of the lights was from a different jigsaw altogether. There was only one way to find out, and that was to find out, and I had plans for that – or rather Rosie Greenleaf did. She had outlined them by way of erotic stimulus while we thrashed about in her increasingly tepid bath, and it seemed to me that we could be on the brink of solving the mystery. What would be in store when we had solved it was another matter, and not one that was going to detain me tonight. I tore up my notes, slotted a rubbishy old film into the video machine, and finished the gin.

In all the time I had been editing Sam's newspaper he had only once before visited me at home uninvited – or invited either, come to that, since he resisted dinner parties where he was expected to break bread with a host or hostess who did not say grace, and Sherry firmly drew the line at that – and that was when he had had his attention drawn to what might have been, but fortunately for me was not, an expensive libel.

This made the second occasion. It was Saturday morning, and Sherry and I were preparing to set out on our usual shopping expedition when she spotted his Jag gliding to a stop outside our gate.

The curtains of the Spruce household opposite twitched. "There goes the neighbourhood," said Sherry.

I watched uneasily as Sam's chauffeur hopped out and shoe-horned our chubby proprietor out of the back. "What does he want, I wonder?"

"You'll know soon enough, darling. When proprietors visit their editors it means they're either going to be promoted or fired. I'll put the coffee on."

"I shouldn't bother – this is going to be short if not sweet," I said, observing Sam waddle purposefully up the drive, his demeanour being best expressed in the phrase, "What I have to say can be said just as well standing up, thank you."

"You were right," said Sherry three minutes later when our guest had just as briskly departed. "So what was all that about?"

"Nothing much," I said fatuously.

Sherry gave one of her pitying sighs. "Kettle, newspaper owners, even small, fat owners of small-town newspapers, do not drop in on their editors on a Saturday morning to discuss the

likely winner of the first race at Plumpton. So you might as well
tell me what's going on."

"I suppose I might as well," I conceded ruefully, "considering
you were listening behind the door."

What Sam had to say, after he had explained with no attempt
at conviction that he just happened to be in the neighbourhood
and that some matters were best discussed at informal level well
away from the office, was that he was on to my affair with Rosie
Greenleaf. Or such was Sherry's reading of the conversation.

While not actually saying, "I'll come straight to the point,"
Sam exuded the air of having said it. "What can you tell me
about a Mrs Greenleaf, Oliver?"

Dangerous ground; but at least it was dangerous ground well
signposted. I said with very careful nonchalance, "Farmer's
widow. Appeals Secretary of the Bonfire Society and a first-rate
fund-raiser. Runs the Farmers' Ladies Circle. Nothing else
known."

"Character?" asked Sam sharply.

"Outgoing. Gregarious. Fun-loving, I'd say." I thought I had
better add for the sake of verisimilitude, "Something of a merry
widow." Without asking Sam what all this was in aid of, I let my
expression pose the question.

"She came to see me last night. A first-rate fund-raiser you say.
I'm inclined to believe you – she left with a cheque for a thousand
pounds."

I whistled. Though no tightwad, Sam was not an easy touch.
"She is a very persuasive lady," I conceded. "Perhaps I should
take some tips from her before I present my next budget."

"Take a tip from me instead," said Sam, already at the door. I
hoped Sherry would not fall into the room as he opened it. "In
your dealings with this Mrs Greenleaf, be very careful. If she's all
you say she is, she could very well mean trouble. Believe me,
laddie, I speak from experience."

Wondering whether Sam's experience of trouble had contrib-
uted in any measure to his religious conversion, I escorted him
out to the Jag. A domestic inquest followed, then Sherry and I
drove in sulky silence to the Cherrytree Shopping Mall where
her last word, or so it was to be hoped, was, "Don't say I didn't

warn you."

Leaving Sherry in the clutches of a pack of diminutive Brownies seeking financial backing for a hoppa-hop-hop along the High Street in aid of some furry friends, I hurried over to the Euro-inn Dolphin Arms Hotel and rang Rosie. Resisting her invitation to join her in a hay rick, it being such a lovely day, I said, "The plan, Rosie, the plan. I think we'd better make it Monday evening."

9

Inland Revenue staff raised more than £100 for the Cystic Fibrosis Fund with a three-legged egg and spoon race in which the contestants were tied together with red tape.

Children from the Merrydale Estate Community School, collecting for the premature babies unit at Badgers Heath Hospital, persuaded shoppers to join in the hokey-cokey outside the Early Learning Centre.

Customers of the Wheatsheaf, East Hustling, will be donating the contents of their swear box to the Little Sisters of the Poor.

Handcuffed to a giant Mr Magoo on roller skates, computer software salesman Alan Colley (28) set off on a one-man marathon run to Brighton to raise money for a guide dog for the blind.

Students of Badgers Heath Polytechnic's Faculty of Media Studies and Print Technology, concerned for the plight of the homeless, have pledged themselves to sleep in cardboard boxes for a week.

If their cardboard boxes were out of doors – and I made a mental note to tick off the reporter who had dozily omitted to find out – then I felt sorry for them. It had been raining all day and seemed set to rain all night – the thin, spiteful rain we often get in our part of the world. At least you could say for it, on this mid-September evening, that it was unlikely to turn to sleet before my mission was either accomplished or aborted. As to which it would be, only time and the relentless drizzle would tell.

Concealment rather than shelter being my priority, I had positioned myself under the dripping boughs of a chestnut tree just beyond where Rosie's driveway led into the farmyard, rather than under the eaves of the barn where our hoped-for intruder

128

would most likely position himself. Barn and chestnut tree afforded excellent views of Rosie's bedroom window. Surveying the brilliantly-lit but at present curtained oblong, I experienced disturbingly voyeuristic stirrings. They were of insufficient strength, however, to extinguish the deep-felt hope that Rosie was not proposing to make a regular erotic hors d'oeuvre of keeping me outside in the streaming rain while she performed a striptease in the window.

It had been a long day and a long evening. The morning had got off to a bad start with Sherry issuing a warning as she climbed into her car to drive back to London: "On the subject of Rosie Tealeaf or whatever she calls herself, I don't know how far you're entangled and I don't think I want to know, but you'd better get yourself disentangled before I get back here on Friday." That came as something of a jolt. She hadn't mentioned Rosie since just after our visit from Sam on Saturday, and I had taken her silence to mean that while not conniving at my little fling she was more concerned that I should watch my step than that I should start spending my evenings at home with a mug of cocoa. Her ultimatum, as it sounded like, meant that if I did announce myself as disentangled I should have to admit to having been entangled, and whatever Sherry said now about not wishing to know about it, there would be a lot of awkward questions to answer, or to avoid answering. It was very worrying.

Then there was Sam. Not that, touch wood, he had mentioned Rosie again, but at our regular Monday morning conference he had expressed a wish to meet Nick Crabbe. Leafing through Nick's latest Bananaskin Week memo, a rough proposed time-table of the week giving cunningly due prominence to the Youth Prayer Rally *pièce de resistance*, Sam said, "This young livewire has ideas coming out of his ears, Oliver. He'll go far." I forbore to mention that Nick had already been far, and blotted his copybook: I would hold that in reserve in case Sam took too much of a shine to him. But editors settled in their ways do not like their proprietors taking too close an interest in their young livewires. That was worrying too.

That evening's Bonfire Society meeting had been gruelling. First there was the sad resignation of Miss Bellows due to ill-

129

health: I was authorised as Treasurer to write my first cheque – to Interflora for a bunch of roses to match those I always imagined to be growing round her door. Nick Crabbe was duly co-opted on to the committee, and since he happened to be on the spot covering the meeting for the *Herald*, or more accurately was just outside the door in accordance with protocol while the votes were counted, he was thrown straight in at the deep end, namely the next item on the agenda which was Bananaskin Week.

Getting the go-ahead for the Bonfire Society to sponsor the week was relatively straightforward, although it took the best part of an hour to convince our resident gloompot Percy Spruce that while we were all well aware of the perils inherent in the possibility of continual rain, war in the Middle East, higher interest rates, and public indifference together with the rival attractions of television and the danger of killing the goose that laid the golden egg, we did feel on balance that Bananaskin Week was a tolerably good idea. Nick Crabbe and I wisely eschewed all mention of the Youth Prayer Rally tie-in and the motion was finally carried. But then just as we were about to move on to my Treasurer's report, with the glad tidings that Rosie's Appeal Fund had now passed the £5,000 mark, Eric Barlow, who had seemingly been asleep throughout the preceding debate, took it into his addled head to pull out his pocket diary and ask, "What dates are we talking about? I don't want it to clash with Alcohol Concern Week because I've a prior arrangement to remain arse-holed from Monday to Saturday."

"Chair, would you remind members that there are ladies present?" humphed Reason. Rosie stifled a giggle, while Betty Spruce caught my eye and blushed as she saw me remembering her at her most unladylike over at Mill Farm.

What dates *were* we talking about? Apart from hoping it would be as far off as possible, say a year next August, I had never given the question a moment's thought. I suppose I imagined we were talking about spring or summer, giving Nick Crabbe time to get his act together.

To my intense surprise he had other ideas. "What's wrong with the week of Bonfire Night?" he carelessly floated. It took only a moment to see that he was absolutely right. November 5 this year fell at the weekend and so the Badgers Heath Bonfire would be a fitting climax to Bananaskin Week. By way of a bonus, it would also put Sam's Youth Prayer Rally in the shade. It would leave us exactly seven weeks to get the event organised from scratch but that was Nick Crabbe's problem.

"I second that," I said.

The ensuing debate takes up seventeen pages of that evening's minutes, most of them summarising the doubts, misgivings and apprehensions of Percy Spruce who contended that November would be too cold for sponsored jelly wrestling; but after an exhausting two hours, Nick Crabbe's proposal won the day.

Down in the Dolphin Arms lounge bar later I allowed him to buy me only one large brandy by way of celebration before loudly asking if I could give anyone a lift. As I escorted our only non-mobile member off the premises, it seemed to me that we ran a gauntlet of knowing looks.

And now here I was under the spreading chestnut tree below Rosie's bedroom window with the rain seeping down my collar. Ten more minutes of this, I reckoned, and then we could call it off. Shivering, I speculated on my chances, upon shedding my wet clothes, of getting into a hot bath before Rosie pounced. I recognised them as slim.

Driving with deliberate slowness through the dark lanes and side roads I had established that neither Nick Crabbe's Escort XR3i nor any other vehicle was following me. Maybe our phantom photographer didn't fancy getting raindrops on his camera lens. It was a foul night and in his shoes I should have opted for staying home and browsing through what after all must by now be quite an impressive portfolio. The vicious rain stinging my face like shards of razor blade, I cut the ten minutes down to five minutes, then to one minute. I counted to sixty and then braced myself for the quick dash across the muddy farmyard to Rosie's back door.

I had stepped out from under the chestnut tree and was gingerly negotiating my way around the puddle that had formed at my feet when I became aware of the sound of crunching gravel. I had heard no car engine and seen no headlights but then round at the back of the farmhouse I was not best placed to do so. They

were positively footsteps, and creeping footsteps at that. I dug
out the handful of small stones I had been nursing in my raincoat
pocket and – our prearranged signal – tossed them up at Rosie's
bedroom window. Then I slithered back into the shadow of the
chestnut tree.

Simultaneously, Rosie's light snapped on and our visitor came
into view, or what passed for a view on a filthy, moonless night.
As he picked his way across the mud to the shelter of the barn, his
black or dark blue raincoat shone like oilskin in the shaft of light
filtering down from the slight gap in the curtained window. That
ruled out Nick Crabbe: he wore a Burberry, as of course he just
would. I knew I had seen that dark raincoat before but I couldn't
place it. Never mind: all would be revealed soon enough –
directly all had been revealed by Rosie.

Peering out through the chink in the curtains she waited until
her audience had got himself settled under the eaves of the barn,
where we had guessed he would establish his position in the front
stalls so to speak. With a flourish, Rosie then threw back the
curtains and stood for a moment, arms outstretched, the lighted
window framing her generous figure like the proscenium arch of
a strip-club stage. The show was about to commence.

Rosie had opted to wear, after consultation with me, the most
modest dress in her wardrobe, a virginal white number that
buttoned up to the throat and left everything but her contours to
the imagination. She now began, in a brazenly leisurely manner,
to unbutton it. She had wanted to do this to music but I had
vetoed the idea.

Tearing my gaze from Rosie over to the barn, I caught the glint
of what could only be a flash gun as the intruder raised his
camera. This meant he was working with reasonably sophisti-
cated equipment rather than your common or garden instant
clicker. A proficient photographer, then – perhaps even a professional one. Dangerous.

I had decided, I had no very clear idea why, to wait until he had
taken at least one photograph before sprinting across and collar-
ing him. Perhaps I imagined it would be hard, caught-red-handed
evidence; although in retrospect I would have thought the camera
itself was evidence enough. Or perhaps, like him, I wanted to see

a little more of Rosie's floorshow before taking any action.

The unbuttoning part of the act finally accomplished, Rosie slowly peeled off her dress and let it drop to the floor, revealing an equally virginal pink underslip. Down came one shoulder strap and then the other, and then this too shimmered to the floor as Rosie ever so casually turned to present her back to the window.

She had mischievously refused to tell me what she would be wearing under the slip, saying that she didn't want our uninvited guest to have all the fun. It proved to be yet another version of the outfit I had seen Betty Spruce modelling for the Farmers' Ladies Circle, although this time in red. It sat rather better on Rosie's ample figure than on Mrs Spruce's ampler one.

Rosie turned to face the window again, sensuously caressing her body from bust to hips. She was enjoying this. So, I had to confess, was I. I could not speak for the rest of the audience but the fact that he had yet to flash off his camera seemed to suggest that he was reasonably transfixed.

Rosie stepped momentarily out of shot, as it were, returning to the window with a hairbrush from her dressing table. Turning now this way and now that, she began, with languorous gestures, to brush her hair. As she bowed her head and applied the brush to the locks cascading around her neck, her full breasts slipped out of their satin moorings and there was a flash of light from the shadow of the barn.

It was something like a twelve yard dash over to the barn and I reckoned I could be across there and have my arm around his throat before he knew what was happening. I reckoned, though, without the mud. Leaping out from under the chestnut tree I slipped and slithered, lost and regained my balance. It was enough to alert him. Luckily for me, instead of making for the far end of the farmyard in his panic, and running off into the darkness of the fields where I should have surely lost him, he charged forward the way he had come. As in some crazy field game I lurched towards him and shouldered him, hoping to send him sprawling into the mud. This time not so luckily for me, the clash just would have to take place on the one strip of firm ground in the whole farmyard. He staggered, thrusting out an arm either

133

to stabilise himself or in the hope of landing me in the mud, and careered off again. I lunged after him, grabbing his sleeve, and was able to yank him towards me, affording a momentary glimpse of his terrified, gleaming wet face before he could tug himself away and, still clutching his camera, more or less skid across the farmyard mud to the gravel drive where I heard his crunching footsteps retreating at speed. There was little point in pursuing him: I could wait, now. Besides, there were distractions. The rain was bucketing down anew and, at her bedroom window, Rosie was continuing her striptease unabashed. Tossing in my palm the button I had wrenched from Dennis Reason's raincoat sleeve, I picked my way through the puddles to the back door, warmth, shelter, and the creature comforts.

"Fiery crosses!" Nick Crabbe had surprisingly breathed, like a man possessed.

Laying down his cheese knife, Sam Dice gave him a long, hard look before asking sharply, "Young man, do you have visions?"

"Only one, sir, but she's leaving me for someone with a bigger salary," jested Nick, nearly losing the Brownie points he had just earned. Briefing him for the occasion, I had forgotten, or perhaps omitted, to tell him that our proprietor does not like jokes.

It was once again my turn for Sam's rotating dinner for his editors and their deputies. On this particular Tuesday, Douglas Boxer had cried off on the grounds of suffering from one of the frequent periods of sick leave to which he was a martyr. For once, I believed his migraine or hay fever or ingrowing toenail could be genuine: he would not willingly have passed up his six-weekly opportunity to lick Sam's boots. It was at Sam's suggestion, meaning Sam's command, that I was fielding Nick Crabbe as substitute – "Bring that bright young lad of yours over and let's have a look at him."

Apart from raising his eyes to heaven in rather the wrong spirit during Sam's grace, Nick had carried himself off well during the meal so far. We would soon enough put a stop to that, I complacently told myself. He was wearing a double-breasted dark suit far better cut than mine but marginally, and tactfully, less better cut than Sam's, and he conversed respectfully but easily as if accustomed to dining with newspaper proprietors every week of his life. On religion, the chief topic of Sam's dissertation during the grapefruit starter and the cottage pie-type main dish (on which Nick was careful to compliment Mrs Bishop), he did not put a foot wrong. While allowing Sam to have the floor on the need to get young people back into the churches, he managed skilfully to get enough words in to suggest that he personally went to church two or three times a week, though without troubling to reveal that these visits were exclusively in search of parish news from the Rev Basil Brush and other local ministers. On the Youth Prayer Rally, to which obviously we had been working up, he gained Sam's approval by listening attentively to all his observations and then not only agreeing with them, á la Douglas Boxer, but endorsing them with some little comment of his own, the equivalent of the glacé cherry on Mrs Bishop's grapefruit. He listened straightfaced to the revelations of St Urban. I said little. My turn would come.

It came with the bread and butter pudding. "Now about this Bananarama Week," began Sam, greedily tucking in. Neither Nick Crabbe nor I corrected him. "When should we make the announcement, Oliver?"

"I thought in about a couple of weeks, Sam."

"A bit premature, laddie, isn't it? Mark you, I don't know what date you've got in mind, but I would have thought if it's going to culminate with our Youth Prayer Rally, what better time than Easter?"

Easter. Easter. I had not thought of Easter. "We did think of Easter, Sam," I said as silkily as I could. "We gave it very serious consideration. But then Nick came up with . . . " About to say "a better idea", I re-drafted it to "another idea", and beamed across at Nick Crabbe to indicate that now was the time for him to dig a large hole in the ground and jump into it.

"We've got the Bonfire Society to agree, sir," said Nick, phrasing it just about as badly as I could have wished, "to coincide Bananaskin Week with the Badgers Heath Bonfire."

"What?" Had Sam not already wolfed down his bread and butter pudding, he would have spluttered a mouthful of it across the table.

135

"Nick believes we should roll up Bananaskin Week, the Bonfire and the Youth Prayer Rally in one great big celebration," I translated helpfully.

It was a sign of Sam's agitation that he began to attack the cheeseboard. Sam normally does not touch cheese, on the grounds that it stops him from dreaming.

"Oh, but we can't have this, Oliver, we can't have this at all. If you have your Bananarama Week coinciding with your Bonfire, then your Bonfire's got to be the climax of the week, wouldn't you say?"

"Yes, I would say that, Sam."

"But I thought we'd agreed the Youth Prayer Rally was to be the climax of the week?"

"The climax before the Bonfire, sir," put in Nick.

"That's an anti-climax, laddie. Now I thought this was all cut and dried, Oliver. We discussed it only on Sunday."

"But at the Bonfire Society meeting on Monday, Sam, Nick persuaded the committee that Bananaskin Week, the Bonfire, and – "

"Yes, yes, yes, we've heard all that already. What's this young man got to say about it? Speak up, laddie."

I had been avoiding Nick Crabbe's eye but now I looked across at him to savour what I imagined would be an expression of concentrated hatred. Instead, he appeared to be in a spiritual trance. And it was then that he said, "Fiery crosses!"

"Come again, young man?"

"Fiery crosses, sir!" Nick rose to his feet as if to address a meeting. Using his hands to eloquent effect, possibly with the object of persuading Sam that he had a little of the evangelist in his blood, he continued, with as much fluency as anyone of his generation could command, "So, the climax of the week as I believe all of us round this table have agreed, all right, has got to be the Youth Prayer Rally, all right, and for which by the way, considering the time of year we are talking about, I very highly recommend the concert hangar at the Flying Club, I've got some provisional costings, Mr Dice and, er, Oliver, and I consider personally it's very much the best venue going."

"Never mind the venue, laddie, what are these fiery crosses

you've brought on to the agenda?" Sam crammed a wedge of Cheddar into his face. For myself, I noted that Nick Crabbe had addressed me by my Christian name for the first time ever. He was getting above himself only to go under any minute now, I ruminated enjoyably. What, Sam had asked, did he mean by fiery crosses? He was literally thinking on his feet and had probably not the faintest idea – or so, mistakenly, I hoped.

"We stage the Bonfire as planned, all right? At a given signal a hundred, maybe two hundred young people file past the fire with petrol-soaked wooden crosses which they set alight. Carrying their fiery crosses, they lead this great procession away from the Bonfire, over the Heath and down to the Flying Club, with people joining in all along the way. It could be really spectacular."

It was then that Sam asked Nick Crabbe if he was subject to visions.

I had to hand it to him. It really was a vision. I could see the television coverage now. So could Sam. Rising, he vigorously pumped Nick's hand as if presenting him with an award.

I wished we could have had Percy Spruce on hand to ask what if it rained, or, if it didn't rain, what if the fiery crosses set the gorse on fire? Racking my brain for a put-down, the best I could come up with was, "You don't think it smacks a bit of the Ku Klux Klan?"

A mistake. Still standing, still clasping Nick's hand, Sam turned on me reproachfully. It was a little tableau of the faithful spurning the scoffer. "You will persist in negative reactions, Oliver. You won't raise your sights. What's that verse I told you about?"

"'Two men looked out of prison bars, one saw the mud hole, the other saw the stars,'" I quoted obediently, smiling across at Nick to persuade him that we were fellow-conspirators indulging Sam's little whims. He did not respond.

"You should learn a lesson from my old mother, laddie. As she always tells me when I'm getting over-critical, 'If you can't say anything good about a thing, don't say anything at all.'"

Sam finally relinquished his grip on Nick Crabbe but remained standing, a welcome sign that the audience was just about over.

"It's good to hear that your mother is still with us, sir," said Nick in a fair imitation of the Douglas Boxer grovel.

"Still with us, young man? Of course she's still with us – have you never heard of life eternal?" A paternal arm on Nick's shoulder, Sam led us out to the hall. "She came round, when was it, last Friday," he continued conversationally. "She'd been looking at the paper, Oliver, and to be quite blunt about it she doesn't care for some of these photographs you've been using. Too clever-clever by half."

My photographer Gavin Pyle had surpassed himself with a study of three schoolgirls, the winner and runners-up in a poetry competition, whom he had portrayed peering through a goldfish tank like the witches in an aquatic production of Macbeth. "I'm afraid he does go over the top sometimes," I conceded. I had better have a word with Gavin. One more visitation from Sam's mother and he would have to go.

It had been a tolerably successful evening as Sam's evenings went. Nick Crabbe had had his little triumph while I had had my nose rubbed in it, but if it kept our proprietor happy I could afford to be magnanimous, or anyway to appear so.

The *coup de grâce*, however, was to come. At the door Sam said, "How much am I paying this young man, Oliver?"

I told him. I knew I had the figure right because I had refused Nick Crabbe a raise only a few days earlier.

"Give him another thousand a year. He's earned it."

On the road back to Badgers Heath, Nick overtook me with a triumphant blare of his three-tone horn and a flash of headlights. I think it was meant to be symbolic.

From the minutes of the Badgers Heath Bonfire Society Standing Committee, September 25. Apologies for absence: Mr D. Reason . . .

But I am getting ahead of myself. In opting to play a cat and mouse game with Reason I was by no means sure, at first, who was the cat and who the mouse. Talking it over with Rosie after my farmyard vigil – a good deal afterwards, since the evening's preliminaries had excited her even beyond her own prodigious norm – I tended to agree with her, changing metaphor, that we should let sleeping dogs lie. This would not preclude me from giving the sleeping dog a swift kick when next I saw it, nor from putting in a dry-cleaning bill for my mud-spattered clothes.

I half-expected to hear from Reason the following morning: either a telephoned apology and the sex offender's standard whingeing explanation that he had been overworking and was subject to strain in his marital relations; or he would come straight to the point with an invitation to examine, on a sale or return basis, a packet of interesting photographs. The latter contingency was happily the more far-fetched one. There are easier ways a bank manager of criminal bent can supplement his income than by creeping around graveyards and muddy farm-yards in the night hours. Besides, Dennis Reason simply wasn't the type. He was, as I reminded Rosie, a pillar of Badgers Heath society – which took me back to my first possibility: for it is the pillar of society, as Rosie in turn reminded me, who is most likely to be found wandering off the sexual straight and narrow.

But one day followed another with no word from Reason, and he certainly wasn't going to hear from me. I could have done with getting my hands on those negatives but I heeded Rosie's counsel, with yet another change of metaphor, to let him stew in his own juice. By Friday, however, when Sherry was due home for the weekend, I was in something of a state of jitters. What if Reason called up, or worse, called round, when my wife was present? Having a guarded telephone conversation with Rosie was all very well, but trying to have one with someone who might seize the occasion to cause me embarrassment and thus assuage his own was another matter. Besides, the prospect left me in no frame of mind for a calm and diplomatic handling of any further examin-ation of the Rosie question which Sherry might care to pursue.

As it happened, Sherry rang me at the office late on Friday afternoon to report that she was unexpectedly on her way to Heathrow to catch an evening flight to Paris to interview some concert idol she had been trying to pin down for months, and so couldn't get home this weekend. These situations did crop up from time to time and I was philosophical about them – in this case more philosophical than usual, although it did occur to me that if her interview wasn't until the next day, as it evidently wasn't, she could just as easily have come home for the night and flown from Gatwick. It occurred to me further that if the interview fell down and her journey was in vain, it wouldn't be for the first time and she would have spent a weekend in Paris on just about as watertight an excuse as it was possible to devise. But I didn't want to go into whys and wherefores just now. Procrastination may be the thief of time but it is a generous provider of peace of mind. That there would have to be a showdown of sorts with Sherry sooner or later I knew, if I cared to face up to it, but her surprise absence this weekend would at least make it later rather than sooner.

A less surprising absence, on Saturday lunchtime, was that of Dennis Reason from our usual exclusive gathering in the lounge bar of the Euro-inn Dolphin Arms Hotel.

I bumped into Eric Barlow in the High Street – or rather, he bumped into me, having propelled himself rather too quickly out of the doorway of what he called his half-way house, the Black Horse, midstream between the Goat and Compasses and the Dolphin Arms – and we entered the hotel together.

"Hello, our man done a bunk with all our life savings, has he?" was Barlow's jest as we noted that our quorum was one short. Reason almost invariably arrived third after Basil Brush and Len Quartermouth MBE FIAV, having learned from experience that with this placement he incurred the least risk of having to buy a round for the five of us. I had certainly not expected him to be present. Now I wondered if there could be some substance in Barlow's facetious suggestion. So there was, in a way – Reason had indeed done a bunk, though not with the takings. Basil Brush and Len were eager to impart the news.

"I'm afraid Dennis has had rather a bad blow," announced Basil.

"It seems his mother has been taken very ah."

"A stroke, poor thing. She's not expected to recover."

"As you may or may not be ah, she's been living alone just outside ah, and he's had to ask for leave of absence to get her into a nursing ah and look after her, ah, affairs."

Very convenient. "When did you hear about this?" I asked.

"On Tuesday morning," said Basil Brush. But of course. "He

sought me out at the church to convey his apologies for missing next Monday's meeting." And several subsequent ones, I shouldn't wonder. "He was in a terrible state, poor chap."

"That's funny," said Barlow. "I saw him opening up the bank Tuesday and he didn't say anything to me."

"Probably he wouldn't," said Basil smugly. "Grief counselling is rather more in my line, I think you'd agree, Eric."

Basil expanded on his bulletin, translating some of Len's earlier ahs and ums. Reason's mother lived outside Norwich, and it was to that city he had repaired with the story that he had to get her out of a National Health ward and into a private nursing home. Although warned by Basil that she could linger on for months, he had every intention of staying near at hand until the end. They had, it seemed, been very close.

Norwich was far enough away and a big enough place for Reason to be able to evade an interview with me for just about as long as he wanted. His abrupt departure meant that I could consider him on the run and thus rule out blackmail; but, more out of curiosity than concern, and discounting the possibility that his mother really had conveniently suffered a stroke, I wondered how on earth he could have squared it with his wife. "Oh, darling, I've rather stupidly been caught out taking dirty pictures so I'm afraid I'll have to lie low for a while . . . "

"Has Mrs Reason gone with him?" I asked.

Len Quartermouth MBE FIAV gave me a curious look. "For the editor of the local ah, if I may ah, Oliver, you seem somewhat out of ah."

"I thought you knew, I thought the whole perishing town knew!" explained Barlow. "A small place like this and you don't know our Dennis's wife left him, what, three months ago?"

"Now we don't know that," Basil intervened. "All we know is that we haven't seen Mrs Reason for some time and Dennis has let it be known that she's looking after her invalid mother in Worthing."

"How good they are to their mothers, the Reasons," I said, feeling very cheered up. "My round, I believe."

10

Memo from Nick Crabbe to Editor. Re: Bananaskin Week.

Just to give you an update five weeks before lift-off.

The preliminary announcement in Friday's *Herald* has already had a terrific impact, with scores of calls and letters offering participation, both from individuals and organisations, and ranging in age from a little girl of four who wants to contribute her 20p a week pocket money to an old lady of 85 who is offering her pension for the week. I am arranging for them to be pictured together once you have found a replacement for Gavin Pyle. A photographer on permanent attachment to Bananaskin Week is a No 1 priority and I am sure you will be recruiting one as a matter of urgency.

The thing is already beginning to snowball and I suggest we install a Bananaskin Hotline to take offers of help. If we could hire a temp to look after the Hotline and act as my secretary it would ease my mounting workload.

Many of the calls we have been getting are in the shape of pledges from groups organising sponsored events such as a tug o' war, slave auction, pickled onion and crisp eating contests, human chess, crazy golf, back-to-front dressing comp, welly throwing, shaving firemen's legs, sweeping Cherrytree Shopping Mall with toothbrushes, sitting in the stocks for a day etc etc etc. These pledges already amount to nearly £20,000, yes TWENTY THOUSAND POUNDS (Owl Insurance's social club alone is pledged to raise £1,000 which will be doubled by management if they reach target), and I suggest we run the story big in this week's issue – though maybe we should play down the offer of an agricultural college student bonk-in!

Seriously, the Badgers Heath Care Group for the Blind are to stage a Braille Bible read-in and I think we should carry this as a separate item to soften our readership up for the thrilling news that Bananaskin Week will have a religious element. I do not know when you intend announcing the Youth Prayer Rally but I would say the later the better – let's get the fun ideas coming in first. Natch, I appreciate the timing of the blurb is not entirely in your hands.

To raise a delicate question, could you confirm that Douglas Boxer is no longer on the Youth Prayer Rally as he seems to think otherwise? While I need all the help I can get, there is a danger of too many chiefs and not enough Indians, and I now have the Prayer Rally being organised in detail by a sub-committee from the Bonfire Society, chaired by myself. If Douglas wants to add his input he is more than welcome, but he will have to report to me.

I understand that Mrs Greenleaf's Appeal Fund now stands at over £6,000 and I wonder if some of this could be released to cover current expenses – mainly the cost of 200 balsa wood crosses for which the suppliers want cash up front. I am not convinced that balsa wood is the best material, as these burning crosses have to be carried two and a half miles, but I am checking this out with the fire brigade . . .

There was a lot more of this but I barely skimmed through it. Nick Crabbe was becoming insufferable – even more insufferable, that is, than he had already been before being anointed with a £1,000-a-year pay hike by Sam Dice. With only five weeks to go before Bananaskin Week I had had to take him off reporting duties to be full-time organiser. It was a project to be worked on behind closed doors, but since we had no doors to close in our open-plan office I was letting him operate from his flat, where he had installed a fax machine from which he was bombarding me with memos – all of them, with overtones of impertinence, telling me how to do my job.

The infuriating thing was that he tended to be right, both in his news judgement – the £20,000 pledges story really would get us off with a bang – and on editorial decisions that were none of his damn business. He was perfectly justified in hinting, however

143

snidely, that I had picked a fine time to fire our brightest photographer, but I had no option. Gavin Pyle had turned in a birthday
portrait of a centenarian so dramatic in its use of shadow that it
looked like a picture of the Grim Reaper or perhaps Sam's late
mother on visiting day. I should not have printed it but her son
was one of our biggest advertisers. Sam was on the phone within
two minutes of receiving his advance copy of the *Herald*. Nick
Crabbe would be glad to hear that I had just taken on Gavin's
successor, a promising young lad whose idea of composition was
to have his subjects pointing at something like the remains of a
chip pan fire and grinning at the camera.

Nick was also right to insist upon Boxer's nose being kept out
of the Youth Prayer Rally. Left to Boxer, or even interfered with
by Boxer, the Rally would never have got off the ground in time
for next year's Bonfire, never mind this year's, and while this
might be good news for the paper it would not be good news for
the paper's owner. I had been meaning, in any case, to have a
word with Douglas Boxer, and now was as good a time as any.

I found him in his Swiss cheese plant-enshrouded space,
jangling the change in his pocket and studying a wall calendar
which, for want of a wall, was Blu-Tacked to the side of his filing
cabinet. Bananaskin Week had been highlighted in yellow. Other
dates, probably Boxer's proposed days off for sick leave, were
highlighted in blue.

"Only five weeks to go," said Boxer with a concerned inflec-
tion as I barged through the greenery. "Not long now, Oliver."

"Not long in terms of what's got to be done," I said, congratulating myself on at once spotting an opportunity for coming
straight to the point. "But a very long time in terms of trying to
get a paper out with one good man off the diary."

"You mean Crabbe? I don't see why he shouldn't combine
what he's doing with his normal reporting duties."

"Just as you tried to combine getting the Prayer Rally off the
ground with sitting on your arse shuffling bits of paper," I said
rudely. I had made little attempt to hide my contempt for Boxer
since he had chickened out of the editorship of the *East Sussex
Advertiser*. "It's a full-time job, cock."

"Then why does he reject every offer of help, I should like

144

to know?"

"Because he knows what he's doing." With some effort I refrained from adding, "And you don't, cock." Poor Boxer was about to be humiliated enough already.

"Whether he does or not, and only time will tell," persisted Boxer, "it was I who sold the idea to Sam Dice."

Yes, cock, and now you're going to pay for it. "Whoever sold what to whom," I said, now jangling my own change, "the fact remains that I'm fielding one man short. I'm sorry, Douglas, but I'm going to have to put you back on reporting duties."

I had expected a stunned silence and I got it. Boxer raised me in the change-jangling stakes by jangling both pockets simultaneously. I believe he carefully sorted his pound coins into the left hand pocket and his silver into the right.

His best response, when it came, would have been, "But I've never been on reporting duties!" which would have exposed my little plan for the one hundred per cent spite it was. He chose rather to say, or bleat, "But I'm the deputy editor!"

"I'll take care of the deputy editing for the next few weeks," I said kindly. "This is shoulders to the wheel time, Douglas. We've both got to take our coats off and get cracking – or in your case put your coat on and get cracking. There's a coroner's court this afternoon, and then you can pick up the church notes from Basil Brush."

"I'm sorry, Oliver, I know we're short-handed, but I can't go along with this at all."

"All right, then, you edit the fucking paper and I'll go on the road myself."

For a moment, as a wild yet wistful glint flashed through his eyes, I thought he was going to take me up on the offer. Not Boxer. "It's all very well, but what are the staff going to say?"

"They're going to say you should have joined the *East Sussex Advertiser* when you had the chance," I said, rubbing it in. "Either that or they're going to say good old Douglas, mucking in with the rest of us."

"I could go to the proprietor, you know."

"Over my head? Sam wouldn't like that, cock. Coroner's court, two o'clock."

And with a feeling of mission well accomplished I trampled through the greenery and ambled back to my own part of the jungle.

I had left Nick Crabbe's update memo on my desk. To get it off my back I scribbled, "It's your show – go ahead" across it. That would create the impression of giving him *carte blanche* while at the same time not committing myself to anything. I was about to toss it into my out tray when, scanning through it to check that I had not given him the go-ahead on anything I might not wish him to go ahead with, I came across a paragraph calculated to take the edge off the glow of pleasure I was experiencing at having cut Douglas Boxer down to size:

"Steve Selby, the alternative wheelchair comedian, is playing Crawley this week. I don't suppose you would want to make another expedition to catch his act but he would be happy to make a side trip to Badgers Heath if you could spare an hour to meet up, as we never managed it last time round. Steve is very keen on including Bananaskin Week in his busy schedule and would be the perfect warm-up man for the Youth Prayer Rally. He has very kindly offered to throw in his services for free, which would be a big saving for us, but while I am happy to make all the arrangements for his stay here, there are one or two things he would like to discuss with you personally."

Such as a guaranteed two-page spread in the *Badgers Heath Herald* plus page one grinning portrait by our new photographer. I brightened. I could put Douglas Boxer on the story.

Not unexpectedly, considering that Bananaskin Week now loomed, that evening's meeting of the Bonfire Society committee went well into extra time. What truly was unexpected was that when I drove Rosie home she neglected, for the first time ever, to invite me in, pleading exhaustion and a violent headache. So it was that when I arrived home at nearly one in the morning, to find Sherry's weekend bag in the hall and Sherry herself curled up on the living room sofa with a brandy and soda, it was with a sense of great injustice that I realised that all the circumstantial evidence was against me when just for once I had spent a blemishless evening.

Babbling imprecations against Len Quartermouth MBE FIAV
for allowing the meeting to drag on interminably, and scattering
the room with Bonfire Society minutes and documents as proof
that I really had attended it, I poured myself a stiff brandy. It was
ironic that I did not sound convincing even to myself.

"There's no need to look so guilty, Kettle," said Sherry,
savouring my discomfiture with a private-joke smile. "I rang
Rosie Greenleaf's number when I got home an hour ago and a
man's voice said she wasn't there."

What man's voice?

"Why didn't you say you were coming?"

"I didn't even know I was coming until my Heathrow flight
was cancelled because of engine trouble and I managed to grab
the last seat on the last flight out to Gatwick. I rang you from
Charles de Gaulle airport but of course you were at your
meeting."

"How was Paris, by the way?"

"Bloody."

There she seemed prepared to leave the matter. I felt an obligation to plough on.

"Well, it's very nice to see my wife on a weekday evening, but
why did you try to call Rosie Greenleaf?" And what man's voice?

"I thought if you hadn't been able to find the time to row
yourself out of whatever you've rowed yourself into, I could have
given you a bit of a push."

That was straightforward enough, anyway. But what man's
voice?

Speculation on that score, which in any case couldn't get me
very far since my chief suspect Nick Crabbe would still have been
sitting in the Tudor Room of the Dolphin Arms when a man's
voice answered Rosie's telephone, was extinguished by the
stomach-churning scenario of likely consequences had the meeting run to its usual length and my arrangements with Rosie to
their usual excess, and Sherry's enquiries had found me in one of
the several positions so ably captured by Dennis Reason.

"A push in which direction?"

"Don't worry, I shouldn't have made a scene."

"Then what would you have said?"

"Oh, just something on the lines of, 'Tell my fucking husband he's wanted at home.' Why weren't you both there anyway?"

I sometimes forgot to keep it in mind that my wife was a highly-skilled interviewer. "I've told you, because the meeting droned on until after midnight," I said before I could stop myself. At once realising my blunder, I floundered on, "That's to say, that's why Rosie wasn't there. Why I wasn't there was because had the meeting finished earlier I should have been here."

"Balls. You're round at Mill Farm every Monday, Wednesday and Thursday."

"Who's been telling you that?"

"Oh, Kettle, don't be more witless than you can help. How many times a week do I call you?"

"Once or twice, I guess."

"Usually, yes. Of late I've been calling you four nights a week – and on three out of the four you've always been out."

It did not seem wise to persist with, "Yes, but who tipped you off in the first place?", the answer to which, if she cared to volunteer it, could only be Nick Crabbe. Instead I said feebly, "Why have you been ringing me so often, anyway? You never used to."

"I never used to because I thought I could trust you."

"So you've been ringing to check up on my movements?"

"Of course I have! What's wrong with that? It's standard practice in marriage, isn't it?"

"It's never been standard practice in ours. Supposing I'd taken to ringing *you* several times a week and found you not there?"

Sherry helped herself, but not me, from the brandy decanter. "Are you pissed, Kettle? If you ring me at the Barbican it doesn't prove anything one way or the other, whether I'm in or out. If I'm out I could be in bed with somebody and if I'm in I could be in bed with somebody. Whereas if you're not at home after the pubs close, there are very few places in Badgers Heath where you could be."

Accusing me of being pissed when she could barely stand to pour herself another drink seemed a little unfair; but she could have been right – I had sunk a few gin and tonics before the Bonfire Society meeting, and I had had nothing to eat – for my response was on the self-pitying side:

"So you're allowed to check up on me while I can't check up on you? Hardly an equitable arrangement."

"Don't be so bloody childish. I'm off to bed."

As so often in my exchanges with Sherry, what promised to be a head-on clash had somehow got diverted into the sidings. There had still been a fair amount of noise but they had been shunting noises; we were both avoiding out-and-out confrontation. Or at least I was, for the sake of a quiet life. Sherry, at a guess, would have preferred to let things drift on, being very much a status quo sort of person – but she didn't want Rosie Greenleaf to be the status quo.

Did I, though? While the mystery of the lights had been spinning itself out I had felt I owed some measure of allegiance to Rosie in case we found ourselves in the same blackmailing boat. Now that it had been ostensibly cleared up, did I owe her anything? She had said herself that she didn't want a heavy relationship – "it's just appetite style of thing" – and while she seemed fond of me, I had no doubt at all that she could quickly become fond of someone else. If she hadn't already done so, that was. I asked myself again, which man's voice?

Perhaps, as my wife kept trying to tell me, my fling with Rosie Greenleaf had gone as far as it ought to go. Perhaps I should sleep on it. Indeed, considering that Sherry was dead to the world when I followed her to bed a few minutes later, I didn't have much option.

I had never been in Nick Crabbe's flat before. Perched up in the rafters of the prestigious converted tea warehouse off the High Street, it was very much the stylish bachelor pad, with a range of Scandinavian-looking furniture, designer rugs and good modern prints way beyond his present salary bracket even after it had been topped up by a grateful proprietor.

Nick and his crony Steve Selby were drinking Mexican beer out of the bottle as Nick let me in. Out of breath after climbing four flights of steps, I remarked to the alternative wheelchair comedian as we shook hands, "We could have met somewhere with a wheelchair ramp."

"He came up in the goods lift," explained Nick.

"I wasn't thinking of him, I was thinking of me."

Steve Selby gave a joshing, teeth-baring laugh. "Hey, who's the comic around here?" The rug over his knees created a wheelchair effect even though he was sitting in an armchair. The wheelchair itself was parked in the hall. I imagined he could stagger a few steps.

Nick poured me a reasonably stiff gin and tonic while prattling on boastfully about how Bananaskin Week was capturing the hearts and minds of Badgers Heath's trendsetters – pledges still pouring in and companies falling over themselves to back their employees' sponsored tomfoolery and get their names in the paper. The phones had not stopped ringing.

"Better not tell Steve how much we're raking in or he may change his mind about waiving his fee," I joked. My second quip of the evening – maybe I felt a compulsion towards drollery in the presence of one who styled himself a comedian.

"Steve has some thoughts on that, boss," said Nick, his non-jocular response signalling that he was anxious to get down to the nitty-gritty. He opened another bottle of Mexican beer and sprawled in an executive-type tube chair. His air was irritatingly proprietorial – not only of the flat and the furniture but of the occasion.

"OK, I don't know how much Nick has told you about my angle on this," began Steve Selby.

"Not a lot," I said cautiously, looking to Nick for guidance. For all I knew he had spelled out the alternative wheelchair comedian's position in a ten-page confidential memo which I had never got round to reading.

"OK, now when we talk of waiving my fee, Oliver – may I call you Oliver?"

"Please do." I felt like adding, as a condition, that in return he might refrain from beginning every speech with "OK".

"When we talk of waiving my fee, that assumes I would have been charging a fee to begin with. I want you to know this, Oliver. Everything I earn on these gigs, less expenses and my personal running costs, goes to the Children of the Brazilian Rain Forest."

"Yes, so I've heard." I wondered how liberally he interpreted expenses and personal running costs. My snap conclusion was that they would be pretty generous, but it was none of my business.

"The least I can do, right? Those kids are our future and our tomorrow. Unless we do something today about tomorrow, it isn't going to happen, OK?"

Clearly he had parroted this gibberish many times before and had plenty more pokerwork motto phrases where they came from. I began to think after all he would be a good choice for the Youth Prayer Rally. If he kept off the four-letter words he would get on well with Sam.

To my relief Nick stemmed what threatened to be an endless flow of ecological platitudes. "Steve's hoping that if he becomes involved we could give a helping hand to the Children of the Brazilian Rain Forest."

"I don't see why not." The Bonfire Society supported every kind of charity, usually dividing the proceeds of the annual celebration between half a dozen or so more or less worthy causes chosen from a mass of supplicants by the committee. Presumably Bananaskin Week would follow the same procedure, though with more largesse at its disposal. I saw no reason why the Children of the Brazilian Rain Forest should not get their bite, if their credentials were good.

Stupidly I said, "Tell me a little more about this charity," and Steve Selby moistened his lips with Mexican beer to begin his spiel.

"OK, how much do you know about the Yanomami Indians?" he began rhetorically. I replied with a hopeless shrug, following this up with a gesture to Nick Crabbe to refill my glass.

"OK, they're the original friends of the earth, right? For ten thousand years, maybe more, they've been tilling their land right there in the tropical rain forest between the Orinoco and Amazon basins without harm to the environment. Then came the rape of the rain forest, right? Right . . . "

It was a prepared pitch, a lantern lecture without the slides. I had to give it to Steve Selby that he knew his stuff. At least he sounded as if he did, for as not much of a newspaper reader – I only edited one – I was in no position either to challenge or confirm his assertion that the children of the rain forest, not to mention their parents, were in a bad way.

"Why have we not seen any of this on television?" I did think to ask.

"You will, Oliver, you will. There are satellite news teams out there as we speak and any day now a hidden famine on the scale of genocide is about to explode into our living rooms." On the facts he had spilled out this seemed to be pushing it a bit but I recognised that he had a competing charity to sell. "And all for what, Oliver? To exchange good pure rain for acid rain, to pollute the skies with greenhouse gases, to hasten the destruction of Planet Earth."

"Sounds a good cause," I conceded when at last I managed to get a word in.

"It isn't a cause, it's a crusade." It was certainly his crusade. There was a fanatical gleam in his dark eyes and his black beard was flecked with spittle.

"All right," I said. "Get me a few facts and figures, annual report, where the money goes, how much goes to the kids and how much on administration – that's very important."

"Right! On that point, Oliver, would you believe ninety pee in every pound goes directly to the Yanomami rehabilitation encampments? That's higher than almost any other charity you could name."

"Impressive. So if you'll let me have the usual bumph – "

"I have it right here in my briefcase. Maybe you'd like to – "

"Give it to Nick," I said hastily. "Then I'll put it up to the committee, and if they endorse it, your Children of the Rain Forest should get a fair slice of the Bananaskin Week proceeds."

Nick and Steve exchanged what I categorised as a significant glance, although it could equally have been described as a conspiratorial one. They had clearly rehearsed what was to follow.

"Ah," said Nick.

"We want them to have the whole cake," said Steve.

"Impossible."

"It's not impossible, boss," cried Nick, leaping to his feet and going into the same routine of evangelical gestures which had helped him screw a thousand-a-year raise out of Sam Dice. "The Bonfire Night proceeds have gone to a single source on at least two occasions, to my knowledge."

It was true. A few years ago we had given the entire takings to an earthquake fund which had seized the popular imagination, and on another occasion we had given our all to a famine appeal fronted by an international rock star. We had hoped the international rock star would come to Badgers Heath to accept the cheque, but this had not happened.

"But Bananaskin Week will be on a much bigger scale," I pointed out. "It wouldn't be fair to put all our eggs in one basket."

Nick seized eagerly on the metaphor. "But just look at how many eggs there are, boss. What makes the Children of the Rain Forest so exciting is that it's the charity that's got everything. It's got starving kids, it's got the destruction of a simple peasant culture, it's got threatened wildlife, it's got wasted resources, it's got global warming . . . What's that slogan again, Steve?"

"Save a child and save the world."

"That's the beauty of it, boss. In doing something for those people all those thousands of miles away we'll be doing something for humanity on our own doorstep."

"Right," concurred Steve Selby. "We've all heard the saying charity begins at home. Here's a charity that ends at home." Another user-friendly old saw.

They were beginning to come on like a couple of street market hucksters. "Let me think about it," I said to shut them up, but Nick was in full flow.

"Please do think about it, boss. It's just what we need to get Bananaskin Week off with a bang. No piddling about with a couple of grand for this organisation, a couple of grand for that. One big charity, one big cheque. We could get the Yanomamis' tribal leader over to receive it, in native dress. Fantastic pictures. And guess who we could get to present the cheque. Big name. Someone who's very keen on green issues."

"Prince Charles, right?" said Steve Selby. "Why not? He can only say no."

They were beginning to convince me. As to why they were

working so hard to convince me, I was in no doubt. Steve Selby was on the take. It was not unusual. The Bonfire Society had long experience of dealing with charity administrators, and more than one of them had been suspected of dipping into the till, usually by way of inflated expense accounts and luxury perks. So long as it wasn't too blatant and they weren't seen riding about in Rolls-Royces shortly after receiving our contribution, we preferred to turn a blind eye. A scandal wouldn't have been good for the Bonfire Society and it wouldn't have been good for the charity.

So I would assume that Steve's claim that ninety pence in the pound found its way to Brazil was something of an over-estimate, and that his expenses for Bananaskin Week would not bear too close a scrutiny. What Nick Crabbe was getting out of it I wasn't too sure. He had had considerable experience of expenses sheet fiddling himself and maybe Steve Selby was cutting him in on the deal. Or maybe he was just after a bit of self-advancement. If Bananaskin Week was a hit and we did manage to get a royal personage to come down and hand over the cheque to a Yanomami Indian chief, there would be no stopping Nick. Certainly the *Badgers Heath Herald* couldn't hold him and that, from the viewpoint of an editor always uneasy as to who might be following him up the ladder, could only be counted a blessing.

"So what do you reckon, boss?"

"It's not a decision for me alone, cock. You've got to persuade the rest of the committee."

"I'm working on it."

He was, too.

"Ooh, just there, no, a bit lower down. Ooh, I'm ever so sorry about Monday, precious, only I really was whacked. Unusual for me I know, we must have been overdoing it, I didn't think it was possible, ooh, don't stop."

"As it happens it's a good thing I didn't come in on Monday, Rosie. Sherry came home unexpectedly."

"Oh, well you won't have gone short, then," said Rosie with casual vulgarity.

"She rang the farmhouse, apparently. While we were still at the committee meeting."

"Did she? Ooh, that's lovely, ooh, it tickles. Whatever for?"

"To see if I was here."

"It's a good thing you weren't, then."

"Somebody was, though. She said a man answered."

"That would have been Harry, my pigman. He's been doing some odd jobs for me."

"What odd jobs?"

"Ooh, are you getting jealous, poppet, you are, aren't you, you're getting jealous? I'll tell you what, Ollie, there's a very special odd job wants doing and I've been keeping it specially for you."

11

Bananaskin Week celebrations will include a mile-long conga –
"The Longa Conga" – through Badgers Heath shopping streets
by members of the Heath Hall Youth Centre.

Badgers Green Clarion cycling club hope to raise £5,000 for
Bananaskin Week by pedalling 5,000 miles – one mile per pound
– non-stop. But the cyclists will be going nowhere – their fixed-
wheel bikes will be mounted on stands in the windows of
Bancroft's department store.

The Mermaid fish and chip saloon, Old Town, will donate all
its takings during Bananaskin Week to Bonfire Society charities.

Police have stepped in to ban service station attendant Darren
Filby (23) from lying in a glass coffin with five boa constrictors in
aid of Bananaskin Week. They say the stunt could cause traffic
pile-ups. Instead, Darren will tour the county in a hearse in a bid
to get his glass coffin filled with money.

Credit International staff restaurant helper Wanda Philips (19)
hopes to raise money for Bananaskin Week from workmates by
having two bananas tattooed on her bottom . . .

The stories were flowing from Douglas Boxer's VDU as fast as
he could key them in. For the second time in his long career, he
surprised me. When I had told him I was putting him back on
reporting duties I had known full well that he had no reporting
experience at all, but had gone straight from a polytechnic
journalism course into sub-editing the gardening notes, and had
risen without trace to occupy his present cardigan-cocooned
sinecure. But a decade of snipping items out of other newspapers
for the *Herald* to follow up had given him a sharp eye for news.
De-ossified, he was proving to be quite a good reporter.

He was not only to surprise me still further, he was to astonish me.

It was Friday, always a slack day, except of late for Nick Crabbe whose flat was now an engine of activity, with half the voluntary workers of Badgers Heath scurrying backwards and forwards at his bidding. Pledges for Bananaskin Week had already more than doubled, and a pledge coupon we had printed in that day's *Herald* – a cunning idea of Nick's – would bring more promises of cash flooding in as well as increasing sales. Rosie's Appeal Fund was not very far off target and so the Bonfire Society would have no difficulty in paying its bills for the Week's extravagances and indulgences. The only question was whether Badgers Heath, after this extended spasm of generosity, could afford to pay its mortgages and school fees. That was not my problem. I was well pleased, and I proposed to treat myself to an extended lunch at the Euro-inn Dolphin Arms Buttery.

To reach the stairs down to the car park I had to pass the office space of my temporarily erstwhile deputy. I came across him lurking behind his Swiss cheese plants. While I had had to demote him to reporter for the time being, I had not had the heart to turf him out into the newsroom with the other hacks. I was glad now that I hadn't, for he was doing a not-half-bad job, and if I could not manage to avoid catching his eye as I passed, I might even tell him so.

"Could I have a word, Oliver?"

"So long as you make it snappy, cock – I'm on my way to lunch." Now that it came to it, I could not bring myself to praise Boxer to his face. It would be too much of a break with precedent.

"I think I'm on to a very good story."

"Good, but won't it keep? We don't go to press again for nearly a week."

"It's something I need to consult you about."

"All right, consult away."

"Preferably not in the office."

An excess of geniality combining with a slight feeling of remorse at having begrudged Boxer his crumb of praise, I heard myself saying, "What are you doing for lunch?" I regretted it even as I registered his reaction of utter incredulity, but at least an ostentatiously private tête-à-tête at a corner table would keep the usual wasps' nest of councillors, shopkeepers and businessmen at bay while I wrestled with my overcooked chicken. We took Boxer's car. Now I wouldn't have to count my drinks.

As self-conscious but gratified as any junior reporter invited to break bread with his editor, Boxer ordered drinks from one end of the bar and food from the other – the system perfected by the Dolphin Arms Buttery for serving the maximum number of lunches with the minimum inconvenience to its staff – and followed me to our table bearing his small low-alcohol lager and my large gin. While we listened for the number to come up, tombola style, that would entitle Boxer to return to the bar and take on the duties of a waiter, I tried to prod him into office smalltalk. It was not his forte; and besides, he was far too keyed up, either about the very good story he was on to or with the rare excitement of the occasion. It must have been the first time Boxer had taken lunch with his editor since joining the paper, certainly since I had joined it.

To put him at his ease and pass the time in a marginally more profitable way than flaking the crust off a stale bread roll, I paid him the small compliment I had suppressed earlier.

"That's not a bad crop of yarns you've got into this week's paper, Douglas."

"Thank you, Oliver, but I believe I'm sitting on a better one."

"So you say. Want to tell me about it, keeping your voice down?"

Boxer looked around the crowded Buttery with overdone casualness. Satisfying himself that he knew no one in the room, although failing to recognise that I knew practically everybody in the room, he said, "How well do you know Mrs Greenleaf?"

"What's that to you, cock?" I asked sharply though not too curtly. He probably had an angle on her Appeal Fund, and she had probably mentioned my name to persuade him to build up the story.

"She's running a – "

"*Seventy-four!*" A screech from one of the waitresses, as the Dolphin Arms chose to call them, drowned the last word, although I had a pretty good idea that I had caught it.

"She's running a what?"

"A brothel. There's our food."

While Boxer, glowing with self-importance at having such a bombshell to deliver, got to his feet and set about his serving duties, I reviewed my reaction. Mindboggling though the news was, the mind boggled less at the revelation than at the source of it. The possibility that the Farmers' Ladies Circle was not all it should be had already crossed my mind. From the odd hint dropped by Rosie I had gathered that some of the Farmers' Ladies were not above entertaining what used to be called gentlemen callers. On how professional and organised a level these diversions were indulged in I had not cared to enquire. Presumably Douglas Boxer was about to enlighten me. But intriguing though the story was, I would be almost as intrigued to know, considering the sheltered life he had been leading, how he had got hold of it.

Boxer returned to our table with our underfed chicken in a basket and the bottle of house white I had instructed him to get to wash it down with. I would allow him to put the bill on his expenses: to entertaining contact for exclusive story.

Gnawing at a stringy chicken leg I said, "No one can possibly come here for the food so they must come for the conversation. You do realise, Douglas, that we are sitting in the clearing house for all the gossip in Badgers Heath?"

"I'm sure we can't be overheard."

"Even if we can't, why didn't you want to tell me what you've just told me in the office?"

"Walls have ears."

"We don't *have* any fucking walls."

He was right about our not being overheard, though. My riposte did not raise a blink from either of the two nuns sharing a frugal cheese sandwich at the next table.

I gave Boxer time to cram his mouth full of game chips, or potato crisps as they were described in the other bar, before continuing, "All right, cock, let's have it. Where did you get this yarn?"

"Tip-off," croaked Boxer, spluttering crumbs.

"Who from?"

Boxer looked as if he would have liked to say all guardedly, "A source," like a proper reporter. He caught the scornful look on my face and said, "An ex-colleague of yours from the Bonfire Society, as a matter of fact. Miss Bellows. She said she owes us a favour."

"She does."

"I called in at her cottage to check a rumour that she was going to have to have her cats put down because of a lack of funds. You know she runs the cat sanctuary?"

"Famous for it."

"Happily a handsome anonymous donation gave them a last-minute reprieve. It makes a nice little story."

It would make a better one, I thought, if Miss Bellows' benefactor turned out to be her sister in Brighton celebrating a lucky streak on the roulette wheel.

"Very touching, cock. Get to the knocking shop angle."

"Well." Boxer licked his lips, probably more to rid them of chicken grease than in anticipation of the salacious tale he had to tell. "Miss Bellows lives in Voles Bottom, just down the lane from Mill Farm. She tells me she often cycles past the farm. And as you may imagine, she doesn't miss much."

"No, I don't suppose she does." I reflected that what with Dennis Reason and his camera and Miss Bellows on her bike, not to mention the leering presence of Harry the pigman, my dalliance with Rosie could not have been more exposed had we chosen – as Rosie had more than once suggested – to disport ourselves on the front lawn.

"There have apparently been a good many comings and goings in recent weeks, according to Miss Bellows."

"Comings and goings of which sex?"

"Both men and women."

"Names?"

"She refused to name names. But she said several of them were well known around Badgers Heath."

I threw down a gristly chicken bone in disgust, both at it and at my intrepid reporter. "Well known around Badgers Heath? *I'm* well bloody known around Badgers Heath and *I* visit Mill Farm on occasion. So what?" The question was a bold one but I was in no trepidation as to the answer. If Boxer had anything on his editor he would have taken the story not to me but to Sam Dice.

"Quite, and obviously there could be good reason for any number of visits by any number of people. So I thought I'd better check my facts."

"I should bloody think so, cock. This has the makings of the biggest libel action in local history." In the very unlikely event, I added under my breath, of a word of it ever reaching the columns of the *Badgers Heath Herald*. I was already rehearsing my little speech reminding Boxer, truthfully enough, that we were a family newspaper and that any attempt to emulate the racier Sunday tabloids would have our proprietor on us like the Avenging Angel. But first I wanted to hear what he had found out about the alleged goings-on at Mill Farm. "So how did you go about checking these so-called facts?"

"Miss Bellows said that much of the activity at the farmhouse took place on Sunday afternoons. So last Sunday I kept watch."

"Where from?" I was always interested in possible vantage points for observers of life at Mill Farm.

"There's a walled field opposite the farm. It affords a very good view up the drive to the house." I wished I had been in a frame of mind to notice details of that sort when I first began to visit Rosie. It would have afforded a very good view of Dennis Reason getting out of his car and saved us all a lot of trouble.

"Go on."

"Between three and half past, five ladies arrived, three by car, one by bicycle and one on foot. They were all in their thirties, I should judge, and provocatively dressed."

"You're not giving evidence, cock – not just yet, anyway. What do you mean, provocatively dressed?"

"They looked like tarts."

"Did you recognise any of them?"

"No, although the faces of two or three of them were vaguely familiar. I suppose I must have seen them out shopping."

"For black silk knickers, no doubt. What about the men?"

"There were six of them, all middle-aged. They arrived in separate cars at about ten-minute intervals from half past

161

three onwards."

"Who let them in?"

"The same lady who let the women in earlier. I think it was Mrs Greenleaf but I couldn't be sure. I've never actually met her and she was rather far off."

"What was she wearing?"

"I can only describe it as a French maid's outfit."

Having consumed their communal cheese sandwich, the two nuns at the next table were gathering up more possessions than I was aware that Little Sisters of the Poor were allowed to own, and were about to pass close by us on their way out. I decided to give Boxer a rest from his narrative by despatching him to the bar for another bottle of the house plonk.

I digested what he had told me so far. The evidence was circumstantial but it was damning – for anyone wishing to damn Rosie Greenleaf, that was, as I did not. As Boxer returned and recharged our glasses I said, "All right, cock, from what I've gleaned up to now they could have been an amateur dramatic society meeting to rehearse their production of *No Sex Please, We're British*. What happened next?"

"Well, nothing. It came on to rain very heavily so I went home."

"And that was that?"

"Not quite. When I got back I looked up Mrs Greenleaf in the telephone directory and rang her up. A man's voice answered."

A man's voice. "And?"

"I asked to speak to Mrs Greenleaf but he said, 'Oh, I'm afraid she's tied up at the moment.' Now I don't know quite how to put this, Oliver, but innocent though such a remark can sound he said it in what I would call a suggestive sort of voice, as if he wanted to imply a *double entendre* without actually spelling it out, if you see what I mean."

I did. Tied up at the moment. Bondage games had never featured in Rosie's sexual stock in trade but I supposed there was a first time for everything. "We seem to be in orgy country here, cock. So what did you say to that?"

"I said, 'I hear there's a party going on today.'"

Enterprising. "You'll make it to the *News of the World* yet,

162

cock. And did he bite?"

"I'm afraid not. He mumbled something about calling back later and hung up."

Raising his glass in an absurd silent toast, Boxer seemed to be indicating that he had reached the conclusion of his investigations. At any rate he did not continue.

I said, "And this was last Sunday?"

"That's right."

"And today's Friday."

Recognising the implied reproof he said apologetically, "I know. To tell the truth, I've been trying all week to pluck up the courage to march up the drive of Mill Farm and knock on the door, but I couldn't bring myself to do it. Last night I even got as far as the farmhouse gate but I couldn't think what on earth I'd say when she answered the door."

I cast my mind back to what Rosie and I had been doing last night. She had been in experimental mood and had wanted to make love on the stairs. Had Douglas Boxer knocked on the door and Rosie had answered, he would have found her wearing rather less than the French maid's outfit he had briefly caught sight of on Sunday, and he would have been afforded a glimpse of his editor sitting on the stairs wearing only his socks.

"You could have made an excuse and left," I said.

"I wish he *had* knocked, so long as he had his cheque book with him," said Rosie with her earthy chuckle. "We only needed another hundred pounds to reach the target."

"You're incorrigible, Rosie."

"If that means what I think it means, you won't be surprised if I get dressed."

"Perhaps you don't know what it means after all. Why do you want to get dressed when I've only just got here?"

"I just fancy doing it fully-clothed for once."

"You're incorrigible all right, Rosie."

This was the following day, Saturday, Sherry having once more given the weekend a miss and flown off to New York. She seemed to be establishing a new pattern and I wasn't sure I liked it. We already had a pattern and it had been working very well until she had taken it into her head to resent my liaison with Rosie. Perhaps now was the time to call it a day with Rosie. The fact of her running the best little whorehouse in Badgers Heath would furnish me with the perfect excuse – not on moral grounds, but on the grounds that as editor of a newspaper owned by a God-fearing puritan I could no longer afford to consort with a lusty widow who at any moment was liable to be driven away in a police car and charged with keeping a disorderly farmhouse.

She was dressing as sensually as I had ever seen her undressing. A sexoholic again, I decided that perhaps now was not the best time after all.

Besides, I needed a long talk with Rosie. I had got Douglas Boxer's side of the story and now I wanted hers. Not entirely out of vulgar curiosity: if she ever did land up in court there was no way I could keep the case out of the papers and it would be as well to have the background and a bit of local colour. Meanwhile Rosie's secret, if it could be called a secret with men streaming in and out of the house at all hours, was safe. It had taken little to convince Boxer that he was treading on extremely dangerous ground and that if the merest whiff of the story appeared anywhere in print he would find himself in the deepest of hot water with the libel lawyers. By way of rewarding his initiative and compensating for his frustration I then promised to relieve him of further reporting duties – I could always put my showbusiness editor in to bat and fill the showbiz pages with old publicity handouts, so that no one would notice the difference – and reinstate him as my deputy, safely behind a desk again. When next I visited Mill Farm I didn't want to find Douglas Boxer lurking behind the wall across the lane.

"Let me get this straight, Rosie," I began when next there was an interval in the afternoon's proceedings. "You're saying that you and the Farmers' Ladies Circle turned Mill Farm into a bordello to raise money for the Bonfire Society Appeal Fund?"

"I told you they'd make good fund-raisers, didn't I? Ooh, that was good, it's a funny sensation doing it with your things on, it makes you feel as if you're out of doors."

"But how did your clientele come to hear about you?"

"Word of mouth, pet. Although I say it as shouldn't we come

very highly recommended. And of course, between you, me and the bedpost," Rosie giggled, "one or two of our ladies were already providing a discreet service to select callers in a private capacity style of thing, so that gave us a start."

"And how many do you have on your books, out of interest?"

"Enough – all of them very respectable, we've never had to turn anyone away."

"I'm amazed you haven't had the police round, Rosie."

"Oh, we have. A chief superintendent – he's been coming every week."

"Friends in high places, eh? You have the devil's own luck."

"It's not luck, pet, it's sheer hard work when there's four or five of them here at once and they want us to put on a bit of a show style of thing. Still, it's all been worth while – you do realise we've reached that £10,000 target a fortnight ahead of schedule, don't you?"

"I'm sure we're all very proud of you, Rosie. And what do you intend to do now?"

"Take my clothes off again."

"I mean you and the Farmers' Ladies. Are you going to divert your efforts to some other good cause?"

"Ooh, I don't think so, precious. Enough's enough, it's been fun while it lasted and it made a nice change, but you can have too much of a good thing. Besides, we want to take up dress-making."

It was a great relief to hear that the Farmers' Ladies Circle was reverting to more orthodox activities, but there were one or two questions arising. One of them was of a delicate nature.

"Rosie, I hope you don't mind my asking this, because it's none of my business, really – but as you seem to have been running the show, I was wondering if you – er – how should I put this?"

"Took part? Ooh, no, pet, no way, unless you call joining in the occasional game taking part." I didn't care to ask what these occasional games might be. Clearly not dominoes. "No, I was the madam style of thing, wasn't I? More your supervisor. I tell a lie – there was one client who asked for me specially but that was only a couple of times and it was on a visiting basis. Why, you don't mind, do you, Ollie?"

"Not at all." Nor did I. The more Rosie had distributed her favours the easier it would be for both of us when the time came to part company. "There's something else, Rosie. Last Monday night when you wouldn't let me come in – "

"Last Monday, last Monday, let me think." Last Monday was a long time ago in Rosie's sex diary. "Oh, yes, I remember. I'm ever so sorry about that, pet, but Janey, Suzie and Beverley had one of the clients in for a bit of slave treatment. Usually he comes on a Saturday evening but he had a previous engagement."

"So when Sherry rang and a man's voice answered, that was this client speaking, was it?"

"It must have been – because he likes to dress up as a maid and go round the house with a feather duster, so naturally he'd see answering the phone as part of his job, while he's here. I'm surprised your good lady didn't recognise his voice, but of course, you're neither of you big churchgoers, are you?"

Churchgoers. The Parish Church of St Michael and All Angels. I couldn't believe it. "Rosie, you can't mean – ?"

"Well we're not talking about the curate, are we, because as far as I know he's gay, so you can come to your own conclusions. Mind you, all this is confidential."

"I wasn't going to put it in the paper, Rosie." If only I could. Vicar Wore Frilly Apron. The Rev Basil Thrush (48) was dressed as a housemaid and wielding a feather duster when a *Herald* reporter called at Mill Farm, Voles Lane, on Monday . . . "I never thought he was that way inclined," I said after taking almost a full minute to take in Rosie's interesting little news item.

"You'd be surprised at some people's inclinations," she said, rolling her eyes. "I'm sure it's been good for him, coming here. Gets it out of his system style of thing."

"Not that I'd breathe a word, but I'd love to hear what Len Quartermouth had to say if he knew."

"Not much he could say, is there, seeing as he's been coming round every Friday lunchtime himself ever since we opened for business?"

"Quartermouth? With his MBE and his FIAV? But for God's sake, Rosie, his daughter's one of your – "

166

"Not while he's here. She does a visit to a bed-ridden retired admiral in West Merdley on Fridays."

"And does she know her father's a client?"

"She knows he comes here, but she doesn't know what he comes here for. He's a Miss Whiplash freak, is our Len. It's the same arrangement with Betty and Percy Spruce. Betty's never here when Percy comes over but unbeknownst to him she's well aware that he's one of our regulars, even though she doesn't know what his little speciality is."

It was odd how quickly I had adjusted to the revelation that I appeared to be living in the south-east's answer to the Reeper-bahn. Occasionally I read exposés of wife-swapping parties and suchlike in sleepy market towns and picture postcard villages, and so I was well aware that there was a vigorous hidden sex life in our national make-up. But what with Dennis Reason and now the Farmers' Ladies, it was beginning to appear that Badgers Heath would romp to the top of any regional league table of sexual deviation that might be drawn up.

"And what *is* his little speciality?" I asked, frankly prurient.

"Percy's into bondage, more's the pity. I wouldn't mind, but he likes to tie me up as well and the ropes burn your wrists something rotten."

This would be one of the occasional games Rosie had mentioned. "Anyone else we know?"

"Plenty, provided it doesn't go beyond these four walls. There's poor old Eric Barlow for one, I don't know why he bothers to come because he's long past it, poor thing. And then let me see, who else have we got . . . "

Rosie proceeded to list some of our little community's leading citizens and their sexual predilections. I was riveted to begin with but as she worked her way down to smaller fry my interest waned and I found my mind wandering back to the names she had first mentioned. Not counting the absent Dennis Reason – had he, I asked myself, captured any of these group antics on film? – the entire Bonfire Society Standing Committee seemed to be involved in Rosie's farmhouse bordello, either as partakers of its services or, in the case of Rosie herself and the dark horse Mrs Spruce, providers of it. Except one.

"What about Nick Crabbe?" I asked, remembering a certain evening when his blue Ford Escort XR3i had been parked in the driveway. "Has he been coming round at all?"

"Only the once, and he got a free sample style of thing. Sorry and all that, pet, but it was the least I could do, considering it was all his idea."

12

One of the afflictions of Sam Dice upon his senior executives was a yearly get-together at one of the less agreeable south coast hotels. He called it his annual conference and I always had the feeling that he would have liked us all to wear lapel badges. It was something between a pep talk and a pray-in, with Sam thanking the Lord for rising sales figures, and blaming his editors and circulation managers for falling ones. The day's exhortations began with a working lunch and finished with an early working dinner, after which Sam repaired to his suite to continue his devotions in private and to receive such VIPs from the other side as wished to consult with him, while his staff were left to their own devices. These usually consisted of sinking a great many large ones in the hotel bar.

This year the venue was Worthing, the hotel had even fewer stars than usual, and for once I did not join my colleagues in the evening stampede. The bar, a vast echoing drinking barracks designed to cater for about five hundred thirsty holidaymakers, was not to my taste, and besides, there was a certain coolness between myself and my fellow-editors. Sam had insisted upon them all giving maximum coverage to Badgers Heath's Banana-skin Week with particular reference to the Youth Prayer Rally, and they understandably blamed me for this unwarranted intrusion upon their editorial territory.

I strolled out of the hotel in search of a near-to-decent pub and presently found myself in a short street that seemed to be lined with licensed premises. Hesitating between the Blue Lion, the Feathers, the Swan With Two Necks and the Chequers, I became retrospectively aware that out of a corner of my eye I had just seen a familiar figure entering the Trafalgar Inn at the bottom of the street. Probably one of my colleagues, escaping like me from the horrors of the hotel bar. On a one-to-one basis I was prepared to put up with a spot of joshing or even a barb or two at the expense of Bananaskin Week, for the sake of a bit of company. I followed him into the pub, spotted him at the bar where he was ordering a drink, and recognised first by his black raincoat and then by his left profile that I had found Dennis Reason, our absconding bank manager and amateur photographer.

I came up and stood directly behind him, so that if he chose to make a run for it again, he would find me barring his way.

"Well met, Dennis. Your round, I believe."

He had already identified me in the bar mirror and did not turn round. His face twitched.

"You're the last person I expected to see in these parts." I expected I was. The attempt at a light touch failed dismally. His voice shook. "What brings you to Worthing?"

"Perhaps I wanted to return your raincoat button."

Reason didn't reply – a marginally better response than "I don't know what you're talking about", which was what I was anticipating. Maybe that would come later. I said, as the barmaid showed signs of interrupting her conversation with one of her regulars to attend to us, "It's been a long day, Dennis, and I need a large gin and tonic. After that I need another large gin and tonic, and then you and I are going to have a long talk – either here or somewhere else, it's up to you."

Considering we were in a street full of pubs there were surprisingly few quiet corners in the Trafalgar Inn. We sat ourselves at a table where, being well within earshot of other drinkers, we could only engage in stilted smalltalk about Badgers Heath and the Bonfire Society. These forced pleasantries left me almost as embarrassed and uncomfortable as Reason himself and I badly needed another drink, but I wasn't going to risk him making a getaway while I went up to the bar.

I said, draining my glass, "Come on, let's move on."

"Is this necessary?" protested Reason as we made for the door. "I've got nothing to say to you, you know." He had the air of a man who had been arrested for some unspeakable offence – as, in a manner of speaking, he had. I steered him towards the sea front. Maybe it would be easier for him to talk out of doors, in the semi-darkness; though why I should want to make it easy for him I didn't know.

We walked in silence until we came to a promenade shelter not seemingly reserved for the exclusive use of winoes.

I thought I had better start the ball rolling. "And here was I thinking you were in Norwich, looking after your sick mum," I said with weighty facetiousness as we sat down.

"Which is what you were intended to think," said Reason in a low, sulky voice. "In fact if it's any of your business I'm staying with a brother in London until I get myself sorted out."

"So what are you doing down here?" Even as I put the question I remembered that his estranged wife was said to live in Worthing.

His tone continued to be resentful, as if I were intruding upon his privacy. It turned out I was. "If you must know, I came to see Margot. My wife. To ask her to take me back — beg her, if I had to. She showed me the door. Understandably — she thinks I'm filth."

His voice quavered again and though I was looking fixedly ahead I had an impression of heaving shoulders. This really was way beyond the brief I had given myself but I did have to ask, "Because of the pictures?"

Again I remembered that I already knew the answer, or so I thought: Mrs Reason had gone home to her mother long before Rosie and I had commenced our photogenic activities. So I was surprised when he said, "Yes."

An old reporter's trick is to refrain from asking the obvious supplementary question, upon which the subject of the interview will break the awkward silence by volunteering a more satisfactory answer than one would have otherwise got. I waited.

After a few seconds Reason ventured hesitantly, "She found them where I kept them hidden in my little darkroom. They were in an album just like all my other work — I thought they were safe, she never went in there. But she had to go looking for some holiday snaps to show one of her friends, and of course she picked out the wrong album."

"But these can't have been the pictures you snatched of Rosie Greenleaf and me." And thank God for that, I reflected, reviewing some of the photo opportunities in which Rosie and I had engaged.

"No, they were of – I'll just say other people. It's been a hobby of mine for some time." The confession seemed to be having a soothing effect on Reason's vocal chords. At any rate, speaking in a firmer voice now, he made his unusual hobby sound as if it equated with model railways or collecting stamps.

"So that's all it was, was it – a hobby?" I said, going along with this bland gloss on what had so shocked Mrs Reason. I had no wish to delve into the murky psychology of the man's secret compulsion. "You'd absolutely no thought of blackmail?"

"Blackmail? Why do you say that?" The voice sharpened noticeably.

"It's been known, Dennis."

"You're a very long way off the mark, my friend. I'm in no position to blackmail anyone, for the very simple reason that I'm the one who's being blackmailed."

Before I could digest this intriguing piece of information, Reason added uncertainly, "Or I should say I think I am." Upon which a particular name flashed instantly into my mind – a name which had developed a habit of cropping up these days wherever there was to be found a mystery wrapped in ambiguity.

"Who by?" I asked.

"That young man I warned you against. Nicholas Crabbe."

"It's chilly sitting here," I said. "Let's walk."

By now Dennis Reason wanted nothing more than to get the whole business off his chest. Once I had got him to start at the very beginning he needed very little further prompting.

He had always been a keen amateur photographer but until a few months ago had confined himself to those studies of Norman churches, village duckponds and so on that get bought by jigsaw manufacturers. Then one hot afternoon, in the course of taking a few shots of a windmill up on the Downs, he had spotted in his lens a young couple doing in a grassy hollow below the windmill what young couples have been doing in that grassy hollow since long before there was any windmill there. That was the start of it.

Mrs Reason was not noted for her over-abundance of warmth and affection – mercifully, this was the briefest of background notes – and so her husband now took to patrolling the Downs with his camera in search of vicarious thrills. Disappointingly for him, he came up against a rainy spell. Not to be discouraged, he decided one dark night to try his luck over on the Merrydale council estate with the new flash attachment he had bought. Here he found richer pickings, particularly down a back lane over-looked by bungalows with picture windows. (It sounded to me, as we tramped on along the sea front, that Reason was somewhat relishing this part of his narrative.)

Pretty soon, with his long-lens Nikon, his flashgun and his dark raincoat, he was a fully-fledged Jekyll and Hyde – respected bank manager by day, drooling photographic voyeur by night. Fortune was on his side and there were no narrow squeaks, unless one counts his wife's unfulfilled threat, before packing her bags, to take her find to the police. With her disgusted departure, Reason grew bolder and began to spend most of his evenings on the prowl, not only around the housing estate but anywhere with an uninterrupted view of a well-lighted and uncurtained or half-curtained bedroom window.

Presently he was drawn to the converted tea warehouse off the High Street where Nick Crabbe has his flat, and it was here that his luck ran out. He knew (as I myself should have known had I kept my ear closer to the ground or put two and two together or both) that Nick was having a secret fling with Mrs Molly Farmer, the daughter of Len Quartermouth MBE FIAV, and one evening mounted the old iron fire escape which still graced the back of the building with the idea of catching them at it. The strap of his camera case caught on the end of the banister rail, causing him to lose his balance and stumble against a dustbin. Nick threw up his bedroom window to investigate the clatter, and recognised him. The next morning Nick Crabbe turned up at the Three Counties Bank requesting a private interview with the branch manager.

No wonder Reason needed so little prompting. He had already told the whole story, or the story so far, to Nick when confronted in his office. He now seemed in danger of going over the same ground again by recounting to me how he had explained himself to Nick when invited to account for his behaviour. I cut him short by asking, "So what did he do?"

"Well, that's it – he didn't do anything, or even threaten to do anything. He was very calm and courteous, deferential even. He said everyone was entitled to their little foibles, that he'd heard of far more shocking deviations in his court reporting days, and that so long as I steered clear of his flat in future and kept my mouth shut about him and Mrs Farmer, I'd heard the last of the matter.

"Of course, I didn't believe him for a moment – he was too smooth by half. I thought any day now he would be back at the Bank demanding a huge low-interest loan or something of the sort, and I should have to agree. Not a bit of it. He did contact me, very shortly after Ted Greenleaf's funeral, but only to suggest that if I were still taking my 'happy snaps' as he put it, I could do worse for myself than keep an eye on you and Mrs Greenleaf."

"Did he say why he wanted to give you this useful tip-off?"

"No, and I didn't ask. I assumed he owed you a grudge – some people can be quite vindictive towards their employers."

"Quite, and it sometimes happens the other way round. So that was when you followed us into the churchyard, and subsequently took to hanging around outside Mill Farm," I said, feeling rather like a character in a detective story.

"I'm afraid so."

For Rosie's sake I thought I'd better get clear on one other matter while I was about it. "Did you ever spy on Mill Farm when I wasn't there but other people were?"

"I don't know anything about any other people." A missed opportunity, then.

"No, I expect my evenings with Rosie alone were enough to steam up your viewfinder."

We had reached the edge of the town by now. Reason brought me to a halt under the last street lamp. "Oliver, I'm sorry about all this, truly sorry, if that means anything at all to you. I hope you can see that I'm not the person I was, I'm a sick man. But while I can't undo what's been done, if it makes you feel any easier in your mind I can swear to you here and now that I have destroyed every one of those photographs, and the negatives. I went straight home and burned them the night you caught me redhanded in the farmyard."

All but the set he had deposited with Nick Crabbe – that had to be a strong possibility. There would be time to go into that later. We turned on our heels and headed back towards the centre of Worthing. Even if we had to pace the sea front until dawn I would get the whole story out of him.

"You're not saying Nick let it go at that. What was the next development?"

"The next development was that he buttonholed me outside the bank one lunchtime and in that smooth way of his said that while it was none of his business, he was rather surprised that I was continuing to serve as Treasurer of the Bonfire Society. He said it was an important office in the town and although my private life was my own, on reflection I'd probably agree with him that there were surely others more deserving of the honour, and shouldn't I find some excuse to step down?"

"How odd," I said. "Almost exactly the same words as you used to Miss Bellows."

"Yes. They originated from the same source."

"But how could Nick Crabbe have known she was swindling her own cat sanctuary – unless of course you told him?"

"I'm sorry to say that out of weakness, and in breach of trust, that's what I did. Crabbe said he had good reasons for wanting to serve on the Standing Committee himself, and that he would take it as a favour if I could persuade one of the existing members to stand down – someone, if a little arm-twisting were required, whose affairs might not stand too close a scrutiny. Poor Miss Bellows, I'm afraid, fitted the bill."

We were still on a very quiet stretch of the promenade. What I had just heard from Reason had brought him as close as he had been so far to having his teeth knocked down his throat. Then I remembered a small detail of my recent conversation with Douglas Boxer.

"Did you by any chance make an anonymous contribution to Miss Bellows' cat sanctuary quite recently?"

Reason's answer saved his skin. "It was the least I could do."

"All right, let's get back to Nick Crabbe. Did he put you up to nominating me to succeed you as Treasurer?"

"Yes, although I didn't need much convincing."

"Again, did he say what he was up to?"

"No, but I imagined it was to do with pushing through that pet Bananaskin Week scheme of his – he needed friends in high places. He's very ambitious, as I once said. Ruthlessly ambitious. That's why I advised you to take care."

"And while Nick was re-arranging the Standing Committee to his own satisfaction, he didn't lean on you in any way? Didn't threaten to shop you to the police or expose you to your head office if you didn't toe the line?"

"No, never. But exposure was always on my mind. As I've explained, this thing is a sickness – has been a sickness I should say, I hope I'm cured of it by now. I've taken ridiculous risks, and I finally got my come-uppance. So when you say did he threaten me in any way, he didn't have to. I was always conscious that he could expose me any time he pleased. Yet he never once stood over me and said he would do this and this if I refused to do that and that. He wasn't even making demands of me, he was merely asking favours."

"And you're quite sure you destroyed those pictures and negs of Rosie and me?"

"Positive."

"Didn't give a set to Nick Crabbe?"

"I would never have done that, Oliver, believe me."

"Ho bloody ho."

"Really. Truly."

I believed him, or I thought I believed him. If he did turn out to be lying I was sure I would know soon enough. Nearly back at the starting point of our evening perambulation, we were approaching quite a promising-looking pub. We had passed it once and I did not intend to pass it again.

"I need a drink and I should think you do too. Come on." As we crossed the road I added gruffly, "For what it's worth, I wouldn't have shopped you either, Dennis. I might have strangled you but I wouldn't have shopped you."

"I'm very grateful, Oliver. That did begin to get through to me as I began to pull myself together after that terrible evening. But two people knowing my shabby little secret is two too many.

176

Head Office have been very kind and promised me another branch when I've recovered from my nervous breakdown. I shall be writing to Basil Thrush resigning from the Bonfire Society on health grounds."

"Have you really had a nervous breakdown?"

"Fortunately for my career, my brother's doctor prefers to describe it as a slipped disc." We were at the door of the pub. Reason hesitated. "Look, on second thoughts, Oliver, I won't have that drink after all. Thank you for being so understanding – I hope all goes well with you. I shall miss the Bonfire this year."

And before I could stop him he had darted back across the road and was walking with great determination along the sea front towards the pier – perhaps with the intention, it did seriously cross my mind, of throwing himself in the sea. In the circumstances it was not for me to intervene, although in retrospect I do see that it would have been no bad thing to have given him a helping hand off the end of the pier.

Meeting Basil Brush, Len Quartermouth MBE FIAV and Eric Barlow for our customary Saturday morning drink, I was hard put to choose whose gaze to avoid first. I could not look at Basil, playing up his tankard-clutching, pipe-sucking parson of the people act for all it was worth, without trying to picture him mincing around Mill Farm in his lace cap and apron and flicking his feather duster at Rosie's bric-à-brac. Mercifully, imagination failed me. Equally preposterous was the image my mind's eye attempted to dredge up of the ponderous, po-faced Len draped over the back of one of Rosie's uncut moquette easy chairs to receive twelve of the best from Janey's riding crop. I had less difficulty in conjuring up a picture of Eric Barlow sitting glassy-eyed in one of those same chairs, nursing a huge Scotch, surrounded by half-naked, seductive women but, in Rosie's words, long past it. This almost homely tableau registering without effort, I let my eye dwell on Barlow to the exclusion of the other two.

I imagined that Basil Brush and Len Quartermouth were unaware of one another's inclinations – Rosie had assured me that complete discretion was the rule of the house, except on what she called her party nights when her friend the chief superintendent of police might find himself in the same bed as the manager of the Cumbria, Badgers Heath and Acorn Building Society, with Betty Spruce sandwiched between them. Yet both Basil and Len, usually ostentatiously relaxed and in breezy off-duty mode on these Saturday lunchtimes, seemed ill at ease. So, come to that, did Barlow, although in his case it could just as easily have been alcoholic dyspepsia.

Add my own self-consciousness at having to join my three companions with their guilty secrets on file in my head, and the atmosphere was on the awkward side. I was glad when Len Quartermouth MBE FIAV turned out to have an auction of agricultural machinery to conduct that afternoon, so was anxious to cut the smalltalk and get down to the official business of our unofficial little steering group.

"The day is fast approaching, gentlemen, when we must apply ourselves to the question of who is to be the ah. There have been several ah."

All of us knew at once what he meant, for the subject had been working its way up to the top of our hidden agenda for some weeks now. We were dealing with our annual choice of Victim, as we termed the illustrious personage whose effigy was ceremonially committed to the flames each year. There had been several nominations.

Len produced a list of the names that had been put forward by various stalwarts of the Bonfire Society. They were the usual crop of obvious minor celebrity *bêtes noires* of the moment – political figures, TV chat show presenters, a drunken actor, a pushy American pop star. We barely glanced at it. Although all the five hundred members of the Society are entitled to vote on who should be the eventual Victim, like everything else to do with the Bonfire Society the choice is fixed by the Standing Committee, and the Standing Committee was fixed by what Miss Bellows had rightly identified as "the clique". We would pick the Victim, whose name would be planted among half a dozen completely hopeless candidates on the voting form, and our decision would carry the day.

Basil Brush opened the bidding by suggesting the captain of the year's disastrous Test side. Eric Barlow, with one of his snorting guffaws, asked whether, having lost one lot of Ashes, we really wanted to manufacture another.

Len Quartermouth MBE FIAV mentioned a Hove minicab driver who had been in the news lately by virtue of having strangled thirteen of his women passengers. Basil thought such a choice might be construed in some quarters as in poor taste. I pointed out that the man had yet to be tried and found guilty.

Eric Barlow, as he did year after year, nominated his ex-wife, at which we all smiled thinly but said nothing. In fact Mrs Barlow had been dead for five years but if he was ever reminded of the fact, Barlow always said, "She's overdue for cremation, then!" and laughed immoderately.

As for my own nomination, taking one thing with another Nick Crabbe seemed as suitable a candidate as any, but I supposed I had better put forward a name better known to Badgers Heath at large. I was in no doubt as to who my alternative choice should be. I had, in effect, had my instructions.

Sam Dice took his inspiration from the angels and his late mother but I took mine from Sam Dice. "You are writing very little about Satanism, gentlemen," he had reproached his editors at our Worthing seminar.

Someone – not I – was emboldened to point out that while there was a lot of sensational talk about the cult in the national media, none of us had yet come across it in our own circulation areas.

Our proprietor did not take to the negative approach. "It is here! *He* is here!" declared Sam, rather confusingly pointing a plump forefinger upwards. "Wherever the Lord is, there is his arch-enemy. Since the Lord is omnipresent, that makes Satan omnipresent too, I would have thought a child of six could have worked that out. Instruct your reporting staff to keep a sharp look-out for signs, gentlemen. Dead cockerels, black candles, you know the sort of thing. See what you can drum up, and if you can tie it in with some timely display advertisements for Hallowe'en pumpkins, so much the better."

I could not promise Sam dead cockerels but I could deliver up Satan to the annual Bonfire. Sam would like that. It would show him, too, that Nick Crabbe and Douglas Boxer were not the only ones around the *Herald* office with bright ideas. It was time, I was beginning to think, that I began to re-assert myself in Sam's eyes.

And so when Len Quartermouth MBE FIAV asked, "And what is Oliver's ah?" I promptly said, "The Devil."

"At least it's someone we know," commented Eric Barlow after a short and possibly stunned silence.

But the Rev Basil Thrush, after a few moments' highly visual agonising, began to nod his head in sage approval. Continuing to nod it, he said, "Good choice. Good choice. Good choice," and would probably have gone on repeating the endorsement indefinitely had not Len intervened to elaborate, "*Very* good ah, and most appropriate for your Youth Prayer ah." At the last meeting, Nick Crabbe and I had more or less shanghaied the committee into accepting the Youth Prayer Rally as part of the Bananaskin Week package. They did not have much choice anyway, since Sam Dice was the nominal President of the Bonfire Society, as indeed he was president or patron of most of the voluntary institutions in Badgers Heath.

It could have been guilt arising from their Mill Farm exploits that motivated Basil, Len and Barlow to accede so readily to the Devil as a suitable candidate for cremation. At any rate, accede to it they did, which would mean that the rest of the committee would accept it too, which meant that we had our Victim. We moved on to next business.

Len Quartermouth MBE FIAV now looked decidedly shifty.

"Now it's by no means usual to discuss the, ah, apportionment of funds to the various ah in any detail until after the ah, when we have a clearer view of what monies are available, ah; but, ah in this year's peculiar ah, representations have been made about the so-called Children of the Brazilian Rain ah."

The peculiar circumstances, we were to understand, were those of Bananaskin Week and its unprecedented swelling of the coffers. What Len really meant by peculiar circumstances, it seemed more likely to me, were those touching on Nick Crabbe's involvement in all our lives. By representations having been made he meant that he had been got at. So, it was to prove, had Basil and Barlow. So, I would have had to concede if challenged, had I.

Just how I had been got at I could not quite put my finger on. That was par for the course with Nick Crabbe, devious young bugger that he was. Following my revelatory conversation with Dennis Reason, which in turn had followed upon my revelatory conversation with Rosie, I had pondered long and hard on how to deal with him but had come up with no conclusive answer – and that was par for the course too. Nothing that he had done could be construed as straight blackmail. Although he had a hold over Reason, as Reason himself had said he had merely been asking favours. He had got Miss Bellows off the Bonfire Society committee to make way for himself, and he had got Reason to quit as Treasurer to make way for me. Favours. He had put Reason up to taking compromising pictures of Rosie and me, and this – for having slept on it, I was no longer so sure that Reason had not handed a set over – gave him a hold over me. Yet he had not used it. When we had next met, immediately upon my return from Sam's Worthing summit conference, I had thought of tackling him head on, to get whatever there was to be got out into the open. But in my usual procrastinating style I had decided to wait and see which way the cat would jump.

It did not so much jump as roll over at my feet waiting for its tummy to be tickled. Nick was bursting with self-congratulation, not only at the way his Bananaskin Week pledges were going – the £100,000 mark about to be reached and the sky now seemingly the limit – but at the boost the exercise was giving to the *Badgers Heath Herald* or, as I would have interpreted it, his own ego. Nick was becoming something of a local celebrity, a regular on the local phone-in programmes and TV and radio news slots. (To his credit – in the literal sense, since it did not go unnoticed by Sam Dice – he never failed to give a plug to the *Herald*.) In the lounge bar and Buttery of the Dolphin Arms Hotel, more hands now sycophantically pumped his than pumped mine. There were some regional press awards coming up and he had put himself in for Campaigning Journalist of the Year. Nick, having come down in the world with his professional demotion from Fleet Street to Badgers Heath, was on the up and up again and maybe this was what it was all about.

"So have you thought anything more about the Children of the Brazilian Rain Forest, boss?" he finally enquired upon realising that compliments from me would not be forthcoming.

It was a question I had been expecting and I had speculated on what his reply might be if I told him that in my considered view the Badgers Heath Friends of the Bat or the Very Loud Talking Books for the Deaf Fund took priority over a far-away rain forest of which we knew little; or if, more bluntly, I came right out and asked him what his little game was. The trouble was that such a question ought to have been rhetorical and I should have known already what his little game was before issuing the challenge – but I didn't.

I contented myself with, "I'm not at all happy with throwing everything we raise at one big charity, and I'm quite sure I'd have difficulty in pushing it through the committee."

"I don't think you would, boss. In fact I know you wouldn't."

"You've talked to them, then?"

"I've talked to them."

"And you think they'd agree?"

"I know they'd agree."

Had he then hinted, ever so subtly, to Basil, Len, Barlow and the rest that he knew all about the hanky-panky at Mill Farm? Perhaps he had no need to – the bordello, as Rosie had said, had been his idea in the first place; perhaps it had been on his sleekly murmured recommendation that Basil and Co had been sucked into it in the first place. And once again you couldn't call it blackmail because, as with Dennis Reason, it was pretty well certain that there had been no threats. It was manipulation. He was manipulating us – and perhaps for motives equally difficult to pin down, although they probably had some connection with the ego – just as we in turn manipulated the Bonfire Society.

And now, like a puppet on a string, Len Quartermouth MBE FIAV was dutifully dancing to the twitch of Nick Crabbe's little finger.

"I'm not sure how much any of you know about this ah," he was saying unhappily.

"A good deal," said Basil Brush glibly, keeping his eyes fixed on the pineapple ice bucket along the bar counter. "It's a well-run charity with a cracking good track record, and I'm satisfied in my own mind that it does a great deal of good in an area of the world that has never benefited from any of our previous donations." He chuntered on in this vein at length. While I had no doubt that he was simply parroting what Nick Crabbe had told him or thrust into his hand by way of glossy brochures, I would say for poor Basil that at least he probably believed what he was saying.

"What do you think, Eric?" I asked when Basil had finally had his say.

It was Barlow's turn to look anywhere but at his friends. "I think I'll have a large drink," he said, and called for a round.

"But seriously, Eric, it's a big decision."

Barlow said nothing until his drink arrived, when he threw back most of a large Scotch in one gulp. Then he said something that would have sounded strange had not all present, without acknowledging the fact, known exactly what he was talking about. "I'm probably the only one standing here who doesn't give a toss one way or the other. Give it all to these rain forest kids, give it all to Ethiopia where the government will piss it against the wall, give it to the dogs' home if you like, but for Christ's sake, excuse my French, vicar, let's stop going on about it."

In the uncomfortable silence that followed, Len Quartermouth MBE FIAV, who I noticed had taken no part in the debate himself, elaborately consulted his watch. Mumbling that time waited for no ah, he summed up with what for him was astonishing alacrity.

"So all in favour say ah."

"Aye," said Basil. Barlow nodded grumpily. I raised a finger. As the minutes for the following Monday's committee would confirm, with not so much as an objection from Percy Spruce that the money might be eaten by white ants when it reached the rain forest, it was cut and dried.

But before that decisive committee meeting took place, I was to come across Eric Barlow again. Following my usual Monday morning conference out at Sam's place I was driving towards the Dolphin Arms for my equally usual well-needed restorative when

I saw Barlow darting into the Goat and Compasses even as the barman unbolted the doors. On impulse I parked the car on one of the many parcels of waste ground where bits of the old Town had been pulled down in readiness for a comprehensive development scheme for which the money had long run out, and followed him into the pub.

I had never been in the Goat and Compasses before and upon entering and appraising it, I could see that instinct had advised me wisely. It was a strictly utilitarian tavern with a nicotine-stained ceiling, bench-lined plank walls adorned with brewery advertisements, a plain wooden bar, a worn lino floor and two or three rickety tables. It made the Harvesters look like an upmarket cocktail bar and for once I could see the case for gutting old clapped-out public houses and doing them up as theme pubs. Any theme would have been an improvement on the Goat and Compasses' present one of unrelieved gloom.

Nor, to the best of my recollection, had I ever had a private conversation with Eric Barlow before. For all his bad jokes (and occasional good ones) and gregarious-seeming ways, he was essentially a loner, spending more time staring into a glass, I would have guessed, than in the company of friends. Except that he lived by himself in one of the few old former artisan cottages remaining in the old Town, I knew little about him, not even what he'd done for a living, much less why he didn't continue to do it considering that he must only have been just on the wrong side of sixty. Someone had said he used to be an antique dealer in a small way who had come into some money. That seemed likely enough: he was quite cultured in a rough sort of way under his boozy exterior, and he was never short of the price of a drink.

He was already a good half way through his first large Scotch of the day as I entered the bar. Without yet greeting me, and as if it was our long-standing custom to meet daily at the Goat and Compasses, he ordered a large gin and tonic, at the same time pushing his own glass across the bar to be refreshed.

Only then did he grunt, "'Morning. It's not your Dolphin Arms but we do you a better class of customer."

"I can believe that."

"So what brings you down here, then? Slumming?" asked

Barlow after we had raised our glasses and he had drunk deeply of his.

"I was just passing."

"A lot of the Dolphin Arms set do that, but they don't usually come in."

"To tell you the truth, Eric, I wanted a word."

"Yes, I thought you might."

The old soak had a shrewd head on his shoulders, which was why we had him on the Bonfire Society committee. Since he plainly knew perfectly well what I had come for, there was no point in beating about the bush. I had no set piece worked out, but without it having kept me awake all night I knew roughly what I wanted to say.

"About tonight's vote. You know you could veto it if you had a mind to?"

"Why should I want to do that?"

"If you didn't go along with the idea of giving all the money to the Children of the Rain Forest."

"Do you go along with it yourself, mate?"

"Not entirely, no."

"Why don't *you* veto it, then?"

Good question, but one which breached the unspoken agreement we had all entered into at the Dolphin Arms on Saturday to keep our heads well below the parapet as regards the events at Mill Farm. Not that I had ever been a party to Rosie's bordello arrangement, but Barlow would assume I had, and I could not very well plead non-culpability on the grounds that I was only ever received at the farmhouse by *la patronesse* herself.

"I think you know why, Eric," I said.

Barlow was stirred sufficiently to put down his glass – an unusual move for him. "No, I bloody don't. What would happen? Go on – for the sake of hypothesis, supposing you voted against it, I voted against it, the whole bloody lot of us voted against it – just what would bloody happen?"

What indeed? If he cared to put it like that, and it was typical of Barlow that he did, then I had no idea what would happen. What *could* happen? What could Nick Crabbe do? Tell our wives? Send anonymous letters to Sam Dice, Basil's Bishop, Percy

185

Spruce's partners, the police? Petition Buckingham Palace to recall Len Quartermouth's MBE? What good would it do him?

Barlow answered his own question. "And I thought it was only conscience that made cowards of us all. If any of us had a scrap of bloody conscience we'd vote the way we saw fit. But we won't, because we're all afraid of having our dirty linen washed in public."

I ordered large refills. Barlow was already slurring his words – maybe he had started the day with a few fortifiers at home before venturing out, or maybe, like so many drunks, he only needed topping up to reach the alcoholic Plimsoll Line again.

"You didn't sound afraid on Saturday, Eric," I reminded him. "And you don't sound afraid now. If as you said you don't give a toss one way or the other, why are you going to vote in favour?"

"Because I'm too old and pissed to rock the boat, and because it doesn't matter two shakes of a pig's bum whether the money we raise goes to this particular charity or to provide false teeth for the cannibals of Papua, New Guinea, and anyone who thinks otherwise doesn't know what the Bonfire Society is in aid of, or this Bananaskin Week stunt either, come to that."

The second double Scotch had done the trick and he was quite drunk.

"I'm not with you, Eric."

"Of course you're bloody with me, if you'd bother to sit down and work it out. What's the whole object of the Bonfire Society?"

"Well," and I hoped I didn't sound as if I were humouring him. "Originally it was simply to provide Badgers Heath with the best and biggest bonfire for miles around on November the Fifth; but nowadays, like everything else around here, it's to raise money for charity."

"Bollocks. The whole object of the Bonfire Society is what it's always been, and that's to make everyone feel good. It used to make them feel good just to stick a rocket up Hitler's arse and watch the bastard burn, but now they want to feel good by shoving a tenner in an envelope and thinking they've saved the bloody whale or bought a new bed for the bloody hospital or sired a bloody guide dog."

In the absence of the barman who had gone down to the cellar,

Barlow went behind the bar and with practised ease replenished our glasses, depositing some money on the cash register.

"But they actually do accomplish all these things you mention," I argued. "If you're going to say a lot of the money is squandered in administration and so on, all right, but some of it does get through and it really is true that without these charities a lot of people would starve."

"And fifty pee will feed a family of ten in Bangladesh for a year, but that's not the bloody point, mate. The bloody point is that it makes *us* feel good. Just look at this bloody town – no unemployment, no crime to speak of, no slums, money coming out of our bloody ears, we've got it bloody made. But then night after bloody night there's pictures on the box of kids looking like stick insects, so what can we do about it? File and forget, that's what. If this town really cared the population would be down to three – we'd all be out playing doctors and nurses in the middle of bloody Africa. But there's an easier way. Write a cheque and we've got the world off our back. And there's a bloody bonus, mate. It gives us a rosy glow."

"Any harm in that?"

"None at all. I'm just saying it does us more good than them. That's why it's better to give than to receive. Bananaskin Week? Why not call it Badgers Heath Week? Down the hatch."

"Cheers."

13

Badgers Heath Diary. Sunday: Thanksgiving Service at the Parish Church of St Michael and All Angels, conducted by the Rev Basil Thrush, to celebrate the beginning of Bananaskin Week.

Monday: Official opening ceremony in council car park, when a Celebrity will release the first of 1,000 labelled balloons entered by Badgers Heath schoolchildren in the Great Balloon Race. March past by youth organisations with massed pipe and xylophone bands. Street theatre in Cherrytree Shopping Mall. Individual sponsored events. Kiddies' Bouncing Castle (all week).

Tuesday: Winter Craft Fayre, council car park (if wet on deck four of Cherrytree car stack). Flying Fools Free Fall Display Team, Badgers Heath Flying Club. Animal-free Circus, behind Bancroft's department store. Miss Bananaskin, first heats, Bancroft's cafeteria. Floodlit American football: Badgers Heath Cowboys v Gatwick Dodgers. A Night to Forget Silly Bar-B-Q including wet fish duelling, Agricultural College grounds. Sponsored events.

Wednesday: The Bananaskin Glide: new dance demonstrated by Monty and Yvonne Cousins of Two-to-Tango Dance Studio, Bancroft's cafeteria. Schools five-village jogging marathon. East Croydon Caribbean Steel Band, Cherrytree Shopping Mall. Hang-gliding Fly-past. Medieval joust. MotoCross. Fire Brigade Abseil Team display, north wall of Owl Insurance Co. Funny Walks competition, High Street. Sponsored events . . .

I put Nick Crabbe's latest draft programme on my spike. There would be a dozen more round-ups pouring out of his busy fax machine before Bananaskin Week dawned. He was having trouble finding his celebrity to kick the week off, I was satisfied

188

to note. A dozen big names had turned him down, his pal the alternative wheelchair comedian Steve Selby had to be held in reserve for the Youth Prayer Rally grand climax, and Nick was reduced to trawling the local TV and radio stations for anyone approaching personality status. We would probably finish up with the newsreader.

I had to hand it to him that failing a monsoon or other Act of God as prognosticated by Percy Spruce, Bananaskin Week was already a guaranteed success. Pledges had long been into six figures and every day Nick's fax spewed out an endless catalogue of the latest in bizarre sponsored events. It was beginning to look as if pretty soon there would not be a living soul in Badgers Heath who was not committed to running the length of the High Street while carrying a sack of horse manure, swallowing a record number of raw eggs, knitting a twelve-foot-long scarf in boxing gloves, playing the mouth organ non-stop, lying in a trough of sheep dip in an Edwardian bathing suit, growing or shaving off a beard, taking off four stones in weight, joining in a shopping trolley dash, wearing pyjamas to school, being voluntarily tarred and feathered, sitting garnished with carrots and onions in a cannibal cooking pot, flagpole squatting, or indulging in some equivalently outlandish activity.

It was all in a good cause, of course, but the remarkable thing was that Badgers Heath had as yet no idea what the good cause was; for while it had been agreed within the Bonfire Society that the Children of the Brazilian Rain Forest should be the sole beneficiaries of Bananaskin Week, the fact had yet to be made public. I was reminded of something Eric Barlow had said in the course of his whisky-sodden ramblings at the Goat and Compasses: "All you need say to get this town dipping into its pocket is one word – 'charity'. It's bloody Pavlovian. They don't ask which charity, in fact if you ask me they'd rather not bloody know which charity. They hand over the cash and that's it till next time. It's like moving your bowels every day."

And it wasn't only that we wanted to feel good, as Barlow had several times reiterated with varying degrees of warmth, it was that we wanted to be seen doing good. You could not say of Badgers Heath, as it pursued its relentless regime of sponsored runs and sponsored walks and sponsored swims, that it wore its heart anywhere but on its sleeve, as visible as a Day-glo good conduct stripe.

These reflections arose, I knew, from my uneasiness over the Children of the Brazilian Rain Forest. Had anyone checked the organisation's credentials? I certainly hadn't. Despite Barlow's assertion that no one cared where the money went, there was, according to the odd TV news documentary I had half-watched, a growing concern among fund-raisers that too much of it was being siphoned off in overheads, lavish expenses, inefficiency and even straight fraud. Did the Children of the Brazilian Rain Forest fund have any record for maladministration? Was it even a properly registered charity? It was Basil Brush's job as Bonfire Society secretary to go into all that, and he claimed he had, but there was a certain amount of bluster in his assurance that all was as it should be.

Sooner or later, I had often told myself as I allowed the *Herald* and the Bonfire Society to drift into what for all I knew could be the set-up for a giant scam, Nick Crabbe would have to show his hand. But he didn't need to: he had us all eating out of it.

Completing one more circuit in what by now had become an almost daily ritual of going round in circles, I put the subject out of my mind and, calling for coffee and canteen toast, unzipped my briefcase and took out a small bundle of personal mail. The previous night's exertions with Rosie had led me to sleep through the alarm, with the result that I had fled the house breakfastless, scooping up my letters from the doormat as I went. Sam Dice had a habit of ringing in the first minute of office hours.

The practice of the Badgers Heath branch of the Royal Mail is to deliver all the second class mail by the first post and leave the first class mail for the second post, and so most of my letters were circulars, all of them either asking for money or offering to lend me money. The ones demanding money predominated: Badgers Heath's reputation for openhandedness must have spread far beyond its boundaries, for we were on the mailing lists of most of the brand-name charities and good causes from Africa Aid to the Save the Zoo Fund. I binned them all, giving first preference to the famine appeal which, in promptly acknowledging the cheque

I had impetuously scribbled in response to a picture of a child looking even more undernourished than the skeletal norm, enclosed a direct debit form with a request to keep the contributions rolling in. The reason fund-raisers were so called, I had long ago decided, was that they kept raising the stakes.

That left me with one bona fide letter, a Basildon Bond affair with the address hand-written, or rather hand-printed, and addressed in rather quaint fashion to O. KETTLE ESQR. I slit open the envelope.

Although I was well-used to finding anonymous letters in the editorial mail at the *Badgers Heath Herald*, this was the first time I had ever received one addressed to me at home.

It being of a personal nature, I judged that rather than a mere anonymous letter it could be classified as a poison pen letter.

The tone was offensively polite or politely offensive:

Sir. To serve on the Standing Committee of the Bonfire Society is an honour and a privilege. You have besmirched that honour and abused that privilege. It is time to step down and place the office you hold in worthier hands. A suitable opportunity to do so would be at the last meeting before the annual Bonfire, after which, as you are aware, the Committee is obliged to put itself up for re-election. Should you ignore this advice and seek to remain on the Committee, then the writer will be forced to place before the membership at large certain facts. It is to be hoped this will not be necessary, if only for the sake of your Wife, with whom the writer has no quarrel. In the words of Oliver Cromwell, "It is not fit that you should sit there any longer! You shall now give place to better men."

It was unsigned as such letters tend to be, but there was no need of a signature. Even had I not recognised the familiar wrapped-in-mothballs style of her occasional notes on the history of the Bonfire Society, there was no mistaking the crabby hand, for all that she had elected to write in block capitals, of our former archivist, Miss N. D. Bellows.

Perhaps I did Miss Bellows' stilted literary style an injustice, for it was to prove that she was capable of some versatility.

*　　　*　　　*

The previous evening having been Rosie's Farmers' Ladies Circle night, when I trusted they had adhered to their intention of switching their group activity to dressmaking, I awoke refreshed and early the morning after receiving my anonymous missive. I was preparing myself a hearty breakfast to make up for yesterday when the doorbell rang. Probably the postman with too much junk mail to go through the letter box. Possibly even a recorded delivery follow-up from Miss Bellows.

Walking through the living room to the hall I chanced to glance out of the window in time to see Harry, Rosie's pigman, performing a three point turn with the Range Rover bequeathed to Mill Farm by the late Ted Greenleaf. Knowing that Rosie did not drive, it did not require much putting together of two and two to guess that it would be Rosie rather than the postman, or even the pigman, I would be greeting as I opened the front door.

"Ooh, I hope you don't mind me popping round to the house, Ollie, but I've had ever such a shock."

Not so much a shock as the one I was enduring, or going through the motions of. Like every philanderer I had a recurring waking nightmare of mistress turning up on front doorstep and making a scene. But quickly I realised that my apparent shock was but a reflex action, that I really had nothing to fear, and that what I was in truth experiencing was but harmless astonishment.

For one thing, Sherry was 3,000 miles away, having that weekend flown back to New York, which these days appeared to be her second home or rather her third home. For another, if the Spruces were peering through their net curtains across the street, it would be a classic case of kettles betraying pots should they have anything to say about Rosie's unexpected visit, either to Sherry upon her return or to anyone else. As for the rest of the neighbours, there was nothing so very strange about one prominent member of the Bonfire Society committee calling upon another, especially on the threshold of November, as we now were. And it was not as if I had opened the door in my pyjamas.

"Come in, Rosie."

For the sake of complete peace of mind I could have wished, as I helped her off with her coat, that she had dressed more modestly for the occasion. If she was not completely naked under her

clinging lycra blue dress she was not far off it. Ushering her into
the living room I had to restrain my hand from wandering down
her spine, and the same thought leapt unbidden into my head as
was, I could depend upon it, already firmly lodged in Rosie's.

"Ooh, what a lovely room, pet, you do have a nice home I
must say, is that the dining room through there? Ooh, I like your
sideboard, it puts my poor Welsh dresser to shame, and this must
lead through to the kitchen, ooh, now this is nice, it's like
something out of the Ideal Home Exhibition. And this'll be your
little study style of thing, very cosy, very cosy indeed. What's it
like upstairs?"

I laughed, in order to derail this train of through before it
gathered momentum. "Never mind upstairs, Rosie. Let me get
you some coffee and then you can tell me all about it."

Pouring Rosie's coffee, and making a mental note to remember
to scrub the orange lipstick mark off the cup when I washed up, I
speculated on the possible nature of a shock so great that it had
brought her to my door. The only theory I could come up with,
while rustling up a plate of biscuits to satisfy my unexpected
guest's sweet tooth, was that the police had been round – police
other, that was to say, than her friend the chief superintendent.

I was a long way off the bull's eye but not altogether off-target.

Having reassured Rosie that it was quite in order for her to
come to the house in an emergency, while at the same time trying
to impress on her my hope that her emergencies would be limited
to this one-off occasion, I asked her what the problem was.

Rosie helped herself to the last of the biscuits. "It might be
something or nothing style of thing, pet, but I wanted you to see
it for yourself. That's why I took the liberty of calling round
instead of ringing you up."

"If you *had* rung up I could always have dropped in at the farm
on my way to the office," I said helpfully, for future reference.

"I know, love, but I was in such a state I couldn't think
straight."

Clamping a piece of shortbread between her lipstick-stained
teeth, Rosie rummaged in her handbag and fished out a Basildon
Bond-type envelope addressed to her in capitals. I had worked
out seconds beforehand what it must be.

It was almost a pastiche of the traditional poison pen letter as investigated by slow-witted constables in sleepy villages before the arrival of the private detective from London. Its author had excelled herself.

"Whore! Harlot! Jezebel!" was its salutation. It was understandable enough that it should have given Rosie ever such a shock. Penned in green ballpoint and heavily underlined in red – Miss Bellows evidently believed in horses for courses – the letter began with a reminder that Ted Greenleaf was still not cold in his grave, then went on to command Rosie to ask herself what might he have done had he been alive to see her turn Mill Farm into a house of lust and sin. My guess, from what Rosie had told me about him, was that Ted would have cheerfully left her to it while he got on with his VAT returns. The Bellows view, however, was that he would have first cut her throat and then commenced on a programme of mutilation that was described in some detail.

Reading on, I was surprised that Rosie hadn't been more upset than she was. The letter went on for four closely-printed pages without let-up, each sentence more bloodcurdling than the last. It made Miss Bellows' restrained effort to me read like a *billet doux*.

"Pretty strong stuff," I said as I finished reading it, noting that in true classic style it was signed "A Wellwisher".

"Is it like that all the way through?" asked Rosie naively.

"What – haven't you read it all?" No wonder her distress was so underplayed.

"Only the first page. I would have thrown it on the fire, only being as I was going shopping this morning I hadn't bothered to light it."

"So you didn't get to the last paragraph?"

"No – what does it say?"

"Well, Rosie, it says that taking one thing with another the writer feels it's high time you resigned from the Bonfire Society committee." I didn't think I had better add the rider that failure to do so would result in her having acid thrown in her face when she least expected it.

"But I was going to do that anyway, now that me and the girls have got that ten thousand pounds together!" protested Rosie.

"So why should anyone want to write horrible things like that to me? I mean to say it's not as if I was *refusing* to step down, pet. Honestly, some people!" From Rosie's hurt but altogether reasonable tone, you would have thought that all she had suffered from Miss Bellows was a catty remark in the fish queue.

"If it makes you feel any better, Rosie, I've had one of those letters too."

"And what did yours say?"

"More or less the same as yours," I white-lied.

"Why people can't mind their own business! What did you do with it?"

"The same as I'm going to do with yours – put it through the office shredder. Now don't think about it, Rosie."

"But who can have sent it, Ollie?"

"Someone who's sick. There's a lot of it about. Put it out of your mind." I could not judge what might have been the fate of Miss Bellows had I revealed her as the culprit. Rosie would either have had her thrown in the duckpond or would merely have cut her dead when next they met in the post office, it was hard to say which.

I would dearly have liked to know, if only to see how expertly she had tailored her prose to match the personality of her victims, how Miss Bellows had couched the letters she had undoubtedly penned to Basil Brush, Len Quartermouth MBE FIAV, Eric Barlow, and – presumably in separate envelopes – the Spruces. And Nick Crabbe? Or had he put her up to it. If he had, it could only have been with Miss Bellows' willing co-operation. Those letters had the hallmark of one dedicated to her art.

Having got her problem off her heaving chest, Rosie began to relax. She leaned back in her easy chair and crossed her legs, revealing rather more thigh than I was comfortable with in the sanctity of my own home. Pouring her more coffee, I brooded on how to get rid of her. It still needed a good hour before I had to set off for the office but she was not to know that. I looked fixedly at my watch.

"Is Harry coming back for you, Rosie?"

"No, I told him you'd very kindly drop me off on your way to work. You don't mind, do you, precious?"

195

"Not at all." I could always chat to the cleaners or catch up on my expenses.

Rosie got to her feet and reached for her bag. For a wild moment I thought she was ready to leave without demur. In a wilder one I recognised that this would have been completely out of character.

"Ooh, this coffee's going straight through me, which way's your bathroom, pet?"

"Top of the stairs." Just the mention of the word "stairs" had an aphrodisiac effect. My heart was pounding.

"That sounds straightforward enough, poppet, but if I don't come back down again you'll have to come looking for me, because you know what it's like in strange houses, you can sometimes get lost."

"Now Rosie," I said weakly, but I knew it was I who was lost. The sexoholic had often pictured Rosie on his own bed, in his own bath, on his own floor, across his own desk. The flesh and the spirit were in willing tandem.

I had seen little of Sherry in the last few weeks. Every second weekend, it seemed, and sometimes two weekends in a row, her presence was required in foreign parts, where she was securing ever starrier interviews with the great and glamorous. She was making an impact on the newspaper world and I was pleased for her. I was also glad that her preoccupation with her work was at the moment taking precedence over her preoccupation with Rosie Greenleaf. I really did mean to make the break with Rosie, not least because I could not see Miss Bellows resting on her laurels, and if she continued to monitor my visits to Mill Farm, an anonymous letter to Sam Dice might be next in the series. I had marked Bananaskin Week as a suitable time to terminate my little arrangement with Rosie. The fireworks display would be a fitting climax to several months of exhilarating if exhausting physical pyrotechnics, and Rosie would be free to explore pastures new or, if I knew her, meadows and churchyards new. From the odd hint Rosie had dropped, the chief superintendent of police, unless he had been nobbled by Miss Bellows, seemed a firm favourite.

Meanwhile relations with Sherry, when she did come home, were of the armed truce variety. Neither of us invaded the other's neutral space: she did not enquire how my disentanglement with Rosie was going and I did not enquire how she spent her leisure hours on her frequent trips abroad, or why she had to fly to New York to interview celebrities who turned out to be in London the following week. We had the odd meal at the Old Forge, had a few neighbours in for drinks, watched television, and perfunctorily made love. Given that ours had always been something of an arm's length relationship, it was easy to lull myself into the conviction, or perhaps it was the pretence, that not very much had changed.

It therefore came as a considerable surprise, the weekend following Rosie's visit, when over Saturday breakfast Sherry said to me, "Look, if you're meeting your chums at the Dolphin this morning, you won't mind if I don't join you? The freezer's positively creaking with groceries so I don't really need to struggle round that God-awful Cherrytree centre or fight off those bloody little vultures trying to hijack my shopping trolley, and besides, I want to pack."

"You've only just unpacked," I pointed out mildly.

"Yes, but I mean seriously pack. I'm off to New York."

"How long for this time?"

"Well, for good, if it all works out. And if it does work out that means leasing an apartment, which is going to cost an arm and a leg, so that'll mean selling the house. Do you think Percy Spruce would put it on the market for me?"

My first thought, upon cottoning on to the fact that my wife was telling me she was leaving me, was that she had broken the news with such style. I felt a pang at what I was losing, and another at the immediate, certain realisation that it was too late to do anything about it now.

All I could do was to say what I imagined would be expected of the shattered but not altogether surprised ex-husband to be. "So what's brought this on?"

"You mean you really want me to spell it out why I'm going?"

"If it's not too much trouble."

"You won't like it."

"Try me."

"All right. One reason is that I really do want this New York job – it's a new magazine, and they want me as their star feature writer, but it does mean folding up my tent and living there. Another reason is that I've decided you're such a complete arsehole. Would you pass the marmalade, please?"

This I thought was overdoing the stylish angle rather, but I tried to play it the same cool way.

"Shall we take your two points in the order given?"

"If you like. If we stayed together you'd have to move to New York with me and I don't think you'd take to that, even if you were prepared to kiss Sam Dice goodbye. You'd have to find a job there, because there's no way I could keep the two of us in gin, and I'm afraid you'd find that rather difficult. I don't want to come the glitzy cosmopolitan, Kettle, but for New York, you haven't got what it takes. Sorry to put it on the line like that."

"That's quite all right," I said, trying not to feel stung for the second time in as many minutes. "I never had what it takes in London either. Maybe that's where we went wrong."

"We didn't go wrong, Kettle, *you* went wrong, with that bloody woman! How the hell could you? It's like hearing my husband's going around with a barmaid. Haven't you got *any* style? At all?"

"It's funny you should say that, because only a moment ago I was thinking what consummate style you have yourself. So whoever may have been your guests at the Barbican from time to time, I suppose they ranked a little higher on the social scale than the barman at the – "

"Oh, put a sock in it!" snapped Sherry with a good deal of contempt. I didn't blame her: it was a cheap remark. "For the record, the only relationships I've had with other men since we moved down to this dump have been strictly on the wining and dining level, even when I've been at the other side of the Atlantic where I could have been hopping in and out of bed like a rabbit for all you knew. If you think otherwise, that's because I've lazily indulged your childish fantasy of having an ultra-sophisticated wife who beds anything she fancies and probably keeps a toy boy on the side. You've believed I was having affairs because you wanted me to have affairs."

This was true enough, but now was no time for self-analysis. Besides, as the conspicuous loser in this particular round, I was anxious to move on.

"If it comes to that, Lydia" – I only reverted to her rarely-used Christian name when things got starchy – "you always had what I'd call a very laid-back attitude about what I might be getting up to in your absence, not that I was getting up to very much before Rosie Greenleaf came along."

"I assumed you were having the occasional fling but I didn't want to know about it. I'm away quite a lot and I told myself that contrary to all the evidence you were probably only human. But I didn't bargain for you taking up with the town tart. Christ, Kettle, it's not even as if you'd fallen stupidly in love with her. If you wanted sex that badly you could have got it without my ever hearing about it. What do you think Brighton's for?"

I felt that I ought to be defending Rosie's reputation, but was too preoccupied, for the present, with my own. Perhaps there was something in Sherry's succinct character reading earlier.

"How *did* you hear about it, as a matter of interest? Nick Crabbe, I suppose."

"You've got Nick Crabbe on the brain. If you really want to know, it was Dennis Reason."

"What did he say, exactly?"

"What the hell does it matter what he said exactly? Christ, that's so bloody typical of you, Kettle. I tell you I'm leaving you and all you care about is what the bloody bank manager said about you."

"I've a reason for asking." Just piecing a jigsaw together, darling.

"He said you were visiting Mill Farm regularly and he wished I'd intervene before there was any trouble."

I knew just what Dennis Reason had meant by trouble. He had meant before he was caught taking his "happy snaps" as Nick Crabbe had called them. He had wanted temptation to be removed from his reach, and in taking the initiative for its removal he had ruined my marriage. Still, that was that bit of the jigsaw completed.

Sherry was right. There were more important issues here than who had exposed my affair and why. "Supposing I told you I've stopped seeing Rosie?"

"It wouldn't make any difference because I've quit my job, I'm going to New York, and anyway you'd be lying."

"Not if we put it in the future tense. I'll tell her on Monday it's all over."

"It's always in the future tense, Oliver. That's the whole trouble with you – everything's in the future tense. I gave you the chance to put it in the past tense but you wouldn't take it. You could have told her it was all over when I first warned you against her, when you first knew that I was on to it; and it wasn't that you didn't want it to stop, it was that you couldn't be bothered stopping it, you thought it would somehow end itself or that I'd stop going on about it and it would all blow over. You know what your motto should be? Never put off till tomorrow what you can put off till the day after."

It was as accurate an analysis of my character as I was ever likely to get from even the most astute astrologer, and it explained among other things why I had been a sitting target for Nick Crabbe and his Bananaskin Week and his Children of the Brazilian Rain Forest. But all that concerned me just now was that Sherry, for the first time in our marriage, had called me Oliver, and I had been calling her Lydia. Now I really knew it was all over.

Sherry's resounding little curtain speech, as it was evidently meant to be, was accompanied by bangs and crashes as she loaded the breakfast things on to a tray. Now moving into the kitchen to stack the dishwasher, she called, "By the way, has Mrs Thingy been coming in?" Mrs Thingy was Sherry's name for our cleaning lady, whom she had never met and was now unlikely to.

"Yes, why – hasn't she done the kitchen floor?" I called back, marvelling that we could engage in domestic trivia at a time like this.

"Oh, the kitchen floor's all right but she can't have vacuumed under the bed."

After a decent pause, and on pretext of going up to the bathroom, I went upstairs, flushed the lavatory and then went and looked under the bed. The red silk knickers, though I had no recollection of her wearing any, could only be Rosie's. Unscrupulous women have been known to leave such souvenirs behind as a means of driving a wedge between a lover and his wife. In justice to Rosie, when she had finally left my house she had probably no recollection of having been wearing red silk knickers either.

From the minutes of the Badgers Heath Bonfire Society Standing Committee, October 23. *Item 7*: Resignation of Mr D. Reason.

The Rev B. Thrush (Secy) reported that he had received a letter from Mr D. Reason regretfully tendering his resignation from Standing Committee for reasons of health. While it was not clear whether it was Mr Reason's own ill-health or that of his mother that was the cause of his resignation, it would be received with great sadness, and the Secretary was sure Standing Committee would wish him to reply to Mr Reason thanking him most warmly for all his past endeavours for the Society and wishing him, or his mother, a speedy recovery.

It was agreed that such a letter be drafted by the Secretary.

Chair (Mr L. Quartermouth MBE FIAV) said that while the personal statement he had been intending to make fell strictly speaking under the umbrella of Any Other Business, the present heading on the Agenda, dealing as it did with a Member's resignation, seemed as good a point as any to put it forward, if Standing Committee would indulge him.

Mr Quartermouth MBE FIAV, now speaking in a personal capacity, said that owing to pressure of work and the increasing amount of form-filling and time-consuming returns required of the business community by an unthinking Whitehall bureaucracy, he too had reluctantly decided that the time had come to step aside. He had been a member of Standing Committee for seventeen years, serving as Chair for the past twelve. They had been rewarding years, enjoyable years, he would even say golden years, but enough was enough and the day was approaching when he must hand over the gavel to a younger man. He would sincerely thank each and every Member of Standing Committee, through their unfailing courtesy and consideration, for making his task as Chair if not an easy one then an easier one than it would otherwise have been.

Stating that the Chair's statement would have been received with surprise and sorrow, the Rev B. Thrush (Secretary) said that now was not the time to pay tribute to those qualities of chairmanship that had guided Standing Committee through many a stormy passage – that opportunity would come at next week's Roast Potato Supper – but he could not let this saddest of moments go by without proposing the warmest vote of thanks to a jolly good fellow under whom it had been a pleasure and a privilege to serve.

A vote of thanks to the Chair, proposed by the Rev B. Thrush (Secy) and seconded by Mr P. Spruce, was carried unanimously.

The Rev B. Thrush (Secy) said that while on his feet he also would like to make a short personal statement, with the Chair's permission. The Rev B. Thrush's curate at St Michael and All Angels, the Rev K. Butterfield, was leaving the Parish in order to walk round the world in aid of lepers, with whom he would subsequently be doing missionary work. The Rev B. Thrush did not know when a replacement curate could be forthcoming, since there was a shortage of new blood in the Established Church. In addition to this increase in his workload, he was having to move the Tuesday Prayer Guild meeting to Monday evenings, Bonfire Society committee night, since Tuesdays were now earmarked for choir practice. The Rev B. Thrush concluded that between having to resign his living or resign from Standing Committee, he would unhappily have to plump for the latter.

Mr E. Barlow asked through the Chair if that meant the Secretary was resigning or not resigning.

The Rev B. Thrush said that reluctantly, he had no alternative but to resign from Standing Committee.

Mr P. Spruce said he would like to propose a vote of thanks to the Rev B. Thrush.

Mr E. Barlow expressed the view that if each and every Member of Standing Committee who resigned was going to get a vote of thanks, Standing Committee would be sitting long after closing time.

Chair said that while licensing hours did not enter into the matter, time was marching on and he would ask Members to

confine themselves to essential business. Votes of thanks, testi-
monials and the remainder could wait for the proper occasion,
which as the Secretary had said was the Roast Potato Supper.

Mr P. Spruce said in that case, while he had the floor, he would
like it to be known that he would not be putting himself up for re-
election on next year's Standing Committee. He had served on
Committee believing that he was serving a Bonfire Society, but
now he found himself, he did not know quite how, serving a
Bananaskin Week. Furthermore he and Mrs Spruce, having
talked over certain domestic matters that were nobody's business
but their own, had decided to join the Jehovah's Witnesses, and
this would be a considerable drain upon their time.

Mrs P. Spruce stated that she could only go along with what
her husband had just said, and she was very sorry but she would
not be standing for re-election.

Mr O. Kettle (Treasurer) said that he had some sympathy with
Mr Spruce. With the advent of Bananaskin Week, the Bonfire
Society had become almost big business. Even though he personally had had a hand in bringing about this important change in
the Society's role in the community, he did not feel able to carry
on as Treasurer once the inaugural Bananaskin Week had been
launched. He felt the post would be better filled by someone who
had more experience with figures, an accountant perhaps. In any
case he could see it coming close to a full-time job, and he had a
paper to run. Mr O. Kettle therefore took this opportunity to give
notice that he would not be seeking re-election, not that he had
ever been elected in the first place since he was an ex-officio
Member.

Mrs R. Greenleaf (Appeals Secy) said she did not know what to
say. It was not so much that she was resigning like all the others
as that she had never intended to stay in the first place, once she
had reached her Appeal Fund target which she had only taken on
in memory of her late husband, this being the least she could do.
She had had a ball and had not regretted a moment of it, but it
was time to move on. Time and tide waited for no man. The
Appeals Secretary had a lot of people to thank from the bottom
of her heart, but the Chair had ruled out votes of thanks so she
would leave it at that and sit down.

Mr E. Barlow said if the rats were leaving the sinking ship, he hoped there was room in the lifeboat for a little one.

The Rev B. Thrush (Secy) asked if he should enter this observation in the minutes as an intimation of Mr Barlow's intended resignation.

This being affirmed, Chair asked whether any other Members wished to speak before he moved on to Any Other Business.

Mr N. Crabbe said that speaking as a new boy he had listened with respect to everything that had been said. He was sure that his colleagues had made the right decision. Bananaskin Week represented a new dawn for the Bonfire Society and what it required now was new blood. Mr Crabbe could see the day dawning when Bananaskin Week became a national, even an international institution but having played some small part in launching it, however hastily and inadequately, he felt he should now withdraw from the limelight and leave it to others to carry on with the good work.

The speaker added that he had taken the liberty of ordering three bottles of champagne from the lounge bar downstairs, and with the Chair's indulgence he would now ask Members to be upstanding and drink a toast "to Bananaskin Week — may it be a roaring success".

The toast having been drunk, and there being no other business, the meeting was adjourned.

14

The first morning of Bananaskin Week, contrary to the forebodings of Percy Spruce, dawned not wet, not foggy, not windy, not bitterly cold, but dry, sunny, and with a champagne sparkle in the air.

It was a good start. The previous day's curtain-raiser – Basil's Thanksgiving Service – had gone as well as Basil's services ever did and had attracted bigwigs such as the Lord Lieutenant of the county and a handful of MPs and country squires. The fact that they all regretted their inability to fall in again at the council car park this morning was neither here nor there. We had enough local VIPs to fill the platform, myself among them, Nick Crabbe – thanks to my studied failure to put his name forward – not. Every minute of the week promised to be crammed with activity. No one had let us down. Common sense had finally triumphed over a threatened farce with the Council designating the High Street one way going down from the Heath while the marching bands, drum majorettes and floats for the opening day parade were programmed to proceed along the High Street up to the Heath. All was well.

It was such a brilliant day that I decided to walk up to the town centre. Opening the front door I located the source of the hammering noise that had commenced while I was putting on my overcoat. The two workmen engaged by Spruce & Partners, Estate Agents, to attach a large FOR SALE notice to my front gate, or Sherry's front gate as I would now more accurately have to call it, cast only a passing cloud over my blue horizon. The house was too big for me anyway. There was a flat in one of the surviving Victorian villas overlooking the Heath which I had my eye on, all mod cons and within walking distance of the Euro-inn Dolphin Arms Hotel. I was used to fending for myself and the bachelor life had its attractions. Perhaps my lease on Rosie's affections could be extended indefinitely until some other prospect beckoned. I tried not to think about Sherry.

Out on the pavement I found myself greeting the moon-faced Kimberley Spruce, clad in her best frock and clutching a red balloon. All the children of Badgers Heath had been given the day off to join in the Great Balloon Race and generally make a nuisance of themselves. I fully expected Kimberley to touch me for fifty pence for one of her many sponsored leisure activities, none of which seemed to reduce her girth; but instead she was staring fixedly at the sky, the steely November sun glinting in her owlish spectacles. Casually following her gaze I glimpsed, before the sun dazzled my eyes, what I thought must be the Goodyear blimp that sometimes cruised over Badgers Heath on its way to Brighton. But there was no engine sound. Then I remembered that Nick Crabbe had sought my approval for a hot air balloon to be part of the festivities. I had agreed, subject to his getting the thing for nothing.

With a hearty word or two to Kimberley, I was about to stride off when she pointed upwards and asked, "What's that, Mr Kettle?"

"A hot air balloon, Kimberley. Haven't you ever seen a hot air balloon before?"

"Yes, but what does it *say*?"

Bananaskin Week, it was to be hoped. Or perhaps we had had to settle for a soft drinks advertisement as our part of the bargain. Shielding my eyes against the cold sun I looked up again and now got a proper view of the object overhead as it serenely floated by. It was a giant condom, the size of the Hindenburg, perfectly contoured. Stencilled on its side in large black letters was the slogan SAFE SEX.

Their task completed, the two workmen were returning to their van. Observing Kimberley and me with necks craned, they too looked heavenwards.

"Fuck me!" exclaimed one of them.

"Is that what it says?" asked the myopic Kimberley.

"More or less, darling, more or less!" chuckled the other. Shaking their heads in disbelief, the two workmen drove off.

Sam Dice would go berserk. He would go higher up in the air than the flying condom itself. It was now changing direction and floating off towards the town centre so that all the assembled dignitaries, Sam among them, could have a good look at it. Its port side, I could now see, was emblazoned with the words AIDS ACTION AIDS YOU. Given that Sam believed Aids to be a plague inflicted upon mankind by a wrathful Jehovah, this could be a firing job. The question was, who would be fired? Nick Crabbe, if there was any justice; but when it came to errors of judgement as foolhardy as this I had seen enough editors' heads roll to know that there was no justice. I could of course get some satisfaction from firing Nick Crabbe before Sam Dice fired me, but a more constructive step would be to get the giant condom out of the sky before Sam saw it.

There was no point in trying to ring Nick: he would have been out and about on Bananaskin Week business since dawn, and I had foolishly refused to allow him a mobile telephone. I would just have to hope to locate him at the opening ceremony, where I now regretted denying him a platform pass. Praying that Sam would not be moved to look upwards in the course of his morning devotions, I headed for the town centre. The great floating condom, bobbing and weaving overhead, seemed to be following me.

The High Street was criss-crossed from end to end with the flags of all nations, many of them nations responsible for creating the very conditions that Badgers Heath's charitable impulses hoped to assuage. The flags were interspersed with banners strewn across the street by traders and other interested parties, identifying themselves with Bananaskin Week or, under the influence of a strong Spruce-type element in our cautious community, warning against its possible excesses. GO BANANAS WITH BANCROFT'S, BIN YOUR BANANASKINS and KEEP EYES PEELED – THERE'S A BAG THIEF ABOUT IN BANANASKIN WEEK were among the slogans I noticed. The lamp posts were hung with bunches of plastic bananas and the shop windows either dressed with banana-related displays of

merchandise or boarded up. One clapped-out little shop, a former fishmonger's intermittently occupied by Oxfam or Age
Concern while waiting for the fag-end of its lease to run out, was
now operating as the Bananaskin Week Victim Support Centre,
offering stress counselling to those finding themselves over-
whelmed by the week's activities. As the shadow of the giant
condom flitted across the High Street, I thought only half-ironi-
cally of dropping in for some advice.

Metal barriers lining the route of the opening day parade
separated the crowds, three or four deep on either side, from the
performers and exhibitionists roaming the street. These were
mainly dressed either as clowns or as a character known as Bertie
Banana, the whimsical logo devised for the Week by the Badgers
Heath Polytechnic Faculty of Art, Design and the Humanities.
The clowns were engaged in under-rehearsed juggling, falling
about and water-throwing while the Bertie Bananas jangled collecting tins. This entertainment, if such it could be called, was
augmented by schoolchildren and youths performing the sponsored tasks by which, among hundreds of others, they had
pledged themselves to raise large sums of money. Hula-hooping,
tap-dancing, skipping, trampoline-bouncing, head-shaving,
statue-posing, handball-throwing, skull-banging with a tin tray,
these too were accompanied by collection box wavers in fancy
dress working the crowds. To be abroad in Badgers Heath this
morning you needed to be weighed down with loose change. I
had only got as far as the church and already I had been relieved
of every penny I had on me except for folding money.

Across the street I spied Eric Barlow sneaking into the Goat
and Compasses a full half hour before opening time. With the
Aids Action condom hovering above my head like an inflatable
sword of Damocles I was sorely tempted to join him, but an
escapologist was performing in the middle of the street, and to
pass by him would mean being expected to throw coins into a hat
when I had no more coins to throw. The escapologist, as he
writhed about in his straitjacket, chains and handcuffs, was
explaining breathlessly to the crowd that they too could break
the bonds that bound them by believing in the Word and becoming Christians. Sam would approve of his act. I made a note to

tell Nick, when I could find him, to get our photographer down here.

By turning off through the churchyard to the car park behind it and following the drab service roads linking one shoppers' car park with the next, I managed to reach the Cherrytree Shopping Mall without being accosted further for funds. To get across the Mall, which at this moment was dedicated to a display of may-pole dancing, cost me a five pound note which I brandished ostentatiously before stuffing it into a collecting box, in the hope that as many stray collectors as possible had seen me paying my whack. By keeping my eyes firmly on the ground, I managed to reach the Dolphin Arms without further outlay. It still wanted a few minutes to opening time but, emulating Barlow, I knew the barman well enough to be able to persuade him to serve me a much-needed gin and tonic before the ordeal of joining Sam Dice on the platform and waiting for a quivering, podgy finger to point accusingly at the giant flying condom. "They haven't un-locked the cash till yet," reported the barman as I produced a tenner, now my smallest denomination. "But if you put some-thing in the Bananaskin Week box, Mr Kettle, we'll call it evens, all right?"

The Dolphin Arms car park leads into the council car park which, thronged with balloon-toting children, teenagers in a variety of sub-military uniforms ranging from the Air Cadets to the Salvation Army, policemen, programme sellers got up as Bertie Banana, and sundry adults in mufti, and overlooked by a makeshift platform crammed with local worthies, presented a miniature imitation of Tiananmen Square on May Day.

The platform, I was relieved to observe as I pushed my way forward through the crowd and picked out the cherubic figure of Sam Dice wedged between the Chairman of the Council and the Chief Executive, as the town clerk now chose to style himself, was protected from the elements by a canvas awning. When last sighted, the floating condom was over the Cherrytree Shopping Mall. So long as it stayed on that side of the High Street, it was not visible from the platform. To put it another way, so long as Sam remained on the platform there was a fair chance that he would not see the floating condom; therefore, for once in my editorial career when dragged to these civic functions, I hoped the speeches would go on and on. But where was Nick Crabbe? There was a press box of sorts below the platform but he was not in it. Who, then, was going to take down the Chairman of the Council's remarks? I certainly wasn't.

I climbed up on to the platform and caught Sam's eye. He turned to greet me with the words, "So Mrs Kettle's off to Sodom. I hope she's doing the right thing." I had thought it wise to drop Sam a line to let him know that Sherry was taking herself off to New York before he heard it on the grapevine. I did not of course mention that she had left me; with any luck, we would get the divorce through without it coming to his notice – certainly he would not learn about it from the pages of the *Badgers Heath Herald*.

To the puzzled-looking Chairman of the Council, Sam was explaining, "Mrs Kettle's chosen to go and work in New York. I call New York Sodom, and I call San Francisco Gomorrah." As he spoke, a great white hot air condom as big as an airship floated gently, gracefully into view, its flank bearing the slogan AIDS ACTION AIDS YOU. Thankfully, Sam was now looking at his programme. I kept my fingers crossed.

To a ragged fanfare from the Boys' Brigade xylophone and flute band – a difficult exercise in the absence of trumpets – the opening ceremony got under way. The master of ceremonies, otherwise the Chairman of the Council's official steward, introduced his boss who in turn, after some rambling remarks about Badgers Heath's enviable record for never failing to respond to a good cause – quite a creditable performance, really, considering that neither he nor Badgers Heath yet knew what the good cause was – introduced the celebrity guest.

The best available celebrity Nick Crabbe had been able to rustle up was the weatherman from the local TV station. At least he was a recognisable personality, as a loud round of applause testified, and he seemed an experienced opener of fêtes and functions. He launched confidently into his patter, obviously a set piece which he tailored to each occasion, in which he thanked his audience for their warm welcome and sunny outlook, noted that the many infants present seemed mainly dry and bright, guessed that a knot of pensioners must be in their low seventies, and hoped they did not find him fresh or windy. Sam, who was never a one for jokes, looked restless. I willed him not to look upwards. The overhead giant condom seemed no longer to be moving, in fact it was so immobile that I feared it had been tethered over Badgers Heath for the week like a barrage balloon. Where the hell was Nick Crabbe? As the weatherman continued his meteorological burblings, my eyes roamed the crowd. I looked down at the press box. Standing by it, one of the Bertie Banana figures, his bright yellow sheath bearing a big blue oval label with the slogan GIVE TILL IT HURTS, was scribbling in a spiral notebook. It was Nick Crabbe.

I sidled off the platform and edged my way round to the press box, where I tapped Crabbe on an arm protruding from his bananaskin outfit.

"What the fuck are you doing in that gear?" I whispered fiercely.

"Just a minute, boss," said Nick, whispering in return. "I've got to get this down."

"Bugger the speeches, you can make them up like you make everything else up," I retorted, louder this time. There were scowls and tongue-clickings from the mutinous-looking reporters, all of them corralled from Sam's other papers, who populated the press box. I led Nick out of earshot to the edge of the crowd. If Sam spotted us he would think I was briefing him, as in a manner of speaking I was.

"You look a complete prat, cock."

"I suppose I do, boss, but it's all in a good cause as we say around here. I'm doing a telly interview for South-east Round-up at half past twelve and they wanted me dressed as a banana. And of course they'll mention the paper. Great publicity."

"Never mind that – what about *that* bloody thing?" I jabbed my thumb skywards. The giant condom bobbed mockingly.

"You sound as if you don't approve, boss."

"No, I don't approve. If Sam claps eyes on it, which he's about to do any second now, he'll go raving mad. Get it down."

"You authorised it, boss."

"You didn't tell me it was a fucking floating French letter, did you?"

"It was a choice between this and one in the shape of a whisky bottle, and I didn't think Sam would like that. Look at it this way, boss — we've got it all week for absolutely nothing."

"No, cock, let's look at it this way — if that monstrosity is still visible when Sam steps off that platform, you're fired."

From a marionette-like jerk of his arms I could tell that Nick was shrugging under his bananaskin covering. "You're the boss, boss."

He was about to move off, but then hesitated.

"I don't know whether you particularly want to listen to this guy, boss, but I'm wondering if you'd mind walking back to the flat with me. There's something I wanted to have a word with you about."

"Every time you want a word with me," I snarled, remembering our original conversation on the threshold of the Dolphin Arms Hotel that had led to the seething jamboree that surrounded us, "you land me right in it."

Nick Crabbe then said something very strange.

"I still think we should have a word, boss, before you're further in it than you've ever been before."

.

To anyone who has never been blackmailed by a banana, I would describe the experience as novel. The ludicrousness of the situation pulls against one's inclination to take it seriously until the surrealist horror of it all gradually superimposes itself on one's consciousness. It is like waking up from a bad dream, only to find that it is not a dream at all.

This was it, then. Just as I had persuaded myself that Nick Crabbe had nothing else up his sleeve, he was about to produce the ace of spades, a dozen silk handkerchiefs and a rabbit.

The flat in the converted tea warehouse resembled the operations room of one small principality at war with another. All the furniture had been pushed aside to make way for half a dozen hired trestle tables piled with papers, where Nick's helpers had toiled for weeks. The walls were covered with thumb-tacked charts and day-planners. A glimpse through the bedroom doorway afforded a view of a bank of filing cabinets.

As nonchalant in his ridiculous banana costume as if he had been wearing blazer and flannels, Nick was ringing the Flying Club from one of a dozen-strong battery of telephones whose trailing leads criss-crossed the carpet. Having given instructions to have the hot air condom balloon grounded, he replaced the telephone and went into the bedroom. Still with no idea what he was about, except for the sure knowledge that the moment of confrontation had come, I irrelevantly registered that when he walked, the bananaskin outfit waddled from side to side, giving the impression that he was taking part in a conga, possibly the Longa Conga that would soon be snaking along the High Street.

Extracting a manilla folder from one of the filing cabinets, Nick steered his crescent-shaped plastic banana back into the living room where I was perched uncomfortably on a minimalist tubular metal and plywood office chair, and placed it on the trestle table in front of me.

"I have some photographs I'd like you to see, boss."

"Yes, I thought you might," I said leadenly. At once it seemed pathetic and absurd that I had ever trusted Dennis Reason not to have given a set of his pictures to Nick Crabbe — not that I could have done anything about it, apart from throwing him into the sea, even had I steadfastly refused to take his word for it instead of dithering between belief and disbelief. Always a student of my own reactions, I recorded, not far from uppermost in a seething mass of emotions, a voyeuristic quickening of the pulse at the prospect of contemplating a pornographic portfolio of Rosie and myself. This, I supposed, was the erotic equivalent of fiddling while Rome burned.

I opened the folder. There were about a dozen large colour photographs of the size standard to newspaper picture desks — almost certainly the product of my own editorial darkroom. I leafed through them. That they were not representations of myself with Rosie I realised at once. It took a little longer, in my dazed condition, to recognise that the naked, barrel-shaped figure stretched out on the diving platform of his own swimming pool was Sam Dice. The plumpish woman attending lasciviously to his needs I mistook for a moment, remembering vague though unsubstantiated rumours, for his housekeeper Mrs Bishop. Then

213

I saw it was Rosie. Dully, I went through the pictures one by one. They had all been taken in broad daylight, presumably on Mrs Bishop's day off, and on the same occasion, forming as they did a familiar sequence from Rosie's extensive repertoire. Each photograph conveyed the impression of having been consciously posed, by Rosie though not by Sam. In the last one she was smiling directly to camera.

I had never seriously examined my feelings about Rosie, and so I was surprised at my deep sense of betrayal. It suddenly seemed clear that she had all along been in complicity with Nick Crabbe, and that hurt. As to what they were in complicity about, I had yet to learn. That would be any moment now. For this one moment I could only grieve over Rosie's duplicity while marvelling at Nick's Machiavellian scheming.

Something about the photographs struck me as I fanned them out on the trestle table, watched in silence by the bananaskinned Nick Crabbe who might, from his nonchalant air, have been showing off his holiday snaps. They had all been taken with a long lens, obviously from the edge of the golf course adjoining Sam's property. They were all so to speak worm's eye view shots, the photographer having been on or very close to the ground, shooting up to the diving platform. I could readily imagine him lying in a bunker to achieve the desired angle. I had never seen the end results of Dennis Reason's voyeuristic prowls but these were definitely not his handiwork.

"So how much did you pay Gavin Pyle for this little lot, cock?"

"Oh, nothing at all, boss," said Nick, quite boastfully. "I happened to come across him in the darkroom one day, developing some tasteful snaps of gentlemen showing all their naughty bits. He's heavily into the gay hard porn scene, did you know that? Plus he thinks he owes you a grudge for firing him. So he was happy to oblige."

The latter motive of the former *Herald* photographer for doing what Nick told him to do left me baffled. "Where does his grudge against me come into it, cock? If he knew he had a grudge against Sam Dice who told me to fire him, I could understand it, but he doesn't. I'm not in any of these pictures and frankly what Rosie Greenleaf gets up to is her own affair."

"I realise all that, boss, but you see I'm hoping you'll see your way to giving me some money for the negatives."

This made even less sense, unless he was looking to me to act as Sam's middleman. Something told me he wasn't, that I myself had been selected as the victim, as surely as we had selected the Devil to roast on Bonfire Night. It was bluff when I said, "You've come to the wrong shop, cock. If you're after blackmailing some-one, go and blackmail Sam Dice. That's if you've got the nerve."

"Yes, I did think of that, boss," said Nick conversationally as between one reasonable man and another. "But I didn't think he would play. He'd almost certainly go to the police."

That was a reasonable prognosis. "So what makes you think I'll play?"

"You haven't got Sam's moral fibre."

That was true enough too, but having had a character analysis from Sherry I was in no mood for additional material by Nick Crabbe. "Leaving my moral fibre aside, if you wanted to black-mail me, cock, wouldn't you have a better chance of success with those pictures you got Dennis Reason to take?"

"That was the original idea, boss, but then he panicked and got rid of them. I would have persuaded Gavin Pyle to take over the assignment but by that time I reckoned you had a pretty fair inkling of what was going on, so it was too risky. But you know the old saying, boss: when one door closes . . . Out of the blue Rosie told me how Sam had slipped from his pedestal and given her one in exchange for a zonking great cheque for her Appeal Fund. So. She didn't take much persuading to go back and do it again out of doors, and from all I gather, neither did Sam. He's a bit of an old rogue on the quiet, our guv'nor."

Sam's roguery was another thing we could leave aside. "So she knew Gavin Pyle was going to take these pictures?"

Crabbe had the nerve to offer an apologetic cough. "Well no, since you ask, boss, she thinks I took them. She mightn't have agreed if she'd known anyone else was involved."

Privately I begged leave to doubt that, but it was neither here nor there. Rosie had deliberately set Sam up for the most incrimi-nating set of pictures I had ever set eyes on. It was unforgivable. She was as bad as Nick Crabbe himself.

But I still didn't understand. "You've yet to tell me why I should stump up a single penny for a dozen pictures of a couple frolicking in the buff, even though one of them is my proprietor. As I say, if you want to sell them, go to him. If I had a taste for porn I could get it cheaper in Soho."

Patiently, as one outlining the rules of a game to a learner, Nick began. "The best way to explain, boss, is to spell out what'll happen if you don't play ball. First off, I take these pix to one of the Sunday tabloids, right? So right, they couldn't use any of them as is, but any good touch-up artist can make them fit for a family newspaper and they'd still be sensational. They'll appear on the same day as the Youth Prayer Rally, or should I say the same day the Youth Prayer Rally would have taken place if Sam hadn't hurriedly cancelled it and left town. He'll be ruined, boss, it's as simple as that. Rosie's got nothing to fear because she's no reputation to lose, but Sam, sanctimonious Sam, would be finished. He'd most likely sell the Herald Group and retire to the Hebrides."

I still could not see the blackmail potential for me personally in all this. Indeed, as I contemplated life without Sam on my back, the threatened prospect even had its attractions. "So what, cock? The worst thing that could happen so far as I'm concerned is that a new owner might bring in his own editor. I've a good track record, and there's a lot of local weeklies in this country."

"None of which would touch you, boss, when you've had your moment of glory at the Old Bailey. You see, if I do have to sell these pictures to one of the Sundays, I've every intention of doing it under your name."

The cocky young bastard imagined he had me over a barrel. I thought quickly.

"Good try, cock, but all it needs is a phone call from me to a handful of picture editors to alert them that an impostor using my name may be contacting them, and they'll either throw you down the stairs or call the police."

"Yes, that could be a bit of a loophole, boss," agreed Nick Crabbe, as if we were having a civilised editorial discussion about one of his madcap stunts like Bananaskin Week. "But you see, I wouldn't go to any paper direct, I'd use one of the picture agencies, only you don't know which agency. And quite frankly, as you must know yourself, boss, once these pix land on an editor's desk he won't give a toss where they originated."

I still wasn't beaten, or such was my fond delusion. "All right, so Sam Dice makes his enquiries and finds that pictures of himself cavorting bollock naked have been sold by someone calling himself Oliver Kettle. At worst, if he won't listen to my side of the story, it's the end of a beautiful friendship – where's the criminal offence?"

"Well, you see, boss, he'll have had one of those Unless You Do As I Say letters telling him to draw a hundred grand out of the bank in notes and await further instructions. Which he'd either ignore or take to the Old Bill."

"Whereupon Oliver Kettle, so-called, goes and flogs the pictures. So where's the cheque? Why isn't it in my bank account?"

"But it will be, boss. I should tell you I've opened an account in your name at one of the Big Four banks in Mayfair – better not say which one. All right, so maybe a handwriting expert might be able to tell the difference between my Oliver Kettle signature and yours, but I don't intend to be here for the law to question. On the other hand, when they start questioning you, you're going to find you're in so much shit you can't row your way out of it even with the proverbial paddle."

This seemed an additional, or supplementary, threat. "In what way?"

"Time enough for that, boss. But what do you think of the story so far? Pretty watertight, I'd say, unless you can see any snags?"

With Nick bending over me in his bananaskin suit, we could have been discussing the last-minute arrangements for the grand opening day parade. I had one more card to play. "There *is* a slight snag I can think of, cock. How much do you say you want for these pictures?"

"Rather a lot of money, boss."

"Ah, well, there I'm afraid I have to disappoint you. I don't have rather a lot of money, cock. I don't even own the roof over my head. Of course," I went on, essaying a joke, "I don't know what's in my Mayfair account."

"Not nearly enough for me, boss. Worry not, though – it's not going to come out of your pocket."

It was all falling into place. The last piece in the jigsaw, one of those bits that are always so obvious once you look at them the right way up and have the surrounding pieces to slot them into.

"So the idea is to milk the Children of the Brazilian Rain Forest fund, is it? What a complete bloody shit you are, Crabbe."

Crabbe ignored the insult. He asked blandly, "What children of the Brazilian rain forest?"

This was too much even from him. There must be some bounds to the bloody ingenuity he had brought to this plot.

"You're not going to say this charity doesn't even exist?"

"Oh, it exists all right, boss – I couldn't have pulled all those colour brochures and bumph out of thin air, now could I? It's quite a small outfit, run by a young couple up in Edinburgh. Steve Selby heard about it when he was doing a gig up there. Someone told him they were running a little merchandising racket in rain forest T-shirts – the punters thought they were flogging them in aid of the charity, whereas it was in aid of the mortgage and the cost of a new sun lounge extension. But ever since they heard we were on to them, they've been keeping their heads down."

"So you and Steve Selby are in this together, are you?" I asked inanely, stating the obvious.

"You could say that, boss. But you do see how you're placed, if you don't feel up to co-operating, don't you? It was you who sold the Bonfire Society on Bananaskin Week. It was you who suggested all proceeds go to the Rain Forest Children. It's all in the minutes. What are the punters going to think when they realise it's a bent charity?"

"What are they going to think when they realise you've disappeared with the cash like an absconding bookie?"

"They're not going to know, boss. Just like you've got an account in Mayfair you didn't know about, the Rain Forest fund has an account in Brazil it doesn't know about. In Rio, where incidentally for future reference we have no extradition treaty. So when it gets around at the end of this week that megahack Nick Crabbe is leaving Badgers Heath to take up an offer he can't refuse, any audit will show that the loot has gone directly from the Bonfire Society account at the Three Counties Bank to the Children of the Brazilian Rain Forest account in a highly-respected bank in Rio, which is exactly where you'd expect to find it. All above board. No problem."

"And just how much are you hoping to get away with?"

Nick Crabbe, perhaps belatedly realising how incongruous he must look in his Bertie Banana outfit in the context of this discussion, or perhaps feeling hot from the exertion of his intense one-to-one fund-raising drive, decided at this point to unzip his plastic bananaskin, which he stepped out of to reveal himself in a Children of the Rain Forest T-shirt, probably commandeered from the wretched couple up in Edinburgh, and clinging lime-green cycle shorts. The transformation was not an improvement. Nor, on the common sense level, was Nick's reply.

"Now we're getting down to the nitty-gritty, boss. I shall be wanting a quarter of a million."

"Don't be ridiculous."

"What's ridiculous about it? We've already got as much as that guaranteed in pledges alone, let alone what we've been raking in in cash. By the end of the week we should be well past the three hundred thousand mark. So any surplus," added Nick Crabbe magnanimously, "you can give to Oxfam, Save the Children, Save the Whale, Save Oliver Kettle, save who you like."

"So I write a cheque for a quarter of a million to the Children of the Brazilian Rain Forest, and you waltz off to Rio de Janeiro with it, is that the plan?"

"Something like that, boss."

I tried a little more bluffing. "But the cheque will require two signatures."

"I happen to know that's no longer necessary."

"Yes, of course, you organised it, didn't you?" I remembered, recalling the manipulative ease with which I had replaced Dennis Reason as Treasurer, and how Reason had persuaded everyone except Miss Bellows, shortly to be replaced herself by Nick Crabbe, that there was no need for a second signature. I grabbed a straw. "But there's one more snag after all, cock. Half those pledges won't be honoured for weeks yet. You can't bank the cheque until there's enough cash in the account to cover it."

"Oh, I see," said Nick as if this point had never occurred to him. "And what you're saying is that the minute I've gone you'll stop the cheque?"

I nodded. I knew he would have an answer for this one too but it was worth a try.

With what was probably meant to be a self-deprecatory smile, although it looked more like a sneer to me, Nick Crabbe went on, "Luckily Dennis Reason is a very accommodating bank manager. He'll see that the cheque is honoured."

Had I really got him this time? "But Dennis Reason isn't coming back. He's being transferred to another branch."

No, I had not. "That fell through, boss. He returns to Badgers Heath this coming weekend. I had a chat with him only the other day."

Poor old Reason, paying the price at last; and probably still believing he was just doing Nick favours. And after clearing a cheque for a cool quarter of a million before a good half of the money pledged was in the bank vaults, he was going to have a tense few weeks of it. Still, that was his headache. I had my own.

Looking back, I still wonder if I could have called Nick Crabbe's bluff. If it had come to something approximate to the worst and I had gone down with the sinking Sam, I would surely have taken Nick down with me; and in the event of any court proceedings there was a sporting chance that I would only be branded a fool while he would be branded an unscrupulous, scheming, blackmailing scoundrel. But I caved in, because it was easier to cave in than not. Sherry would have understood, if not sympathised.

The decision was made the easier by the fact that in the interests of milking another massive squirt of publicity out of Bananaskin Week after it was all over, we had yet to announce where all the money raised was going. Badgers Heath was giving to charity, and as Eric Barlow would have put it, no one really gave a toss which charity it was. Everyone who had given would feel virtuous, and as Nick Crabbe had pointed out there would as likely as not be a surplus for other charities after he had taken his lion's share, so the week would not have been a complete waste of time. And next year a new committee would build on our example and organise an even bigger Bananaskin Week where hundreds of thousands of pounds would be raised for famine relief or flood victims or East European orphans. We were saving the world, weren't we?

I had given Nick custody of the Bonfire Society cheque book to write out cheques for some of the Bananaskin Week bills that had to be paid, courtesy of Rosie and the Farmers' Ladies. He now produced it, and while he stacked the photographs of Sam Dice and Rosie in their folder and locked them back in his private filing cabinet, I scribbled my signature on half a dozen cheques.

Pay Badgers Heath Balloons & Novelty Co four hundred and sixteen pounds 60p.

Pay Nichols & Sons (Scaffolding Hire) Ltd one thousand eight hundred and nine pounds.

Pay Office Supply Centre plc seven hundred and eleven pounds 95p.

Pay Best Deal Joiners & Carpenters Ltd three hundred and fifty one pounds 50p.

Pay Dorothy's Pantry twelve pounds and 45p.

Pay Children of the Brazilian Rain Forest two hundred and fifty thousand pounds only.

Giving a miss to the so-called Grand Parade of floats, of which a twelve-foot beetroot-coloured papier mâché effigy of the Devil complete with horns and pitchfork was the centrepiece, and checking the skies for flying hot air condoms, I set off out of the town centre. I badly needed a large gin and tonic, but not in the Dolphin Arms where I guessed Basil Brush, Len Quartermouth MBE FIAV and Eric Barlow would be assembling.

Behind the Cherrytree Shopping Mall I spotted a taxi decanting four moppets dressed respectively as a banana, an orange, an apple and a pear, who were being shepherded by their minder to a fancy dress competition where they would presumably feature as a joint entry representing a bowl of fruit. I took over the cab and told him to take me to the Harvesters. Since I had put my entire staff on covering Bananaskin Week the office pub should be soothingly empty.

So it was, the only other customer being Harry the pigman,

sinking his morning pint. It was only upon acknowledging his half-witted leer with a curt nod that it belatedly occurred to me, such had been my preoccupations, that I had not seen Rosie at the opening ceremony.

"Where's Mrs Greenleaf today, Harry?" I asked as the landlord served my sticky gin and tonic. From the pigman's reply in his incomprehensible country burr I just managed to extract the words "bed" and "flu". Knocking back my drink I left Harry guzzling the half I had caused to be tipped into his pint glass, and by the skin of my teeth caught the passing Shoppahoppa that would deposit me at the top of Voles Lane.

It was an impulsive visit. I had already written Rosie off, the moment Nick Crabbe had shown me those photographs. But I had been so surprisingly dismayed by what she had done to me that I wanted her to share some of the hurt. And delivering a tongue-lashing would make me feel better.

Rosie answered the door in a towelling bathrobe, under which she sported a pair of her late husband's pyjamas. She was, as she would have put it herself, a sight. Her hair was in rollers and she was dabbing her reddened nose with a bunch of screwed-up Kleenex. There was no danger of my being seductively deflected from my purpose, but Rosie always earned full marks for trying. "Ooh, it's you, pet, ooh, what a surprise, I did ring you at the paper but of course you'll have gone straight to the opening, I'm ever so sorry to have missed it but I was hoping you'd come over afterwards and here you are, ooh, I must look like something the cat's dragged in, why don't you wait downstairs while I slip into something a bit more becoming, ooh, Ollie, you're just what the doctor ordered."

I decided to get straight to the point before the promised transformation scene weakened my resolve. Beckoning her into the living room I said, "There's no need to get dolled up for me, Rosie, I shan't be here for long. I've something to say to you. Nick Crabbe showed me those photographs this morning."

"Which photographs, pet?" It was not bluff: she seemed genuinely to have forgotten. Then she remembered, and looked guilty and confused. "Oh, those photographs. It was only a bit of fun, Ollie, and he swore blind he wouldn't show them to a soul, ooh, just wait till I see him."

I wasn't going to be taken in by this. "How much did he pay you, Rosie?"

"How much did he pay me? Let me see, it was five hundred pounds."

At least she wasn't beating about the bush now. "Then all I can say is he got you cheap. You could have held out for many times that amount."

"Ooh, I don't think so, pet, he's not made of money. Besides, it wouldn't have been fair, seeing as I was enjoying it as much as he was."

"I'm sure you were."

Rosie now began to look concerned. "You don't half sound cross, pet. You don't really mind, do you? I mean to say I did tell you I'd been round to Mr Dice's a couple of times, though naming no names what with wanting to be discreet style of thing, and you said it was quite all right. And if you're worried about the photos, well I suppose I might have gone just that little bit too far, but five hundred pounds is five hundred pounds, when all's said and done."

"And blackmail is blackmail, Rosie."

She gave me an odd sort of look, as if she genuinely didn't understand what I was talking about. It then struck me that possibly she didn't: for a simple soul Rosie was quite a mistress of euphemism, and anyone who could pass off a brothel as a social club for farmers' wives could certainly find an equally innocuous term for blackmail. The word was probably not in her vocabulary. Perhaps Nick Crabbe had persuaded her that it was merely an exercise in inertia salesmanship.

I spelled it out for her. "I'm saying that Nick Crabbe is a blackmailer and that you're his accomplice. He gave you a lousy five hundred quid for that steamy photo session, Rosie. How much did you get for letting Dennis Reason spy on us – thirty pieces of silver?"

We were both facing one another in Rosie's uncut moquette easy chairs. Shaking her head in bewilderment, she buried her face in her hands and as her shoulders began to shake I thought at first she was laughing. Then I saw she was weeping. Mopping the

223

tears with her wad of tissues she sobbed, "How can you say such a thing, Ollie? What do you take me for?"

I said in a hard voice, unmoved, "I've already told you what I take you for."

Again she shook her head, this time in disbelief. "Then you just don't know me, you just don't know me at all. I've never harmed anyone in my life, not purposely. I wouldn't hurt you, I wouldn't hurt Mr Dice, I wouldn't hurt anybody. All right, you can say it was wrong of me to allow those photos to be taken, but you know what I'm like, yes you do, it's the kind of thing I'll do for a laugh or a thrill style of thing, but take money for it? Blackmail? What are you talking about?"

She sounded as if she believed herself. I spelled it out again, this time putting hyphens between the letters. "You say you set up those incriminating pictures but you didn't take money for doing it. What do you call that five hundred pounds? Bus fares?"

Rosie smiled wanly to herself, and another fat tear ran down her cheek, leaving a sooty trail of yesterday's mascara. "You daft pudding!" she said softly. "That five hundred pounds went straight into my Appeal Fund! That's what I did it for!"

She could have been speaking affectionately, but she wasn't. I had never seen Rosie in any but an effervescent mood and it was unnerving to see her so upset.

"I'm sorry, Rosie. Sorry sorry sorry. What a bloody fool I am. I should have known."

Too late. She had got to her feet. I rose too: as I had discovered when Sherry had told me she was going, it can be extraordinarily humiliating to be metaphorically handed one's hat while remaining seated.

"And so you should be sorry sorry sorry, and yes you are a bloody fool, Oliver, and yes you should have known. I know I'm not much but I thought I meant more to you and you knew more about me than to come round making accusations like that."

"What can I say, Rosie?"

"There's no need to bother saying anything. Just go, if you don't mind, and don't ever come back. You can let yourself out — I'm going upstairs for a lie-down."

I missed the Shoppahoppa by seconds and there wouldn't be

another for an hour. It was four miles to the office. Miss Bellows, cycling tight-lipped down towards Voles Bottoms, did not acknowledge my lacklustre wave.

15

By the evening of the Fifth of November, Bananaskin Week had more or less, while still raking in the money, taken a back seat to Badgers Heath's traditional Bonfire Night. There were still a few Bertie Bananas strutting about, but most of the plastic banana-skin outfits had proved not to have staying power and their split remnants were to be found in skips and litter bins. The customary Guy Fawkes masks, wide-brimmed hats and cloaks now pre-dominated. Badgers Heath, however, was still being urged to give until it hurt, for all that the budgetary pain barrier must long ago have been reached. The intermittent splutter and bang of prema-turely-released fireworks punctuated the persistent seismic creak of layer upon shifting layer of coins shifting in their rattling collecting boxes.

As always on this red-letter night the Heath resembled a fair-ground with three great marquees for the Roast Potato Supper, and smaller tents for officials, first aid, the Bananaskin Week Victim Support team, and the sale of beer and soft drinks. Duly-licensed hucksters had set up their hot dog stands, hamburger stalls and traditional franchised toffee-apple carts, while un-authorised hucksters were being moved on by security guards. The great Bonfire, twenty-five feet high and topped by the giant, now firework-stuffed papier mâché effigy of the Devil, awaited combustion within a cordon sanitaire of metal crush barriers. A smaller compound, stacked with a hundred wooden crosses – paraffin-sprinkled deal rather than petrol-soaked balsa wood, on the urgent advice of the fire chief – rather eerily suggested the supply depot for a World War I military cemetery. Far, far across the Heath, over the Flying Club, two searchlights swept the sky like the trademark for Twentieth Century Fox. Later they would converge into the sign of the Cross for the Youth Prayer Rally as the procession of fiery, paraffin-dipped crosses approached over the brow of the Heath.

Nearer to hand, but at a safe distance from the mob converging around the Bonfire, and again protected by metal barriers and patrolled by guard dogs, and with its own attendant fire engine and ambulance, was the huge ammunition dump of rockets, Roman candles, Catherine wheels and suchlike gasp-inducive explosive devices, all awaiting the lighting of the blue touchpaper along with this year's set piece, a gigantic, dancing Bertie Banana animated by fire crackers. The crowds streaming up from the High Street or across the Heath from the tidy suburbs took up their accustomed positions in the straggling queues for refreshments or the Portakabin toilets, or they jostled for the privilege of finding themselves in the prime danger zone when, as would inevitably happen, the crush barriers were finally toppled and those in front were pushed towards the Bonfire flames by those behind. Others positioned themselves on the rough temporary grandstand, admission one pound, that promised the most comfortable view of the fireworks display. With any luck, this would be the one year it did not collapse. Packs of teenagers, a proportion of them at least, it was to be hoped, the audience for Sam Dice's Youth Prayer Rally, roamed the Heath letting off squibs at the feet of unsuspecting girls and generally looking for trouble. Lost children wandering piteously in circles, clutching sparklers that were all but extinguished by their tears, heard their names crackling over the loudspeaker system and cried the more. Overall hung the stench of frying onions.

One of the perks of being members, albeit retiring members as we now all were, of the Standing Committee was that we had our own hospitality tent, exclusive to ourselves, our wives in the case of those of us who still had wives, and the odd guest. Having neglected to fortify myself at the Dolphin Arms en route, I headed for it directly I reached the Heath. As expected, Eric Barlow, Basil Brush and Len Quartermouth MBE FIAV were already propping up the bar together with, less expectedly, Percy Spruce. Basil's, Len's and Percy's womenfolk, following Badgers Heath's standard etiquette for social occasions, were sitting by themselves at a table, sipping lemonade. Rosie Greenleaf was not among those present, which rather saddened me, for like her late husband she liked her fireworks, and it could only be on my account that she had stayed away.

On the other hand it was perhaps as well, for among our guests was Sam Dice, who from remorse or embarrassment or both would surely have had the greatest difficulty in looking Rosie in the eye. Recalling some of the more graphic *tableaux vivants* as captured by Gavin Pyle, I certainly had difficulty in looking my proprietor in the eye. He was talking to Douglas Boxer, who had been endowed with temporary VIP status by virtue of having been prevailed upon by Nick Crabbe to organise the procession of fiery crosses. For myself I should have called this a risky piece of delegation, but apparently it had all been meticulously rehearsed with the one hundred blazer-clad, clean-living young people bussed in by an organisation of Christian enthusiasts known as the Living God Tabernacle, and all Boxer had to do was blow three blasts on a whistle to start off the drill.

As for Nick's own role in the proceedings, he planned to be down at the Flying Club to greet his fellow-conspirator Steve Selby the alternative wheelchair comedian. It puzzled me somewhat that they continued to go through the charade of Bananaskin Week now that Nick Crabbe had got his hands on his bumper cheque, but I reasoned that had the chief organiser decamped earlier in the week it would have raised the same kind of questions as sometimes arose in our surrounding villages when slate club treasurers went AWOL just before the scheduled Christmas Club payout.

I thought I had better do my duty by Sam before joining Eric Barlow and the others. I had had it from his chauffeur waiting outside the tent that he was not staying for the Bonfire but proposed taking himself off to the Flying Club concert hangar for a quiet lie-down in his dressing room to prepare himself for the Youth Prayer Rally. Doubtless he would be receiving his late mother, together with St Urban who, as he was reminding Douglas Boxer as I approached, shared with my deputy the credit for the evening. I hoped Boxer realised that if he made a cock-up of that fiery cross procession, he would not be able to devolve the blame on St Urban or even on Nick Crabbe whose bright idea it had been in the first place.

"I'm just saying to Douglas," said Sam, having exchanged greetings, "I found myself in a marble hall last night. 'I dreamt that I dwelt in marble halls' – d'you know that song, Oliver? Only this wasn't a dream, it was more of a vision."

I tried to exchange a covertly sardonic glance with Boxer, but he was too busy preening himself. His hour had come.

"And in that vision I was privileged to have words with our old friend St Urban, who sends all his best regards and blessings," continued Sam. "He said he had every confidence that the Youth Prayer Rally tonight would be a turning point for this town. A turning point, that's what he said, Oliver and Douglas. Well, wish me luck, laddies." With this Sam put down his glass of the Malvern water I had got in specially, and picked up his hat. As I delivered him up to his chauffeur, so he delivered what I took to be his parting shot. "Mother was there too, by the way, in this marble hall I've been telling you about. She wants to know when you're going to do something about the crossword."

But it was not his parting shot after all. Over-riding my diplomatic, all-embracing explanation that some people would always find the crossword too easy while others found it too difficult, Sam went on: "But going back to St Urban, he did give me a friendly word of warning. Watch out for satanic forces. Now what d'you suppose he meant by that? No, don't interrupt me, laddie, I'll tell you what he meant by that. He meant that where you find the force of the Lord you'll also find the force of evil, pulling against it, as I've reminded you more than once. I notice none of my editors have dug anything up on satanic rites, despite the tip-off I gave you all down in Worthing."

"We're working on it, Sam." I had given the non-story to Douglas Boxer as his last assignment before reinstating him as deputy editor. He had, unsurprisingly, turned up nothing.

Having said goodnight to Sam, I really had no option but to rejoin Boxer, who was now standing forlornly by himself, twiddling an empty glass, and steer him over to my Dolphin Arms drinking companions at the bar. He was a touch awkward in company but I reckoned he might hit it off with Percy Spruce.

Eric Barlow, who I reckoned must have spent the best part of the day in the Goat and Compasses, affably called for a round, tried to pay for it, and then remembered that we were the guests of the Bonfire Society. "As but once a year we are entitled to be, considering the hard work we have put into ah," intoned our retiring Chair as we drank a toast to the retrospective success of Bananaskin Week and the prospective success of Bonfire Night and its recent addendum, the Youth Prayer Rally.

"And at the Roast Potato Supper later, we mustn't forget a toast to our absent friends," said Basil. "Mrs Greenleaf is still down with flu, I'm afraid, and Miss Bellows I don't suppose will be with us, and – "

"Miss Bellows is wandering around outside," volunteered Douglas Boxer with a meaningful look embracing the whole company. "She said she wouldn't come into the hospitality tent but would pray for you all at the Youth Prayer Rally."

"Strange lady," mused the Rev Basil Thrush, who was as suspicious as any agnostic of parishioners praying off their own bat. "And then another absentee of course is poor Dennis Reason – "

"Poor Dennis Reason is back," put in Eric Barlow. "I saw him opening up the bank this morning, Sunday of all days. Must have been putting back the cash he scarpered with."

Or juggling a certain account around in readiness to process a cheque for a quarter of a million pounds that could not yet be met from its resources. "How odd," said Basil. "I'd no idea. How is his mother?"

"She wasn't with him," said Barlow owlishly. "I expect she was having a lie in."

Our absent friends accounted for, Percy Spruce confirmed my impression that he and Douglas Boxer were kindred spirits by turning to him and saying, with a sigh of foreboding, "Well, I hope your proprietor knows what he's doing tonight, Mr Boxer."

This would in normal circumstances have been Boxer's own line, but since the Youth Prayer Rally was his baby and Sam was his employer, pride and loyalty prevailed. But the frosty reply "He usually does, Mr Spruce," accompanied by a bleak smile, was the best he could manage in Sam's defence.

"I'm not thinking so much of the Youth Prayer Rally as such," said Percy, "as this procession of blazing crosses that's to start it off. Has it been properly thought through, I wonder? I can see many pitfalls."

"Did he say pitfalls or pratfalls?" slurred Eric Barlow, whose wit was deserting him in tandem with his wits.

"Now Percy," I said firmly. "It's all been properly organised. They're not going to set themselves on fire, they're not going to set anyone else or anything else on fire, and they're not going to set the Heath on fire. No one is going to go up in flames. Everything's taken care of."

"Except certain elements," insisted Percy Spruce darkly.

"You mean rain?" queried Len Quartermouth MBE FIAV, misunderstanding. "But surely the weather forecast was most ah."

"I mean outside elements. Troublemakers."

"What troublemakers?" I asked sceptically. We had had a gratifyingly trouble-free week so far.

"Well," said Percy, who under cross-examination seemed to be wavering somewhat. "It *is* a highly emotive religious occasion, and one *does* hear of – well, I can only say *elements*, hotly opposed to Christian rigmarole as they themselves would have it."

"We've discussed this, haven't we, Percy?" interjected Basil helpfully, and I thought a mite sheepishly. "While we must always be on our guard, I'm bound to say there's no evidence that these young tearaways are in any way an organised force for evil."

"What young tearaways?" I asked sharply.

"Satan's Soldiers," said Douglas Boxer with authority. "It's just one of these youth cults, like the old mods and rockers."

I was not up on youth cults. Boxer was supposed to be my youth expert. But I stiffened, as would any of Sam Dice's editors, at the very mention of Satan. "Who are Satan's Soldiers when they're at home, cock? They're not into devil worship and all that, are they?"

"Oh, nothing like that, Oliver – they just roar around on

231

motorbikes. Mark you," said Boxer, "they were credited with vandalising a graveyard in Brighton two or three weeks ago."

"Vandalising a graveyard? Fuck me, cock!" I exploded, quite forgetting the Rev Basil Brush's presence. "Why wasn't I told about this?"

"Not in our circulation area," said Boxer with wooden complacency.

What promised to be a fertile discussion about Boxer's career prospects — mine too, if this story ever reached Sam's ears — was curtailed by the whine and then the distant exploding thud of a powerful rocket, the signal that the bonfire celebration was about to commence. We trooped out of the refreshment tent, Eric Barlow still clutching his glass.

It was as orderly a Fifth of November as I could remember. Half a dozen stewards, dressed for no good historical reason as nineteenth-century Peelers, lit the Bonfire with burning brands plucked from a brazier. The crowds, good-humoured and well-behaved, dutifully oohed and aahed as the fire began to crackle through the mighty pyre of tree branches and demolition site lumber and the first salvoes of starburst shells from the fireworks display point turned the sky red, then white, then blue. Toddlers were hoisted on shoulders to watch the flames lapping up towards the feet of the giant papier mâché Devil, secured to the very pinnacle of the Bonfire like a grotesque fairy on a blazing Christmas tree. If the technological incendiaries from the Polytechnic Faculty of Science who each year construct the Bonfire were accurate in their calculations, it would be a good hour before we saw the Devil consumed in his own flames, since he was granted temporary protection by a ring of kindling around his feet which had been soaked in water. This brief reprieve provided us with ample time to watch the fireworks for a while, amble into one of the marquees to partake of the Roast Potato Supper, then pour out on to the Heath again to see the Devil go up in a welter of fire crackers. The disposal of the Victim would bring us to the fireworks display's Bertie Banana grand set piece finale, followed by a farewell salute of ninety rockets, one for each year of the Bonfire Society's existence.

The fireworks were well up to standard and I watched them for a good five minutes before re-joining Eric Barlow back in the hospitality tent. By the time we had drained the gin and whisky bottles respectively, the crowds were drifting into the marquees for their Roast Potato Supper. Two of the marquees were self-service affairs for the riff-raff, the third was reserved for the five hundred members of the Bonfire Society – those who pay an annual subscription and take on some of the chores – plus the committee and a smattering of civic dignitaries. The food was the same, though. Actually the Roast Potato Supper is a bit of a misnomer. The tradition goes back to the early days when the townsfolk would bring their own potatoes and roast them over the Bonfire; then we got more organised and more commercial, until what we had now was effectively a fast food franchise, and what you got was a baked potato with a choice of filling. You could have a baked potato with cottage cheese, a baked potato with chilli, a baked potato with tuna and sweetcorn, or a baked potato with prawn cocktail, none of which I cared for. But there was beer. Putting my arm around Barlow's swaying shoulders, I steered him into the Bonfire Society marquee.

The fare may have been simple but the place was laid out like a banqueting hall, with five long banks of trestle tables covered with white cloths, and a top table featuring the usual gang. I left Barlow slumped in the end seat, where he promptly knocked over a jug of beer, and took my place between Mrs Basil Brush and Mrs Len Quartermouth.

I had no sooner sat down than I was seized with a desire to get up again and remove myself from the marquee. The mesdames Thrush and Quartermouth were not the easiest of conversationalists, and my having got through the best part of a bottle of gin did not make the going any better. The very sight of a great bowl of baked potatoes stuffed with congealing chilli made me feel ill. I took a gulp of beer and that made me feel worse. Looking up the table in search of a carafe of water, my eye fell on Len Quartermouth MBE FIAV, who was shuffling a pile of notes. I had my excuse. Len's habit was to give the same old speech of thanks year after year to all those to whom ah and all those without ah, and the *Herald* never bothered to report it. On this occasion, with the entire committee resigning, I suddenly realised that there would be a good deal more speechifying than usual and that I should have to print at least a representative selection of platitudes. But I had no reporter present. On the not altogether bogus pretext of going to find one, I mumbled my apologies to the ladies and staggered off towards the fresh air. Eric Barlow was asleep with his head on the table, to the disgust of Mrs Spruce sitting next to him, and I wondered momentarily whether to arouse him and get him out too. I was to wish dearly that I had.

Out on the Heath, the crowds had thinned considerably, a good wedge of the spectators having deployed themselves to the marquees. Those whose tastes, or pockets, did not run to the notoriously pricey Roast Potato Supper, mainly teenagers, queued for hamburgers and hot dogs, or meandered about the Heath, chomping. The Bonfire crackled merrily, with steam from the dampened section now billowing up to the Devil's waistline and giving him the appearance of a pantomime demon king springing out of a trapdoor in a puff of smoke. In the Bonfire's glow, a few families were contentedly picnicking out of paper bags.

Although I had my entire staff covering the event, I couldn't see any of my reporters anywhere. They were probably all eating. In any case, it was already too late. From within the Bonfire Society marquee I heard the sharp rap of our outgoing chairperson's gavel, followed by the introductory ums and ahs of Len Quartermouth MBE FIAV. I would have re-drafted Douglas Boxer to reporting duties but he was eating with the clean-limbed young cross-bearers of the Living God Tabernacle, who had their own tent. There was nothing for it: I would have to cover the damned speeches myself. Fortunately I was feeling better.

As, with a last gulp of raw night air, I made my way back across to the Bonfire Society marquee, I stopped and listened as I caught a distant humming sound which, fast coming closer, was already obliterating the dronings of Len Quartermouth MBE FIAV. The noise was coming from far down the High Street, but approaching the Heath. In a moment it had swelled to the sound of a thousand-bomber air raid. Then I saw the bank of headlights, as piercing as the criss-crossing searchlights over the Flying Club. Then I saw the motorbikes, heavy and shiny, bumping like tanks across the Heath towards the Bonfire.

There were a good hundred of them, manned by just the kind of youths and not-so-youthful young men you would expect to see churning up a public open space with that type of machinery. Dismounting and kicking their bikes on to their stands in a twenty-deep, five-wide column like an army convoy, they began to advance with that arrogant yet sheepish swagger of the archetypal English yob. I had no difficulty in recognising them as Douglas Boxer's Satan's Soldiers, for such was the emblem stamped on their identical T-shirts, over which they wore identical black bomber jackets stencilled with the words BRIGHTON CHAPTER. To complete the uniform they sported identical black crash helmets, of approved standard design except that they were embellished with what appeared to be Viking horns.

There were few policemen or security guards about: the great majority of them, like my reporters, were taking the opportunity of the Roast Potato Supper lull to have their own refreshment break. Those who were in evidence elaborately posted themselves in strategic positions in case of trouble, but none of them directly approached the interlopers, of whom it had to be said that apart from their very presence being offensive and threatening, the only damage they had so far perpetrated was to leave a few tyre-ruts in Council grassland.

The atmosphere of menace they had introduced to the environs of the Bonfire was in any case considerably evaporated by the sight of about two dozen of their number meekly queuing for the lavatories in a more or less orderly manner. Others, no doubt feeling peckish after their long drive, got in line for junk food and fizzy drinks, and one, who had disappeared into the shadows in a sinister manner, returned eating candy floss. The tension relaxed. The policemen and security guards, while still keeping a sharp eye open, began to wander about again.

Their numbers thus largely dispersed on one harmless diversion or another, a remaining hard core of about twelve Satan's Soldiers swaggered nearer to the Bonfire, defying anyone in their path to obstruct their progress but otherwise still not doing anything the so far outnumbered police presence might care to apprehend them for. They were an ugly bunch, faces round and shiny from too much lager and too much greasy food, fingers tattooed with HATE on the right hand and HATE on the left – a variation on the now conventional HATE and LOVE – and adorned with knuckledusters. The heads of those who had removed their helmets were uniformly bald, but probably not from the same motives as had moved much of the youth of Badgers Heath to suffer sponsored head-shaving for Bananaskin Week.

Still they offered no direct aggression. The one I took to be their leader, being heavier, older and considerably more stupid-looking than the others, was staring fixedly up at the papier mâché effigy of the Devil who was still basking in a cloud of steam atop the Bonfire. His companions clustered around him, following suit. Since all of them were rhythmically chewing gum, the effect was reminiscent of cows looking over a wall to watch the trains go by.

Finally the leader gave voice: *"The fucker's gonna catch fire in a fuckin minute, gerra fuckin pole!"* But the question seemed rhetorical. There were in any case no poles to hand, and no one made a move to find one. One of the picnickers sitting near the Bonfire, a middle-aged accountant-looking type with his pursed-lipped wife and two scared children, unwisely made so bold as to protest, "Language, do you mind?" The only response, from one of the leader's acolytes, was an indifferent "Piss off," followed by a belch. The incident was closed. A policeman who had drawn near to cock an ear to these exchanges wandered off again.

As so often with riots, a small thing sparked it off. In this case the small thing was the slight, forlorn-looking figure of Miss Bellows, whom I had observed once or twice ambling aimlessly about the Heath by herself. She was wearing, over her usual severe attire, a transparent plastic raincoat of the type sold by opportunistic street traders during sudden showers, complemented by a transparent plastic pixie hood and an umbrella with a handle carved in the shape of a cat's head.

Completely ignoring, indeed seemingly unaware of, the Brighton Chapter of Satan's Soldiers, Miss Bellows had taken it into her head to pace out the perimeter of the Bonfire. As she drew near, the leader of the pack sniggered something to one of his henchmen.

"Wossat, Codger?" enquired another.

The one addressed as Codger sniggered again and repeated, louder this time: *"Looker this – fuckin walkin french letter!"*

Miss Bellows, who was now abreast of the group, stopped in front of Codger, raised her cat's-head umbrella, struck him smartly over the head with it, and went on her way with great dignity. Since he was not one of those who had removed their helmets, the blow could have done him no harm, but it gave great satisfaction to the accountant type, who commented loudly to his wife, "That just serves him right!" This was the trigger.

The Satan's Soldier who had invited Codger to repeat his sally lumbered over to the picnicking family, who were sitting around a blanket on which their food was laid out. Taking careful aim, he kicked a plate of sausage rolls high into the air. With a cry of "All right, that's quite enough of that!", the accountant type tried bravely if rashly to scramble to his feet, only to be pushed in the face and sent sprawling into the family picnic. The nearby policeman ran to the scene and was deftly head-butted. A security guard dashing to his rescue, baton raised, was intercepted by one of Codger's team and kicked to the ground.

Within seconds, the action had escalated to a point where it was taking place on several fronts at once. The substantial body of Satan's Soldiers who had been about their comparatively lawful business came charging towards the Bonfire as if summoned by corporate sub-intelligence. Stray local teenagers clutching hot dogs and hamburgers, already resentful of the invasion, now joined in the fray, tripping up and putting the boot in, or having the boot put in by, any Satan's Soldiers within battling range. Egged on by Codger, the original squad of acolytes were meanwhile tearing down the crush barriers and hurling them into the Bonfire. My impression that Codger's instruction to *gerra fuckin' pole* was rhetorical now proved mistaken, as half a dozen of the Brighton Chapter's burliest appeared brandishing scaffolding poles from the temporary grandstand overlooking the fireworks display. Swinging them around their heads like cabers, they flung them at the figure of the Devil surmounting the Bonfire. Even as the Devil toppled down into the flames, discharging fire crackers in all directions to the consternation of parents fleeing with their screaming children, hordes of policemen poured out of their refreshment tent and were at once locked in battle. As two of them grappled with Codger, Miss Bellows came to their assistance with her cat's-head umbrella. Unfortunately misjudging her aim, she knocked off first one policeman's helmet and then the other. One of the Satan's Soldiers, coming to Codger's rescue with an iron bar he seemed to have about his person, felled both officers with a single blow apiece.

Attracted by the commotion, people were by now streaming out of the marquees and beer tents, with some of the younger element, emboldened by drink, deciding as they observed the confusion that now would be as good a time as any to start overturning hamburger stands and hot-dog carts. I spotted none of my fellow committee members among the mass of Bonfire Society members crowding out of our marquee, and would not have been surprised to learn that Len Quartermouth MBE FIAV was still plodding through his speech. Over the shouts and screams and the machine-gun rattle of the papier mâché Devil's fire crackers could be heard the ululating wail of sirens as every police car and ambulance in Badgers Heath hurtled to the scene.

With the affray now in full swing, Douglas Boxer, his recently-awakened reporter's instinct alerted, had stepped out of the Living God Tabernacle refreshment tent to see what all the fuss was about. Dabbing his lips with a paper napkin he took in what he could of the violent passing show and then, for reasons at that moment beyond my comprehension but which retrospectively I see may have marked the commencement of a half-baked plan to march his little army of blue-blazered cross-bearers to safety, he blew three blasts on his whistle.

If such was his motive, then he reckoned without the iron discipline of the Living God Tabernacle. The signal indicated to the clean-limbed ones that the moment had come to dunk their wooden crosses in the Bonfire and then carry them like standards in torchlit procession to the Youth Prayer Rally. That was what they had rehearsed and that was what they were now pro-grammed to do, regardless of distraction. Flanked by stewards or minders in tracksuits they came filing out of their refreshment

238

tent at the double, like an Olympic team into the stadium. Ignoring the fact that most of the youth of Badgers Heath who were scheduled to follow them to the Flying Club concert hangar were now fighting, helping themselves to hamburgers and cans of drink, throwing missiles or being rounded up by the police, they sprinted in single file around the perimeter of the mêlée.

As the Living God Tabernacle sacrificial lambs trotted past me in the glow of the far side of the Bonfire where I had prudently removed myself to comparative safety, I observed on each and every face the bright hypnotic stare and the fixed seraphic smile of the born-again Christian. They were like automatons. Perhaps the police should have stopped them but the only police presence this side of the Bonfire was a bearded inspector, who, from his staring eyes, seemed himself to have been born again.

Like cattle to the slaughter, they were checked one by one by their stewards into the compound where their wooden crosses were stacked. Proceeding through the compound into what would have been the sealed-off Bonfire area had not our Brighton visitors dismantled the safety barriers, they plunged their crosses into the flames and then, zombie-like, fiery crosses raised, cantered obediently into the arms of Satan's Soldiers. A cry from Codger of *"Looka these fuckers! Gerrem!"* and the war between good and evil commenced.

I did not stay to see which force would triumph. Blazing crosses were being systematically impounded by Codger's troops and hurled like javelins into the crowd. The Living God Tabernacle side were valiantly fighting back, but with their bare fists, almost Queensbury rules style. The Christian soldiers approach seemed to puzzle the opposing side, each of whom was armed with some handy weapon such as a studded belt or makeshift cudgel. Douglas Boxer was an early victim, felled by a scaffolding pole. As the gallant blazered army went down like dominoes and police cars began to screech across the Heath, I decided to follow the general tendency of the crowd and depart.

I edged away from the Bonfire, avoiding eye contact with anyone who might be spoiling for a fight. A fiery cross described a flying arc above my head and landed on the Bonfire Society marquee. The marquee was fireproofed but the guy ropes were not. One section of the marquee sagged as a set of guy ropes were burned through. Another section caved inwards as a stray youth, inspired by what he had just observed, sawed at other guy ropes with a Stanley knife. Other youths, at a loose end now that Satan's Soldiers seemed to be engaged in an exclusive war with the Living God Tabernacle, adopted a guy rope each and cut away assiduously, one of them hindered by Miss Bellows who was belabouring him with her umbrella. As the huge marquee billowed in on itself like a gigantic collapsing soufflé and I walked away, the last detail that registered in my smoke-reddened eyes was the sight of Miss Bellows being frogmarched into a police van.

16

Badgers Heath is not Dartmoor and I would not have thought it
possible to get lost on it, but I managed it. With most of a bottle
of gin inside me I had thought it best not to drive to the Flying
Club. I had been told that it was only half an hour's walk across
the Heath and I had the crossed searchlights to guide me like the
star of the east, and so I set off to follow the route that would
have been followed by the torchlight procession, had the torchlight procession not been helping the police with their enquiries. I
had thought of ducking out of the responsibility altogether, confining myself to a telephone call to the concert hangar to inform
Sam that in all the circumstances he had better start his Youth
Prayer Rally without us; but if I did not face the music now I
would have to face it tomorrow, and I should most likely want to
keep tomorrow free to look for another job. Probably it would
count in my favour if I started by congratulating Sam on St Urban
having got it absolutely right about satanic forces.

I am no walker but it was a pretty easy trek to the brow of the
Heath, although a bit of a climb. A clear path had been trodden
through the gorse by generations of hikers and there was no
danger of taking a wrong turning. The brow reached, however,
set a problem. Here, having risen a couple of hundred feet or so
to form a modest promontory, the Heath dips sharply to dissi-
pate itself in the back gardens of the avenues of semis and
bungalows below. While I could now see the lighted runway of
the Flying Club beyond the playing fields at the edge of this
residential suburb, and while I still had the searchlights as my
beacon, I would have to choose between half a dozen straggling
paths that led down to different parts of the housing development

below. Furthermore, without the lights of the town centre behind me, augmented by the Bonfire and the headlights of dozens of police cars, ambulances and fire engines, the slope down to the playing fields was pretty dark.

I cast one last look back. The Bonfire was still blazing away, though very probably by now without an audience, since the tendency of the Badgers Heath police when confronted with trouble is to seal off the area with tape for days on end. Surprisingly, a crescent moon was glowing brightly over the far edge of the Heath – surprisingly, that was, in that there was already a crescent moon ahead of me. Then I realised, as the supplementary moon shimmered and danced, that it was in fact an outsize Bertie Banana, the finale set piece of the fireworks display, computer-programmed to light up at this moment come rain or riot. As the dancing, fire-cracker-spurting banana fizzled out, and rocket fire began to fill the sky, I chose the footpath that seemed likeliest to lead down to my destination and, to the sound of distant ricochets, began my descent.

It was not so much that I had chosen the wrong route as that the path simply fizzled out half way down, leaving me to flounder through the darkness as best I could. With the gorse scratching my hands and attacking my ankles and snagging my clothes, and with sodden feet – for I had at some point trodden in a rain puddle that had accumulated in a small hollow – I could only follow the contour of the slope as it led me down, farther and farther from where I wanted to go, to the back gardens of a suburban street.

Leaning against the back fence of a semi-detached house where a light burned in an uncurtained bedroom window, and praying that I would not be mistaken for Dennis Reason who for all I knew had prowled this area, I took stock. By following the gardens round I should eventually arrive at the playing fields and thus at the Flying Club; on the other hand it was muddy down here from rainwater trickling down the hillside, and I could very well be walking into a bog. Far simpler to cut through one of these back gardens to a solid pavement and then, setting my course by the crossed searchlights, head for base.

I chose a house that was in complete darkness and which had

an acceptably shinnable fence, and in a few moments, shaken somewhat by the barking of a dog next door and the possibility that its owner would come out to investigate, was walking down the garden path to the street.

I was, the street sign said, in Heathview Gardens. The search-lights were due east and all I had to do was keep on walking. What the street sign did not reveal was that Heathview Gardens was a cul-de-sac. I turned back and retraced my steps until, a little way past the garden gate from which I had started, I came upon a street junction. I turned right into Heathview Way.

Heathview Way was only a short street and so it did not take me long to discover that this too was a dead end. Again I retraced my steps and continued along Heathview Gardens to Heathview Rise. Having established that Heathview Rise was another dead end I went on to add Heathview Crescent, Heathview Close and Heathview Walk to my collection of non-starters. Finally Heathview Gardens led me to a grassy roundabout which gave me the option of turning left into Heathview Approach, right into Beauregard Avenue, or continuing along Heathview Gardens. Since Heathview Approach could only lead back to the Heath itself, and since anyway I had lost faith in the whole Heathview series, I plumped for Beauregard Avenue, for all that owing to the curvature of the road it would lead me farther away from the searchlight cross in the sky than ever. All I wanted was to get out of this introspective estate of cul-de-sacs and take my bearings from there.

Beauregard Avenue was a very long thoroughfare, but at least the longer it was the less likely was it that it would fizzle out in a privet hedge. I trudged on for about half a mile, and then I had my first and only stroke of luck of the evening. Ahead of me was a shopping parade, and in the parking bay adjoining it was a double-decker bus.

As well as not being a big walker I am not a big runner either, but I broke into a shambling trot and made the bus just as the driver climbed into his cab and the conductor extinguished his cigarette before pressing the bell. I was prepared to board it whatever its destination, but it proved to be going past the side of the Flying Club en route for the Merrydale housing estate.

A few minutes later, having shown my press pass to the security man on the side gate, I was walking – limping, rather, since it had been a hard slog – across the deserted airstrip towards the concert hangar. Although the runway is lit for emergencies, there is no night flying at Badgers Heath; all the light aircraft were in their hangars and the only other airworthy vessel was the great bulbous Aids Action condom, swaying and creaking on its guy-ropes. Beyond it were the two dazzling searchlights, their beams locked in a St Andrew's cross.

I had wasted a lot of time and it was long past the hour when Sam's Youth Prayer Rally had been scheduled to begin. I hoped he would have got something of an audience from such of the faithful as had elected to come straight to the concert hangar instead of making the pilgrimage across the Heath. I would creep in and stand at the back, and explain everything later. But first, I suddenly realised as I reached the other side of the airstrip, I urgently needed to answer a call of nature. My exertions had sobered me up but they had done nothing for the state of my bladder. I could not possibly hold out until I reached the concert hangar, even though it was but five minutes' walk, or a two-minute dash, away. There was another hangar alongside it. I headed for the privacy of its huge corrugated-iron flank.

I all but stumbled against the abandoned wheelchair. It was parked in shadow just by the short flight of steps that led up to a doorway in the side of the hangar. Subliminally recognising that wheelchairs for the use of invalid passengers were a standard feature of airports, I did not even pause to wonder what it was doing there, much less register it as the probable property of Steve Selby, the alternative wheelchair comedian; my first priority was to relieve myself. It was not until I was in luxuriant full flood that I noticed that the door above the wheelchair was ajar and that from it could be heard raised voices, those of Nick Crabbe and Steve Selby.

"Look, I'm not going to argue with you, Steve," Nick was saying. "We have a deal, we've had it from the start, and I want that sodding money."

"I keep telling you I don't have it right at this moment, OK?" Steve Selby was saying.

"You said you'd bring it with you."

"Fifty grand doesn't grow on trees, Nick. I'll get the money for you. That's a promise."

I zipped up and tiptoed up the steps. Through the slightly opened doorway I could see Nick and Steve facing each other on a concrete platform overlooking the hangar. Steve Selby was pacing up and down in an agitated manner, and it was plain that he could walk as well as I could; indeed, in my present footsore condition, better.

"It was a promise that you'd have it with you tonight," said Nick. "I'm on to you, Steve. You're not moving out of my sight until I've got that money."

"Or else what?"

"Or you won't know what's hit you, matey."

Common sense told me I should have stayed where I was and gone on listening, but histrionics got the better of me. Flinging open the door and addressing Steve Selby I said, "Fuck me, cock, don't tell me he's blackmailing you too!"

Nick whipped round in astonishment, but he was no more astonished than I was, at Steve Selby's reaction. Raising a hand-gun, which I now saw he must have been brandishing all along, he pointed it at me with the words, "What the hell's he doing here, Nick?"

I know nothing whatever about guns. I assumed that what he was holding would be an automatic. Why it was called an automatic I had no idea, except that it had a reputation for automatically shooting people. Perhaps I was less sober than I imagined, for within seconds I had lurched forward, grabbed the gun from Steve Selby's hand, and was now pointing it at him. The surprise element must have played a considerable part in this uncharacteristic coup.

He was a tall man, taller even than I had judged him to be when I had first seen him on the stage of the concert hangar next door, and he could easily have overpowered me, all the easier since having acquired the gun I had no further plans for it except possibly to hit him over the head with it if he tried to get it back. Instead Steve Selby, closely followed by Nick Crabbe, made a dive past me to the doorway, took the steps in one leap, and dashed off across the airfield.

I followed. Steve Selby leading, the pair of them were heading towards the hot air balloon condom about two or three hundred yards across the airstrip. I did a stupid, impetuous thing. I raised the gun and fired blindly, twice, only in the hope of scaring them – scaring them into what, I had not the first idea. Nick Crabbe staggered a few yards and then fell. Steve Selby kept on running. The security guards, I would have to hope, would think the shots were fireworks going off.

I ran forward and found Nick lying on his back in long grass, gripping his right leg and moaning. There was enough light from the runway to see that I had winged him in the fleshy part of his calf. He was pulling up his trouser leg and it was evident that it was only a superficial wound but that he was bleeding copiously. I know even less about first aid than I know about guns but I did know that the thing to do was to get a tourniquet round his leg and then find a doctor.

"You stupid pillock, boss," Nick groaned as I knelt over him. "You've got it arse-end about – I wasn't blackmailing him, he was blackmailing me!"

"Don't talk," I said curtly, tearing off my tie.

"Why the hell not?"

This was an extremely good question. I simply could not say why not. All I knew was that it was what doctors and priests always said to gangster victims in the old black and white movies I watched on my video machine.

"All right, go ahead if it makes you feel better," I said. Besides, I was intrigued to know what he had to tell me. I started to wind my tie tightly around his leg just above the knee. I hoped it was approximately the right place.

Nick was coughing and wheezing a bit from the pain but otherwise he was articulate enough. "Steve Selby and I were showbiz writers together in Fleet Street before I got my gossip column, right? As you've just seen, he's as fit as I am."

"Fitter," I said drily.

"He started doing gigs himself but he wasn't getting anywhere until he hit on this wheelchair comedian gimmick. I gave him some big write-ups and he began to take off, right?"

Perhaps conversation took his mind off the pain. "Bit risky for a hack, going along with a fraud," I said, pulling tight on the tourniquet. It seemed to be doing the trick: the blood was no longer spurting out as from a pump, but had reduced itself to a steady if still abundant oozing.

"I didn't have any option, boss. You see, in my showbiz days I ran a concert club for the paper – you know the kind of thing, discount tickets for the fans and all that jazz. So natch, I was milking it rotten."

"Natch. And Steve Selby twigged."

"Right."

"You should have told him to get stuffed, cock. You would only have been fired, as I seem to recall you were from your last paper."

"Not this time, boss. We're talking about tens of thousands over three years. It would have been a prison job."

The bleeding had almost stopped. I got Nick to put his finger on the knot while I tied it as tight as I could. He winced as he did so and went into another coughing fit.

"Look, I honestly do think you should stop talking now," I said. "But tell me one thing first. Was Bananaskin Week his idea or yours?"

"His. Like I said, he was holding the concert club fiddle over my head. I had to set the whole thing up and my take would be fifty grand. Now he's got away with a quarter of a million. You shot the wrong man, boss."

"Not necessarily," I said cruelly. "All right, now we've got to get you to a doctor. Do you think you can hobble to the concert hangar if I give you my arm?"

"I doubt it, boss. I've got a hell of a pain in my right shoulder."

"You don't walk with your shoulder, cock."

Nick winced again, then raised his head and fixed me with a look of almost comic disbelief. "Jesus Christ, boss, this is crazy! I'm bloody dying!"

He was, too. I put my hand under his head to support it and it was sticky with blood. I had shot him not only in the leg but in the neck. Cold eyes staring up at me, his head lolled away from my hand and he was still. Something else I had seen the doctors and priests do in those late-night movies was to put their face to the victim's chest to check if he was still breathing. I didn't need to do that: you can tell a person is dead by the fact that he is dead. I couldn't bring myself to close his eyes with my bloody fingers. I stood up. Across the airstrip, momentarily transfixed in the cross-beam of the twin searchlights, the giant condom swayed and hovered and then floated off into the night. Before it passed into the darkness, I thought I saw a figure waving from its passenger basket, but that could have been a trick of the light.

I supposed I had better get the police. I had good contacts among the top brass, Rosie's chief superintendent among them, and they would understand that it was an unfortunate accident. Steve Selby's gun was somewhere in the long grass for them to find. What they would make of the former alternative wheelchair comedian making off in a flying condom that was not his property was not for me to say. It was probably an offence, like taking and driving away a car.

I made my way across to the concert hangar and entered through one of the side doors. The place had an empty feel although I could hear Sam Dice's voice, distorted like the public address messages you hear on railway stations, echoing through the vast hangar. Wandering along a bleak brick corridor I found a men's room where I washed the blood off my hands as best I could when there was only a trickle of cold water and no soap. I looked at myself in the mirror and I looked ghastly. My shoes were caked with mud and my clothes were filthy. I didn't want to find myself in the interview room at Badgers Heath Central in this state, and anyway I remembered now that I had no change for the telephone, since once again it had all passed into the hands of our indefatigable Bananaskin Week collectors, with the exception of my last fifty pence piece which had gone on the bus fare. I decided to wait until I had got home and had a bath and changed before calling the police. The *Herald* plant was not all that far away and I could borrow an office car. Nick wouldn't mind the wait.

It would also not be a good idea to face Sam Dice in this dishevelled condition, either. In fact there was some doubt in my mind as to whether it would be a good idea to face Sam Dice ever again. I would have to think about that.

Woozy and in a state of shock, I came out into the brick corridor again and made tracks, as I imagined, for the exit door. Instead I found, as Sam's echoing voice got louder, that I was heading for the auditorium. Perhaps I could circumvent it. But like Heathview Gardens and its tributaries, the corridor proved to end in a blank wall. However, there was a heavy metal door let into it. I opened it a crack and found that I was looking through the wings to the stage of the concert hangar.

Sam was much too short to reach the microphone and no one had adjusted it for him after the warm-up evangelistic guitarists we had been promised, plus Steve Selby the alternative condom-flying comedian, had done their stuff and departed. Nor did Sam know how to adjust it himself, and so he could probably not be heard beyond the first few rows.

"Now I want to tell you good people," he was saying, "about a very beautiful garden I sometimes visit. Not the kind of garden we have in Badgers Heath with lawns and flower beds and maybe a birdbath or a little ornamental pond, but a biblical garden with mossy rocks and peculiar twisted trees and olive bushes . . . "

Inadvertently I leaned against the heavy door so that it swung open another fraction, enough now to give me a view of the auditorium. Sam didn't have to worry about his microphone problem after all. In that stadium-sized hangar capable of seating thousands, only eight seats were occupied, and those in the first three rows. They were all women, all elderly and drably dressed except for the one member of the audience sitting in the very front row, who was in her thirties and wearing a purple satin suit that encased her ample contours into the shape of an hourglass. Rosie Greenleaf, an anticipatory smile upon her orange-painted lips, was gazing up at the lay preacher's face with that expression of evangelical lust I remembered so well from her husband's funeral service.

You would not think a condom the size of a Zeppelin could vanish into thin air, but there was no mention of a sighting over the Sussex Downs or anywhere else on the local television breakfast news next morning. Nor, unless they were keeping it from their viewers at an hour when children would be watching, did anyone seem to have reported a hot air condom missing. Maybe Steve Selby owned the thing, and Aids Action was as insubstantial a charity as the Children of the Brazilian Rain Forest. I hoped dearly that he had been blown out to sea.

The camera team covering the Bonfire had secured some spectacular footage on the Satan's Soldiers riot and there was a short report on that. There had been many arrests but surprisingly few casualties, except for one fatality. Eric Barlow (63), a well-known character in Badgers Heath, had been found dead in the wreckage of a refreshment marquee which had collapsed on top of him. Poor old Barlow.

There was nothing on the news about another character well-known in Badgers Heath having been found shot dead near the runway out at the Flying Cub. Procrastination had won again and I had yet to call the police, having last night fallen asleep in the bath with a tumbler of brandy. Maybe I needn't ring them at all. There was little activity at the Flying Club on Mondays and Nick's body was effectively hidden in the long grass. Of course someone would find him before long but by that time I would have pulled myself together and there would be nothing to connect the shooting with me. After all, while editors may often threaten the lives of their reporters they do not usually carry the threat out. A wheelchair would be found close by and a wheelchair comedian had gone missing. No need to involve myself at all, unless I chose to as an upright citizen and pillar of the community.

There were decisions to be made and the first decision was whether it was to be gin or brandy for breakfast. I had just poured myself a weakish brandy and soda when, just after nine, the telephone rang. It would continue to ring intermittently over the next hour.

I half-expected this first call to be from Sam Dice, although recognising that he would probably prefer to wait until he had got me face to face at our weekly conference before getting off his chest whatever accumulation of bile, bitterness, rage and disappointment might be on his chest. It was not Sam: it was one Police Inspector Balmforth, a valuable contact of mine who often

rang me with tips in exchange for the occasional lunch at the Old
Forge, where a fat envelope would discreetly change hands at the
coffee and liqueurs stage. Police Inspector Balmforth reported, in
confidence for the present moment, that during last night's Bonfire fracas, a Miss Bellows had been taken into custody for her
own protection. Misunderstanding the purpose of her temporary
loss of freedom, and suspecting that people in high places were
trying to intimidate her as she had put it, Miss Bellows had
demanded to see a detective sergeant and had made a lengthy
statement. As a result of this statement the chief superintendent
had suspended himself from duty. Certain persons mentioned in
the statement — myself among them, Police Inspector Balmforth
felt bound to mention — would be asked within the next few days
to make statements of their own, when it would be decided by his
superiors what action, if any, would be taken.

The next call was from Douglas Boxer at the office. I was
surprised to hear from him, having seen him literally pole-axed
during the Bonfire riot, surely good for a few days' sick leave; but
he assured me he was quite all right, apart from the odd dizzy
spell. Obviously he would keep his dizzy spells in reserve until he
felt like some time off. Boxer wanted to say that as he wasn't sure
whether I would be coming in before my conference with Mr
Dice, both Mr Dice and I might care to know that he had been
totting up the figures and the final total of pledges and contributions to Bananaskin Week had exceeded even Nick Crabbe's
expectations. Boxer hoped the news would in some small
measure compensate Mr Dice for what must probably have been
a disappointing turnout at last night's Youth Prayer Rally.

At about half past nine, when I was on my second brandy and
soda, the Verger of St Michael and All Angels rang, unusually
for him since although like Inspector Balmforth he was a *Herald*
contact, he usually imparted his trifling bits to whoever was
doing the churches beat, in exchange, if their swindle sheets
were to be believed, for a few drinks in the Goat and Compasses.
The Verger evidently considered that he had a choice enough
item to deliver to the top man. His news was that following a visit
from two plain-clothes detectives earlier, the Rev Basil Thrush
(48) had been found hanging from a bell-rope. The Verger had

been alerted by the unauthorised ringing of the church bells. Foul play was not suspected.

I stiffened my drink. It needed over an hour to my weekly conference with Sam, and already I was in no fit state to talk to him. I was not going to get any better, either.

Fifteen minutes or so later, the telephone rang again, with that shrill insistence that telephones seem to acquire when they have bad news to impart. It was Police Inspector Balmforth again. This time he sounded strange and stilted, from which I gathered after a moment that he was speaking in his official voice. A body had been discovered lying in long grass at the Flying Club. It had been identified as that of one of my reporters, Mr Nicholas Crabbe (27), of Unit 17, the Old Tea Warehouse, Badgers Heath. He had died, subject to confirmation by the pathologist, of gunshot wounds. I myself had been identified by one of the Flying Club security guards as having entered the airfield by the side entrance, shortly after which what may have been two shots, although the security guard thought they could have been fireworks, had been heard. Certain enquiries were being made and in order to eliminate me from those enquiries, Police Inspector Balmforth would ask when it was convenient to make a statement. He realised I was a busy man.

I told him I would be along to Badgers Heath Central directly I had finished breakfast, and pouring myself the last of the brandy put on my jacket and then went out into the hall for my overcoat. My briefcase was on the hall table and I picked it up. With no very clear idea in my head – I was in no condition to have clear ideas – I went back through the living room to my study and took my passport out of my desk. I didn't know where I was going or whether I was going anywhere, but considering the all-round situation there didn't seem much time to lose.

I turned off the lights which had been burning all night and was just opening the side door that leads into the garage when the telephone rang for the last time, or the last time so far as I was concerned. It was Sherry, still to my surprise at the Barbican. I had assumed she was already in New York.

"No, and I'm bloody livid. They've been buggering me about over the contract and I'm in two minds whether to tell them to

252

stuff it. What do you think?"

"From the price you tell me they've put on your head," I said, I hoped not indistinctly, "I should think you could withstand a modicum of buggering about."

"I suppose I can, but while I'm sitting here twiddling my thumbs, there's something I just wanted to check with you. I suppose it really is all over between us?"

"You're the one who said it, darling."

"Yes, I know all that, but was I right? Is it too late, even now, to do anything about it?"

"I think it is, Sherry. Far too late."

"That's what I keep telling myself, but I wanted to hear it from you. So there we are, then. How are you coping?"

"Moderately well."

"Take care, Kettle."

"You too, Sherry."

I locked the house and unlocked the garage and drove, as unerratically as maybe, to Gatwick Airport where I left the car in the long-term parking section and got the courtesy bus to the departure hall. I still had no real idea whether this was the start of a long journey or whether I meant to have a cup of black coffee, after which I would ring my friend Inspector Balmforth and tell him that I had been held up but would be along shortly. But then I saw the little monorail that serves the long-haul terminal. On impulse I stepped on it and eleven hours later I was here in Dallas.

I've been having second thoughts about this suicide lark. Sleeping pills are harder to come by than you would think, and although I am on the thirty-first floor of my hotel, the windows don't open. Maybe I'll give it a few more days and see how I feel. This is a big country and I could get lost in it. If they're not too insistent about work permits and all that, I could get a job on a small-time newspaper somewhere, provided I don't have to cover any hundred-dollar-a-plate fundraising breakfasts. Or I could fly home and take what's coming, hoping for a suspended sentence once I've told the whole story just as I've told it here. We'll see. My credit cards are good for a month or so before they put a stopper on them so there's plenty of time yet.

For the record, the Bananaskin Week grand total in pledges and contributions amounted to £304,717. Deducting a quarter of a million for administrative expenses, that leaves a net sum of £54,717. Every penny will go to charity.